Praise for Carolyn Hart

Winner of Multiple Agatha, Anthony, and Macavity Awards

"Carolyn Hart's work is both utterly reliable and utterly unpredictable."
—Charlaine Harris, #1 *New York Times* bestselling author

"One of the most popular practitioners of the traditional mystery."
—*The Cleveland Plain Dealer*

Praise for

Ghost Gone Wild

"The well-constructed plot offers an ample supply of red herrings. Fans of benign ghosts such as those in *Blithe Spirit* and *Topper* will find a lot to like."
—*Publishers Weekly*

"Hart's ghost mysteries . . . are often amusing and never easy to solve. Bailey Ruth's latest is one of her toughest cases."
—*Kirkus Reviews*

"The Bailey Ruth Mysteries are light and fluffy, funny, and a good read. Bailey Ruth is a character you wish you'd known when she was alive and hope is watching over you now that she's an angel."
—*Kings River Life Magazine*

"Bailey is a fun, feisty sleuth who finds herself in humorous predicaments when she forgets the rules of being a ghost. This solid mystery has comedic moments and a surprise ending, providing readers with a thoroughly entertaining story."
—*RT Book Reviews*

continued . . .

Praise for the Bailey Ruth Ghost Novels

Ghost Gone Wild

❧

Carolyn Hart

BERKLEY PRIME CRIME, NEW YORK

THE BERKLEY PUBLISHING GROUP
Published by the Penguin Group
Penguin Group (USA) LLC
375 Hudson Street, New York, New York 10014

USA • Canada • UK • Ireland • Australia • New Zealand • India • South Africa • China

penguin.com

A Penguin Random House Company

GHOST GONE WILD

A Berkley Prime Crime Book / published by arrangement with the author

Copyright © 2013 by Carolyn Hart.
Penguin supports copyright. Copyright fuels creativity, encourages diverse voices,
promotes free speech, and creates a vibrant culture. Thank you for buying an authorized
edition of this book and for complying with copyright laws by not reproducing, scanning,
or distributing any part of it in any form without permission. You are supporting writers
and allowing Penguin to continue to publish books for every reader.

Berkley Prime Crime Books are published by The Berkley Publishing Group.
BERKLEY® PRIME CRIME and the PRIME CRIME logo are trademarks of
Penguin Group (USA) LLC.

For information, address: The Berkley Publishing Group,
a division of Penguin Group (USA) LLC,
375 Hudson Street, New York, New York 10014.

ISBN: 978-0-425-26076-0

PUBLISHING HISTORY
Berkley Prime Crime hardcover edition / October 2013
Berkley Prime Crime mass-market edition / October 2014

PRINTED IN THE UNITED STATES OF AMERICA

10 9 8 7 6 5 4 3 2 1

Cover design by Jason Gill.
Interior text design by Laura K. Corless.

To Kay and Clark Musser,
fun companions and dear friends.

Chapter 1

I passed Julia Child's kitchen and breathed deeply. The aromas were Heavenly. Julia still loves butter. I was in a rambling mood on another golden day in paradise. As my thoughts flitted, so did my presence. Heaven makes joyful pursuits quite easy. If I envision a place or activity, I am there, everything from white-water rafting to a romantic tango in the moonlight. When I murmur, "Come dance with me," to Bobby Mac, we move in unison to the pulsing music, his hand warm against my back. I savor the beat and Bobby Mac and my filmy dress of sea green chiffon. Bobby Mac is gorgeous in a white Guayabera shirt and black trousers, quite a change from his usual cream polo and khaki shorts when fishing from *Serendipity* or his blue work shirt and Levi's when out on an oil rig. As we say in Adelaide, he cleans up real nice.

Do I sense bewilderment? Heaven? Julia Child's kitchen? A tango in the moonlight? Adelaide? Oh yes, all of that and more. If we haven't met before, I'll introduce myself. I am Bailey Ruth Raeburn, late of Adelaide, Oklahoma. Bobby

Mac and I arrived in Heaven when our cabin cruiser, the faithful *Serendipity*, sank during a storm in the Gulf. Bobby Mac has been my man ever since high school, when he was a darkly handsome senior and I was a redheaded sophomore. We lived a happy life, which has only been better since arriving in Heaven.

Heaven is, I assure you, quite Heavenly. Everything good, everything honorable, everything beautiful is here. Earth, as we all know, is beset with sin and strife, which is why I sometimes yearn to return.

Not that I wish to dabble in sin.

Heaven forbid. Instead, I like to lend a helping hand to those in trouble. I remember well that I received boosts, some surprising, some unaccountable, that got me past rough patches in my life. That's why, delightful as Heaven is, I revel in returning to earth as a special emissary from the Department of Good Intentions.

I've been honored to serve as an emissary three times. However, eager as I was to serve once again, my steps slowed.

Just around the curve of a golden-hued cloud, a small train station nestled against a green hill. The station served as the headquarters of the department under the kindly direction of Wiggins, who had been a stationmaster on earth.

I sighed and stopped. I didn't quite have the courage to swing around the cloud and see the small redbrick station with silver rails that ran into the sky.

I studied the intervening cloud, made glorious by incandescent streaks of gold and rose. Have I ever described the majestic puffs of cloud that delineate a change from one destination to another? I'm not talking about cool, damp particles of mist. Heaven's clouds are silky soft, as luxurious to touch as fluff from a cottonwood. I've always loved cottonwoods, and they are everywhere in Oklahoma. . . .

I reined in my thoughts. Cottonwoods were all well and good—and I'm sure it is of interest to realize there is nothing chilling and wet should you plunge into a glorious white column—but there was a time and place for memories of cottonwoods. I was pondering clouds to avoid an approach to the department, even though Wiggins would welcome me warmly. Wiggins has a smile as reassuring as the dancing flames in a winter fireplace, but he is rather a stickler for following rules. His emissaries have a list of strict dos and don'ts. Truth to tell—and Heaven always expects truth—I'm not awfully good at rules. Some might say I am a bit impetuous. Oh, all right. I think fast, move fast, and sometimes I leave rules in my dust.

Perhaps the format of Wiggins's rules best reveals his precise nature. The list, printed in gold letters on glorious parchment, is entitled:

PRECEPTS FOR EARTHLY VISITATION

I like to sing. I quickly donned tap shoes and belted out the list to an eight-count bebop tune.

1. *Avoid public notice.*
2. *Do not consort with other departed spirits.*
3. *Work behind the scenes without making your presence known.*
4. *Become visible only when absolutely necessary.*
5. *Do not succumb to the temptation to confound those who appear to oppose you.*
6. *Make every effort not to alarm earthly creatures.*
7. *Information about Heaven is not yours to impart*—Oops. Scratch all that about Heavenly clouds—*simply smile and say, "Time will tell."*
8. *Remember always that you are on the earth, not of the earth.*

॰s॰

My impromptu dance ended. What would Wiggins think? I laughed aloud. He would appreciate my accurate, though musical, rendition of the Precepts. Slowly, my smile slipped away. In my previous jaunts to earth, how many Precepts had I broken?

A few.

I clicked a tap; actually, eight taps. Okay. All of the Precepts.

How often?

Possibly fairly often.

All right. Insist upon truth. Precepts flouted morning, noon, and night.

I glanced at a bright shaft of crystal opposite the column of cloud and saw myself at twenty-seven, coppery red hair in springy curls, curious green eyes, a spatter of freckles on a narrow face. Five foot five on a tall day. Slender, ready to move, dance, climb, run, play. Twenty-seven had been a very good year for me on earth, and how I looked then was how I chose to appear in Heaven. Everyone in Heaven was the best they'd ever been.

I grinned.

My reflection grinned back.

I should have been ruing each and every transgression of the Precepts, but, despite what might have been perceived (I think uncharitably) as a wholesale flouting of the rules, I believed I'd done the department proud in my three previous adven—*missions* to earth.

I wanted to go back. I loved the challenge of doing my best for a troubled creature.

Okay, more truth.

Lending a helping hand is Heavenly, but protecting the innocent makes me a very happy ghost. There are also side benefits. I had dearly loved my hometown of Adelaide: rasping cicadas in summer, fall leaves that rivaled flame, majestic eagles in a winter sky, the scent of dark, rich dirt in a spring furrow.

I squared my shoulders. Onward to the department. Wiggins's telegram had been enigmatic: *Possible assignment. If you qualify.* I was puzzled. The message didn't sound quite like Wiggins. What qualification was needed? I glanced again at my reflection. Hmm. Perhaps the azure blouse was a little too flattering. There. More of a gray tone. Gray is such a steady color. Boring, but steady. I changed the bright floral print of my sateen slacks to a subdued houndstooth check. Instead of tap shoes, blue sandals. I refused to wear gray shoes. There was a limit to my sartorial sacrifices. Besides, men don't notice shoes. Except for Jimmy Choo.

In the distance, I heard the deep-throated woo-woo of the Rescue Express, the marvelous silver train that carried emissaries to earth. If I hurried . . . But I didn't yet have a mission. I had to face reality. Wiggins had thought of me, but he wasn't sure. Well, I would have to convince him that I was perfect for the task, whatever it might be.

Galloping hooves sounded. The ground quivered beneath my blue-sandaled feet. An ebony horse thundered around the pillar of cloud, pawed to a stop scant feet away. The slender rider sat straight in the saddle, impeccably attired from her black hat and navy coat to her tan breeches and black boots. The horse was all black except for a white crescent on his forehead.

Her face, once seen, was not to be forgotten—high forehead, arctic blue eyes, narrow nose, pointed cheekbones, a decisive mouth, cleft chin. She gazed down imperiously, gestured with her crop. "There's just time to catch the Rescue Express. I have your ticket. You are Bailey Ruth Raeburn, aren't you?" Her tone was impatient.

"Oh, yes. Who—?"

"Are you game or not?" She flung the words in a challenge as sharp as a whip crack.

No one ever said I wouldn't take a dare. There was the time Billy Snodgrass shouted, "Bet you a box of Dubble Bubble you won't jump off the dock." The dock in question was in the nature preserve next to St. Mildred's. Of course I jumped, even though it was January and there was a skim of ice across the lake. I'd arrived home drenched, blue from cold, and only alive because a bundled-up fisherman angling for striper waded out far enough that I could catch the end of his rod. "Bailey Ruth, honey," Mama had sighed, "look before you leap."

Truly, I always intend to do that very thing, but the horse stamped a hoof, the rider reached out for my hand. "I'll get you there."

Perhaps this was the qualification I was supposed meet, a willingness to dare. Of course I would. I swung up and settled behind the saddle and clung to her waist.

The horse rose through the air and we sped from Heaven's golden light into a star-spangled night and there, not far ahead, was the plunging Express.

Words streamed to me. ". . . he's always been such a fool . . . but there are those who love him . . . try to save him from himself . . ."

"Who?" I shouted, but the cry was lost in the rush of space.

With a mighty stride, the horse gained on the whooshing Express, came level for an instant with the caboose.

The rider twisted, thrust a small scrap of cardboard into my hand. "Here's your ticket." A strong arm gripped my elbow, and I was swept out into emptiness.

I grasped the railing and pulled myself aboard the Rescue Express.

The stallion and rider were gone. The immensity of space held me in thrall as billions of stars in shining galaxies dwarfed the Express, made the line of cars seem as small as a miniature train amid swirling flakes in a paperweight.

The door swung open. "Wot's this 'ere?" A conductor in

a dark blue uniform and a braided cap peered out. "Wot's 'appening 'ere?"

I was enthralled by his cockney accent. I wanted to know his story, who he had been and when he'd come to Heaven and whether he'd ever worked on the *Flying Scotsman*. One time Bobby Mac and I . . . But that's another story.

Sandy eyebrows drew down in disapproval. "'ighly irregular, that's wot it is."

"Everything's fine." I always look on the bright side, though I was a little unsettled. Dramatic departures aren't unusual from Wiggins's station—an earthling in dire straits can necessitate haste—but we always chatted about my upcoming visit and reviewed my occasional trespasses of the Precepts.

Honestly, do we have to be so insistent upon accuracy? Cross out *occasional*. Substitute, I regret to say, *wholesale*. But this time would be different. I hadn't had a chance to reassure Wiggins. I felt flattered. Wiggins hadn't considered it necessary to brief me, though I would have thought that his assistant—and I wondered who she was and how long she'd been on his staff—would have given me some idea of who I was expected to assist and why.

The conductor shook his head. "It will run us late, but I'll 'ave to pull the emergency stop." He pulled open the door and stood halfway inside the car, reaching out to his right. "No travelers permitted without proper papers—"

"Here." I thrust the ticket at him.

He took the ticket, poked out his jaw, his face settling in pugnacious lines.

I had my first misgiving.

I recalled with clarity my previous tickets to Adelaide, soft white with the destination stamped in bright red.

The conductor held between thumb and forefinger a jade green ticket with yellow letters. He peered nearsightedly. "This 'ere's torn, so how can we know where to stop? Ponta Delgada? Pontefract? Pontevedra? Pontiac?" He rattled names fast as a 1940s typist in a secretarial pool, took a deep breath. "Pontine Marshes. Po—"

I interrupted. "Pontotoc." I spoke with authority.

He glowered. "There's no such stop."

"It isn't a city, it's a county. Pontotoc." I tried for charm. "I always go home to Adelaide, Oklahoma. That's in Pontotoc County." I forbore mentioning Pontotoc County, Mississippi. After all, Wiggins knew my stomping ground.

The conductor held the torn ticket close to his face, laboriously spelled, "P-O-N-T . . . Could be." He was grudging. "Well, 'tis *almost* a proper ticket. We can give it a try." He lowered his arm. He stood straight, his eyes gleaming. "If there's a spot of trouble down there, the Rescue Express will 'one in sharp as a magnetic needle. She's a gallant old girl, the Rescue Express." His pride in the trusty train was evident.

"Oh, there's trouble, all right." The rider astride the horse had been clear enough. Some fellow who has "always been such a fool" needed to be saved. I slid inside the car and gazed about in admiration. As Mama always said, "Praise a man's prized possession and he'll treat you like a queen." "Such splendid furnishings." I pointed at red velvet cushions in comfortably curved wicker chairs. "Everything is perfect. And I know"—my gaze up at him radiated soulful conviction—"that you'll get all of us to our destinations in good order." Most of the seats were taken. My fellow passengers looked up to smile a welcome. Dress ranged from a Roman toga to colonial breeches to a French Foreign Legion uniform to a late-nineteenth-century gray fawn gown.

A pink flush touched the conductor's sallow cheeks. "Nice of you to say so, and 'ere"—he gestured toward a chair—"you'll be comfortable." He gave me a conspiratorial nod. "I'll pop up to the engineer, add your destination."

I almost called after him. Pontotoc County covered a lot of ground. Then I shrugged. The conductor promised to drop me at a spot of trouble. I'd have to find my way from there.

ᔦ

The moon hung cool and remote, spilling a creamy sheen across a neighborhood of mostly frame houses. Within the city limits, Adelaide has pockets of homes built in the 1930s that are semi-rural with spacious lots. Though the air was nippy, tree branches were thick with leaves. Probably it was early to mid-October. Directly below me a house blazed with lights. Most of the other homes were dark with only an occasional gleam in a window. Rumbling thumps came from the lighted house.

I felt a little chilly, so I changed to a crisp rose blouse, charcoal gray worsted wool slacks, and a wine-colored cardigan. Fashion was such a pleasure. As soon as I pictured the clothes, my costume changed. I added matching rose-colored leather flats.

The conductor had promised to drop me at a spot with trouble, so I assumed the two-story house directly beneath me was my destination. There didn't seem to be any cause for alarm. If there was trouble here, it wasn't apparent. Feeling uncertain, I dropped to the front walk and cautiously approached. Wide open uncurtained windows spilled light onto a porch and front steps. From the windows and open front door, guitar music blasted. I suspected neighbors were grateful for the distances between houses. I supposed it was music. Everyone to their own taste, of course.

In the graveled driveway, a low-slung sports car glistened cherry red in the sharp bright light of an outdoor lantern. Nearby sat a butter yellow motor scooter, which looked like the scooters Bobby Mac and I had once ridden up and down the hills of Bermuda. I floated to the front porch. The music was deafening. Wretched. However, Heaven also loves those who confuse thumps and twangs with melodies.

I drifted inside. The living room had a masculine appeal,

comfortable leather furniture—obviously new and expensive—plain wooden floors, bright posters on the walls, a game table, and, on a golden desk, an iPad. I kept au courant with earthly matters and was now quite adept at computers and iPhones and all manner of electronic advances. I glanced from the table to a rather scruffy young man and wondered how he afforded such a luxury.

The windows lacked curtains. Wooden shutters were ajar. The single occupant perched on a wooden stool in front of a drum set. Lanky and lean, he drummed with abandon, locks of dark hair falling forward, bony face rapt in concentration as he added oomph to rock guitar blasting from the stereo. His foot slammed the bass drum foot pedal so hard, I feared an explosion. Whaba whaba whaba whump. Thutter thutter thutter crump.

I folded my arms and felt a sharp stab of impatience.

He did not appear to be in trouble except for the damage he might be inflicting on his hearing.

Could my ticket actually have been to a destination unknown to me? Had Wiggins realized that I was quite willing to go far afield? However, I'd expressed a preference for Paris, not Ponta Delgada, charming as it sounded.

Well, fuss and feathers, here I was and not a calamity in sight. I studied his face, noting the dark fuzz that indicated a casual attitude toward shaving. The features were a bit too irregular to qualify as handsome, the forehead a trifle large, the nose too narrow, sharp cheekbones, and a pointed chin with a decided cleft, but he possessed a definite appeal. Perhaps a hint of a likeable rebel? Perhaps an air of I'm-gonna-have-fun? He was young, early to mid-twenties. His broad mouth was stretched in a satisfied smile. He was clearly quite pleased with himself.

With a final horrendous tattoo, the assault on the drum set mercifully ended. "Yee-hah!" As he reached to turn off the stereo, he gave a boisterous shout, "Nick Magruder, you are The Man!," and flung the sticks across the room, where they ricocheted off a high padded leather stool at the counter of a wet bar. He ended with an unmistakable rebel yell, a welcome home as warm as a hug.

"Yee-hah!" I responded.

I clapped a hand over my mouth.

His head jerked up. He looked around the room, then dropped to the wooden floor, and in two strides he was at the front door. He flipped on the porch light, looked out. Finally, shaking his head, he turned back into the room. Slowly bewilderment eased from his face.

I began to relax. Human beings are so transparent. They don't tolerate the inexplicable well. In automatic defense, he would satisfy himself that the feminine yell had a perfectly ordinary explanation. An exuberant shout from a passing car. A high-pitched creak from old wood.

A majestic orange tabby strolled into the living room.

I smiled and reached down to pet the huge creature. I gazed at the cat's large, splayed paws. Surely those were almost thumbs! I was startled into exclaiming, "Why, look at your claws—" Again my fingers pressed against my lips.

The cat flopped to the floor and rolled over on his back.

The young man blinked. "Hey, Champ, you got a lady cat stashed around here somewhere?" His tone was falsely genial and a bit overloud.

I darted to a rattan sofa and sank down. In my haste, I forgot the uncarpeted floor. The light sofa lurched and slid backward about an inch, making a distinct scraping sound.

The cat rolled to his feet and padded toward me. Before I could move, he jumped and landed on my lap. Unfortunately, that positioned him with a several-inch expanse of space between his fur and the sofa.

"Here, Champ." I whispered. I gingerly pushed the cat toward the empty center of the sofa.

Sharp claws tightened on my upper thighs.

I managed—almost—to suppress a gasp of pain.

"Hey, Champ." The young man walked nearer. "How

you doing that, chum?" There was a mixture of disbelief and determined heartiness in his voice. "Cats can't levitate."

Desperate situations require desperate measures. I firmly gripped the cat, flowed to my feet and pressed him into his owner's arms. I skittered sideways fast, knocking over a can of Schlitz that had been, in my view, carelessly left sitting on the floor by the sofa. Of course I hadn't noticed the beer. I'd been watching the cat.

The cat growled deep in his throat.

Beer spewed, foaming.

"Okay, buddy, time to go out. I am not getting this." His nice tenor voice definitely sounded strained. "I guess you made those funny noises. Maybe you've got a mouse stuck in your throat. Funny, but I thought you weren't actually on the cushion. You looked like you were floating. Cats can't float. I guess I didn't see you right." This was a mutter. "You didn't need to knock over my beer." Carrying the squirming tom, he hurried to the front door. He placed the cat on the porch and shut the door firmly.

I floated to the wet bar and perched on the counter. I needed to catch my breath.

He walked behind the counter, opened a small fridge, pulled out a new can of beer.

I watched with narrowed eyes. If anybody needed a beer, I did.

He flipped back the tab, lifted the can, drank about half. He heaved a sigh of contentment as he strolled back around the counter. He stopped to look into the mirror behind the wet bar. He gave himself an approving nod. "Nick, old buddy, you got 'em on the run." He threw back his head and brayed with laughter.

I shook my head in dismay. I'm all in favor of good humor, but there was a tone of uncharitableness in his proud pronouncement.

He held the can high in a self-toast. "So they're on me

like june bugs." His voice was defiant, but there was a lost look in his dark blue eyes. "Hey, that's okay with me."

The sound was small but alien, hard to define, something between a rasp and a rattle. Even before I swung toward the front of the house, I somehow knew that I'd found the trouble I'd been looking for.

The blue black barrel of a rifle poked through a hole gouged in the screen of an open window not fifteen feet distant. The barrel moved toward the lanky young man holding his can of beer.

With a shout—and I am pleased to say I thought quickly and screamed, "Police!" at the top of my lungs—I flung myself forward and barreled into him.

Caught completely by surprise, though he was tall and rangy, he toppled backward, crashing heavily to the floor. Beer spewed in an arc and the can fell and rolled across the uncarpeted wood.

A loud crack, and a vase atop a bookcase shattered.

I continued to scream. "Police! Police! Nine-one-one!" Not even the most determined of killers would hang around to find out the meaning of frenzied female shouts.

The rifle barrel was gone. I was about to pop outside to discover the shooter's identity when I realized the young man who had happily played the drums and taken such a satisfied gulp of beer now lay unmoving.

Oh yes, there was trouble in Pontotoc County.

Chapter 2

I dropped to my knees beside Nick. I patted his chest, tugged up his polo. No blood. I ran my fingers across his face. No wounds. "Nick?" I spoke his name more loudly. "Nick, are you hurt?"

My hand slid behind his head. Dampness. I bent near and turned his face. Blood streaked my seeking fingers. Blood oozed from the back of his head. He must have grazed the edge of the wet bar's foot rail when he tumbled backward. But surely he hadn't been shot. From the angle of the attack—my eyes flicked toward the window—a bullet would have struck him from the front.

I lightly touched his throat and felt the steady beat of the carotid artery.

I was almost weak with relief.

My head jerked up. In a flash I was outside, standing by the window with the broken pane. I was alone. Whoever had stood there, rammed the barrel through, steadied the rifle, and pulled the trigger was long gone.

I pressed my lips together. I'd foiled the attack, but the

attacker was at large. The police must be summoned and Nick's injury treated.

I was once again at his side.

Nick's eyelids fluttered. The lashes were long and dark and silky. His eyes opened. He stared blearily up.

"Don't move." I was crisp. My mind was going a mile a minute. "You probably have a concussion. I'll call nine-one-one, and then I'll check outside again."

His eyes snapped wide. "Where are you?" He moved his head from side to side. "Ouch. My head."

"Lay still. That can't be good for you."

Breathing fast, he struggled to his hands and knees, reached out, pulled himself up, and leaned against the wet bar. He wavered unsteadily. "Nutty. Something's nuts. My head hurts. Voices. Nobody here."

"Nick. Listen up." I once taught high school English and had six football players in my class. I can match a drill sergeant any day.

Instead of cowed attention, he gave a yelp that was part panic and part despair. His gaze swept back and forth, seeking the source of that imperious voice. "What was I doing on the floor? How'd I get on the floor? I'm sober. I swear to God, I'm stone-cold sober. I am not hearing voices."

Clearly I'd whacked him like a mole in the instant before the attacker pulled the trigger. Nick had no idea what had happened, and every time I spoke, he edged nearer complete demoralization.

I felt equally demoralized. So far, and I'd not been here for more than a quarter hour, I'd violated Precepts Three and Six. However, in the present situation, I was able to follow Precept Four: "Become visible only when absolutely necessary." If ever necessity demanded my appearance, it was now.

"I can explain everything." As I spoke, I swirled into being. Of course, such an appearance can be rather startling. As colors whirled, I was reflected in the mirror behind the bar. I brushed back a tangle of red curls. I appeared a bit disheveled, but I'd been rather active. I admired the wine-colored sweater, decided the shade should be a tad lighter, and paused in mid-swirl. Lavender was such a nice color.

He clutched the counter and moaned.

I went around the end of the wet bar, found a glass and a bottle of club soda. I scooped ice cubes from the freezer and poured the fizzy soda. "Sit down on a stool." I nodded in approval as he slid onto the leather seat. I placed the glass in front of him. "Drink this. I imagine your head hurts. But don't worry. I'll take care of everything." I spoke soothingly. "I'll call the police."

"The police? Why? What have I done? Lady, I never laid a hand on you." He leaned forward, stared at me as if I might disappear. How insightful of him. "Where'd you come from? You weren't here a minute ago. How'd you get in?"

"Everything will come back to you." I had this nurse thing down pat, just the right pleasant tone: warm, reassuring, and slightly condescending. Now was the moment to take charge. I jerked my thumb toward the ragged hole in the screen. "Someone poked a rifle through the screen and took a shot at you."

Nick slowly turned his head, looked toward the window. "The screen's messed up." He looked puzzled.

Nick might be young, sexy, and attractive, but he was a trifle slow.

He squinted at me. "Who ripped the screen?"

I was patient. "Your assailant." At his lack of response, I shook my head. "The person who tried to shoot at you."

He managed a sickly grin. "You got a great sense of humor. Is that how you got in?"

"I dropped in." I try to be accurate. "Please pay attention. We need to call the police. Now. Where's the phone?"

"Phone?" His face creased.

"We need to call nine-one-one. Your attacker has been gone for several minutes. But the police can start a search."

"I didn't hear a shot. That's nuts." He started to shake his head, winced, gingerly touched the back of his skull. He brought his fingers around. His eyes looked hollow. "Blood!"

He swayed.

I gripped his arm. "Not much. You banged your head when you went down. I pushed you out of the way." I spoke with quiet pride.

"You were here?" His voice fairly squeaked. "I've never seen you before. Where did you come from?"

Heaven admires honesty. However, if I understood the Precepts properly, and in Wiggins's mind there was some question about that, I should avoid sharing information about the department. Therefore, I felt comfortable in obfuscating, always a delectable sport.

"Concussion," I announced with nurselike firmness. If he assumed greater medical expertise than I possessed, I was not responsible for his thought processes. I leaned forward, peered intently into his blue eyes. I held up one hand. "How many fingers do you see?"

"Five."

"Excellent." I beamed at him. "What day is it?"

"Tuesday."

I had no idea, but it sounded okay to me.

"Who is the police chief?" Chief Cobb wouldn't be pleased at the delay in reporting the shooting.

"How should I know?" He sounded bewildered.

Apparently he wasn't active in his community. On the positive side, his ignorance suggested that he wasn't a lawbreaker.

"What's your favorite TV show?"

"True Blood." He gingerly touched his head. "But I don't like blood. How'd my head get hurt?"

I pointed at the railing on the wet bar. "You cracked your head as you went down."

He stared down at his fingers. He looked queasy.

I took him by the elbow. "Here. Wash your hands." I turned on the spigot of the wet bar.

Dutifully, he thrust his big hands into the gushing water.

I grabbed some paper napkins, swiped them beneath the water, gently dabbed at the back of his head.

"Ouch."

"It's a very minor cut. Hold still." I patted the area. "If you have some antibiotic cream, I'll dab some on the scratch." The wound was minor and no longer noticeable.

He turned off the water, grabbed a handful of napkins to dry his hands. "I don't keep stuff like that. How's it look now?"

"Fine. And you're fine."

He turned to look at me. "Yeah, thanks for the help." He moved out from behind the counter.

I followed, feeling impatient. We definitely needed to contact the police, the sooner the better. I scanned the room for a phone.

"The door's that way." He pointed.

As if I couldn't find a front door. I gave him a scathing look. "I'm not going anywhere until we find out who shot at you."

He started to shake his head, winced. "I didn't hear a shot."

"There was a shot. I shoved you. I saved your life. That's why you weren't shot. You took a glancing blow and momentarily lost consciousness"—I thought he had been stunned, but it wouldn't hurt to mislead him—"and that's why you don't remember me."

He studied me.

I saw quick recognition that I was young, redheaded, and female. There was a momentary pulse of attraction, the automatic male appreciation of a desirable woman. But there was no spark of pursuit in his dark blue eyes. As Bobby Mac always puts it so well, he never walks by a beautiful woman without noticing, but his heart belongs to me.

I wondered who owned Nick's heart.

"Now that everything's clear—"

"What were you doing here?" There was a tinge of apprehension in his voice. He clearly hoped he wasn't forgetting anything compromising.

"I'd just arrived. I'm running behind"—I scrambled for a reason to be in a young (I assumed) bachelor's home long after dark—"in my survey for the Chamber of Commerce. I have to turn in my report tomorrow, and your house is one of the last on my list." I'd once served as the mayor's secretary, and I had great faith that the chamber was quite capable of surveying a neighborhood for one reason or another. "However, that's neither here nor there." I spoke with great accuracy. "What matters now is to report the effort made to shoot you." I held out my hand. "Your cell phone."

He reached into his back pocket, stopped, looked puzzled. He patted all of his pockets, then glanced around the room, his eyes searching. "I must have put it somewhere."

Time was fleeting, as it always is when it is of the essence. "Surely you have a regular phone. Where is it?" I, too, glanced around the room. I didn't see a telephone anywhere.

He started to shake his head, stopped with a wince. "What for?"

"No phone?" I suppose my shock was evident.

"Who needs a landline?" He was disparaging. "That's for geezers."

I kept to the main point. "Do you mean we can't call the police?"

He rubbed his temple. "My cell's gone." He didn't speak as if this were a complete surprise. "Maybe it's out in my car. I toss it on the seat a lot. Bulges in my pocket."

He started for the door.

I gripped his arm and admired its muscular firmness. "Wait. I think it's safe enough. Let me take a look first."

He looked incredulous. "Listen, I don't believe in this

OK Corral stuff. But if somebody was sniping at me, I'm the guy to look. What do you think I am, a weenie?"

"I'm better equipped." As soon as I stepped onto the porch, I could disappear. "Just wait right here." I hurried toward the door.

He was right behind me. "Lady, let's cut the drama and the fairy tales. The C of C is a fine group, but I doubt it sends ladies out at this time of night, and even if it did, nobody's handed you a marshal badge."

I stopped and faced him. "Don't be difficult. I am here on a mission to protect your sorry carcass." I slapped my fingers to my lips. Wiggins always feared that his emissaries might forget in the heat of the moment that they were *on* the earth, not *of* the earth and succumb to worldly emotions.

Such as irritation.

I forced a smile. "Truly, it's much safer for me to go out and check the grounds." Since the cat was out of the bag, I might as well be forthright. "See, I'll disappear—"

I glanced at the mirror behind the bar. No matter how often I appear or disappear, I enjoy the quick swirl of colors. At first there is a delicate hint of change in the substance of the air, the merest flicker of pastels. Colors brighten, deepen, and there I am, copper red hair, eager face with a spatter of freckles, obviously up for anything. Disappearing is dramatic, too. I was fully there—in the moment, for all who appreciate Zen—with eager green eyes and a merry smile and fashionable clothes. I admired the cunning trim on my lavender sweater. . . .

My smile slid away.

I stared at the mirror. Red hair. Green eyes wide and staring. Lips parted in dismay. I reached up, tugged at a strand of hair. I fingered a flamingly visible curl and gazed in disbelief.

Nick's expression was desperate. He cracked the knuckles of his right hand. "You got someone I can call to help you out?" His attempt to soothe sounded like a sheep bleating. "Oh damn, I forgot. I don't have a phone." He struggled for air. "Try taking a deep breath. Looking cross-eyed at your hair is pretty weird. Look, why don't you go home?" His voice rose in hope.

I ignored him, pressed my eyes shut. I would think, as I always did, *Disappear*, and I would disappear. I eased open one eye.

Both eyes.

I stared at my unmistakable image in the mirror. I gave myself a little shake. Okay, how about different clothes? I shut my eyes, thought: *Green silk dress, high heels, very high heels with a natty little strap over the instep.*

My eyes jerked wide and gazed in despair at the lavender sweater and charcoal gray slacks. I patted my arm, slapped my palms together, stamped my right foot on the floor. "I can't disappear. My clothes won't change! What am I going to do?"

He gestured toward the bar. "How about a drink?"

I walked toward the wet bar. Nearer and nearer came my image in the mirror. I slapped the countertop, stared into green eyes stretched wide in disbelief. "I'm stuck. How could this happen?"

"Lady, do me a big favor. Walk outside and get in your car and go home. It's been nice to know you. And I'm sorry if I miffed you about the Chamber of Commerce. Whatever your survey is about, check the yeses and I'll make a donation. A great, big, fat donation. Look, it's late." He glanced at the clock. "Almost ten." He spoke as if the hour were incredibly late. I'd be willing to bet he barely started to boogie by ten. Boogie? I'll explain another time. Time! Why was I still here when I'd intended to disappear. All I had to do was think, *Gone*, and I was gone.

The reflection in the mirror was clear and sharp and undeniably there.

"Lady—"

I spoke in a steel-ribbed voice. "Stop calling me lady."

"Who are you? What's your name? Why don't you go away?"

"I would go," I spoke through clenched teeth, "if I could. I can't. Hush for a minute and let me think."

He started for the door.

I beat him to it, yanked open the door, plunged onto the front porch, and yelled, "The police are on the way."

He pushed out beside me.

The only sounds were the rustle of leaves and the distant whoo of an owl.

I turned to go back inside.

He caught my arm. "Do you always yell for the police when you go outside?"

"I am protecting your—" I broke off. Despite the pressures of the world, I would demonstrate that I wasn't *of* the world.

Except apparently I was.

He grinned and was suddenly appealing, his wide mouth turning down in a lopsided smile. "—sorry ass."

I managed a quick smile in return. "Carcass, to be precise." But I didn't have time to be pleasant. I shot one more questing gaze around the yard. If a killer was lurking, he was lurking quietly. In fact, I had no sense of danger, and I have a pretty good instinct for malevolence. "I think you're safe enough now." I trotted down the steps, opened the door to the snazzy sports coupe.

He was close behind me. "Wait a minute. What are you doing?"

I was brisk. "Looking for your cell phone. Ah. Here it is. Now you can call the police. It will be better if I leave before they arrive. It would be awkward for me to be involved."

"La—" He broke off. "I didn't say it." He pointed at the drive, then stiffened. He made a strangled noise in his throat. "Where's your car?"

"I don't have a car." I would have thought that fact was apparent.

"How'd you get here?" His head jerked as he checked out the drive and street.

"Train." I spoke absently. My mind quivered with imperatives: Call the police. Protect Nick. Figure out why I was stuck *in* the world. But first, I needed a pick-me-up. We'd wasted so much time already, another few minutes wouldn't matter. I swung around and walked swiftly to the steps.

He was on my heels. "Train?"

I strode toward the wet bar. I went around the counter, rummaged in the cabinets. "Don't you have anything besides alcohol here? I'm starving." I'd had a rather active time since my arrival, and when I am on the earth, I need sustenance.

Nick reached the counter. "La—" He saw my look, broke off, took a breath. "Let's start over." His voice was agreeable, the kind of tone a hapless male employs when dealing with a difficult woman.

I couldn't find even a cracker. "If I could start over, you can bet I wouldn't have jumped on that horse and caught the Express—" It was my turn to break off as he began to edge cautiously backward.

Clearly he thought I was demented.

I found a jar of maraschino cherries.

I wasn't *that* hungry.

I hoped Wiggins was aware that duty was ever most present on my mind. Wiggins? I didn't have a sense that he was near. He always popped down to remonstrate when I inadvertently flouted the Precepts. "Wiggins?" My voice sounded forlorn.

Nick stopped edging away. "What'd you say?"

"My supervisor. I don't know where he is." Obviously this was where he wasn't.

"Your supervisor at the chamber?" Nick sounded like a man who sighted a fact and intended to pursue it. "I never heard anybody called a supervisor at the Chamber of Commerce."

"Actually, Wiggins is a stationmaster."

Nick looked bewildered.

"At his train depot."

"Of course." Nick's tone was hearty. "The train that brought you here. Sure. I understand."

"You"—my tone was icy—"don't understand anything. However, I am responsible for your safety, and I am here—"

"Oh boy, you can say that again." Nick shoved a hand through his unruly dark curls. "Here I was, playing my drums, not bothering anybody, and the next thing I know I hear your voice and you aren't here and nothing makes sense and my head hurts and then you appear"—he looked uneasy—"and you claim somebody tried to shoot me. That's probably a crock, too."

"Look at the window screen." My tone was steely.

He immediately looked. Somewhere in his past a good woman had started him down the right path: When a woman speaks, salute. Then his eyes slid toward me. "Did you rip it?"

I folded my arms, stood at the tip top of my five foot five inches. "The rifle barrel poked through, and then there was a shot and it smashed that vase on the bookcase."

He turned. His bony face registered shock as he gazed at the broken pieces of the vase. His eyes scanned the height of the bookcase. "If I'd been standing there, a bullet would have got me in the chest."

Finally, I was making progress. "I expect the slug went into the wall." I quickly walked nearer, pointed to a round, blackened depression. "There's the hole. The police may be able to trace the gun." If they ever found the rifle.

He moved with all the grace of a zombie, clutched the top of the bookcase, and stared at the bullet hole: clear, distinct, ominous, and ugly in the pale yellow plastered wall. "Oh my God. You aren't making this up."

I refrained from slapping my temple and shouting, "Duh." Instead I tried to remain equable. "You finally understand. Somebody's out to get you. We'll talk more about that later. Right now, here's what you need to do: Call the police, make a report. I wish I could be here to tell them I saw the rifle, but that's not possible." In previous encounters, I'd been of assistance to Sam Cobb, chief of the Adelaide police, but I'd most often been able to maintain my distance as an unseen helper. As soon as Nick made the call, I would address my unfortunate position. I was definitely too much *in* the world. And I didn't even have a purse. I looked forlornly down. No purse. How was I going to eat? Where could I stay? What was I going to *do*? Where was Wiggins?

Nick came a step nearer. "You sick or something? Maybe I can drop you somewhere."

A brisk knock jerked both of us around to face the door.

A light voice called. "Nick, it's Jan. I came as fast as I could."

Emotions raced across Nick's bony face: shock, panic, utter vulnerability. He swung toward me. "You've got to get out of here. Jan can't see you. She'll think—"

The front door swung open.

Chapter 3

"Nick, I—"

Jan was lovely, chestnut curls and a rounded, kind face with wide-set brown eyes, pert nose, and generous mouth. She wasn't beautiful, but she carried an aura of sweetness. Sweetness trumps beauty any day of the week.

She saw the two of us standing near the wet bar. I suspected she was also intuitive and that she sensed drama, of which there had been plenty in the last fifteen minutes. Nick looked strained and I, no doubt, appeared stressed.

"Oh." She lifted her chin. "I'm sorry. I didn't know you had . . . company."

My hope of dispatching Nick to the police, then slipping away to seek a solution to my own challenges disappeared, unlike me, into an unknowable future.

Yes, the police would have to be informed, but there was no way to adequately explain the situation to Jan unless I admitted my identity as an emissary, and Wiggins—wherever he was—would be utterly appalled if I revealed the truth to yet another mortal creature. Instead, I would have to make it clear that I had no designs on Nick and then possibly she would depart.

Nick looked at me with despair in his blue eyes.

I sprang into action. "Jan, how wonderful to meet you." I was across the room in a flash. "Nick's told me all about you." I hoped his oh-too-revealing face wasn't stricken with terror. I reached out, took her hand.

She was too well bred to resist, though her small hand was limp in mine.

"We're going to have a wonderful time this evening. Nick loves to dance, and he's asked me to teach you both"—I am inventive, but for an instant I was at a loss. Did they dance? What did they dance? What dance wouldn't they know?— "how to"—a deep breath—"shag."

"Shag?"

"Shag! Here we go. Watch my feet. Triple step, triple step, rock step."

Nick's face brightened.

I gestured to him. "Come on, Nick. Take Jan's hand." I sang "Under the Boardwalk." Have I ever mentioned that I love to sing?

"Oh." Jan looked surprised, then pleased. Stumbling and laughing, they followed fairly well.

A door slammed. Quick footsteps came nearer. A dark-haired young woman burst into the living room through the kitchen door.

I broke off in mid-lyric.

Nick and Jan stumbled to a stop. Nick's face looked like that of a midnight traveler confronted by a vampire. Happiness seeped out of Jan's face, replaced by repugnance.

The newcomer was pretty in a flamboyant fashion, but her features were marred by discontent and too much makeup. A low-cut red satin blouse, intended to be provocative, appeared skimpy, as did skin-tight jeans. She flung out one arm in a posture that rivaled Bette Davis on an emotional rampage and stared at Nick, her gaze beseeching. "I come"—her voice was husky with emotion—"and what do I find? You and two women. How could you do this to me?"

Jan shot Nick a glance of disgust. "I see you had other plans tonight. Why did you text me?" Her voice wobbled in disappointment and chagrin. "Oh well, it doesn't matter."

"Jan, wait a minute—"

Head held high, Jan rushed across the room. The screen door clattered shut behind her.

Nick strode after her.

The new arrival hurried across the room, caught his arm. "You sent for me. You apologized. You said we would be together now. Only to betray me—"

Nick's face flushed. "I'm not betraying you. Everybody knows you run around on Brian. So I took you out a few times. That doesn't mean anything. I don't owe you anything. And I didn't send for you."

Nick pulled free and plunged out onto the porch. "Jan, wait . . ."

Nick's accuser pressed a hand to her lips. Tears trickled down her cheeks. Nick might not feel he owed her anything. She clearly didn't agree.

I felt a pang of sympathy. She was obviously a mess, but I had a sense life had not been gentle with her. I moved to the door and looked out.

I joined Nick. He was at the foot of the steps, hands balled into fists, as a blue Camry jolted toward the street.

A battered pickup truck making explosive sounds, likely from a defective muffler, careened into Nick's drive.

"Jan, watch out!" Nick's shout was frantic.

In an instant of peril, Jan's car veered off the drive to avoid the pickup.

The pickup's horn blared. The exhaust backfired again as the pickup jolted to a stop. The driver's door slammed. "Where is she?" A barrel-chested man hurried toward the front porch. "Don't tell me she's not here," he yelled at Nick. "She said she was going to her mom's, but I called and she isn't there."

Nick hunched his shoulders. "You damn near hit Jan. Are you crazy, Brian?"

The young, balding man in a torn T-shirt, faded Levi's, and scuffed boots thudded onto the porch. He moved with the ferocity of a charging bull, but his face held misery and aching disappointment.

Nick shot me a panicked look and raced up the steps as Brian slammed into the living room.

Dimly I heard the sound of another car's motor, likely from behind Nick's house. I ran up the steps and inside. "Oh my, oh my, oh my. What a to-do this evening." I spoke loudly as if everyone in the vicinity might be hearing impaired. I guessed the departing car held the girl with the haggard face, who was making a strategic withdrawal. Likely, she was driving without lights until she'd eased a block or so distant from Nick's.

Brian stood in the center of the room, his head swinging in a slow circle. "Where is she?"

I grabbed Nick's arm. "Honey, what's the matter?"

Nick's response was scarcely flattering. He looked like a man snared by an octopus.

I pinched his side.

He jerked away.

I folded my face in a pout. "I declare, I don't know what's happened to our *romantic*"—heavy emphasis—"evening." I patted Nick's arm, which was as rigid as a steel beam. "Honey, don't you worry. I'll take care of everything."

The burly young man's face creased in bewilderment.

I moved toward him with a smile. "You must be Brian."

He made an angry sound in his throat. "Where's Lisa?"

I heard a strangled sound behind me. I put my left hand behind my back and made a waggling gesture, indicating, if Nick had the wit to understand, that he should leave the driving to me.

"You just missed her." I had no doubt this was the forlorn young woman's husband.

There was a definite groan from Nick.

Before Brian could gather his muscles to leap and put a throttlehold on Nick, I looked sweetly up at Brian. "Poor dear. Your wife apparently thought you were here. She came and pled with us to say where you were. Perhaps you'd better scoot home and reassure her that you are fine."

Brian blinked, his expression surprised.

I felt a stab of pity at the sudden glisten of hope in his eyes.

Some of the tension eased out of his big shoulders. "Lisa was worried about me?"

"Worried as can be. Nick and I assured her we hadn't seen you all evening."

Brian massaged the side of his branch-thick neck. His eyes narrowed. "You been here with him"—he jerked his head at Nick—"all night?"

"Every minute. We love spending time together." I increased my volume to drown out Nick's growl. "I told Lisa we understood how important you are to her and assured her we understand how much she cares about you. I had to forgive her"—I gave a tinkling laugh and a gentle head shake—"for pretending to be interested in Nick. It's just a ploy to get your attention. The best thing for you to do is pretend you don't care. Why, if you act as if you're interested in someone else, Lisa will be so jealous, she'll do everything in her power to get you back."

His face furrowed. "I've always been true to Lisa."

Uh-oh. Talk about unintended consequences! I certainly had no intention of encouraging the man to violate his wedding vows. Wiggins would be appalled.

I didn't sense a pulse of indignation near me. I couldn't

even picture Wiggins's handlebar mustache quivering in dismay. *Wiggins, where are you?*

I pushed back my feeling of abandonment and hastened, I hoped, to clear up any misunderstanding. "Certainly you have been faithful. Just as she has been." Not being sure, I crossed my fingers on the hand behind my back. "Perhaps now you'd better hurry home after her."

He started to turn, then stopped and glared up at Nick. "You're a sorry louse. Taking advantage of a woman when she's down." Brian squared his shoulders. "I'd knock you halfway to Dallas—"

I lightly touched Brian's muscular arm. "Every minute they spent together, Nick was building you up to Lisa." I glanced at Nick and wished he didn't have such an unpleasant expression on his bony face. I was sure he could be attractive if he tried. "Didn't you do just that, Nick?" I wiggled the fingers on my hidden hand, the old "come on now, play along" gesture.

Unless Nick preferred have his sorry ass kicked halfway to Dallas, he needed an attitude adjustment and maybe a dash of my creativity.

Nick's face had a decided prunelike stiffness, but he muttered, "Yeah. I think Lisa"—pause—"well, she wasn't interested in me"—pause—"she kind of seemed to want to kick up her heels"—pause—"like"— He looked at me. A moment of shock rippled across his face as he realized he couldn't bring up my name, because he didn't know my name—"like the lady"—I detected a touch of malice in his voice—"says, Lisa's kind of messed up thinking about you and her."

Oddly, I was impressed with his honesty. He wouldn't lie, even though his rangy frame didn't appear to be a match for Lisa's muscular, aggrieved husband.

"Yeah. Well, gee, I guess you meant well. I got it all wrong. So"—Brian's voice was gruff—"sorry I busted up your evening." He gave me a shy nod. "Glad you and him are an item." He swung around and moved swiftly across the room. He banged through the door. In a moment, we heard the roar of his truck.

I gave a whoosh of relief.

Nick glared at me. "It will be all over town that I've got a redheaded girlfriend. Jan will never talk to me again."

For a man whose sorry ass had not been kicked to Dallas, he was exceedingly ungrateful. "We can deal with that."

"We"—his voice was deep in his throat—"are not going to deal with anything. You need to go home."

Home.

"I don't have a home." My voice was shaky. Tears burned my eyes. I was half-scared, half-mad, and feeling way too much *in* the world. "It's all the fault of that woman on the horse. I should have demanded to talk to Wiggins, but she looked so grand in her riding habit. She had such an aristocratic face and the most vivid blue eyes. She looked as if she could see right through me. She said you were such a fool, but there were those who loved you."

Nick reached out, grabbed the back of a straight chair. He appeared to be struggling for breath. His voice was strangled. "What color was the horse?"

"Black. Black as a chunk of coal. He glistened. A gorgeous creature." My tone wasn't admiring. If I ever found the horse and its rider, I'd demand an accounting. But if I couldn't disappear from the present, I couldn't count on climbing aboard the Rescue Express to return to Heaven.

"All black?" There was faint hope in his voice.

I pictured the horse and its rider. "Except for a big white splotch on his forehead shaped like a crescent."

"Oh God." Nick looked haunted. "That's McCoy. Her horse, The Real McCoy." He swung around and headed for the stairs, took the treads two at a time.

"Nick!" Where was he going? He and I had to talk. I was here on his behalf, and I needed help in return. I hurried to the base of the stairs and folded my arms. If he didn't come down again quickly, I would pursue him.

The stairs reverberated as he thudded back down the steps, again two at a time. He clutched in one hand a silver photograph frame. He skidded to a stop in front of me, took a deep breath, thrust out the frame.

I studied the photograph with widening eyes. The woman pictured on the jumping horse was older than the rider who had directed me to catch the Express. The woman in the photograph had silver hair and a thinner face, but there was no mistaking the cool blue eyes, pointed chin with a distinctive cleft, and long, thin nose. She and the horse had melded into one, moving together as the horse rose in the air to jump.

I was excited. "That's she."

"You mean it's her." He sounded glum.

I almost corrected him, but decided grammar wasn't important at this point. I tapped the glass. "Who is she?"

Nick managed a sickly smile. "Come on. Explain the joke. Did you know her a long time ago? Did she leave a bequest asking you to come here and shake me up?"

Bequest. I sighed. "She's dead, of course."

He looked relieved. "So you did know her. Did you ride together? Or travel or something?"

"I never saw her in my life or in Heaven until she came thundering up to me on that beast and sent me down here to help you."

"Heaven." He offered the word experimentally. "You really mean"—there was a trace of a gulp—"Heaven?"

"I mean Heaven."

He turned away, walked unsteadily across an oval braided rug, and flung himself onto a plaid sofa.

I pattered after him, settled at the opposite end, and, just for fun, sang "My Blue Heaven." "Bobby Mac and I used to do a great duet."

He drew himself up in a defensive posture, gazed at me as if I might suddenly produce a Heavenly choir.

"Bobby Mac's my husband."

"I didn't know ghosts were married."

I smiled brightly. "I've probably told you too much. But that's the situation. I'm a ghost."

His chin jutted out. "I don't believe in ghosts."

"You will." My tone was mild. "I am here because you are in danger." I pointed at the bullet hole in the wall. "Now, who was the woman on the horse?"

He gazed down at the photograph. "Delilah Delahunt Duvall. She lived in Adelaide when she was a kid, but moved to California after college. She died last year. In an accident climbing Liberty Ridge on Mount Rainier."

"Mountain climbing? She did that as well as ride?"

"Aunt Dee rode, climbed, white-water rafted, caved, scuba dived, gambled, and wrote thrillers, and along the way she collected lovers on five continents. Aunt Dee never took no for an answer and always said yes to a challenge." Nick sounded weary.

"I see." I was afraid I was beginning to understand. The telegram from Wiggins had been counterfeit. Nick's aunt Dee had nosed about the department and found my name. Any thriller writer would consider it child's play to purloin information from Wiggins's old-fashioned paper files, which were kept in accommodating unlocked wooden filing cabinets. It was possible she sometimes served as an emissary. However, Wiggins was always insistent that emissaries not contact family members who knew them. In my first adventure, I'd aided a great-niece, but I had never met her previously. Possibly Aunt Dee was simply aware of the department's activities. In any event, if she'd wanted to send help to Nick, obviously she would have hunted about in the files for someone connected to Adelaide, and so she had sent the spurious telegram and waylaid me as I was en route.

I felt chilled to the bone. Wiggins had no notion I was here. None. Even worse, assuming she cared, Aunt Dee had no way of knowing that I was marooned, unable to disappear, and adrift in a world where each person needed a proven identity to function. Oh, woe.

"If anybody could hijack somebody from Heaven, it would be Aunt Dee. That's for sure. But look, you're kidding me, aren't you? You knew her, and that's why you're here. You can't be a ghost." But he edged farther away from me.

I squeezed my face in concentration. Perhaps the incidents of the evening had only temporarily derailed my ability to appear and disappear. I took a deep breath, and thought, *Gone.* My elegant rose leather loafers remained firmly planted on the floor and in full view.

I tried again. This time I spoke aloud, forcefully. "Gone." The stylish loafers were fully visible on the floor.

I sighed. I was an emissary without a link to the department. "Like it or not, and I definitely don't, your aunt Dee bamboozled me. *Hijacked* sums up my situation very well indeed." An untethered astronaut in space could not have felt more adrift than I.

What was worse, I had no idea in this world—and obviously not in the next—how to reconnect. I'd been in tight spots on my previous missions, but I'd always had my ace in the hole, the ability to appear and disappear at will.

Now . . .

I popped up from the sofa and stared at my image in the mirror behind the wet bar. I looked good. This was no time for false modesty. My morale needed every morsel of affirmation I could manage. I smoothed back a coppery red curl. My eyes looked a trifle strained, but the lavender-colored sweater, rose blouse, and charcoal gray slacks were quite flattering. I especially admired the scalloped collar of my blouse. I lifted my chin. I was Bailey Ruth Raeburn and, whether Wiggins realized my plight or not, I would do my best for Nick.

"All right. We play the hand we're dealt." I spoke decisively.

Nick looked alarmed. And worried. Very worried.

"Since I don't have any money or transportation, I'll have to stay here—"

He began to back away. "No way. I can't explain to Jan why the shag dancer started living with me. Nuh-uh. You have to go someplace."

I folded my arms in exasperation. "Let me put it in words of one syllable: I have no cash. I have no car. I have no identification. I have nothing."

He fumbled with his back pocket. "Money is no problem. Lady, I'll give you money." His face brightened. "How about a plane ticket? And cash. Tomorrow I'll get you ten thousand dollars and you can fly away. Have you ever been to Tahiti? You'd—" His face fell. "No ID. Yeah. Scratch a plane. No passport, I guess."

I didn't bother to answer. Earlier I'd thought he had a core of honesty. Obviously not. Ten thousand dollars! Where would a scruffy young guy like him get ten thousand dollars? He was just trying to get me out of his house. He would have promised the moon if I'd have listened.

He began to pace. "I'll buy a car, get you a snazzy one. You can take the car and the money and drive away."

My smile was slightly pitying. He was in error if he thought I was naive enough to believe his offers of money. I shook my head, gestured toward the bullet hole. "I'm here. Here I stay."

He slammed a hand on the top of the wet bar. "Not here. That sure sounds like a setup to me. You got somebody around taking pix? I'll bet this is a con, all this stuff about Aunt Dee. For all I know you knew her somewhere and you came here to screw money out of me."

I raised a eyebrow. My tone was scathing. "I suppose you are just rolling in money! You don't look old enough to manage anything better than a lemonade stand. One look at your patchy beard and polo with a ripped pocket and Levi's with the knees out and it's obvious you are not a titan of industry."

He stared at me. "You think I'm broke." His voice had an odd tone.

"I think you've got a few years to go before you have an extra ten thousand." As in never.

"What did Aunt Dee say about me?"

I quoted: "He's always been such a fool . . . but there are those who love him . . . try to save him from himself."

He scratched at one cheek. "She didn't tell you what I'd been doing or why I was back in town?"

"There wasn't time." I'd been swept up by Aunt Dee's challenge. Next time I would pause and think, as Wiggins always hoped I would. If there were ever to be a next time. . . .

"So you don't know that I'm seriously rich."

I almost hooted. It was absurd to imagine that this callow, unshaven, sloppily dressed guy had an extra fifty bucks in his pocket. Absurd. . . .

He leaned casually against the wet bar with a cocky smile.

Nick had stumbled all over himself in talking to Brian about Lisa, but there had been a core of honesty in his response.

"You're rich?" I felt stunned.

"You got that right, babe."

I glanced toward the bullet hole. Money might not be the root of all evil—I'm no authority—but its possession or lack has a mighty effect on the course of human events.

He looked like a house croupier raking in the chips. "You ever heard of *Arachnid's Revenge: Featherfoots to the Rescue*?" He studied my face. "Yeah, well, it's my video game. Featherfoot spiders on a rampage, and they catch the bad guys, big hairy flies, in their webs, and there are thirty-two radii and twelve concentric spirals. You've got to fix the web when it's broken and catch at least ninety flies to get to the second level—" He broke off, no doubt realizing I hadn't followed a word. "Anyway, lots of goo oozes out as the flies try to get through the webs, but the Featherfoots are a web ahead." He stopped to laugh at his own wit. "It's a hairy,

hairy game, and I got bought out for a cool nine million."
He slid onto a bar stool, propped an elbow on the counter.

I stared. "How old are you?"

"Twenty-four."

"You said you came back to Adelaide. Where were you?"

"Austin. I went to school there, but I didn't finish. I was
halfway through my junior year when I started working on
Featherfoots again. I first had the idea in high school.
Everybody laughed at me. Like they always did." There was
a trace of bitterness in his voice. "Because I like spiders. I
especially like Featherfoots. They are kind of a woody
brown or gray mottled with white. What I really like is they
can hang for hours in a web without moving. And the
webs"—he sounded triumphant—"are always horizontal."
He spread his arms wide. "Cool, huh?"

Nine million dollars. Long live *Featherfoots*.

"Okay. I get it. You created this game and sold it, and
you are rich. Why did you come back to Adelaide?"

If Bobby Mac and I had ever had nine million, or even
one, my destination of choice would have been Paris.

Nick's young face was abruptly pugnacious. "I had some
scores to settle and money"—his tone was arrogant—"makes
me a player. See, nobody ever thought I was a player. Well,
I'm showing them, one by one. I'm having a hell of a good
time. I started with Cole Clanton. He played football." Years
of loathing curdled his voice. "Big Bad Cole." He drawled
the name with venom. "He showed his ass one night on a
campout, but he was such a big deal he turned it around and
pretty soon everybody was dumping on me. See, we were
at church camp and a jumping spider—a *Phidippus audax*—
crawled out of a log Cole was sitting on. He gave a squeal
like a girl and bolted like a stuck pig. The guys started
laughing at him. His face turned red and he grabbed a stick
and headed for the log. He was going to kill the spider. I
yelled at him to stop, that it was a *Phidippus audax* and
wouldn't hurt anybody. I should've kept my mouth shut, but

I said it was a cool spider with eight blue eyes, four big ones on its face, and it could jump fifty times its body length. He kept on going. I tackled him, and by the time everybody pulled him off of me, the spider was gone. Cole had gotten in some punches, and my right eye was swelling up. He pointed at me and yelled, 'Look, one blue eye. I got it. You're a *Phidippus audax*. I guess you got a whole family out here. Gee, Phidippus, how could I have known?' Well, the guys all cracked up. That's what they called me the rest of the way through school. Phidippus."

"So you came back and you're busy getting even."

He gave two thumbs-up. "When money flows, anything goes."

"I see." Indeed, I did. No wonder Aunt Dee hoped I could save Nick from himself. "I suppose there are others who have earned your ire?"

He looked blank.

He might be in his own way a homespun philosopher, with all due respect to spiders, but his vocabulary lacked muscle. Possibly, if time permitted, I might suggest a reading list, starting with "Babylon Revisited," though Nick was obviously not a serious drinker even if he was seriously rich. However, efforts to engender a more charitable attitude could await the successful completion of my assignment.

I felt a little lurch inside.

I didn't have an assignment. But Nick was in danger and I was here. I would have to do what I could. I had much yet to learn about Adelaide's youngest millionaire and who might have wanted him dead, but tomorrow was time enough. For now, I hoped Wiggins would forgive me— *Wiggins, are you there? Are you anywhere?*—if I sought a place to stay. It would be easiest if I stayed here, though the prospect had moved Nick to ferocious resistance. So that was out for now. The attack still must be reported to the police, and I was in no position to answer official questions.

I gave a decisive nod. I caught the movement in the mirror. Wiggins would be proud. I appeared as determined, and I hoped as appealing, as Myrna Loy in the paint scene in *Mr. Blandings Builds His Dream House*.

Nick stiffened.

I reached out to pat his shoulder reassuringly, and he shied like a spooked horse. "Emulate your favorite spider. Be cool. Here's what we need to do."

His rigid face was all angles, mostly jutting cheekbones. He seemed to have an aversion to the plural if it included me.

I was pleasant, but firm. "You must report the shooting. After the investigation is complete, you can join me. I'll . . ." I paused, squeezed my face in thought. Where could I go? "It's such a bother, not being able to be here and there whenever I wish. You must stay here for the moment and I must leave. . . ." Inspiration struck. "I'll take that little yellow scooter outside. Meet me at Main and Calhoun at midnight. Surely it won't take any longer than that to see about the shooting. Until we figure out what's going on, you shouldn't stay by yourself. We can book a double room somewhere."

He looked as horrified as if I'd suggested sharing space with an adder. "Not a chance."

"Your virtue is not at risk. I am a happily married woman. You can sleep in your shorts and I suppose you have a T-shirt I can borrow. After all, there are not only coed dorms but coed rooms these days. So what's the problem?" I smothered a yawn. "On the way, we'll stop for a hamburger somewhere."

Now his face not only jutted, his body locked in a decent imitation of an iron sculpture. "No way."

I moved behind the wet bar, opened cupboards. A can of cashews.

"Come on, Nick, you must call the police. But first, call a motel and make a reservation."

"You want me to use my credit card and have a redheaded babe show up and check in? This is a little town. Word would get back to Jan—" He stopped. "Jan. Hey, that's where I can put you. Jan's mom has a B and B. I grew up next door." He looked a trifle defensive. "Arlene—her mom—is kind of frosted at me right now, but I doubt if she's full, and a body in a bed pays better than a bed without a body. Anyway, Arlene can use the money. Adelaide's booming because of the Chickasaw Nation, but even so, Jan said the B and B visitors are down this year. The economy keeps a lot of people home. I'll call and explain I have an employee who needs a place to stay. Jan will think everything's on the up-and-up if I send you there. Won't she?" The beseeching tone in his voice was pitiful.

"Of course that's what she'll think."

His momentary elation fled. He gazed at me from head to foot. "What could I hire you for?"

His emphasis on the third-person pronoun was not pleasing. Possibly, I thought, I should add to his reading list a self-help book extolling the value of tact. However, a seriously rich twenty-four-year-old probably felt tact was as unnecessary as a landline. But this wasn't the moment to try to improve Nick's attitudes.

He shook his head in disgust. "Who's going to believe I need a redheaded babe to do anything? I've never had a secretary. I'm thinking about a new game, but I'll bet you don't know a thing about vampires. That's what's hot." His face brightened. "I've got this great idea about vampires who vaporize giant squid invading from Saturn."

Great idea. . . .

I clapped my hands together. I don't know if it was the cashews or the prospect of finding sanctuary or the light-at-the-end-of-the-tunnel relief that finally the police would be contacted, but suddenly I knew exactly what to do.

Chapter 4

I shared my plan in a few short sentences.

Nick looked even more disagreeable.

I was adamant. "It's a brilliant ploy. Nobody will dare touch you."

"You've got to be kidding." He gave a kind of snicker.

"I am not kidding."

He made a sound between a moan and a snort. "You look about as much like a private eye as a belly dancer resembles a bishop."

My eyes slitted. "Are you sexist? Why couldn't a belly dancer become a bishop?"

His mouth opened, closed. He took a breath. "I'm not touching that one, lady."

"But you are going to cooperate with me." I tried to maintain a pleasant tone. "Unless you want an unexplained female voice reporting the shooting." I grabbed the cell from his hand, punched 911.

With a yelp, he grabbed it back, lifted it. With a gulp, he muttered, "Nick Magruder here." His glare at me was malevolent. "Nick Magruder. Eight nineteen Mulberry Lane. Somebody shot a rifle through my front window. Nobody's hurt, but there's a slug in the wall. Yeah, I'll be here." He clicked off the phone. "A patrol car's on the way."

"Which side of town are you on?"

He gave a strangled moan. "You're going to pretend like you're a private eye, and you don't even know where you are?"

"Aunt Dee"—my tone was icy—"didn't share much information."

He squeezed his face as if his head hurt. "Aunt Dee. Do I believe you? Actually, there's something screwy here. Tomorrow I'm going to find out all about you and get you out of my hair."

"Tonight comes before tomorrow." I paused to contemplate my observation. Perhaps stress made me even more lucid than usual. "Tonight," I spoke with emphasis, "comes before tomorrow."

"You already said that."

I felt in top form. "It was worth repeating." Such an apposite observation deserved to become a maxim. Possibly after he knew me better, he would appreciate shared wisdom. "Tonight I am here. You don't want me here. But here I stay until you agree to my plan. I need transportation and funding."

From his expression, he would have enjoyed tossing me into a deep pit.

I held out my hand. He was seriously rich, and if he didn't want to be seriously compromised by my presence, he would ante up.

"Okay. You win. For now." He shoved a hand in the pocket of his jeans, shook his head. He stalked to the desk.

I was right behind him.

He pulled out the center drawer. Keys slid toward us. I reached in and grabbed a small pad with a hotel logo and the single pen. Obviously, he didn't use the desk for work.

Nick picked up the scooter key, plopped it in my hand.

From his back pocket, he retrieved his billfold. He flipped it open, plucked out a bunch of bills, thrust them at me.

I counted aloud. "Six hundred dollars. I'll keep a meticulous count of expenses. I'll need clothes, of course. Oh, rummage around and find a suitcase."

"There aren't any clothes here." He looked abruptly mulish. "You can't have any of mine."

"Why would I want your clothes?" I found his thought processes puzzling.

"I don't know. Why do you want a suitcase?"

"When I arrive at the B and B, it will look odd if I don't have a suitcase."

"You're going to look odd anyway, arriving on a motor scooter. Are you going to pretend you drove up here from Dallas on the scooter? Yeah, Dallas private eyes go everywhere on scooters."

I remained unruffled. "There may be a few flaws in my plan, but it gets me out of here."

"You just said the magic words." He dashed across the room, banged open a door, disappeared from view. In a moment, he was back with a canvas duffel bag. "It'll fit better on the back of the scooter."

The bag appeared to be full.

"I stuffed in a couple of pillows so it looks like you've got stuff." He glanced at his watch. "The cops will be here in a jiffy. You need to get out of here. Now." He strode to the door, flung it open. "The B and B's at the corner of Elm and Buffalo. I'll call Arlene as soon as you leave."

I felt a bit pressed for time as well. I definitely wanted to avoid the police. What if I were asked for identification? I grabbed the duffel and hurried to the door. "Remember, I'm your employee. You can leave the rest to me."

"That's what I'm afraid of." He was gloomy. "Don't do anything rash. I'll check with you after breakfast."

I folded my arms, slowly shook my head. "I expect you

to arrive at the B and B as soon as you finish with the police. You will be safer if you are always in the company of others from this point forward."

"You want me to stay at the B and B?" Expressions flitted over his face—irritation, consideration, anticipation. "Yeah, maybe that makes sense." He rubbed his furry cheek. "If Arlene'll let me in. But hey, money's money."

"I'm beginning to think that attitude is what put you in peril."

He cocked his head. "You talk like an old radio show. But if I have to hang out with you, the B and B sounds good."

He didn't care a bean bag about my protecting him, but apparently proximity to Jan appealed mightily. He nodded energetically. "I'll make a reservation for two rooms." As I stepped onto the porch, he stuck his head out the door. "Don't come to my room."

I grinned at him. "Only for business conferences."

He didn't grin in return. Possibly he was humor-impaired.

He massaged his cheek again. "I'll tell Jan's mom you work for me and need a place to stay while you're in town. Oh hey, wait up. What's your name? I have to give Arlene your name."

My name . . . Bailey Ruth Raeburn was chiseled into a stone in St. Mildred's cemetery: *Bailey Ruth Raeburn, cherished wife of Robert MacNeil Raeburn*. There was a nice carving that did justice to the *Serendipity*, and the legend *Forever Fishing*.

In my past adventures, I'd assumed several names. Police Officer M. Loy, a tribute to Myrna Loy, who played Nora Charles to William Powell's Nick; Jerrie Emiliani in a nod to Jerome Emiliani, the patron saint of orphans; and Francie de Sales in honor of Francis de Sales, the patron saint of writers.

The right name came to me in a flash. My mission—even if unauthorized—was clear: I needed to lift Nick out of the mess he'd obviously made of his return to Adelaide as a seriously rich twenty-four-year-old. But, as Mama always told us kids, "Honey tastes better than vinegar," so I would have to use finesse and be adroit. The blessed Hilda, revered abbess of the monastery at Whitby, was renowned for her charm and grace in directing the lives of those in her care. I couldn't aspire to her accomplishments. However, I would do my best. Did I hear a distant tattoo of trumpets? "Tell them Hilda Whitby is on her way."

I felt jaunty as I started down the steps, the scooter key tight in my hand. I had transport and six hundred dollars in my pocket. If I had to be marooned, at least I had enough to keep me clothed and fed for a few days.

Some of the bounce left my steps by the time I reached the scooter. As I swung onto the seat and turned the key, I looked up at the diamond-bright stars in the immeasurable night sky and felt far, far away from Heaven. Previously I'd known with certainty that when my task was done (I usually hoped not too soon due to occasional mishaps), I'd hear the triumphant whistle of the Rescue Express and I would be homeward bound. What if . . . ?

I gave myself a shake. Mama also told us kids not to borrow trouble. As I wheeled down the drive, my hair streaming in the night air, I gave Heaven a thumbs-up. "I'm here, Wiggins. I'll do my best." But I'm afraid the sound of my voice was plaintive.

∽

I parked the scooter on the street, hefted the duffel, and followed a mosaic walkway to the front steps of a three-story Victorian house with a corner turret. Light spilled from ground-floor windows through lace curtains. On the porch, a hexagonal lantern with intricate ironwork offered a welcoming golden glow. Ferns in terra-cotta jars framed the paneled and elaborately carved jade green front door. On the side door panels, peacocks postured brightly in stained-glass insets. A center inset featured a shaggy buffalo.

A white wooden sign hung to the right of the door with the legend *Majestic Buffalo B & B*. Beneath a doorbell, a taped white card instructed: *Ring after ten p.m.*

I punched the bell.

An athletic blonde in her late forties opened the door. Trim and graceful, she had the healthy glow of a tennis player or golfer. She flashed a quick but meaningless smile that didn't reach ice-blue eyes. "Miss Whitby? Nick Magruder called. Please come in. I'm Arlene Richey." Her white blouse was as crisp as though she'd just dressed. Palm-print pale green linen slacks fit her loosely. Her apple green, single-band leather sandals were especially attractive, the band having the fine-grained appearance of bamboo. Her daughter Jan bore not the slightest resemblance to her.

I stepped into a hallway with golden yellow oak wainscoting and geometrically patterned floor tiles. A mirror framed in gold leaf hung above a mahogany chest. A Tiffany lamp sat on a pillar styled after an Ionic column. At the end of the hallway stood an oak grandfather clock. The stairway, with ornate cast-iron floral balusters, was in shadow, but a slim figure stood watching from the landing.

I smiled at Arlene. "I'm sorry to be late arriving. Travel difficulties." I waved them away with a flick of my fingers. I wasn't pleased with the rose red of my nails, but I couldn't, as in the past, think pink and achieve a better result. "Mr. Magruder," I hoped the more formal appellation made clear that Nick and I were not well acquainted, "will arrive as soon as the police complete the initial investigation of the crime."

Arlene looked shocked, but I didn't detect concern for Nick. "Crime?"

Jan clattered down the steps. "What happened?"

"Someone shot at Mr. Magruder tonight. Fortunately, the shot missed him. You arrived very soon afterward. Mr. Magruder insisted the incident not be mentioned. He didn't want you to be worried. That's why we danced." I was businesslike. "I'm a private investigator, not a dance teacher." Announcing myself as a private eye pleased me so much that I feared I was succumbing to worldly ways. However, even Wiggins—if he ever were to know—would have to admit that I was at the moment most definitely not only *in* the world but *of* the world. "My job often requires me to assume different identities, but I've never taught the shag before. Hopefully, when everything is sorted out and Mr. Magruder is safe, we can have another lesson before I leave."

If I ever left. . . .

"Someone shot at Nick!" Jan stood with one hand at her throat, her eyes wide and stricken. "Why?"

"That's what I'm here to discover. My agency is SAM Private Enquiries, Limited." If pressed, I'd give the principals' names: Spade, Archer, and Marlowe. "We have a one hundred percent success rate once we take a case." I am nothing if not positive. "Mr. Magruder contacted us after he received several threatening letters. He didn't keep the letters and ignored the threats until the night he almost crashed into a log that had been dumped onto his private drive." I must remember to inform Nick about the letters and the log, fancies I'd spun as cleverly as a Featherfoot. "I arrived tonight for a personal consultation. The shooting occurred at about twenty minutes before ten. He is dealing with the authorities at this moment. I recommended he rent a room here. He should not remain in that isolated house." I looked at Arlene inquiringly.

She nodded, though her lips were pursed. "He rented rooms for you and for him."

"Staying here will help keep him safe and it will aid me in my investigation."

Jan clasped her hands together. "We'll do everything we can to help."

I gave her a quick, warm smile. "He'll be here soon. I hope you'll let me ask a few questions. The more I learn, the quicker we can find out who is behind the attack. I need to find out as much as I can as fast as I can"—hopefully before Nick arrived at the B and B—"about anyone who might be angry with Mr. Magruder."

Jan bit her lip and looked away. Her mother's cool gaze studied me.

I looked wistfully at Arlene. "Perhaps I might have a snack? I missed dinner this evening."

♋

The sandwich was delectable—thinly sliced rare roast beef piled on a buttery croissant with a layer of Thousand Island dressing. I took a forkful of tangy coleslaw, munched a sweet potato chip. A tall glass of whole milk added to my contentment.

Arlene sat across from me, Jan to my left, at a small oak table in a nook near the swinging door to the kitchen. I finished offering my creatively crafted resume. ". . . and I've been working for three years at SAM. Previously I was with Gilbert, Keith and Chesterton Private Inquiry Agency in Houston." Few people knew that G. K. Chesterton, the creator of the Father Brown stories, was Gilbert Keith Chesterton. For an instant, I felt uneasy. Perhaps I was being too clever by half. I knew enough of the digital world from my previous missions to understand the threat posed by Google. A couple of clicks would reveal that my purported job history was bunk. Oh well, I'd think of something.

Arlene already appeared unconvinced. "What did the letters threaten? A good kick in the butt? If so, he's a candidate."

"Mother! If somebody tried to shoot Nick, it isn't a joke."

"I was there. It wasn't a joke." My gaze held Arlene's until she looked down, her lips compressed. "We were in the living room. A rifle barrel poked through the screen of a front window. I pushed him out of the way before the rifle was fired. Had I not done so, I doubt he would be alive now." I took a last bite, gathered my plate and cutlery. "So I need to know who wants to kick Nick's butt and why. Please give this some thought while I take care of my dishes." I popped up, waved Arlene to her seat, and carried the plate into the kitchen.

Picture tiles with baskets of fruits added a Victorian flavor. Glass-fronted cabinets were painted a serene pale blue. I noted the rose-colored linoleum flooring. There was even a dresser, that icon of a Victorian kitchen. Several framed photos sat on the dresser. One studio portrait pictured a broad-faced man with curly brown hair and a genial expression. I had no doubt he was Jan's father. A cut-glass bud vase sat next to the frame. The vase held one white rose.

I rinsed the plate and cutlery and placed them in a drainer. There was a thoroughly modern notepad and several pens next to an old wall telephone. I hurried to the table, pulled off several sheets, folded and stuffed them along with a filched pen into the pocket of my slacks. What detective would interview sources without taking notes? I reached the swinging door into the dining area. I started to push it open, then stopped, held the panel slightly ajar, and listened.

". . . no wonder someone tried to shoot him." Arlene's voice was acidulous. "He's done nothing but cause trouble since he came back. Old Timer Days is the best idea to hit Adelaide in years. Everybody's behind it, and it's all because of Cole. What right does Nick have to come back and ruin everything?"

Old Timer Days. This lush, rolling, hilly country had been home first to the Choctaws and, after their removal from Mississippi in 1837, to the Chickasaws. As Congress abrogated many of the promises to Indians, white settlers arrived in the 1890s.

Jan's reply was sharp. "You've been listening to Cole. That's always a mistake."

"Cole has every right to be furious." Arlene's retort was indignant. "Claire called him this morning and told him that Nick's buying the property so he can't build the trading post like she promised. It's rotten of Nick. He doesn't care about the Arnold place. All he wants to do is block Cole."

"Cole can't possibly care that much about Old Timer Days." Jan was dismissive. "He knows about as much Oklahoma history as that armadillo who digs up your iris. In fact, I'd bet on the armadillo if I had to choose."

"You never have liked Cole."

"With good reason." Jan's voice was cool. "He isn't what you think he is."

"I know him much better than you do." Arlene's voice was soft. "He has a hard time trusting people. He never had much kindness in his life—his dad dead, his mom dumping him on her brother and his family. The last Cole heard she was somewhere in Bolivia. His uncle is a stuffy old jerk. He thinks Cole is flaky, like his mother. Anyway, he needs understanding. He and I have a good time together."

Jan didn't answer. She pressed her lips together.

Her mother's face flushed. "There's nothing wrong with an older woman and a younger man."

I dared not linger longer, or they might wonder if I was pilfering the silver. I bustled through the swinging door and ignored the tension in the breakfast nook, though the atmosphere was as heavy as an imminent thunderstorm. Jan pressed her lips together. She made no reply to her mother, but there was very likely no good reply that had come to her mind.

I gave Arlene a swift glance. Undeniably she was a youthful and quite firm late forties, but late forties are late forties. I wasn't taking undue pleasure in forever being twenty-seven. That would not reflect a generous spirit. "The kitchen is amazing. The plate rack over the butler's sink is such an excellent Victorian detail." I slid into my place, pulled out my folded sheets and pen, and looked at them brightly. "It's been my experience as a detective that authorities are excellent at investigating homicides. But they are not adept at preventing homicides. My job is to protect Mr. Magruder.

To do so, it is essential that I speak to everyone who has reason to be angry with him. As I understand the situation, and I have had the opportunity for only a brief talk with Mr. Magruder, he has returned to Adelaide as a very wealthy man and it might be said he came home with an attitude."

Arlene looked sour. "He can't wait to tell everyone how rich he is."

Jan rushed to his defense. "That's not fair. He's a success, and he has every right to be proud. The guys who treated him like scum in high school are the ones badmouthing him now."

I asked quickly, "Such as?"

Arlene's lips thinned. "I don't blame them. Nick sneers at anyone who played football. But he hasn't stopped there. He's gone out of his way to try to block Cole's plans for the festival."

"Cole?"

"Cole Clanton." Arlene slipped a cell phone out of her pocket, swept her thumb across it several times, held it out to me.

Cole Clanton's thick brown hair was tousled. His dark eyes looked sleepy. Sensuous lips parted in a half smile, he lounged shirtless on a rumpled bed, propped on one elbow. He looked reckless, sexy, and arrogant.

Arlene gazed at the picture. Desire glowed in her eyes, her lips were parted.

Jan looked away, her expression a mixture of sadness and distaste.

Arlene spoke with energy, oblivious to Jan's discomfort. "Cole's amazing. Everybody's excited about the upcoming festival. He has wonderful ideas." Arlene gestured around the room, her gaze settling on a glass-paned china cabinet filled with Victorian bric-a-brac, ruby red lusters, paper-weights, papier-mâché trays, small statues, china vases, crystal boxes, silver goblets. "We'll serve a Victorian tea every afternoon, and we're selling tickets for a Ladies' Book

Society meeting, and everyone will wear eighteen-nineties dresses. We'll have a review of *The Light That Failed* by Rudyard Kipling. It was published in eighteen ninety, a couple of years after the trading post was built. The Strand Shoppe has picked up twenty or thirty dresses discarded by a costume shop in New York, and the dresses will be for rent with a percentage of the rental going to the festival fund. The Chickasaw Nation Dance Troupe will give a special program at the lake amphitheater, and tickets are selling like wildfire. Bud Hotchkiss has a restored stagecoach and he's going to take groups for rides. Rod Holt, who runs an Old West store, plans to sell replicas of Oklahoma treasure maps. The festival will get a percentage of the profits. And if Nick hadn't messed everything up, Cole was going to put up a replica of the original trading post, but that's all off now. Nick's going to buy the place from Claire Arnold."

I looked up from my sheet of paper. "How did Nick block the trading post?"

"Money." Arlene's tone was dry. "Claire was willing to let Cole set up the trading post, but Nick told her he would buy only if Claire refuses to let Cole come on the land. Nick offered her a lot more than the place is worth, so of course she agreed. Cole's really upset. Claire told Cole this morning that she'd changed her mind about participating in the festival. It's really hateful of Nick. It wouldn't hurt anything to let Cole put up the replica. Nick did it out of spite."

Jan shrugged. "Nick has the money. If that's how he wants to spend it, it's his business. Anyway, I'll be glad when someone buys that place and fixes it up. It was bad enough when Gabe Arnold was alive, but the shrubbery's even thicker now. At least the gates aren't locked anymore and the dogs are gone. Gabe had two German shepherds, and nobody dared ever touch foot inside those walls." Jan looked toward me. "Mom's yard is gorgeous, daylilies and roses and grass like velvet. To have that eyesore next door is hideous."

I was puzzled. "Did Nick grow up there?" I distinctly remember his saying that he'd grown up next door to Jan.

Arlene shook her head. "The Arnold house is on one side," she pointed over her shoulder. "The Magruder house is on the other side."

I made quick notes, but losing out on a place to set up a replica of an old trading post didn't sound like an A-rated motive for murder. I was ready to move on. Sex is a much better motive than a disappointed event planner. I didn't want to compound Nick's difficulties with Jan. Perhaps I could give Nick a boost with Jan but get the information I needed. "Mr. Magruder was irritated tonight when a young woman named Lisa showed up uninvited."

"Lisa Sanford." Jan paused. "Uninvited?" Her tone was slightly breathless.

"Absolutely. He hadn't called her and he wasn't interested in having her at the house. Then her husband arrived. He thought Lisa was involved with Mr. Magruder. I diverted Mr. Sanford by pretending that Mr. Magruder and I were a couple."

Jan's eyes scoured me.

I made every effort to appear as inoffensive and sisterly as possible. "Mr. Magruder was offended—"

"You got that right." Nick strode into the kitchen. He glanced at Arlene. "Front door wasn't locked. Since I'm a guest, I thought it was okay if I came on in." He bit off his words. His thin, unshaven face was taut and his eyes had a flinty glint. "Offended puts it a lot nicer than I would. In fact, I am pretty damn pissed off. I'm playing my drums tonight, having fun, and everything goes to hell. You come"—he pointed at me with an accusing finger and not a shade of warmth, which should have been reassuring for Jan, but didn't augur well for a cooperative effort—"I've got blood on my head, Aunt Dee's screwing with my life, there's a bullet hole in my wall, Jan rushes off because the town tramp blows in through absolutely"—he glared at Jan—"no fault of mine. Lisa claims I called her on my cell. I didn't. But," and he sounded morose, "a little while ago I checked, and damned if there weren't calls to Lisa and Brian and Cole. I didn't make those calls. Somebody must have taken my cell from my car and used it and then thrown it back in the car tonight." He sighed. "At least Cole didn't show up. But Lisa's sad-sack husband barrels up mad as a stuck pig, and, to top it all off, one of the cops—Ed Loeffler—is an old buddy of Cole Clanton's, and he all but calls me a liar."

I was shocked. "Didn't he see the slug in the wall?"

"He looked at the hole, walked over to the window, looked at the ripped screen, turned around and asked me where I was when the shot occurred. I told him I was standing by the wet bar. He got a sneer on his face that looked like a Mafia hit man's, and said, 'I don't think so. If you were standing there,' and he jabbed a finger, 'you'd be dead.' He rocked back on his heels like a gunslinger in a saloon door, and said in this menacing growl, 'There's a law against falsely reporting a crime.' I told him I thought there was also a law against somebody shooting at a man when he's in his living room. He said, 'Yeah, if it happened.'"

"Didn't he do anything?" Oh, if only I could pop to the police department unseen, a ghost on the warpath. But here I was, stuck.

"Oh, sure. He took pictures, wore plastic gloves, eased the slug out, put it in what he called a collection bag. Then he asked me if I was trying to get rumors started about some crazy sniper and ruin Old Timer Days. That's when I got the picture. Ed didn't buy the idea that somebody tried to shoot me. He thought I faked it to scare people away this weekend." He rubbed his cheek. "He's a buddy of Brian Sanford, too. I guess Brian had unloaded about me. Johnny Cain was the other cop. He's a good guy. He never called me Phidippus."

"Was Ed a football player with Cole?"

"Yeah." The answer was short.

"You don't like any of the football players."

His voice curdled with loathing. "You got that right."

I gave him a cool look. "So you came home to settle scores and used your money to keep Cole off the Arnold property and pretended you were interested in Brian's wife to make him miserable even though you didn't care for her." I was sorry to add to Nick's difficulties with Jan, but his actions were what they were.

Nick's stubbled cheeks flushed. "I didn't hire you to preach at me. If Cole wants to have his little celebration on that land, let him scare up the money to buy it. A man can do what he likes with his own property." His bony jaw jutted.

Arlene's voice was hot. "If he got the money, and you know he doesn't have any way to raise it or get a loan, you'd just double your offer."

His grin was ferocious. "You bet I would. As for Lisa, I sure wouldn't have gone with her except everybody knows she runs around on Brian. Everybody but him. She's been sneaking around with Cole Clanton for a couple of years."

Arlene's chair jolted back. She came to her feet. She trembled, eyes wide, lips parted. Her breaths came shallowly. "You're making that up. Cole wouldn't have anything to do with someone like her."

As obtuse as most men, Nick clutched his main point like a caveman with a spear. "You've got to be kidding, Arlene. Everybody in town knows about Lisa and Cole. I saw them at the casino a couple of nights ago. I was talking to some guys, and they said room seven at the Roadhouse Inn is called the L and C Special."

Arlene's face crumpled. She moved leadenly across the floor, her back rigid. In a moment, there was a clattering sound as she started up the stairs, faster and faster.

Nick stood with his mouth open. He looked at Jan. "What's the big deal?"

"I don't think you'd understand. Just like you didn't care that Lisa might be fooled by you. I'd heard people say they'd

seen you with her, and I didn't believe it. I guess I should
have known. All you care about is getting back at people."
Jan's gaze was steely. "I'll get the keys for you and Miss,
uh, Ms. Whitby." She moved fast, hurrying past him, out to
the hall and back again in a flash, carrying two old-fashioned
metal keys on rings with dangling trinkets. She handed me
the key with a pink ceramic heart. "You're in the Sweetheart
Room. At the top of the stairs, turn right and go to the last
door. Breakfast is served from seven to nine." She thrust a
ring with a plastic arrow quiver at Nick. "Good night." She
turned to move swiftly toward the hall.

"Hey, Jan. Wait a minute." He took a step after her.

She kept on going and spoke over her shoulder. "The
Powwow Room. Top of the stairs, third door on your left."
Then she was gone.

Nick stopped and looked miserable. "What'd I do wrong?"

"Possibly everything. We'll talk about it tomorrow. But
quickly, before I go up, who else have you infuriated since
your return?"

He lifted his bony shoulders in a shrug, let them fall.
"How should I know?" He avoided my eyes.

I wasn't about ready to accept his evasion. "You know."

He looked so hangdog, I felt sorry for him.

"Nick, you came home with a bunch of grudges and you
didn't see past getting some payback. You forgot"—Wiggins
would be proud of my tact—"that kicking a bumblebee nest
can get you stung. It's up to me to swat the bumblebee. As
soon as I know the person who tried to shoot you, you can
make amends with everyone else. That will impress Jan."

I'd tugged the right string. He looked hopeful and eager.
"You think so?"

"A very good chance. The sooner I find your attacker,
the sooner you can set everything right." Though I rather
doubted Arlene's faith in Cole Clanton could be restored.
"So, who else is mad at you besides Cole Clanton and Lisa
and Brian Sanford?"

"Yeah. Well." he stared over my head as if the blank wall were mesmerizing. "There's Albert Harris. Just because we used to toss ideas around, he thinks I should split everything with him. No way. I'm the one who designed the game."

"Nothing you and he discussed ended up in your game?"

He was a shade strident. "Sure, I always talked about spiders. But I did the work."

"Anyone else?"

He relaxed. "That's the crop."

"How can I find them?"

"Cole Clanton wangled an office at City Hall since he's the director of Old Timer Days. He parlayed some stories he wrote for the *Gazette* into this Old Timer Days celebration."

"Is Cole a serious student of Oklahoma history?"

Nick gave a whoop. "He's a serious student of sex and whisky. He wouldn't know an old timer if he fell over him. Nah, he's just figured out how to be a big deal without working a lick. It's easier to sit on a cushy chair at City Hall than work on the *Gazette*. He only got that job because his uncle owns the paper. As for Lisa, she's got a job as a clerk at the college library. Brian's mowing yards. He lost his job with a construction company last year. Albert's a reporter at the *Gazette*. I doubt he and Cole were buddies. Cole's way too cool for Albert, and Albert's got a superiority complex that won't stop even though he didn't play football." Nick cracked his knuckles. "If it weren't for the hole in my wall, I'd say this was nuts. Maybe I've rubbed some people wrong, but I haven't done anything to make somebody mad enough to shoot at me." He looked bewildered.

He didn't want to face the fact that he was alive by the merest fraction of an instant. I was blunt. "If I hadn't pushed you, your next of kin would be dealing with funeral arrangements tomorrow." Speaking of . . . There was one more fact I needed to know. "Since you are seriously rich, I assume you have an estate plan."

"Estate plan?" He looked as blank as if I'd started to discuss the charms of a point-collar pale pink blouse that I'd recently worn with a new suit. The jacket had the most adorable narrow lapels. I felt a pang. I was going to be tired of my current costume very, very soon. Sartorial boredom is a sad state of mind.

I focused. "You are rich. Do you have a will naming a beneficiary or beneficiaries? Or have trusts been set up?"

He jammed a hand through his thick curls. "La—Hilda, if that's your name, give it a rest. I'm only twenty-four. I don't need a will."

No will. "Who's your next of kin?"

"My cousin, Bill. Bill Magruder." There was no fondness in his tone. "I sure wouldn't leave him anything. He's a bum. And he hangs around with Cole. I wouldn't give him the time of day, much less money."

My voice was thoughtful. "A bum here in Adelaide?"

"Yeah. He's had his hand out ever since I got back. It's not my fault he has a degree in art history and he can't find a museum job. He's working at La Hacienda, the Mexican restaurant downtown. The only good thing he's ever done is spill a bowl of queso on that cop who sneered at me." A happy smile lighted his face. "Sticky, hot queso."

"Where does Bill live?"

"Those old apartments out near the railroad tracks, the Lilac Arms." He gave a muffled snort. "Who'd name something the Lilac Arms? Can't you see big, fat arms sprouting purple flowers?"

The Lilac Arms had been the latest, most up-to-date apartments when they were built in the 1970s. I remembered them well. To Nick, they would be so far distant in history as to be ancient.

I added Bill's name to my mental list. I was going to be busy tomorrow with both personal and professional tasks. I needed clothing. After all, a woman can't wear the same old tired outfit and function at a high level. Once equipped, I intended to ask provocative questions of the likely suspects. I had no expectation that I would speak to those who disliked Nick and discern like a dowser who had pulled the trigger of the rifle. My goal was much simpler: to warn off a killer from trying again.

Chapter 5

I should have sunk into instant, deep sleep. Heaven knew I'd expended both physical and emotional energy since my arrival. But that was the problem: Heaven didn't know. I lay wide-eyed. Moonlight streamed into the room, illuminating the dressing table, which sat in a bay. White dimity with antique lace fringes decorated the table. Wooden towel rails were well stocked with fluffy pink embroidered towels. In a mahogany wardrobe I'd found two pink terry cloth robes. One now served as a makeshift nightgown. With little expectation of success, I employed my usual method of dress, envisioning an item of clothing in which I then would appear. There was no change in the feel of terry cloth against my skin. The much more appropriate silk of red pajamas remained a hope.

I knew of no way to bring my plight to Wiggins's attention. Possibly he might summon me for an adventure and discover I was not to be found. Until then, here I was and here I would be. Much as I loved Adelaide, I had no wish to become a permanent resident. Without money or identification,

I would be a wretched waif. Nick Magruder could provide income while I sorted out the truth behind the attack on him, but I could not expect him to provide for me when that task was done. In the past, when I had been here as an official emissary, Wiggins often arrived to encourage or chide. Perhaps if I ended up in peril, he would sense my need.

My predicament was enough to make anyone sleepless!

However, as Mama always told us kids, "If you rip your shorts, sew on a patch and hold your head high."

Possibly sleep would come if I got up and found something to read, I thought. I popped up and was halfway to the chest to turn on the lamp when I stopped at a window, my gaze caught by an intermittent flash of light in the thick rank of shrubbery and trees next door. It must now be well past midnight. Absently, I imagined a watch with a buffalo face. My wrist remained unencumbered.

The movement of the light seemed stealthy and vaguely threatening. I wished mightily that I were the old me (although always twenty-seven, mind you) and could at will appear and disappear, moving from one location to the next in an instant by thinking of a destination. Right now, had I been an official emissary, I would think *wooded area next door* and there I would have been.

I began to have a better appreciation of investigators limited by physical boundaries.

Of course, the area with the occasional light wasn't the property of the inn. There was probably no reason for me to be alarmed. So far as I knew, no one was aware that Nick Magruder was in a room down the hall from me. Still, the vagrant bounce of light was not ordinary. A punched-out window screen and a rifle shot weren't ordinary, either.

The window looked out over the second-story veranda. I touched the lower sash, lifted. The sash slid up, noiseless and smooth. It took only an instant to unhook the screen. I started to slip out, realized I was clad only in a terry cloth robe. With a little huff of exasperation, I dashed across the room, donned the now oh-so-familiar blouse, slacks, sweater, and shoes.

From my second-story vantage point, I could see over the tall stockade fence between the inn and next door. The light was sometimes visible, sometimes not. From Jan's description, the Arnold property was thick with uncut shrubbery and heavily wooded. That would explain the occasional disappearance of the beam. Finally, there was a flicker and then a kind of soft glow that was almost indiscernible through shifting limbs.

Nick was going to buy that property. Cole Clanton wanted permission to build a replica of the trading post there. Now someone was creeping about in the deep of night. I wanted to know who was there and why.

I tiptoed to the stairs that led down to the B and B's backyard. As Jan had said, her mother's garden was well kept. Shaded lanterns illuminated October blooming plants—Indian mallow, Chinese lanterns, goldenrod, and mums. I smelled the sweet scent of autumn clematis as I passed an arbor.

Now I couldn't see anything next door, my vision blocked by the stockade fence. I reached a heavy iron gate, which stood ajar. I slipped through the opening and was plunged into darkness. Occasional swaths of moonlight appeared through shifting tree limbs to help me stay on a winding dirt path. I heard an occasional, distant pinging noise. I had a quick vision of a war movie, actors hunched in silence in a hunted submarine as an enemy destroyer passed overhead. I shook my head and had a moment of amazement at the long-submerged memories harbored in my brain. This was no time for daydreaming.

I made a wrong turn and lost the path. I had no flashlight. I was plunged into a tangle of greenery, brush encroaching from both sides, vines and tendrils snaking across the path. I felt my way forward, sliding one foot forward, then the other, my hands spread wide like an insect's antennae to brush aside whip-lashing branches. I tried to move quietly, but the shrubbery rustled. I was thankful that a playful wind rattled leaves somewhere near. The noise of my intrusion could easily be attributed to the wind. I heard an occasional rasp of a still-surviving cicada.

Abruptly, a coyote howled, the shrill wavering sound as shocking as a cross between a wailing banshee and a berserk soprano. The cry seemed to come from behind me. I gave a startled yelp, took a breath, and continued forward. I felt claustrophobic in the intense darkness. I saw a light and veered to my right. I stepped into a moonlit clearing.

There was a sense of movement behind me, but before I could turn, a plastic bag was thrown over my head. My arms were pinned to my sides. I was hefted like a feed sack in a tight, painful grip. I felt an instant of vertigo as I was carried, twisting and struggling, unable to see, enveloped in the plastic, my cries muffled.

Over the sound of my ragged breathing and strangled gasps came the thump of footsteps on wood. Abruptly, I was flung high. I flew through the air to splash into cold water. I flailed frantically and finally freed myself of the plastic sack. I sputtered to the surface. My hand banged against something slimy. It took a heart-wrenching moment for me to realize I was standing waist deep in a fish pond. I flinched as something smooth touched my skin. If my hair hadn't been plastered to my head, it likely would have stood on end like the needles of a threatened porcupine.

In the distance, the sound of running steps faded to silence.

Shivering, torn between fury and relief, I moved toward the edge of the pond, jerking like a marionette each time I was touched by a fish. I scraped one knee crawling out onto the bank, trying hard not to imagine what might have been lurking in the dried stalks that rimmed the water. At least

Oklahoma ponds didn't run to leeches. At worst, I'd probably been nudged by a catfish.

The wind picked up. I began to shake with cold. I gazed around the clearing. There was no indication, at least not in the moonlight, of what my assailant might have been doing. The gleam of the flashlight was gone. Beyond the pond with its wooden bridge and a screened gazebo rose a three-story frame house, utterly dark.

I was confident an intruder had been in the side yard of the Arnold property. When I'd reached the clearing, I'd been grabbed and thrown into the pond so the intruder could escape.

I shivered and turned back toward the overgrown path. Whatever my attacker had intended, I couldn't see a connection between the fitful flashlight in the Arnolds' yard and the shot fired earlier at Nick Magruder.

However, I'd found trouble when I landed at Nick's house. He'd arranged for me to stay at the Buffalo B & B and I'd found trouble again.

Possibly I'm talented.

Possibly I was a shade too curious for my current earthbound status.

I hurried back toward the B and B, clothes squishing, water oozing from my loafers, thinking about Nick and the property he intended to buy simply to thwart Cole Clanton.

∽

The sunlight slanting through the window emphasized the shabby state of the clothes I'd draped over the towel rack last night. Now they were stiff, wrinkled, and stained by moss and algae. The rose blouse looked mottled, the sweater was damp, and the slacks sagged. Trust me, I have never in this world or the next ever worn saggy slacks.

My face wrinkled in distaste. I picked up the blouse reluctantly. Perhaps this equivalent of a hair shirt was to remind me that I was currently *of* the world, not simply *in* the world. In Heaven, my dress would be perfect. Perhaps I would have chosen a long, sunset-orange linen pullover with a ballet neckline and a tiered cream voile skirt and orange leather heels.

I closed my eyes, pulled on the musty-smelling, stained clothing. I took a moment to walk down the hall and slip a note beneath Nick's door. The instruction was simple: *Stay with Jan.*

As a seriously rich young man, he could arrange his day as he wished. I didn't think he would find my order hard duty. The attack at his house had occurred after dark when he had been ostensibly alone. The shooter had not been aware of my presence because I had not yet appeared. During daylight hours in the company of Jan, he should be safe. If my plans went well today, there should be no more attacks.

I slipped down the stairs and hurried out into the early morning. I hopped on the yellow scooter and wove in and out of morning traffic to a strip shopping mall anchored by Wal-Mart. I was at the door when it opened at 8:00 a.m. Normally, to shop is to live; or, in Heaven, to swirl from one outfit to another is simply another sublime aspect of paradise.

However, this morning I darted from rack to rack, from department to department, in a whirlwind of activity. In twenty-eight minutes, I had assembled a wardrobe, everything from undies to blouses, slacks, skirts, two cardigans and a fleecy jacket, three pairs of shoes and costume jewelry, plus makeup and toiletries, all for less than three hundred dollars.

Returning to the B and B, I hurried upstairs and changed into a bright blue shirt, added oval-shaped turquoise drop earrings and a gold-plated chain-link necklace. Navy slacks and flats completed my outfit. I admired my appearance—truly this could not be said to be vanity; it was simply an expression of heartfelt relief—in the framed mirror and whirled toward the door, a new woman. A quick breakfast and Hilda Whitby would be on the case. But first . . .

༄

The front gate to the Arnold property hung askew, the bottom tension-bar band missing. Shrubbery ran amok on either side of a sidewalk with jagged cracks. I stepped inside the gate, shaded my eyes to study a rambling three-story white-frame house, probably built in the 1920s. The big structure had likely housed a huge family or served as a boarding-house. Now, paint peeled, and there was an aura of disrepair and neglect.

I moved toward the front porch with a confident air. As Mama always said, "A dog on his belly won't get the bone." I pushed the doorbell, heard a distant chime. The door opened to reveal a bouncy, pert brunette probably in her late forties. I was surprised. Given the dolorous appearance of the house, I expected an occupant more on the order of an undertaker's assistant. Or a stand-in for Morticia Addams.

"Mrs. Arnold?"

"That's me, honey. Call me Claire. What can I do for you?"

"I'm Hilda Whitby, Mr. Magruder's assistant. He asked me to write up a report on the property. Do you mind if I wander around the yard? He's thinking about landscaping."

She glanced at the greenery run amok. "That sounds like a good idea. Tell him he can send in a crew anytime he wants. I got rid of the dogs after Gabe died. Rufus and Wally were great watchdogs, but they always scared me. My brother has a farm, and they don't mind dogs that don't let anybody get near the house. Kind of a help when you live out in the country. Please ask Nick not to have the shrubs and trees cut too much. My husband never wanted to trim anything." Her smile was quick. "Just like his beard. He had a big, bushy brown beard and looked kind of like a hulk, but he was kind as could be. People thought our place was scary because of the dogs, but Rufus and Wally loved Gabe." She looked around as if seeking a familiar face.

"I'm sure Nick will cooperate."

Claire smiled. "He's real nice. Anyway, I never gave Gabe a hard time about the yard. Let it grow, I'd say. When he died, I kept it the way he liked it." For an instant loss transformed her face with a look of puzzled hurt in her eyes. "But he's gone, and I'll have to tell you I can't wait to sell the place. I don't like living here by myself. It's an old, old house and there's been a lot of misery here."

"Most old houses hold a lot of stories."

"You got that right." Claire nodded agreement. "I agreed to live here because Gabe liked all the stories, even the bad ones. Some of the rooms I hated to go into, but Gabe said nobody could ever call our house boring. Once a gambler owned the place. His old green-felt poker table's still in the basement. Gabe was always looking for the secret room the gambler was supposed to have built, but he never found it. Anyway, I hope the place can stay the way Gabe liked it. Nick said he wouldn't trim a whole lot, kind of keep the wild-and-woolly look. There's a lot of history here. The first trading post was over by that oak." She pointed to her right. "This was part of the Chickasaw Nation, but settlers were coming in anyway. Ezra Porter built the post around 1888. He was married to a Chickasaw. There are lots of Porters still in town. That's the only thing I'm kind of disappointed about in selling to Nick Magruder, but we're going to sign the papers tomorrow. I'd promised to let the Old Timer Days people put up a replica of the trading post, but Nick said that would be a deal breaker. He didn't want anybody on the land for any reason. Yesterday I had to call the fellow who was going to put up the trading post."

"Cole Clanton?"

She looked uncomfortable. "He was mighty upset, said I'd promised him. But like I told him, I don't owe him any-thing. I put the place up for sale after Gabe died, but I hadn't even had a looker. I want to go help my sister, who's real sick. So that's that. I told Cole a few feet doesn't make any difference, and he's thick with Arlene. Maybe she'll let him put the replica up over there. He said that wouldn't be authentic. I could have told him history was bunk. Sure, people say the trading post was here, but it could have been a couple of hundred yards either way. But he got excited about Adelaide's history when he did some stories for the *Gazette* in August. He got stuff out of the old newspapers, and then Rod Holt joined in. He owns Holt's Back Shop."

Arlene had mentioned Rod Holt. "What is Holt's Back Shop?"

Claire lifted her shoulders, let them fall. "Kind of a silly name. It's an Old West store. Rod means back in time. He carries all kinds of stuff. I'd call it junk, everything from washboards to spurs to leather trunks. He's helping plan events for Old Timer Days. He's nutty about old treasures, and he's going to sell maps that show where Belle Starr buried some loot. Cole wanted to set up a replica of the original trading post here, but he has to stay off this property now."

She pointed to her right. "Near that oak, you can see a couple of stones jutting up from the ground. Belle was rumored to have visited the trading post several times in the late eighties. One visit came not long after she and her gang boarded a Katy train near Boggy Depot and blew apart a safe to escape with a metal strongbox containing a shipment of Army gold worth almost two hundred thousand dollars. Who knows what those gold pieces would be worth today? People have hunted for that cache for years. Some people think she buried it near the trading post, but there's an old legend that Ezra helped her bury it near a cistern in what's now City Park. Rod's fixed up a bunch of maps on thick paper yellowed to look like parchment. He's using the old story about the cistern and making lots of maps with directions to Belle's treasure. Each treasure hunter gets a map keyed to some spot near the ruins of the cistern. It's kind of a cute idea. Each map has a different little story to account for why she buried the stuff there. After all, the whole idea is probably hokum anyway, so nobody cares if the maps all have different sites. Rod's going to plant prizes at all the places. That'll be the biggest draw. Not having the trading post here isn't that big a deal. Like I told Cole, they've got plenty of places to feature, and they can do without this one. Maybe it's all for the good. Gabe never let anyone step foot on the land." Again there was a look of loss and pain.

A distant bell chimed. She glanced at her watch. "I got to get on to work in a few minutes, but you feel free to look wherever you want." Her tired face was lit for an instant by an impish smile. "But no digging!"

As soon as the door closed, I headed down the steps and moved toward the thicket of trees between the Arnold house and the B and B. As near as I could guess, the bobbing flashlight had been near the big oak with the ruins of some old structure, which may or may not have been the original trading post.

Between the oak and a caved-in wishing well, its decorative bucket rusted and fallen to one side, I found a trampled area of still-blooming Indian paintbrush, stems crushed and fluted orange and reddish blossoms broken. Not all of the patch had been crushed, but it was easy to see a zigzag pattern near the center of the grassy area.

I went to the far side of the patch of disturbed grass. Now I stood between the trampled area and the oak tree. To my left was a stagnant pond with a wooden bridge. In the morning sunlight, algae looked thick as a crust. There was nothing to indicate I'd been tossed over the railing to flounder in the muck. I tried not to remember the slimy feel of the algae.

Portions of the B and B's second-story veranda were visible through the shifting limbs of the trees. Last night I'd seen a flashlight from my room. Mrs. Arnold could wander about her property anytime she wished, so I was confident the late-night visitor was an intruder. I came up to the edge of the trampled grass. The closer view offered nothing new. Someone had walked over portions of the grassy area, but bent stalks and crushed grass appeared to be the only damage. Why sneak onto the lot late at night to walk about in the thick grass mixed with tall-stalked wildflowers? I had no idea, but my dousing in the pond indicated the trespasser was determined to remain unknown.

I had no idea why someone had skulked about the area last night, but two men had a definite interest in the property: Nick Magruder and Cole Clanton. As far as I knew, Nick had been safely ensconced at the B and B when the flashlight beam was flitting. I would ask him. It might be interesting as well to ask Cole Clanton about his whereabouts last night.

I stopped long enough at the B and B to call the mayor's office. "This is Hilda Whitby, reporter for *Middle News Press*. I'm trying to contact Cole Clanton, director of the Old Timer Days celebration."

A familiar Oklahoma accent was soft and cheerful. "Mr. Clanton's office is on the third floor of City Hall. His extension is thirty-eight, but he's often out making arrangements." The secretary gave me his cell phone. "The celebration is sponsored by the Mayor's Office. The mayor will be here this afternoon. She is the proper person to interview for your story. May I schedule an appointment?"

I remembered the mayor from previous encounters. She had all the charm of a warthog but the financial backing of a banker husband, who provided plenty of cash for her campaigns. "My schedule is full today. I'll be back in touch." I replaced the receiver. Wiggins would have been pleased that I had resisted the unworthy temptation to promise worldwide attention for Old Timer Days, which, of course, would not be forthcoming.

That is, he would have been pleased if he'd had any inkling of my activities. I suppressed a hot pang of panic.

For now, I had nice clothes and a place to stay. What the future held . . .

Sternly, I returned to my to-do list. First, Cole Clanton, then the others who had little fondness for Nick Magruder.

Cole Clanton answered on the first ring. "Hey, Arlene. We can work everything out." He was trying for charm, but there was a hint of desperation in his voice.

I raised an eyebrow. Obviously the telephone in Cole's temporary office had caller ID. He saw that the call came from the Majestic Buffalo B & B. Obviously, he'd spoken earlier with Arlene. Last night she'd run from the dining room, carrying with her Nick's careless revelations about Lisa and Cole.

"Listen, babe." His voice was beseeching. "Lisa doesn't mean anything to me. I swear to you. Nick's trying to cause trouble. I'll be right over and—"

I hung up. Cole Clanton appeared frantic to repair his relationship with Arlene. She must have demanded to know about Lisa and revealed Nick as her source of information. If Cole had been angry with Nick before, he would be enraged now. My intent was to warn off everyone who had reason to shoot at Nick. I intended to inform Cole that if anything happened to Nick, Cole's name would be at the top of the list going to the police.

If only I had been able to disappear and immediately pop to a destination.

I reconnoitered. Jan was in the kitchen and turned with a polite smile, a B and B employee ready to be of assistance.

"Have you seen Nick?"

"I said good morning a little while ago." She evinced no enthusiasm. "He'll be back soon." She was making a factual report. Her tone indicated it was immaterial to her if he ever returned. "He went out to his house to feed his cat."

I felt an instant of alarm. I'd warned him to stay close to others. However, it was unlikely that the assailant would be lurking at Nick's house this morning. "It would be better if he weren't alone today. Perhaps he can give you a hand here."

Just for an instant, concern flashed in her eyes, then she shrugged, possibly dismissing last night's attack as more of a prank than a threat. "Nick?" She raised an eyebrow. "I don't think mopping is one of his skills. When he gets back, he'll find breakfast in the dining room. He's a guest. He's welcome to hang around. I can't wait for him. I'm on my way to the grocery as soon as I finish the dishes." She turned back to the sink.

I scanned the room.

Water gushed from the faucet.

I used the sound to cover my soft footsteps to a closed door. Cole Clanton was en route to the B and B, and I wanted to overhear his conversation with Jan and possibly one with Arlene. I turned the knob, winced at the click. I glanced toward Jan, but she was working at the sink, her back to me. I eased the door open wide enough to slip inside the pantry. I pulled the door almost shut. If I were found . . . I'd cross that bridge when I came to it, hopefully with more success than my bridge crossing last night.

A door squeaked. Arlene Richey slowly crossed my sliver of a view. Last night she'd been an older woman proud of a young lover. This morning she was a woman diminished, eyes red-rimmed in a pale face. "Are the muffins hot?"

"Let me pop them in the microwave. Mom, take the morning off."

"Why would I do that?" Arlene's voice was brittle, a quick challenge to Jan.

Jan took a quick breath, turned away. In a moment, the microwave pinged. "Here they are."

In a moment, Arlene passed me on her way to the door to the dining room.

When the door creaked shut, Jan said violently, "Oh, Mom, he's not worth your pain."

Abruptly, I heard the back door open.

I eased the pantry door open another inch.

In Arlene's phone pic, Cole Clanton had been a man pleased with himself and his world. Now he looked anxious and uncertain. He gazed around the kitchen, started for the swinging door.

Jan's voice was hurried. "Mother doesn't want to see you. Please leave."

"Sure she does. Listen, Jan, that's all crap about Lisa."

"No, it's not." Jan's tone was flat.

His eyes narrowed and his face hardened. "Lisa's a slut. So I took my turn. That has nothing to do with Arlene. Come on, Jan, give me break. Where's your mom?"

The swinging door to the kitchen opened. Arlene stood in the entryway. She gestured at the refrigerator. "Take some apple juice to the old ladies."

Jan looked from her mother to Cole and back again. With a helpless shrug, she walked to the refrigerator and lifted out a pitcher.

When the door to the dining room swung shut, Arlene gripped the back of a kitchen chair. "Get out." Her face was pinched. She looked older. A sheen of tears glistened in her eyes.

"Hey, Arlene." His tone was smooth, cajoling. "Let's sit down somewhere quiet. I can explain. Sure, I hung out with Lisa, but that was before you and I got going."

"No." The single word fell like a stone in a well. "I called some friends. They knew. You made love to me and it was a lie."

His features twisted in quick anger. "We said all along we were just having fun." A flush suffused the back of his neck.

"Of course." Her lips twisted in a pathetic attempt at a smile. "So the fun's over." Her voice was thin. "You go your way. I'll go mine." She whirled and blundered toward the door into the dining room.

He stood with his shoulders hunched, hands balled into fists.

I pushed open the pantry door and stepped into the kitchen. "Mr. Clanton."

He jerked to face me. "Who're you?" His tone was hard. A muscle twitched in one cheek. He was livid with the thwarted, petulant anger of a spoiled man faced with a situation he couldn't control. It took me a little by surprise. Did he care that much for Arlene Richey? Nothing in his demeanor suggested jealousy or great passion. No, he was simply boiling mad.

People who are angry often speak before they think. I decided an up-front attack might afford Nick the most protection. "You were spotted at Nick Magruder's house last night."

He stared at me, his face utterly still. Finally, he spoke, his voice bland. "You got that wrong. I decided not to come." He folded his arms over his chest.

"Why not?"

He shrugged, looked more comfortable. "He texted me, said he was ready to deal over the Arnold place. I figured he didn't want to chump off and pay what he had offered. I decided to let him stew about it. Maybe I would've called him today. Maybe not."

I felt confident that Nick's attacker had taken his cell phone from the front seat of his car yesterday, placed some calls, then tossed the phone back into the car. Three people had shown up unexpectedly at Nick's house: Jan Richey, and Lisa and Brian Sanford. Now it appeared Cole Clanton had been summoned as well. Obviously, the shooter had obtained Nick's cell, texted messages setting up arrivals after the attack, possibly hoping one of the visitors would call the police and thereby be embroiled in a murder investigation.

"What were you doing at Nick's?" His mouth twisted

into a leer. His eyes roamed me up and down. "I guess I don't need to ask. I thought he had the hots for Jan. But you look like fun in the meantime. Maybe we could get together for a drink."

"Not in this lifetime." My glance was dismissive. "I work for Mr. Magruder. If you didn't come to his house, you must have a double."

His eyes narrowed. "No way anybody saw me. I wasn't there." Now his gaze was steady, con-man steady.

I felt a flicker of excitement. I was almost certain Cole Clanton was lying. Although if he had arrived as a rifle was being shot, he might be excused for deciding it wasn't a good moment to come calling. "You were there."

"Who says?"

"I do."

He studied me.

I don't claim to read minds. That isn't a ghostly skill. But, unless I was far off the mark, Cole decided I was bluffing. Maybe he played a good hand of poker. His wariness seeped away. He shook his head as if I were an annoying gnat. "You can't prove anything. Tell your boss—" He broke off, his eyes narrowing. "Are you really working for the jerk?"

"I am investigating an attempt on Mr. Magruder's life."

Cole stared at me with a dark, unreadable gaze. "I heard he claimed somebody shot at him."

"How'd you hear that?"

"Everybody was talking about it at Lulu's this morning."

Lulu's was Adelaide's old-time café with the best hamburgers in town and breakfasts to match.

Cole sounded bored. "It's all over town. Somebody told me it was on the local radio station, and a couple of guys tweeted me about it. They knew I wouldn't be shook up if somebody got him. I didn't take it seriously. Around here, people who shoot don't miss."

I was sharp. "If anything happens to Nick, your name will be at the top of the list for the police."

"You scare me almost as much as Phidippus. So who's got a list and why should I care?"

"I have a list, and I will make that list available to the authorities."

"Are you a cop of some kind?"

"I am a private investigator." I loved the sound of the words.

He appeared to process the thought. "A redheaded private eye. So you and the jerk aren't a twosome. That means Jan's still the chick he's chasing." His tone was thoughtful. He looked toward the screen door. Was he staring at the door or at the property that stretched beyond the B and B grounds?

Cole wanted access to the Arnold place. Nick had thwarted him. Last night, someone shot at Nick and someone trampled grass near the site of the original trading post. Maybe it was a leap too far, but I decided to push my chips into the pot.

My tone was casual. "Did you find what you were looking for at the Arnold place last night?"

He swung toward me, looking like he'd been sucker punched—eyes wide, mouth open, face slack. He moved toward me, stopped a scant foot away, glared down. "What are you talking about?"

I described my adventure at length, finishing, ". . . somebody covered me with a plastic bag and threw me in the pond." If Cole had tossed me from the bridge, I would have expected his bland con-man expression.

Instead, his face was grim. He asked sharply, "What time did this happen?"

"Late. After midnight."

He took a step toward me, his face intent. "What did you hear?"

I couldn't know if he was clever enough to pelt me with questions, thereby underlining his lack of knowledge, or if he was desperately interested in what I knew. Whichever, it wasn't my intent to placate him. "Mine to know, yours to wonder. Unless you were there."

"If somebody was over there last night, it wasn't me." His flat voice had an ugly sound. "Why were you nosing around?" His gaze was sharp and suspicious.

"I saw lights. I was curious."

"Maybe you'd better not be so curious."

I folded my arms, returned stare for stare. "I'll do what I want to do."

Antagonism flickered between us.

Jan pushed through the door from the dining room. She stopped and stared at Cole. "You aren't welcome here, Cole. Please leave."

Cole took his time turning away from me. His face was cold and hard. "I want to see your mom. She's on the committee. I need to put up the trading post over here now."

Jan folded her arms. "You're kidding, aren't you? Do you think she'll have anything to do with you and that stupid celebration now?"

Cole slammed his hand on the kitchen counter. "She's got to help me out." The door from the back porch banged open.

Nick stepped inside. "I thought I heard your loud, obnoxious voice." Nick, as usual, was unshaven. He looked seriously poor in a ratty red polo and worn jeans with one knee shredded and the other grass-stained. His eyes moved from Cole to Jan. "Is he bothering you?"

"Cole, please leave." Jan's voice shook.

Nick's chin jutted. He stepped toward Cole, lifted a hand with fingers curled and thumb stiff and gestured toward the door. "Get out."

Cole's shoulders tightened. "Since when do you own this place?"

"Jan wants you out of here." Nick's voice was dangerously soft.

"So you want to keep Jan happy." Cole's tone was considering. "You'll do anything to make her happy, right?"

Nick glared. "What's it to you?"

Oddly, Cole gave a short bark of laughter. "I think that's nice. I like romance. You screwed everything up for me with Arlene, but that doesn't mean I don't wish you luck with Jan. I guess you'd do a lot to keep her happy."

Nick stiffened, sensing a threat, uncertain what might be coming. "If you bother Jan, I'll beat the hell out of you."

Cole's laugh was derisive. "Sure, you and those furry little spiders you hang out with. Gee, I'm scared." His amusement slipped away, replaced by a combative look. "I got some business to see to, then I'll be in touch, Phidippus." He swung around and strode toward the door.

Nick's hands balled into fists and he lunged after Cole.

I moved fast and grabbed Nick's arm. "Don't be dumb. He's goading you."

Nick skidded to a stop, glared down at me. "You're always in the way."

I didn't take his criticism personally. I was too worried about Cole's triumphant expression as he slammed through the door, his thin lips curved in a cruel smile.

Chapter 6

I swung aboard the yellow scooter. I'd warned Cole Clanton that he faced a police investigation if anything happened to Nick, but there were others who found Nick unlovable: the voluptuous Lisa Sanford; her husband, Brian; Albert Harris, who thought he deserved to share in the riches cascading into Phidippus's pocket; and Nick's bum cousin Bill Magruder, who would be a very rich young man if anything happened to Nick. I wouldn't relax until each and every one realized they would be suspect in another attack.

Seriously rich . . . As a motive for murder, it was hard to pick between sex and money, but money might win by a nose.

❦

Head-high sunflowers, their bright yellow petals brilliant in the October sun, were bunched on either side of the worn front steps. The stately flowers added charm to the shabby old apartment house. I checked the mail slots. More than half were nameless. Bill Magruder was in apartment 6.

The front door opened readily. Midway down the dim hallway, I skirted a cooler outside of one door. My nose wrinkled at the scent of old fishing bait. At apartment 6, I punched a buzzer, held it for several seconds. On the fourth try, the door opened a few inches. "Hey, what's the racket? How the hell can I sleep?"

"Bill Magruder?"

His face screwed up in disgust, a young man peered out. Also unshaven, blond hair matted and uncombed, he was a bleary version of Nick, the same bony face and sharp features. "Didn't you see the sign? No soliciting." He blinked, rubbed his eyes. "Oh yeah." There was a change in tone. "You looking for me?"

Bobby Mac always says redheads have an edge. Perhaps that's true. I smiled, but carefully made my smile simply friendly. I wasn't going to encourage false hopes. "I'm here for your cousin, Nick."

Bill frowned. "What's he want? Is he broke, in jail, bad ass against the wall?"

I raised an eyebrow. "Bad ass against the wall?"

"Sorry if that offends you." There was no apology in his voice. "Nick's put everybody's backs up since he hit town."

"Including yours?"

He gave a little whoop of laughter, though he didn't sound amused. "Babe, he isn't my favorite cuz these days. More moola than a mogul and tight as a tick. If you know him, he's probably told you I've hit him up for a stake. All I want is enough cash to get to LA. I got a friend who's working in the William Morris mail room, and she thinks I can get a spot. I can apply online, but I got to be able to get there. What's a thousand bucks to Nick?"

"He turned you down."

Full lips curved lower than a downward parabola. "Yeah." Bill's nose wrinkled. "Just because I didn't give him some bucks when he was in school and he had to lay out a semester."

"You had money then?"

He shifted from one foot to another. "My mom died and left me some."

"Why don't you use that money to go to LA?"

"I tried to win big at the casino. Some people do."

I forbore to point out that most people don't. Maybe Bill had learned that lesson.

He gazed at me with admiring eyes, then glanced over his shoulder at the disheveled room. "You got a minute, I'll throw on some clothes, straighten things up."

"I'm simply a messenger. Somebody tried to shoot Nick last night—"

Bill's eyes widened in surprise. Of course he would appear surprised if his finger had pulled the trigger.

"—but the shooter missed. If Nick had died last night, you would be rich. However, Nick made his will this morning. His estate had been left to the Oklahoma Humane Society." Bill Magruder would have no reason to doubt my statement, and that removed the motive of murder for an inheritance.

Bill rubbed his head again. "I didn't get in until three. Had to help wash up. A couple of sorry no-shows at the restaurant. Didn't sleep worth a damn. The doorbell made my head feel like a gigged catfish. Now I find a good-looking chick in the hallway who tells me somebody shot at Nick and his money is going to the dogs. Have I got that right?"

"Essentially."

"Yeah. Well, maybe he needs to improve his overall personality. But I sure as hell didn't take a shot at him."

I thought I detected the slightest emphasis on the first person singular pronoun.

"Who did?"

"How would I know?" His expression was suddenly disingenuous.

"If you have information that could lead to Nick's attacker, remaining silent makes you an accessory after the fact."

"Lady, I don't know from nothing. Anyway, it sounds like no harm done." He gave me a wry smile. "Give Nick my regards. And tell the bowwows they're gonna be rich." The door started to close.

"One thing more." I spoke swiftly. "Can you prove you were at the restaurant from nine to eleven last night?"

He kneaded one cheek with his knuckles. "I had a late shift, ten to two. I was here"—he gestured with one hand—"until about a quarter to ten. I wasn't anywhere near Nick. Where did it happen?"

I didn't bother to answer. I looked past him into a dingy, small living room that appeared littered with pop cans, DVDs, and fishing tackle. "Where's your rifle?"

He gave me an odd look. "I am fresh out of rifles. And that's my quota on weird questions for the day." The door slammed in my face.

⟋

Reporters' fingers flashed over laptop keyboards on the gray metal desks that rimmed the *Gazette* newsroom. A balding man with a hypertension flush and an unhealthy paunch sat at a desk in the middle of the room. "Crandall"—his yell was weakened by a wheeze—"where's the copy on that hit-and-run?"

A thin woman in her fifties with huge eyes, a mop of straggly brown hair, and an aura of toughness barked in a raspy voice, "Almost done, Ralph." A long strip of red licorice hung from the corner of her mouth, impeding her speech. She chewed, and an inch of the strand disappeared.

I scanned the room's occupants. A blue-haired woman in her seventies in a navy silk dress flipped pages in a notepad. A mid-thirties man wearing a ball cap backward talked to himself in an indistinguishable mutter as he wrote. My gaze stopped on a mid-twenties man with wiry brown hair, a round face, and an absorbed expression. He typed, paused, typed, gave a satisfied nod. His hand moved to his mouse. He was the right age to have been Nick's high school friend.

I walked swiftly to his desk. "Albert Harris?"

He glanced up. His brown eyes flicked up and down as he computed my age and social class and tabbed me as a stranger in town. I decided Nick's former classmate was a young man who thought fast and would not be easy to fool. His crown of tight curls and chunky build gave him a slightly teddy-bearish appearance, but his gaze was penetrating. "I'm Albert. And you?"

"Hilda Whitby. I'm here about the shooting attack last night on Nick Magruder."

He jerked his head toward the desk opposite his. "Joan Crandall has the crime beat. She covered it, but she's on deadline about a liquor-store heist. If you want to see the story about Nick's peril"—his tone was sarcastic—"I can pull it up. It's short and sweet." He clicked several keys and text filled his screen. I sat in the chair next to his desk and read:

> Adelaide police responded at 9:40 p.m. Tuesday to a 911 call reporting a shooting at the residence of Nicholas Magruder, 819 Mulberry Lane. The police report stated a screen was ripped in a front window of the residence and a bullet was found embedded in the wall opposite the window. The report said no one was injured and Magruder, 24, was unable to describe the purported assailant. No witnesses were at the home when police arrived.
>
> According to the police report, Magruder insisted he had no knowledge of who ripped the screen or fired the shot. According to police, no similar attacks have been reported in Adelaide or in Pontotoc County. However, the police took the slug in the wall into evidence.

෴

It seemed to me that the police report had clearly implied the attack was phony.

"Anything else you need?" He reached out and clicked and the text disappeared.

"I understand you resent Nick's success with his video game."

His eyes narrowed. "It's obvious from the police report that Nick trumped up a fake shooting. What's your game? Are you trying to pin the so-called crime on one of Nick's old friends? Like he had any."

"You don't count yourself as a friend."

"I sure don't. He took our idea and sold it out from under me. Did he cut me in? Not a penny." His brown eyes glittered with anger. "He lied and said it was all his idea, but it wasn't. We talked all about the spiders and how they could be a killer game. He owes me."

"You didn't do the programming."

"So?" He shrugged. "We talked about the idea. It was the idea that counts. I read about his sale in a trade magazine. Nine million dollars. He could have spared at least a half million."

"Where were you last night?"

He leaned back in his chair, folded his arms. "So, why are you asking all these questions?"

"I'm a private investigator hired by Mr. Magruder. Last night?"

He grinned. "Eat your heart out. I was at the Blue Note from nine o'clock to eleven, and I had a babe with me. So tell Nick his ploy is a bust. Now"—he glanced at the wall clock—"I got work to do." He turned back to the laptop.

I stood. I could check out his alibi, but it had been offered with utter confidence. Still . . . "If anything happens to Nick Magruder, expect a call from the police."

He shot me a taunting look, widened his eyes in mock alarm. "You scare me, lady."

∽

Lisa Sanford pushed a book cart in the main reading room at the Goddard College Library. Her blouse was too tight and her jeans too small. Unaware she was being observed, her face drooped in discontent. She was near the wall in a corridor between shelves.

My steps clicked on the tile floor.

She paid no attention until I stopped beside the cart. She looked up. Her eyes widened in surprise. "You." Her voice was startled. "You told Brian I was trying to make him jealous." Her tone was sad. "He was real nice. It was the first time in a long time we ever talked. I told him I didn't care anything about Nick."

There was no suggestion of returning happiness in the drooping lines of her face.

My voice was gentle. "Brian loves you."

"I kind of wish he didn't." Her gaze was weary. "It's too late. Me and him. See, he was real handsome when we were in school. A big football player. I was a cheerleader. We got married right after we graduated. He was fun then. He got a good job with Murray Construction. But he lost his job a couple of years ago. He tried and tried to find something, but there's no jobs out there. Now he mows lawns. We don't have any money. We had to move out of our house. We're living in a dumpy trailer outside of town. Brian's mad at everything. All he does now is mow lawns and drink beer and watch TV. It's kind of funny"—there was a sob in her voice—"you told him I went after Nick to make him jealous. I don't care about Nick."

Brian loved Lisa. Lisa didn't care about him. Or Nick. She'd been linked to Cole Clanton. "You wanted to make Cole jealous." It wasn't much of a leap to reach that conclusion.

She reached down, picked up a book, turned toward the shelf, but not before I saw tears in her eyes. "Cole dumped me for that old woman. How could he do that? He told me not to call him anymore." She shoved the book onto the shelf.

"So you had no reason to shoot at Nick last night?"

She swung back to face me, a hand at her throat. "Shoot at Nick?"

I described the rifle barrel poked through the screen and the shot that had almost hit Nick.

"Gee, that's awful." She sounded shocked. "Listen, I came to his house because I got that text. And so did Brian. Brian acts big and tough, but he'd never hurt anybody. You tell Nick it wasn't us." She plunged past the cart and hurried up the aisle.

As the sound of her steps faded, I wondered about Lisa. Did she really care about Nick? If so, she might have been angry enough to shoot him. But if her heartbreak over Cole was genuine, she hadn't pulled the trigger last night.

Brian Sanford's furious arrival in Nick's front yard indicated at that point in time he was violently jealous of Nick. However, if he had shot at Nick, surely he would never have revealed his anger.

I couldn't be sure about either Lisa or Brian. Lisa could be distraught over Nick's careless treatment of her. She might not care at all about Cole. Was Brian clever enough to pretend anger to indicate he had no reason to worry about an accusation of attempted murder?

Hard fingers gripped my arm.

I was alone in the aisle. I looked frantically about and tried to pull away.

"You are worse than useless. Get to City Hall. Immediately!" The crisp, cultivated voice was sharp and irritated.

I was struggling to breathe. No one was . . .

Oh.

I planted myself firmly and yanked my arm. "Let go." I

wished my voice weren't wobbly. A voice from someone unseen is certainly unsettling and a reminder to me to avoid similarly discomfiting those on earth when I was invisible.

Would I ever be invisible again?

"You are derelict in your duty." The deep contralto reverberated with contempt, but the pressure on my arm eased.

"You are a great one to talk about duty! You shanghaied me, Delilah Delahunt Duvall. Wiggins doesn't know I'm here." Possibly my voice rose in a near shout.

Brisk footsteps sounded. A tall woman with long, straight black hair and a vampire face swung around the bookcase. "Ladies, please. We can't have . . ." Her words trailed off. She stared at me. "Has the other lady left?"

"Other lady?" I looked about me. "I'm alone here." I kept my voice soft and offered a bemused smile. "Perhaps another aisle?"

The librarian backed away. When she was out of sight, I whispered, "Keep your voice down."

A hiss in my ear made me jump. "I had no choice but to corral you if I hoped to protect Nick. I thought you'd be perfect to send back to Adelaide. There was no chance that Wiggins would dispatch you. Nick's folder doesn't have a star."

Nick's aunt Dee obviously knew a good deal more about the inner workings of the Department of Good Intentions than I did. I'd never been privy to how earthly beings were selected to receive support. "How did you know that?"

A huff of impatience. "Any fool studies the course before riding."

I did not take that as a compliment. Who was she to be so high and mighty? "Nick told me about you." My whisper was high and hot. "You sound like a mess."

"We can have this discussion another time." Possibly, the implication was clear, when the next ice age arrived. "Right now you're here, and you're supposed to be keeping Nick safe. You have to get to City Hall before he does."

I folded my arms. "You go to City Hall. You can pop right there. I can't."

"Of course you can." Dee was impatient. "Go poof."

"Easy for you to say. I've been stuck here since last night. I appeared to reassure Nick, and now I can't disappear."

"Oh. That's a problem." She sounded personally vexed.

We were in heartfelt agreement, though she might have addressed my situation with a little more sympathy.

Those cool, strong fingers seized my elbow. "Then I'll have to make do with what's available." Disdain was evident in her brusque tone. "No wonder Wiggins considers you a third-tier choice."

I was wounded to the core. Dear Wiggins would never denigrate an emissary. I was furious. "He didn't say so."

"Possibly not in so many words." The admission was careless. "But you aren't on his auto dial."

I felt triumphant. "He sends telegrams."

"You haven't received one recently." The observation was smug.

"You are odious."

"*You* are wasting time. You have to get to City Hall before Nick does." The fingers yanked, and I found myself propelled down the aisle and across the library lobby by a hard push in the center of my back.

⌒

Aunt Dee's left arm clutched my waist.

The scooter seat scarcely afforded room for two. I felt crowded by the handlebars.

"Faster." The command was accompanied by a sharp pinch to my right thigh.

The scooter swerved to the right. I corrected and we veered left.

Behind us a car honked.

I gave a bit too much gas, and the scooter jumped like a gigged catfish.

A siren squalled.

"Look what you've done." I flung the words over my shoulder as I eased to a stop.

The retort was sharp. "Quick. Gas it. He's out of the car and you can make it around the corner."

"Are you out of your—" I broke off and looked up into the startled face of one of Adelaide's handsomest police officers, Johnny Cain—curly dark hair, mesmerizing blue eyes, chiseled features.

"I beg your pardon, miss?" He stared at me with an uneasy, not to say haunted, expression. This was not our first encounter. On an earlier assignment to Adelaide, he had seen me in the passenger seat of a dead woman's car, though he was unaware of her demise at the time. Later, he'd had a partial glimpse of me as I fled the counter at Lulu's. It would be fair to say neither episode had brought him joy.

I smiled brightly, though I was trying to jut out my chin in hopes of altering my appearance.

"You look like you have lockjaw." The hiss behind me was snakelike.

I whipped my head around, started to speak. My mouth opened, closed. Calmly, I faced Johnny again. "I thought I heard someone behind me. It sounded like a goose."

The pinch was sharp. I managed not to exclaim.

"Lockjaw?" he asked.

"Logjam. That's the predicament I find myself in. Just one of those logjams that we find ourselves in. But that's neither here nor there, Officer. What can I do for you?" It was an effort to keep my chin out as I talked, and it added an odd cadence to my words.

He stared at me, possibly wondering if I was being impudent or, worse, was slightly unhinged. "You were driving erratically. May I see your license?"

"License." I nodded in agreement. "I would be happy to display my license." I spread a hand expressively. "If only,"

I sighed, "I had my license. I know you will understand. Actually, I was on my way to the police station—"

Dee gripped my arm tight as a vise.

"—at City Hall"—the pressure relaxed—"to report that my purse had been stolen." Fortunately, I'd not brought the new purse with me. It reposed in my room at the B and B. I'd tucked the remainder of the money from Nick into a pocket of my slacks. "I know"—I realized I was talking normally and poked my chin out again—"I shouldn't be driving, but what else could I do? Certainly the loss of a purse isn't a crime that requires the dispatch of officers. I felt I was doing my civic duty—saving time for Adelaide's finest—by making my report in person." My jaws ached.

"You're on your way to the department?"

"As fast as I can go."

His broad mouth twitched. "Maybe you might go a little slower." He pulled a small notebook from his pocket. "Name?"

"Hilda Whitby. I live in Dallas, 1427 Carleton Way. I'm visiting Adelaide to make impressions of gravestones of long-deceased relatives. At the cemetery, I dropped into that wonderful old mausoleum with the stone dog and cat." Johnny well knew the Pritchard mausoleum, because he recently had wed a family connection. "I left my purse dangling from a handlebar and, when I returned, my purse was gone. So"—my gaze was pleading—"I'll report the theft now if I may, and I promise to drive more carefully." I poked an elbow backward and took satisfaction in a muffled *ouch*.

As I pulled away from the curb, I noted in the rearview mirror that the patrol car kept pace behind us until we turned into the lot behind City Hall.

⌒

At City Hall, we took the elevator to the third floor, bypassing the police department. As the elevator door clanged behind us, Nick slammed out of an office midway down the hall.

I hurried toward him. "Nick!"

He was moving fast, fists balled, feet stomping, a furious scowl turning his bony face into a good imitation of an enraged hawk.

"Nick!" The cry from Aunt Dee brought him to a startled stop.

His eyes widened. They darted back and forth across the hall. He looked behind him, then he swung toward me. "Knock it off. You had to know Aunt Dee to sound that much like her. Lady, I don't know what kind of nut you are, but I want you out of my life. I got enough problems without some death-obsessed redhead on my case. Take the cash and go. If you show up at the B and B, I'll call the cops, get you arrested for fraud."

Before I could respond, he plunged around me and broke into a run.

Now I was cast out on my own without even the prospect of a place to stay. Obviously, he discounted my claim to be an emissary, but he knew I could not possibly bear scrutiny by the police. I had no papers. I stamped my foot, my patience at an end. "You're a rat," I shouted after him. "It will serve you right if your ship goes down and you with it."

"Did he scare you, too?" A reed-thin blonde peered out anxiously from Cole's office. "I think he's dangerous. I'm going to call the police if he comes back."

"He isn't dangerous. Or a rat." The pronouncement was vigorous, though there might have been an uneven breathiness to Dee's deep voice.

The young woman clutched at the doorjamb. She was trembling. "Mama told me I shouldn't work at City Hall. She said people go bonkers all the time. First you say he's a rat, then you speak in a different voice and say he isn't. I don't know if he's a rat, but he's a wild man." Her voice was shrill. "I've never seen anybody madder." Her china-blue eyes stared fearfully down the now empty hall. "He came crashing in here, yelling for Mr. Clanton. I told him Mr.

Clanton wasn't here but he banged past me and slammed into Mr. Clanton's office and then he came out and rushed at me and I got behind my desk. He was so mad his voice was shaking and he wanted to know where Mr. Clanton was. I said I didn't know and he pounded on the edge of my desk and told me to tell him that Nick Magruder was looking for him and they used to hang people like him and when he got his hands on him—"

I had no difficulty sorting out the pronouns.

"—he was going to wish he was dead."

ᔕ

I tried to slide back an inch on the scooter seat. "You're crowding me."

"If you had smaller hips, I'd have more room."

"My hips are perfect." I spoke with confidence. At twenty-seven, I was slender but curvaceous. Bobby Mac always whistled when I walked past.

"Your hips are irrelevant."

Did I hear a distant whistle?

Only in my heart.

Dee poked me in the back. "Hurry. We have to find Nick."

I clamped my hands on the handlebars. "Why?"

A hand gripped my right shoulder. "He's still getting himself in trouble. It will be all over town that he's threatened Cole Clanton."

"I don't care if he challenges Cole to a duel. Nick's popularity in Adelaide is of no concern to me. Unlike me, you are quite free to pop"—my voice was bitter—"after him. As far as I'm concerned, my job is done. I saved his life last night. I've warned the suspects that the police will be informed if anything happens to him. And now, I want to go home."

Even as I spoke, I knew she was no longer there.

No pressure on my shoulder. I had plenty of room on the seat.

"Wiggins?" Possibly he'd become aware of my marooned state.

No answer.

He always sent a telegram to summon me. But I couldn't send him a telegram. I tried ESP.

It's a long way from earth to Heaven.

I'd wanted to be free of Dee. She was overbearing, exasperating, imperious. She'd pushed me here, yanked me there, and now she'd abandoned me.

Where had she gone?

No doubt she was popping around Adelaide, a spirit on the loose, trying to help her adored nephew.

She could at least have had lunch with me. I was hugely hungry. Dee likely wasn't thinking about food, since she hadn't appeared. It was being in the world that created appetite.

I brightened. As long as I was *in* the world . . .

❧

Lulu's was just as I remembered, the plate-glass window, the counter on one side, four booths on the other, and every seat taken at the lunch hour. I waited a few minutes and slid onto a vacated stool at the counter. I felt better when I'd ordered a hamburger with a thick slice of cheddar, onions, tomatoes, dill pickles, mayo, fries, and iced tea. In Adelaide, everyone drinks iced tea year-round.

I was midway through my burger when I glanced in the mirror. I wasn't surprised to spot Johnny Cain and several other patrolmen in a booth. Lulu's was on Main Street and convenient to City Hall. I noted that he carefully did not look my way. Obviously, he was cutting me slack about my lack of a driver's license and would be sure not to see the yellow scooter parked outside. I scanned the other booths behind me. My feeling of comfort vanished.

Cole Clanton's secretary hunched in the third booth. Face pale, eyes huge, hands gesturing, her mouth moved in rapid speech. Three women listened, their food ignored.

I didn't have to overhear to understand. She was regaling her lunch companions with a blow-by-blow account of Nick Magruder's fiery appearance at Cole Clanton's office. Her expressive face told a tale I should have read when Dee and I were there. Cole's secretary was genuinely frightened.

I took a last bite, but the savor was gone. I'd been so consumed with irritation at Dee and aggravation at Nick, I'd not considered the implications of Nick's search for Cole Clanton. An obviously agitated and upset Nick was tearing around Adelaide looking for Cole. It was a reversal of fortune. Cole had been furious with Nick on two counts, the lost opportunity to buy the Arnold property and Nick's revelations about Lisa to Arlene. Now Nick was livid with anger.

What had prompted Nick's fury?

As Cole Clanton slammed out of the B and B, he'd tossed a taunt at Nick: "I got some business to see to, but I'll be in touch, Phidippus."

I'd told Nick to stay with Jan at the B and B.

I placed a bill by the check and slid from the booth, once again ruing my inability to disappear and arrive immediately at the desired destination.

Because, suddenly, I was frightened.

⚘

As soon as I was out of sight of Main Street, I boosted the throttle on the little yellow scooter. I made it in four minutes flat to the B and B, ran the scooter right up to the back porch, braked, killed the engine. In a flash, I pounded up the back steps and hurried inside.

Jan sat at the kitchen table, her hands clasped tightly together. She saw me and jumped to her feet, her round face apprehensive. "Where's Nick? You have to tell me what's going on."

"He's hunting for Cole."

She was impatient. "I know that. Nick raced out of here after he talked to Cole." She gestured at the kitchen table and two mugs of coffee. "We were sitting there, talking. Everything was fun, the way it used to be when we were kids. I felt safe. And happy." Her voice shook. "When his cell rang, he glanced at it and almost didn't answer. Oh, I wish he hadn't. Then he said, and he was cocky, 'It's Cole. The little man left in a bad mood. Too damn bad. He said he'd call. I'd blow him off, but he'd tell everybody I was running scared. I'm not afraid of him. Now or ever,' and he clicked on the phone."

Jan's expression was suddenly stricken. "Nick's face changed as he listened. It was awful. It was like he'd been slammed hard and couldn't get his breath. I could tell he was looking at a picture. He jumped up and his chair crashed to the floor. He was yelling into the phone, his words coming so fast I could barely understand. He told Cole he was a repulsive, slimy, sick son of a bitch and when he got his hands on him he'd regret ever being born. And then he stood there"—she pointed at the center of the kitchen—"his face red, and yelled, 'You'd better not. I'm coming for you.' He clicked off the phone and started for the door. I ran and grabbed his arm and it was rigid as steel. I asked him what was wrong. He looked down at me and shook his head. 'I don't know what I can do. I'll stop him. Somehow.' He charged out the door and drove away."

I had been right to be frightened. Something had set Nick off, and if he found Cole there might be serious trouble.

Jan flung out a beseeching hand. "I've been crazy ever since he left. And then Rod Holt called and asked for Nick, and when I said he was gone and could I take a message, Rod acted really odd. He said I should tell Nick that Cole

Clanton was in an ugly mood and he'd tried to talk Cole out
of doing something he might regret, but he hadn't had any
luck. I asked Rod what he was talking about and he said well,
it was just a word to the wise, but he didn't want to get
involved and maybe Cole would have second thoughts. He
hung up real quick. I called back and he didn't answer."

∽

Rod Holt's Back Shop was at the tail end of Main Street, a
shabby one-story frame building sandwiched between an
abandoned storefront and a pawnshop. Plate-glass windows
on either side of a rough-hewn wooden door featured
assorted memorabilia, spittoons, two worn saddles, stained
leather chaps, a stack of lariats, enamel basins, several Winchester rifles, a calico bonnet, empty feed sacks, boots, gun
rigs, barbed wire, and branding irons.

A bell clanged loudly as I opened the door. There scarcely
appeared to be a free inch of space, only a narrow aisle
between walls laden with curiosities ranging from Indian
headdresses to old rifles to galvanized iron tubs. I skirted a
late-eighteenth-century claw-footed porcelain bathtub to
reach a counter that held even more clutter, plus jars of hard
candy and beef jerky. Square in the center of the counter
was an intricately patterned Indian basket filled with rolled
up sheets of thick paper. A hand-lettered sign proclaimed:
Treasure Maps. $25 each. Going Fast.

"Hidey." The drawl was pure Adelaide. "Welcome to the
Back Shop. Make yourself to home."

The lighting from wall-mounted gaslights was fairly dim.
It took me a moment to distinguish the lean figure lounging
on a wooden chair tilted back against the wall. A nearby
horsehair sofa was burdened with two sets of molted antlers,
a toy rocking horse, and a late-Victorian wooden toilet seat.

"Mr. Holt?"

The chair clipped to the floor and he stood. In the flicker
of gaslights, he was the image of Doc Holliday, thin with

smoothly cut, jet-black hair and a sharp-pointed mustache. His long-sleeve, faintly yellowed white shirt, string tie, baggy black trousers, and black boots would have attracted no notice in any saloon in the Old West in the 1880s. Dark eyes studied me as he hooked his thumbs in his pockets and nodded. "Don't think I've had the pleasure."

"I'm Hilda Whitby. I'm representing Nick Magruder."

A thick dark eyebrow arched. "I heard about Nick setting up to buy the Arnold place. Are you his lawyer?" His long face looked more animated. "That old Arnold place could be redone like the nineteen twenties if he replaced the recent stuff." He pointed at the claw-footed bathtub. "That would go in an upstairs bath real pretty."

"I'm not sure about Nick's plans for the house. I'm here about a different matter. Jan Richey told me you called Nick to warn him about Cole Clanton. She wants to know what Cole is threatening to do."

He squinted at me, the enthusiasm draining from his face. "It seems to me like maybe Nick might be the right person to tell Jan." He pulled at his mustache. "If she has to know." The last was a mumble.

"Nick stormed out of the B and B to hunt for Cole. We can't find Nick and Jan's worried. Nick is terribly angry."

"Right." Rod's gaze skittered away. He looked toward a set of antlers, and his face twisted in uncertainty.

"Mr. Holt—"

"Rod. Everybody calls me Rod."

"If you tried to talk Cole out of a plan, then you know what he intends to do."

"Oh, hell." He sounded aggrieved. "I had a covered wagon about sold to Cole, an honest-to-God wagon I can trace to the Land Run." The Unassigned Lands in Oklahoma were opened to settlers at noon on April 22, 1889, and fifty thousand hopeful settlers poured into the area from north, south, east, and west, by buggy, wagon, train, and on horse-back. "This wagon left from Purcell. We were dickering when his cell rang." He turned away, reached up to straighten a pair of spurs hanging from a board.

I moved until I could see a portion of his averted face.

He peered at the spurs as if he'd never seen a pair before.

"I can tell you are uncomfortable." I spoke soothingly. "If you know what Cole plans to do, I hope you will tell me. Maybe I can do something to prevent a problem."

He tugged again at his mustache. "I don't want to be caught in the middle of anything. But I guess I got to say what I know." He reached over, moved a set of antlers. "You might as well sit down."

He waited until I perched on the hard-as-a-rock sofa before he settled in the chair. He didn't look at me, fastening his gaze on an Indian basket. "No way you can't hear when people talk on a cell. Of course, I only heard Cole's side, but I knew who he was talking to. Cole kept calling him Phidippus. Everybody knows that story. Long and short of it, women are damned fools sometimes. That's why I couldn't tell Jan. I hope she doesn't ever have to know. I told Cole he was playing with fire. If he puts those pix on Facebook, who knows what Arlene might do?"

Pictures on Facebook. I didn't have to ask the content of the pictures. Women were damned fools sometimes and Arlene had been proud of having a young lover. "Cole took pictures on his iPhone?" How easy to click and post the photos on his Facebook page. How easy and how devastating.

"Cole got ugly, said it would serve Arlene right if everybody in town saw the photos. But he said they were worth more off the Net than on it. Nick is a sap for Jan, and he'd do what he could to protect Jan's ma. In exchange for no pix, Nick was going to have to sign a paper saying he'd sell the Arnold house to Cole for a dollar and maybe, if Nick was lucky, Cole would pay him a couple of bucks. Cole held up the phone and laughed like a hyena, and said, 'I'll give Nick a call every so often, describe another one of the pix.

I'd send them to him one by one, but Phidippus might be shocked. By tonight he'll be begging me to let him hand over the place.' "

⁓

On the back porch of the B and B, I hesitated. What, if anything, could I share with Jan? I gripped the doorknob. I didn't want to tell her about the cell phone photos of her mother, but I needed help. She was sure to know the number of Nick's cell phone. I had to talk to him. Would he agree to meet me? I had a plan. Of course, everything depended upon finding Cole Clanton and the return of Nick's aunt Dee.

The grip on my arm was just this side of vicious. "I've buzzed between this place and downtown so many times I'm dizzy. You've got to help me with Nick."

"You're back!" I tried to pull away, but a woman who could control eleven hundred pounds of horseflesh wasn't going to set me free. "Where've you been?"

"Trying to stop Nick from his lunacy." Her deep voice was strained and discouraged.

I yanked free, then with a swipe through the air found her arm and held on tight. Turnabout. "Where is he?"

"Running around town like a madman. He goes from place to place—the library, the basketball court behind the fire station, the pro shop at the golf club, the *Gazette*. He barges in and asks for Cole with a look on his face that would scare a sumo wrestler. Cole's not there and Nick paces around like a caged lion and finally flings himself outside again. Then he races back downtown and skulks in the gazebo in the park across the street from City Hall. He waits until he gets a call on his cell and then he bolts off again. The calls seem to come right on the hour."

I glanced at my watch. I'd picked up a bright pink Timex at Wal-Mart. A quarter to five. I gestured toward the yellow scooter. "I'll meet you at the gazebo. Pop back and make sure he doesn't leave."

 ❦

I parked in a small asphalt lot and cut across the park at a slant. I glimpsed portions of the gazebo, but most of the structure was hidden. Old maples and firs surrounded the gazebo, offering shade and the illusion of a remote country glade right in the heart of town. Halfway across the park, I was aware of city employees streaming down the broad white steps of City Hall across the street. A few steps more and I entered a dusky path that curved through the trees like a country lane.

The temperature was drifting down into the sixties. I reached the edge of the trees. Nick stood in the gazebo, body tense, shoulders bunched, hands in fists. He was bare-armed in the same ratty polo he'd worn that morning. His age-whitened Levi's sagged on his hips. The dark stubble on his cheeks was heavier. Despite his disreputable appearance, I saw rock-hard determination in his face.

"Nick."

At my call, he swung toward me. He made a gesture of impatience. "I don't have time to talk to you." He looked at his watch. "Get lost."

I walked up the gazebo steps. "What makes you think Cole will show up this time?"

Expressions slid over his face—surprise, irritation, uncertainty, and an underlying anger bubbling hot as lava. "How'd you know?"

"By this time"—my voice was dry—"practically everybody in town has heard you're hunting for Cole Clanton like a sheriff after a horse thief."

"Do they know why?" He barely managed to push out the question.

"Not unless you've told them."

"Not me. But Cole can't resist twisting the knife. He called Arlene, told her what he'd do if I didn't cooperate. He called Jan. I'll make him pay for that. Damn him, I don't care about the Arnold place. He can have it. But he's got to shut up. Who's he going to tell next?"

"We can stop him. But you have to do exactly as I say."

A hot whisper buzzed in my ear. "Get to the point."

I turned toward the sound and snarled, "If you'll resist micromanaging for a half second, I will."

Nick's head jerked, too. He stared at the empty space next to me, made a strangled sound. "Lady, I don't have time for you to act like Aunt Dee's lurking around."

His cell phone rang. Although, to be accurate, the summons wasn't a ring. Rather, quarter notes on the backbeat of a snare drum played with brushes.

An ordinary ring should be good enough for anyone. I have never found making oneself seem special an attractive quality.

Holding the cell in his right hand, Nick glanced at the caller ID. His face hardened.

The call must have been from Cole Clanton.

I grabbed Nick's right arm. "Dee, catch his other hand."

Nick's strangled yelp and panicked stare at his left arm indicated Dee, for once, had followed instructions.

I talked fast, knowing we had only seconds. "Don't let Cole butt you around. Tell him this is the last call you're taking. Take charge. Tell him you'll meet him with a written and signed promise to sell the property to him for one dollar. Answer it now." I let go of his right arm.

He lifted the cell phone. "Nick." He spoke through stiff lips, his gaze fastened on his left arm.

I frantically tried to figure a location that would satisfy my requirements for the vanquishing of Cole Clanton, then realized the gazebo was perfect. "Tell him nine o'clock tonight. Here at the gazebo." The gazebo was downtown, and there were cars up and down the streets. I doubted Cole Clanton harbored any fear of Phidippus, but he may have heard about the threats Nick had been flinging around Adelaide. In that event, the choice should be reassuring. Critical to my plan, however, was the gazebo's isolation in the center of town, hidden from view by the encircling trees. On a chilly October evening, the likelihood of anyone visiting the gazebo was fairly remote.

Nick's voice was thin. "I'm not chasing around town anymore, Cole. I won't answer if you call again. I'll have the paper for you tonight. Nine o'clock. The gazebo."

I reached over and clicked off the phone.

Nick gave another yelp. "What do you think you're doing?"

"Saving Arlene."

The cell rang again. "Don't answer. Shut up and listen."

"Do as she says." Dee's voice brooked no disagreement.

His head jerked to the left. He tried to move his arm and made little progress. "Aunt Dee?" His voice cracked.

"If *she* were more capable, you would never have known I was here. Nick, dear, do as she says. Possibly she has a good idea." There was no conviction in Dee's tone.

I was hot. "If *she* had any character, I wouldn't have to involve her. But I can't disappear and she can. Here's what we're going to do."

Chapter 7

Nick got out of his car behind the B and B.

I parked the scooter beside the back steps. It was chilly now that the day was waning. I'd wear my new thick black cardigan this evening.

Nick waited for me, his eyes flickering uneasily from side to side. He looked even scruffier than usual, hair uncombed, the stubble on his cheeks now bristly, a new tear in his polo.

"Where is she?" His gaze jerked up and down and all around.

I tilted my face and concentrated. Funny how I could tell when Dee wasn't present. "Do we care?"

"She's not here right this minute?" His voice was hopeful.

"We'd know." My tone was sour.

"Look"—he tried to smile—"I love Aunt Dee. She was swell to me growing up. But"—his eyes rounded—"it's spooky to think she's hovering around."

"If it weren't for her, I could hover, too." Clearly, my arrival here remained unknown to Wiggins. Obviously, Dee didn't have the authority to install me as an official emissary. I felt suddenly dizzy. Would she ever tell Wiggins what she had done?

"Are you all right?" He reached out and touched my arm, then yanked back his hand. "I don't get it; you're as real as real. Are you sure you aren't some kind of ventriloquist? Aunt Dee's not really here, is she?"

"You'd better hope she's at the gazebo at nine o'clock tonight. Everything depends upon her."

The kitchen door opened. Jan rushed out. "Nick . . ."

He held open his arms and she came into them. He held her tight. "Honey, I'm sorry. I'm trying to make it right."

"Mother's terribly upset. It's awful. She said there were pictures and Cole called her a couple of times and she's cried until she can't cry anymore. She wouldn't look at me."

He gripped her arms. "I'll get them. I promise you."

She stepped back, looked up at him. "Nick, I'm scared. Mom's gone. I can't find her anywhere."

His face creased in concern. "How about her cell?"

"She won't answer." Jan's voice trembled.

"Leave a message on her cell. Tell her everything's going to be okay. Tell her I'm meeting Cole at the gazebo downtown at nine o'clock and I won't give him what he wants until all the pictures have been deleted."

Obviously, Nick didn't feel comfortable telling Jan the actual plan.

&

After a quick supper of pizza and iced tea, I excused myself and went upstairs, both to provide Jan and Nick with time alone and to get my head together. I changed clothes and settled in a comfortable recliner. Relaxation didn't come. I wasn't worried about the outcome of the evening. If I say so myself, I had everything under control. Except, possibly, Nick's aunt Dee. I didn't know why she'd flitted away or where she was, but Nick's safety was the impetus for all her actions, so I assumed she would be at the gazebo on time.

If all went well this evening, Nick should be fine. His rescue of Arlene would surely be a plus for him with Jan, offsetting his cocky return to Adelaide. Moreover, no more attacks on him were likely. I felt it had been a masterstroke on my part to warn off the likely suspects. Further, if it had been Cole Clanton who'd shot at Nick, once he had the Arnold property in his grasp he no longer had a motive for wanting Nick out of the way. In fact, Cole would be the cock of the walk.

No, my concern was not with Nick.

My concern was me.

Before this evening ended, I must persuade Delilah Delahunt Duvall to alert Wiggins to my plight. Somehow I doubted she would be moved by piteous entreaties. As for forcing her hand, I had no leverage.

"Lolling about in sumptuous comfort." The deep voice exuded disapproval.

I bolted upright, looked toward the fireplace. Yes, I'd taken advantage of the wood and kindling to light a cheerful fire. Why should I be apologetic? "I wouldn't need a fire if I could disappear."

"Your mistake was to appear in the first place." Disdain was evident. "When I am on a mission, I make it a point of honor never to appear unless there is no other choice. I'm quite sure I could have handled everything without appearing if it had been possible for me to come back to help Nick. But Wiggins hadn't put a star on his folder. And Wiggins is such a stickler about avoiding contact between a recently deceased emissary and family."

"Honor? Who are you to talk about honor? How honorable was it to trick me onto the Rescue Express and land me here without a return ticket?"

There was a heavy sigh. A cushion in the sofa opposite

me was suddenly depressed. "I'll be kicked out of the department." Her deep voice was as doleful as a dirge.

"Oh." I understood. She'd transgressed and was terrified that Wiggins would ban her from the Department of Good Intentions. I understood her concerns. Possibly her transgressions were beyond his approval. I cleared my throat. "You could spend more time riding McCoy."

"McCoy always rode like a dream. He still does. But, you know, I need challenges. Heaven's quite wonderful. Everything is perfect. But I miss excitement. I need a chance to use my wits. Working for Wiggins makes me feel alive."

I walked across the room, swept my hand until I felt her shoulder. I gave her two pats. "I understand." I dropped onto the cushion next to her. "But"—and I tried to sound reasonable—"you can't leave me high and dry."

There was no answer.

"Dee, I've fixed everything for Nick, and tonight you can make everything right for Jan's mom. You'll help me, won't you?"

The cushion next to me was no longer depressed.

But I was.

৵

I pushed open the kitchen door.

Jan moved jerkily away from Nick.

Had they been in an embrace? I hoped so. Jan's cheeks were slightly pink. I gave them an approving smile.

Nick angular black brows rose. He shook his head. "You look like a cat burglar. Black sweater buttoned up, black slacks, black socks, and shoes. All you need is a face mask and the cops'll arrest you on sight."

"I have no intention of being seen by the police or anyone else." I glanced up at the kitchen clock. Seventeen minutes after eight.

Jan looked, too. "Mom's been gone for hours. Why doesn't she come home?"

Nick's voice was gentle. "Jan, you're driving yourself nuts. You left a message. You told her not to worry, that I was going to meet Cole and get rid of the pictures. How's your mom about checking her messages?"

Some of the tension eased from Jan's round face. "She checks them all the time. I guess it's okay. Maybe she's waiting to find out if you succeeded. Nick"—she reached out, touched his arm—"you don't suppose Mom will come to the gazebo?"

He looked stunned. "Call her again. Tell her not to come. That might set everything off."

Indeed it might.

Jan quickly dialed, waited, left a message. "Mom, don't go to the gazebo. Nick will handle Cole. They've already agreed. It's all settled. Nick will let Cole have the Arnold place and Cole will get rid of those pictures. You don't need to worry anymore. Please"—Jan's voice shook—"come home."

The minute hand moved.

Jan began to pace. "I wish she'd come home. I'm frightened."

"Nick's going to take care of everything." I was being generous, but I've never been one to insist on taking credit. Success depended upon me and Nick's unscrupulous aunt. Dee oozed gall—to insist she made it a point of honor never to appear! But Delilah Delahunt Duvall was amply endowed with gall.

I glanced again at the clock. "Nick, we'll leave at eight thirty."

Jan swung toward Nick. "I'm coming."

"No." My voice was crisp. "Let Nick handle this. I'm afraid you'd tell Cole exactly what you think of him."

Jan flushed. "He deserves to know that he's despicable."

"Another day." I held up my hand. "If you make him mad,

your mother might suffer. Stay here. Nick will call as soon as everything's done."

"I'll call you first thing, Janny. And then I'll come back." He gave her a reassuring look.

She turned away. Her body was rigid, her hands clenched.

That was the way we left her.

As I followed Nick across the porch, I was grateful for the warmth of my sweater. All the way to the steps, I expected to hear the door bang open behind us and Jan hurry after us.

The door remained shut.

I was relieved at Jan's acquiescence. Now the path was clear. I foresaw no obstacle to success. I felt buoyant.

Buoyant? As if I were floating?

Hope flickered. Maybe my long spell of "here you are, tough it out" was over. Was I once again an emissary in full, able to disappear at will and arrive immediately at another destination? I stopped on the steps, waited for that ineffable sense of "now I'm not" to occur.

I glanced down at my black slacks. The light from the porch was bright enough to reveal them in their stubborn reality. With little hope, I thought: *Gazebo.*

Nope. I wasn't there. I was here. I glared around the shadowy backyard. Not, of course, that I would see her, since *she* could be invisible. "Dee, you owe me big time."

Nick's head jerked around. "Where is she?" He rushed to me, grabbed my elbow. "Don't make noise. What if Jan comes out? I can never explain."

I folded my arms, glowered. "Don't worry. Dee's not here. But if I ever get my hands on her, she's going to rue the day." Big talk, but who had the advantage? I was whistling Dixie. "Come on." I knew I sounded petulant, but Nick didn't understand my desperate status. "Let's go."

He opened the driver's door, stopped. "Are you sure you have to come?" His voice was glum.

"I may be needed to provide a diversion."

He shook his head. "Your plan's nuts. Cole's not going to let you grab that cell."

I felt that Nick sometimes didn't really focus. "He'll never see me. Dee will get the cell phone."

"Oh yeah. My dead aunt. You're always talking about Aunt Dee, but I don't see her. I just see you."

He couldn't know this was a sore—very sore—topic.

"I think you're making it all up about her." His features weren't clear in the dark, but his voice was combative.

"You know something, Nick?" My tone was barely civil. "I'd rather be helping Featherfoots than you. You lack the charm of a Featherfoot, and I doubt you have the IQ of a Featherfoot."

"Don't knock Featherfoots." His voice was hot. "You should see them sneak up and jump on their prey. You can't jump fifteen feet can you?"

"Not now."

That went right over his head. I could jump the world in a single bound when I was invisible.

"A Featherfoot can jump several times the length of its body." He was triumphant.

I almost snapped, "Good for Featherfoots," but refrained. Instead, I was pacific. "Featherfoots are amazing. However, tonight you have to count on me and your aunt." I slid into the passenger seat.

He flung himself behind the wheel, but made no move to start the car. "My aunt. My sainted aunt. She's dead. She's not here. Drop that for now. Tell me what happens at the gazebo. Run the plan by me again."

"It's very simple." I was soothing, as if explaining one plus one to a five-year-old, who, I felt sure, would have been on board much more agreeably than Nick. "A block from the park, you drop me off. I'll slip through the dark and come as near the gazebo as possible. You meet Cole. You promise him the paper agreeing to sell the Arnold property to him for one dollar."

Nick patted his pocket. "Got the paper here."

"In return he agrees to delete specific photographs from his cell phone. However, nothing is ever really deleted, so we have to get the phone. That's the only way Arlene will be safe. Cole can't be trusted."

"That's for sure." He sounded grim. "How do we know he hasn't already zapped the pix to his laptop?"

"Dee will have to check for us."

"Oh, sure. Easy as pie."

"Why not? You said she wrote thrillers. She has to know about computers." I might not be charmed by Dee, but I had no doubt she was competent.

"She's dead." His tone was flat.

I wasn't ready to cover that ground again. "Leave everything to me. We need to concentrate on the cell phone. Insist he show you the phone so you can watch him make the deletions. That will get the cell out of his pocket and into his hand. Now, it is essential"—I was emphatic—"that you stand at least four feet from Cole."

"Four feet?"

"When the cell phone is taken, he will know there is no way you could have grabbed it from him."

Nick pressed the ignition. He curved around in the drive, drove too fast into the street. "Okay, la—Hilda. I'm four feet from the jerk. You're lurking in the shadows outside the gazebo. Who grabs the cell? A Featherfoot?"

I was firm. "Aunt Dee." He seemed to have difficulty mastering simple concepts. Possibly his brain synapses only worked in regard to Featherfoots.

"That's what I thought you were going to say. There are no invisible genies in this world. You faked me out, imitating her voice."

"Who held your arm?" My tone was sweet.

"I guess I got a cramp. Anyway, if she's going to save the day, where is she?"

I didn't want to make him nervous, but I had no sense of

Dee's presence. I twisted to look in the backseat. Not that I would see Dee if she were there. I was beginning to worry. Of course, there was still plenty of time.

"I'm sure she'll show up." I tried to sound blithe. I don't know if I fooled him.

Chapter 8

As the taillights of Nick's car disappeared. I tried to recall the layout of the park. Thick woods bordered the gazebo except for an open expanse on the south. Paths wound through the trees to a pond on the north side of the park. Willows bunched between the pond and the back of the gazebo. A large open lawn stretched from the gazebo's entrance on the south.

I ducked into the trees. Soon I was in deep darkness, far from the occasional lampposts along the street. I waited for my eyes to adjust, then moved carefully, wary of unexpected holes and fallen branches. A breeze rustled the leaves of the maples. I smelled the woody scent of firs. An owl hooted not far away, the mournful cry prickling my skin. Twice I heard unexpected crackling and stopped, listening hard. It might have been a deer.

I reached the edge of the woods. I was standing to the east of the gazebo and I had a good view of the entrance. The nearest lamppost was some thirty feet from the steps, so the gazebo itself was shadowy.

Footsteps sounded on the concrete walk. Nick hurried toward the entrance. He reached the gazebo, rattled up the steps. As the minutes passed, he moved restlessly back and forth. Occasionally he lifted his arm. I supposed his watch had a luminous dial. He yanked his cell from his pocket, bent over it, fingers moving. He waited, watched, then shoved the cell back into his pocket.

I considered moving behind the gazebo, where weeping willows afforded a deep patch of shadow, but I wanted an unobstructed view of the interior. I found a pine tree about fifteen feet east of the entrance. I knelt and scooped up a couple of sharp-edged cones, tucked them in each pocket. I could pelt Cole with cones if Dee had any difficulty wresting away the cell phone.

Where was she?

I took a deep breath and did my best owl imitation. "Dee-eee-eee-eee."

"Only a fool would take that for an owl's cry." Her deep voice dripped with disdain.

I was so relieved she was here, I bit back what I would have liked to say. I swept out my hand, found her, gripped her arm. I pulled her close and whispered, "Nick's going to insist Cole take out his cell. You need to be right there, ready to grab it."

"I do not require repeated instructions." She was acerbic. "I know quite well what to do. Once I get the phone, I'll zoom straight to the lake and toss it in."

With a twist, she pulled free from my grasp. I was once again alone in the shadows. But I felt excited because Dee was in the gazebo with Nick, ready to play her part. Everything was in place to confound a particularly unpleasant man. I had no doubt that Dee would play her role to perfection. Cole Clanton didn't have a chance.

I pictured her leaning casually against a pine railing, probably in her riding gear, possibly holding a crop. Was McCoy nearby? Did I hear the snuffle of a horse?

Suddenly I stiffened.

Nick ducked his head as if something had brushed against him. His face puzzled, he reached up, touched his tangled mop of hair, shook like a dog coming out of water. I had no doubt what had happened. Dee had reached out to touch his dark curls.

"Don't spook him." I willed the thought to her.

But I was touched. She dearly loved the young man standing there.

Footsteps sounded. The clock at City Hall began to toll the hour. Cole Clanton strolled into view on the main path. He passed beneath the lamppost nearest the gazebo. He moved unhurriedly with a noticeable swagger, the conqueror coming to claim the spoils of victory. His mouth twisting in triumph, Cole thudded up the steps, stopped a few feet from Nick.

"All right." Nick's voice was gruff. "I've got the paper."

Cole folded his arms. "Have I told you what a hot ticket Arlene is?"

Nick took a step toward him, fists bunched. "Stop the trash talk."

"Who's gonna make me? I can say and do whatever I want, Phidippus." Cole's tone was mocking.

Fighting for control, Nick drew in a breath, rocked back on his heels. He forced out the words, his voice harsh. "I'll give you the paper as soon as you delete those photos." He drew a folded sheet from his pocket.

"Not so fast, Spider-Man." Cole pulled out his cell, held it to one side. "You hold up the paper, bring it close enough for me to read. Then we do a duet: I hand to you, you hand to me. I get the paper, you delete the pix."

Nick looked uncertain, possibly remembering my insistence that he stay at least four feet from Cole. Slowly, he took one step forward.

Abruptly Cole's wrist was bent back. He gave a shout, but the phone was out of his grasp and dangling in midair.

"What the hell?" He jerked his head toward Nick. "What's going on? You can't—" Cole broke off and stared at Nick, who was a good three feet distant and, in fact, backing away, and clearly had nothing to do with the seizure of the phone.

Cole looked frantically around, seeking the phone.

Nick's face was a study in disbelief as the phone sped through the air toward the back of the gazebo.

Cole made a strangled noise and lunged in pursuit of the phone, which disappeared into the darkness.

An explosive crack shattered the night silence.

Cole staggered.

Another shot rang out.

Cole gave a cry of pain, clasped one hand to his upper thigh. He wavered, took one unsteady step, then crumpled, blood splashing as he crashed heavily to the gazebo floor.

Nick shouted and moved toward the fallen man.

After a stunned instant, I ran toward the gazebo. Distantly I heard a shrill scream and knew it was me.

Nick knelt beside Cole, reached for his hand.

Out of the darkness, a rifle spun toward Nick, striking him across the face. Nick lurched to one side, grappling with the weapon. He lost his balance and landed on the floor next to Cole.

I reached the gazebo as Nick flung the rifle away and rolled to his knees.

"We have to get help," I cried. "Call nine-one-one."

Nick fumbled with his pocket, drew out the cell. "Did you see who shot him?" He pressed the numbers. "A man shot in the park. The gazebo—" His voice was ragged. "Nick Magruder. Man shot. Send help."

The night was suddenly alive with crisscrossing lights. Beams settled on the gazebo. Nick was clearly visible, the lights pinning him in a glare. I was on the other side of Cole, deeper in the shadows. Nick was still on his knees, holding the cell phone. I crouched by Cole, his hand in mine, seeking a pulse.

Sounds of running feet. Shouts. "Police. Hands up. Police."

How could help have come so quickly? Then I understood. We were across the street from the police station. Two shots had been fired and heard. Police knew the sound of gunfire, and they reacted quickly.

Nick still knelt by Cole. "We have to stop the bleeding." He peeled off his ratty polo.

I laid down Cole's arm. I had found no pulse. One of Cole's legs jerked. I feared the movement meant little, a final quiver of a dying body.

Help was coming for Cole, but there was no help for me. In only minutes, I would be asked questions I could not answer and only too quickly the truth would be known. There was no Hilda Whitby from Dallas.

"Dee!" My shout was desperate.

Spears of harsh light from the police officers' Maglites came nearer.

"Bailey Ruth," Wiggins's deep voice commanded. "Come. At once."

I disappeared.

Hilda Whitby was no longer in the gazebo. I gazed down at the fallen man and at Nick, breathing fast, shaking, but keeping the shirt pressed against welling blood.

"Stand up. Hands above your head." The shout was brusque, demanding compliance.

Nick looked over his shoulder. "He's bleeding. I'm trying to stop it, but the blood keeps coming and coming." His voice shook.

Gun in hand, a policewoman warily circled the downed man and Nick as a muscular policeman trained his gun on Nick. "No weapon, Sergeant. I'll take over until the medics get here." She approached warily, the gun waggling at Nick to move away. She was on the floor, one hand pressing Nick's shirt against the wound, the other holding the gun steady on Nick as he slowly stood and lifted his arms. As he pushed up from the floor, his hand left a reddish smear. Blood stained both of his hands and one knee of his jeans.

Stark white Maglite beams harshly illuminated the interior of the gazebo. The muscular sergeant held his gun in both hands, pointed unwaveringly at Nick. "Got you covered, Officer."

Half-blinded by the lights, Nick lowered his arm to shield his eyes.

"Up, up, up." The sergeant spoke quickly.

Nick raised the arm. "He needs help. He's been shot."

"Don't move, man. Medics are coming."

I was poised to push the policeman's gun away from Nick. Surely he wouldn't shoot Nick. Every muscle in the officer's body appeared hair-trigger tight. Of course, it looked to him and the other officers like they'd captured a criminal red-handed.

Nick glanced up at his hands with a sick expression. "I didn't shoot him."

In two strides, a second officer moved to Nick's side. He ran his hands over Nick, lightly, quickly. "Unarmed. Stay where you are."

The officer kneeling by Cole returned her gun to the holster. Still pressing the bloodied shirt to the wound, she lifted a flaccid arm, touched the wrist. Her face squeezed in concentration. Finally, she spoke. "No detectable pulse. Severe wound to upper thigh, apparently femoral severed, massive blood loss. Second wound to the chest."

Sirens shrilled in the street. Running steps sounded. An ambulance drove squarely up the center path.

"He's dead?" Nick glanced toward Cole with a look of horror.

I looked, too, and was swept with regret. Cole had caused trouble, but he had been young and alive and now his time here was over.

The officer in charge spoke rapidly. "Inform the chief.

Apparent homicide in City Park. Rifle near the body. Possible suspect in custody."

"Suspect?" Nick's voice wobbled. "Listen, somebody shot him. Don't just stand there. You've got to find him. The shot came from behind the gazebo."

"Handcuffs." The order was crisp.

In an instant, Nick's arms were behind his back, and handcuffs clicked.

The officer placed his gun in a holster, handed the Maglite to a patrolman. He walked up to Nick. "We'll be taking you to the station for questioning. You have the right to call a lawyer."

"I didn't shoot him. The shots came from there." Nick jerked his head toward the dark mass of willows.

"Hey!" The shout was loud. "I'm press." A stocky young man about fifteen feet from the gazebo tried to step around a wiry police officer. "I got a right to be here. Press. The *Gazette*. Albert Harris."

"Get back, buddy." The tall, thin cop barred the way. "I don't care who you are. You're interfering with a crime scene."

Albert leaned to one side for a better view. "Hey, Nick, what are you doing here? Who's—?" Albert broke off, stood stiff and still. "My God. Blood . . . That looks like Cole." He stared, his round face slack with shock. "Nick, did you shoot him?"

"I didn't shoot him." Nick's voice was strident. "I don't know who shot him."

The officer approached the reporter. "Back up, buddy. You're in the way."

Albert backpedaled a few feet, shouted, "Who shot him? Where are they? Has the killer been arrested? Nick, why'd they handcuff you?"

The officer glared at Albert. "This is a crime scene. Back off."

Under cover of the officer's gruff command, I heard Wiggins's sharp whisper. "The Express is coming."

I whispered in return. "We can't leave Nick now."

There was a huff of exasperation, then silence. I had no sense that Wiggins was nearby. He had let me remain, but who knew for how long.

"I want you at least twenty yards from the steps. Keep your mouth shut." His expression grim, the officer turned away from Albert.

In the gazebo, a sergeant spoke to Nick. "Name?" He slipped a video camera from his belt loop, turned it on.

"Nick Magruder." Nick squinted against the brightness of the Maglites.

"Address?"

"Eight nineteen Mulberry."

"Mulberry. You the one that called nine-one-one about a shooting Tuesday night?"

"Yeah. I sure as hell did." Nick was combative.

The sergeant's gaze moved back to the dead man and the rifle lying on the gazebo floor. "Another rifle." The tone was thoughtful. "Who's the dead man?"

Nick glanced at Cole's body, closed his eyes briefly. He opened them and met the sergeant's stare with dogged determination. "Cole Clanton. I didn't shoot him, and you idiots are standing around and the guy who shot Cole's in the next county by now." Nick gazed at the darkness of the willows. "The shot came from there."

The sergeant's stolid face remained unmoved. His voice was terse. "Describe the shooter."

"I didn't see him." Nick saw disbelief in the tough faces around him. "Listen to me, will you? I was up here with Cole and he turned away from me and moved toward the back of the gazebo. There was a shot and Cole staggered. Then a second shot. Cole fell. I ran to help him. I was looking at Cole, not that way." He nodded toward the willows. "Then somebody threw the rifle at me."

"How'd somebody throw a weapon at you and you didn't see the person?"

Nick tried to keep his voice steady. "I was down beside Cole. I was trying to help him." He looked queasy. "That's when I got blood on my hands. I was helping him." His voice shook. "I wasn't hearing anything or seeing anything. It was like I had roaring in my ears. The gun hit me. I never saw it coming. I kind of fell to one side." He looked at Cole's body. "I tried to help him." His voice was shaky.

"All right. Edge back a few feet and walk toward the steps." The sergeant turned to a female officer standing next to him. "Get on protective foot gear. We can't touch the body until the ME gets here and makes it official, but I want a visual search made of the interior, then record the scene on video. Is crime lab on the way?"

"Yes, sir."

"Listen, I can prove I didn't shoot him." Nick talked fast. "I have a witness. She can tell you where the shot came from. She—" He was looking around the gazebo. "Hilda? Hey, Hilda, where are you?"

Their faces expressionless, the police officers watched Nick.

Nick gazed back and forth. He tried to move to the steps. "Don't move."

Nick looked frustrated, half-scared, half-mad. "She must have panicked and run away."

The officer drew out a small pad. "Name."

"Hilda Whitby."

"Description."

"Redhead. About five five. Maybe twenty-five, twenty-six."

"Wearing."

"Black outfit. Sweater, slacks, shoes."

"Relationship."

Nick blinked. "She works for me."

The sergeant looked around the gazebo, out into the darkness. "At night?"

"Business." Nick was uneasy. If he said I was a private detective, that would require explanation.

It was my turn to blink. Someone shot at Nick and missed, thanks to me. Someone shot at Cole and didn't miss. Surely the two attacks were connected, but who would try to kill both Nick and Cole?

"What kind of business?"

"She was looking into some things for me. She'll be at the Majestic Buffalo B & B. You can find her. She can tell you I didn't shoot him. Someone else did."

"Sergeant, no woman came out of the gazebo." An officer stood on the gazebo steps. "We got here right after the shots. We ran across the park. I heard the shots as I was walking to the side entrance of City Hall—"

The sergeant nodded. City Hall, home to the police department, was directly across the street. The side entrance was about twenty feet from the street. Once across the street and into the park, the officer would reach the main walk in less than a minute.

A chorus of voices rose. ". . . nobody came away from the gazebo . . . didn't see anybody . . . only the guy and the victim in the gazebo . . . had a clear view . . ."

Behind the police, Albert held a cell phone to one ear. He was talking fast.

I popped near enough to hear.

". . . heard shots when I was coming out of the office." Albert's voice was high and shaky. "Cole Clanton's dead. In the gazebo. The cops are holding Nick Magruder. I don't know what happened. The cops won't let me get near. Yeah. Well, you're the crime reporter. I was going to hog the show when I heard all the commotion, but Cole was my friend. I don't want to do the story. Yeah. I'll wait for you." He slid the cell into his pocket and watched the gazebo, but his gaze was strained and his face drawn.

"All right, people." The sergeant held up a hand and the cops fell silent. "We'll sort things out later." He gestured to the trim policewoman. "Go to the B and B. Find this woman and bring her in."

Nick looked relieved. "She can tell you."

I felt stricken by guilt. I couldn't appear and vouch for Nick. Hilda Whitby's brief moment had passed. Once questions were asked, there would be no refuting the fact that there was no private detective agency of that name in Dallas and no Hilda Whitby.

I had to do something to help him. *We* had to do something, Dee and Wiggins and I. Dee surely was nearby, because she had alerted Wiggins to my impending capture. I also felt certain Wiggins was close at hand. He had every intention of seeing me aboard the Rescue Express.

I looked at Nick, shirtless, his arms pulled behind him, but he appeared more relaxed. He thought it was only a matter of time until he was cleared.

I had put Nick in a deep and dangerous hole. I couldn't leave him there.

Softly, I whistled, "I've Been Working on the Railroad." I hoped Nick would make the connection.

The park and gazebo hummed with activity. A crime van drove across the grass, parked only feet away from the gazebo.

My light, soft whistle was, however, clear and distinct.

The sergeant looked around. "Hey, knock off the whistling."

I continued.

Abruptly, a warm hand touched my cheek. "Shh."

"Wiggins!" I was so excited his name came out in a yelp.

"Unprofessional," came a hiss close to me.

"Shut up, Dee."

"Ladies," Wiggins implored.

"So, hey, wait a minute," the lieutenant bellowed. "If somebody thinks this is time for a comedy routine, cut it out."

I wouldn't say Wiggins yanked me. Wiggins is always a

gentleman. However, I was clutched by one arm and up we zoomed until the gazebo was far beneath us and we hung in the sky against a backdrop of stars.

"Delilah Delahunt Duvall." Wiggins spoke her name grimly. "Do not return to the gazebo."

I took pleasure that the name so announced was not mine. I recalled a wonderful author, Doreen Tovey, who wrote charming books about life with her Siamese cats. It always seemed that her boy Siamese were, to put it politely, a challenge, and her girl Siamese were well-behaved and prim, often emphasizing in a Siamese wail, "I'm a Good Girl, Am I." I felt uncannily like a Siamese princess. I would have to ask Wiggins if cats—

"Bailey Ruth Raeburn."

Uh-oh.

Steel wheels clacked on rails, the rumble coming nearer and nearer. A deep-throated woo-woo-woo, rising and falling, signaled the Rescue Express was en route.

"Ladies"—there was no warmth in his tone—"when we board—"

"I can't leave now." Dee's bold voice was determined. "Nick's in terrible trouble."

"Neither can I." For once Dee and I were in agreement. "Wiggins, we can't desert Nick. He thinks I will be able to prove he didn't shoot Cole. The police won't be able to find me, and they'll discover there's no private detective from Dallas named Hilda Whitby. Then they won't believe a word Nick says."

Wiggins was disapproving. "Appearing always leads to problems."

"That's what I told her." Dee sounded quite proud. Now it was her turn to be a virtuous Siamese princess.

"I wouldn't have stayed visible," my voice was hot, "if I'd been an official emissary, and we all know whose fault that is."

"Ladies." It wasn't brusque, for Wiggins is never brusque, but his tone definitely brooked no further bickering.

The smell of coal smoke carried across the sky. The clack of wheels on the rails was loud, the woo-woo of the horn compelling.

Wiggins made a soft whuff of indecision.

I had a quick vision of Nick: bony face, stubbled cheeks, sloppy clothes, cocky, seriously rich, good-hearted. "Nick was trying to do good tonight. Wiggins, if ever a man needs help, it's Nick."

"Please don't send me away." Dee's voice was tremulous. "Of course, I shouldn't have tricked Bailey Ruth, but I knew something awful was going to happen to Nick. McCoy was fractious. When McCoy ducks his head between his knees, trouble's coming. I was certain you wouldn't send me—all that nonsense about no contact with family members—but I thought she'd be better than nothing."

I was incensed. "Who saved Nick's life?" Did the woman have no gratitude? Did she appreciate the swirl of panic that had engulfed me when I wasn't able to disappear? Did she care?

"That was well done." Her grudging tone had all the warmth of a polar ice cap.

"Thank you." I can drip sarcasm with the best of them. I pictured Katharine Hepburn in *Pat and Mike*. For good measure, I swirled into a pants suit reminiscent of her style, a gray pinstripe and an orchid silk blouse. I immediately felt much more comfortable. Orchid suede ballerina flats completed my transformation. I might not have been able to see my apparel, but a vibrant sense of good fashion infused me with energy.

"Stop bickering." Wiggins's tone was more hopeful than commanding. Wiggins cleared his throat. "Nonsense?" He was clearly perturbed.

"Dear fellow," Dee spoke kindly, "you might let me take a shot at the Precepts. I could update them in a heartbeat."

"The Precepts are what they are." Wiggins is a man who would cling to his country railroad station and Teletype no matter the changes on earth. But I was sure he applauded emissaries who adapted to the mores of the times in which they moved. I was rather proud of my familiarity with cell phones, iPads, iPhones, and the aptly named Web, with its electronic tentacles that enmesh the globe.

Nick was likely en route to the police station as we chattered. "Perhaps the shots in the gazebo are more relevant than a shot at the Precepts. Wiggins, I can help Nick. Dee's a hindrance."

"Hindrance!" She was outraged. "That's absurd."

"Dee won't appear when she's needed, and she flits off without a word."

"I've never been able to tolerate ineptitude. Bailey Ruth was no help today in finding Nick in time to stop him from making threats against Cole. Now those chickens will come home to roost."

I snapped, "If he weren't seriously spoiled as well as seriously rich, he'd have the good sense not to broadcast his moods."

"Nick didn't know someone was going to shoot that odious young man." Her defense was passionate.

"Ladies." Wiggins's patience was at an end.

I could scarcely hear him over the woo-woo of the Rescue Express. The scent of coal smoke tickled my nose. The clack of iron wheels pulsed nearer.

"Nothing about this episode"—his distaste was evident—"reflects well upon the department. Certainly the two of you lack a collegial spirit. The department prides itself upon cooperation, quietness, *remaining unseen*"—the emphasis was strong—"effort. Faced with an unpalatable choice, I believe the department's goals will be better met if Bailey Ruth accepts the assignment. Come, Dee, we'll board the Express, and then we can discuss your highly irregular acts."

"I can't leave Nick!" Her husky voice quivered with despair. "He's only twenty-four. He needs me." She might have racketed around the world, felt at her best astride McCoy, loved men and left them, but her cry revealed a woman who cared above all for her dark-haired nephew, who was at the bottom of a pit without a rope.

"Oh, for Heaven's sake." Wiggins, bless him, is a sucker for a woman in distress. "Stay if you must. Do what you can. But mind, you and Bailey Ruth must cooperate."

The Rescue Express, gleaming in the moonlight, swung by, pausing for an instant. Then, with a burst of speed, the train rose in the sky and streaked away like a meteor. "Remember the Precepts" came the distant cry.

With the immensity of the star-spangled sky arching above us, the departure of the Express emphasized a deep and peaceful silence.

"Dee?"

"Here." She sounded invigorated. She'd won her battle. As if reading my mind, she shouted exuberantly. "Wiggins is a fine fellow. Now, I must be off to help Nick."

"Hey, wait a minute. It's the two of us. . . ."

Delilah Delahunt Duvall was gone.

❧

Nick's face was pale and drawn. He moved restively in the hard wooden chair, rubbed knuckles against his bristly cheek. I was relieved to see there was no longer blood on his hand. No doubt the stained hand had been filmed and tested for gunshot residue particles before he was fingerprinted and permitted to wash. A too-large orange jumpsuit slopped over at the shoulders and sagged at his waist. His bloodied polo and blood-smeared jeans must have been taken into evidence. The jumpsuit would be dispiriting, but I imagined Nick preferred it to his own stained clothing.

"Would you like a cup of coffee, Mr. Magruder?" The familiar voice was impersonal, but polite. Detective Sergeant

Hal Price sat behind a high-wattage lamp turned toward Nick. I always felt a quiver of delight when I saw Hal Price, a lean blond with slate-blue eyes, a man who appreciated redheads. If my heart didn't belong to Bobby Mac, I would be smitten.

I had assisted Detective Sergeant Price and Police Chief Sam Cobb in previous visits to Adelaide. Both had glimpsed me despite my best efforts to escape their notice. Could I help it that occasionally my actual presence was essential? I especially enjoyed appearing as Police Officer M. Loy, my tribute to the auburn-haired actress who will always be remembered opposite William Powell in the Thin Man movies.

Price was flanked by the officer who had been in charge at the gazebo and a fortyish policewoman who held a notebook and pen. Chief Cobb stood near the back wall with his arms folded, his well-worn brown suit wrinkled. His heavy face was impassive beneath grizzled black hair. He was a big man with a quietly commanding air. Both a tape recorder and video camera sat on the desk.

"Mr. Magruder, I'd like to hear again about the meeting you set up with Mr. Clanton. What was the purpose of the meeting?"

Nick looked wary. "We had some business to take care of."

The chief was pleasant. "What business?"

Nick spoke carefully. "Cole wanted some property that I was going to buy."

"The Arnold house." Price tapped his pen on the table. "It's pretty well known around town that you made a bigger offer to keep Clanton from obtaining the property."

Nick looked truculent. "There's no law against that."

Price appeared interested. "Why did you want the property?"

Nick looked uncomfortable. "Yeah, well, I thought I'd like to have it."

"Why?" Chief Cobb asked.

Nick shrugged. "I imagine you know why. I didn't like

Cole. He wanted to put up a replica of the original trading post. I thought it wouldn't hurt for him to find out he couldn't always have things the way he wanted them."

Price said mildly, "Would you say there was bad blood between you and Mr. Clanton?"

Nick's stubborn honesty glinted in his eyes. "He was a jerk. But"—his anger was evident—"I know a lot of jerks, and I don't shoot them. I was having too much fun making him mad."

"Good clean sport? But today, you changed your mind." The chief's eyes were gimlet sharp. "Why?"

Nick's bravado faded. His eyes flickered. "Yeah. Well, Cole and I had been in touch today and I thought maybe I'd let it go. I didn't really want the place."

"What contact did you have with Mr. Clanton?" The even tenor of his voice made the question seem negligible.

Nick turned over a hand. "Yeah. Well, we talked a couple of times."

Price picked up a folder from the table, flipped through it. "People keep up with the news, Mr. Magruder. Information gets around fast. Apparently local radio and TV have already broadcast news about Mr. Clanton's murder. We asked media to suggest that anyone with information contact Crime Stoppers or send tweets. We've had several responses."

Nick tried to appear at ease, but he began to crack the knuckles of one hand.

"We'll check everything out tomorrow, get witnesses. From what we hear, you were all over Adelaide today, trying to find Mr. Clanton. Why were you angry, Mr. Magruder?"

"A misunderstanding." Nick's voice was stiff. "We worked things out."

Price closed the folder. "You say you and he spoke several times. It's interesting that your cell phone contains several texts to his cell phone number."

Nick slowly nodded.

Cobb moved fast for a big man. He came around the table, stood within a foot of Nick. "What did you do with Mr. Clanton's cell phone?"

Nick's eyes flickered.

Of course he remembered the exchange that had been about to be made, the agreement to sell the property to Cole for a dollar if Cole removed Arlene's photographs, Cole pulling out his cell phone, the cell phone plucked from Cole's grasp and moving through the air to the back of the gazebo, Cole jerking about, the crack of the rifle.

"I didn't take Cole's cell phone."

Price shook his head. "We have your cell. You texted him at 8:58. The shots were heard at 9:07. Shall I remind you of your texts?" Price picked up a sheet and read aloud, " 'Are you coming?' His reply: 'Got the paper?' Your reply: 'Signed and ready.' A few minutes later he was dead. Where's his cell phone?"

Nick hunched his shoulders. "I didn't do anything with his cell phone."

Price was grim. "Somebody got that cell phone, Mr. Magruder. Otherwise why didn't we find it in his pocket or in the gazebo?"

"I didn't take it."

Price snapped, "Who did?"

Nick looked weary, shook his head.

"Some of the texts you sent him contained threats."

Nick stared at the floor.

"Let's go over it again, Mr. Magruder."

"Look"—Nick sounded tired and truculent—"I've told you and told you. Somebody else shot Cole. Haven't you talked to Hilda Whitby? She was there. She'll confirm everything I've said."

Chief Cobb's eyes narrowed. "We haven't found Ms. Whitby yet. Let's hear your version again. Tell us what happened from the time you arrived at the park."

"I already told you. I parked the car in the lot." Nick

sounded long-suffering. "I walked up to the gazebo—" He stopped with an odd expression on his face. His head jerked to the left. "You're not here. I got enough problems without you."

His left arm rose.

He tried to pull his arm back. "Let go. Come on." His voice was anguished.

Chief Cobb stared, his thick brows drawn into a frown.

I sped to Nick's side, swept out a hand, brushed against a tweed jacket. Excellent material. Did Dee like a British country-house look? So far, I'd seen her on earth only in a photograph. Perhaps she had good taste, even if she lacked charm. I caught her sleeve. "Hush," I whispered. "You're making a scene."

"I'm trying to help him," Dee hissed, shaking me off. "Nick, don't say another word until you get a lawyer." She spoke aloud, her deep voice commanding.

Nick flinched and grabbed his shoulder. I guessed she'd poked him for emphasis.

I bent down and whispered in Nick's ear. "That's good advice. Shut up and I'll get her out of here."

Nick made a strangled sound. His face stricken, he looked from one side to the other, but, of course, no one was visible near him. "Go away. Both of you."

Cobb's voice was gruff. "That's enough, Magruder. Maybe you do female impersonations in your spare time, but you're in big trouble, and smarting off won't do you any good."

I tapped Nick's cheek. "Ask for a lawyer. Then we'll leave." I tried to speak softly, but in the taut silence of the observers, my voice was clearly heard.

Nick clapped his hands to his head. "All right. Yeah. I want a lawyer."

Cobb folded his arms. "You can call a lawyer. We're holding you on suspicion of murder. Maybe a night in a cell will help clear your head."

Chapter 9

The brightly lit cell was spartan—two bunks, cement floor, metal toilet.

"This is dreadful." Dee's voice shook.

"Don't worry." I spoke with more confidence than I felt. "We'll find out who shot Cole."

Nick stared wildly around the cell. He looked very young, his dark curls tousled, his stubbled face strained.

"Oh, sure." Dee's tone was scathing. "Private Detective Hilda Whitby! You've made a mess of everything."

"I didn't make a spectacle of myself in the interrogation room."

"Did you intend to hang there and let him talk and talk without a lawyer? I should have done something sooner."

Nick was breathing hard, as if he'd run too fast, too far. "Nobody's here. I got to keep my head together. Nobody's here." He cracked the knuckles of one hand.

Dee snapped, "Don't do that, Nick."

Nick slid a hand over his eyes. After a moment, he

splayed his fingers to peer around the cell. "That's what you always used to say. Aunt Dee, are you really here?"

"We're both here." I reached out and patted his shoulder.

He dropped onto the bunk, hunched his shoulders. "Either I'm nuts or I'm haunted."

Nick was utterly demoralized. He needed encouragement. "Dee, we have to prove we are who we say we are."

"There you go again." Dee was derisive. "You're hell-bent to appear."

"I do hope not."

I wasn't certain, but I thought I heard a faint wisp of laughter. Then came a definite sigh. "Oh well, I'm on my last mission anyway. Wiggins won't trust me again. So what does it matter if I appear?" She sounded glum. With that, she swirled into being—deep blue eyes, narrow nose, distinctive cleft chin, tall, slender, and utterly confident.

"Oh." I was admiring. "I like that jacket. Speckled black tweed! Much more eye-catching than brown."

"Just a little thing I picked up from Saks." Three-quarter-length ribboned cuffs added a definite flair.

I gave some thought and appeared in a new outfit. After all, I'd been deprived of fashion for several days. I looked down and smoothed the sleeve of a deliciously supple pink leather jacket. Nothing heavy, mind you. I changed my mind in mid-swirl from ivory straight-leg slacks to charcoal gray with matching gray leather loafers.

Nick was as far back in the bunk as he could manage.

I moved over to sit beside him, gestured for Dee to join us. She dropped down on his other side.

I touched his left arm.

Dee touched his right arm.

He was as rigid as the bars that held him captive.

Running footsteps sounded in the corridor.

Dee was sharp. "Here comes trouble. That's what happens when emissaries appear. You know it's against the rules."

I wasn't troubled, though the steps were pounding nearer. "Nick needed to see us, but," I said more quickly, "it's time to disappear."

I disappeared.

"Who knows what will happen now." Dee's tone was waspish as she faded from view.

"Shh." I hoped Dee might become a bit more optimistic. I would do my best to share a little sunshine with her. "All will be well."

"That'll be the day." A huff. "We need to talk to Nick and now look what's happening."

Two officers arrived, a heavyset woman with protuberant brown eyes and a tall, gangly older man with a handlebar mustache. She reached out, pulled at the door, which remained immovable. "Two women were in here. We saw them on the monitor. Where'd they go?"

Nick turned his hands over. "I don't know."

The man moved past her. "I'll check."

Her face grim, the officer—I glanced at her name tag: *Officer L. Nelson*—used both hands to grip the bars, shook again. "Tight as a drum."

The second officer returned. "No way out. Nobody in the hall." His name tag read: *Officer R. Maitland*.

"We saw them. We heard them. Where are they?" Officer Nelson grappled with the impossible.

"Maybe I just thought about them and you saw them." Nick waved his hand. "It's a variant on the validity of physical objects created by brain waves. The door's locked. I'm here. Who knows? They may come back. You can watch them on the monitor, but they won't be here if you come look." He gave a wolfish smile. "Have a good night."

I heard soft laughter from Dee.

"You laughing at us?" Nelson glared at Nick.

"Lady, I didn't make a sound. Nobody"—he spoke loudly—"ought to make any sounds."

I hoped Dee was chastised.

Nelson's heavy face was hard. "You telling us not to say anything?"

Nick looked beleaguered. "Not you."

"Then who you talking to?" Maitland's voice was rough.

Nick's eyes gleamed. "When I think, physical manifestations may emanate. I'm simply telling them to stay away." There was definite emphasis on the command.

"Come off it," Maitland sneered. "How dumb do you think we are?"

"Officer, I have no doubt about your capacity to see what is in front of you."

Maitland looked puzzled, uncertain if he was being insulted.

Like a dog with a bone, Nelson repeated, "Nobody's here." She spoke with a hint of bluster. "Obviously, if nobody's here, we didn't see what we thought we saw. Probably something's wrong with the monitor. But"—she gestured up the corridor—"let's look again." She swung away.

Maitland's face flushed. He turned to follow her. "You saying I don't got eyes? I'm telling you nobody's down the hall and there's no way out and his cell's locked up tight."

I moved out into the corridor.

Maitland stopped two cells down. "Hey, Bud. You see anybody come this way."

A man rolled over in his bunk, shaded his eyes. "Can't a man get any sleep around here?" His slightly slurred voice was aggrieved. "Nobody's been here. But make that guy down the way turn off his radio."

Officer Nelson stalked to the cell. "What radio?"

The prisoner blinked. "I don't know. I heard a couple of women talking. Had to be radio or TV. I don't see why I can't have one if somebody else does."

"You aren't in the Ritz, Bud." Nelson spoke to the prisoner, but her eyes slid toward Nick's cell.

"Like I don't know that? Anyway, make those women shut up." He rolled back toward the wall.

Maitland stood with his arms akimbo. "I don't get it."

Nelson looked indecisive, then jerked her head at Maitland. "Nothing more to do here."

I followed them out of the cell area. As the heavy door closed behind them, Nelson jerked a thumb over her shoulder. "That guy's a troublemaker. Maybe he likes to talk in girlie voices. There's nobody around. Probably there's something funny with the monitor. Anyway, he's locked up. Let's get some coffee."

Back in his cell, Nick sat like a statue, staring at his knee. "Aunt Dee, I can feel your hand on my knee and I know you are trying to encourage me, but it's making me nuts. I can't see you, then you and that redhead appear, and then you're gone again." He cracked his knuckles. "But I get it. You really are ghosts. That means I'm in deep"—he paused—"deep trouble. Hilda, if that's her name, is bouncing around in the ether, and I don't have an alibi, and I'm going to end up tried for murder."

"Nonsense. Dee and I will find out who killed Cole." I spoke more loudly than I'd intended.

His head jerked toward the sound of my voice. "Keep it low. I don't need the *Police Academy* cops back. So"—he folded his arms—"are you really a private detective? A dead one?" There was a faint note of hope in his voice.

I didn't think my experience as a high school English teacher and later as a secretary at the chamber would impress him. Telling the truth didn't require telling everything. "I've had some investigative experience." I spoke with quiet pride. "I've helped Chief Cobb here in Adelaide. Nick, you're exhausted. Try to sleep now." Actually, a respite would likely help Dee and me as well.

"Sleep . . . Yeah." He rubbed his face. "Listen, my cat comes in at night and sleeps on my bed. He'll be at the door waiting for me."

Nick's mind had to be pummeled by anxiety, fear, and disbelief. He'd seen a man die and now found himself a suspect in that death. None of this would ever have occurred to him in his wildest nightmares. Yet he worried about a battle-scarred tomcat waiting for a door to open.

Dee had said, ". . . but there are those who love him . . ."

I felt a rush of affection. "We'll see about Champ. We'll make sure he's fed until you're home again."

"Home." Nick's voice was hopeless. "Yeah. Well, if I don't get out, maybe Jan will take him. He's a great guy. He wants to be talked to, but don't pick him up. He's got a bad hip. And maybe when you talk to Jan . . ." He stopped, looked even more discouraged. "But you can't talk to her. I mean, the cops are hunting for you, Hilda. Plus, if I got it right, it's against the rules"—he sounded a little puzzled—"to be seen. I guess there's no way to tell Jan I didn't shoot Cole. I mean, I hope she knows that, but I'd like for somebody to tell her."

Dee was brusque, and I suspected beneath her stern exterior was a heart that cherished romance. "We'll tell her. Somehow."

"Of course we will. Don't worry about Jan." Nick needed sleep. Perhaps we could ease his mind at least a little. "Write her a note."

He turned his hands over in defeat. "They took everything. My billfold, my cell phone, a pen."

"We'll get . . ." My voice trailed off. Dee and I could speed through walls and doors, but to bring him a sheet of paper and a pen required opening the locked entrance to the cells. "Don't worry. Dee and I will make sure Jan knows you are all right, and you are going to be all right. We'll go there first and then we'll take care of Champ."

∽

The lower floor of the B and B was dim except for a Tiffany lamp on a hall table. The cream, jade, and crimson art glass added cheer. The last fading notes sounded from the grandfather clock at the end of the hall. It was a quarter to eleven.

I spoke softly, sure that Dee was nearby. "The police must have already been here. Let's check upstairs for Jan."

All of the bedroom doors were closed. Jan stood at the end of the hall, her hand on a doorknob. She tried to turn the handle. "Mom, unlock the door. The police are gone." She twisted again. "I know you came in the back way and slipped up the stairs. I have to talk to you." She shook the knob. "Mom, where were you tonight?"

"Dee." My whisper was faint, too soft to be heard over Jan's entreaties.

Dee tapped my arm.

I bent toward the touch, whispered, "Go into Arlene's room. Find out what's happening. I'll wait until Jan goes downstairs, then I'll appear and talk to her."

I waited to see if Jan prevailed. She tried again. The knob didn't budge. Finally, she turned away from her mother's door and walked toward the stairway, her round face creased in an anxious frown. She walked heavily down the stairs.

When the kitchen door closed behind her, I swirled into being. Regretfully, I replaced my elegant pink and gray outfit with the black sweater, slacks, and shoes I'd worn to the gazebo. I consoled myself that the change was temporary. I pushed open the door.

Jan whirled. "Mo—" Eagerness was replaced with shock. "You! Where have you been? The police are looking for you. You have to call and tell them you're here. They said you don't exist, and they wanted me to tell them who you really are. I don't care who you are." She sped across the floor, gripped my arm. "They're holding Nick. They think he shot Cole. They don't believe you were there. But you went with him. Why didn't you help him?"

"Jan, I'm doing my best for Nick. He understands that I can't appear to talk to the police right now. I'm working undercover. I have every intention of informing the police of the killer's identity. Nick is innocent, despite what the police think. I was there, and someone shot Cole from the weeping willows behind the gazebo."

Sheer terror flickered in her eyes. She whirled away from me, walked to the counter, placed her hands against the rim as if clinging for support.

I followed, lightly touched her rigid shoulder. "What time did your mother get back here?"

Jan jerked to face me. "Mom didn't shoot Cole. I know she didn't." She tried to sound confident, but her voice was shaky.

"The police will find out if she was at the park. She'd be much better advised to contact them and describe what she saw."

Jan took a deep breath. "I'll tell her."

I looked into eyes brimming with fear. "Ask your mother if she wants an innocent man to go to prison."

"Mother wasn't there." It was a prayer.

I turned and walked to the hall door.

"Wait." Jan started after me. "The police want to talk to you."

"I'll contact the police when I have information that clears Nick. If you want to help him, don't tell anyone I came here." I pushed through the door. As it closed behind me, I disappeared and flowed back into the kitchen.

Jan rushed to the telephone, grabbed up the receiver, then slowly replaced it in the holder. "Oh Nick." Tears slid down her cheeks. "Nick, I don't know what to do." She whirled away from the counter, began to pace.

She wasn't going to report my return, hoping that her silence would be best for Nick. But she wasn't afraid only for Nick. Arlene had known that Nick was meeting Cole in the gazebo. Had Arlene been in City Park, too?

∽

Arlene's bedroom was pure Victoriana. Another time I would have been enthralled by the pine Georgian fireplace and its flowered-tile insert of urns with roses and ferns. A reproduction of a Sargent painting hung above the massive carved mahogany bedstead. A Japanese screen stood in one corner of the room. Filmy muslin edged with lace draped a dressing table, which sat in a bay window framed by dark red velvet drapes. Bric-a-brac decorated several small tables, all with lace cloths.

I was puzzled. Jan had stood at her mother's door, asking for entry. Where was Arlene?

"Dee?" I spoke softly.

"Over here." Dee's reply was equally soft. "She's in the bathroom. She's dreadfully upset."

The bathroom door creaked. Arlene stepped into the bedroom. Her black silk dressing gown with golden embroidery was lovely, but in the privacy of her chamber, her face revealed shock, despair, and fear, eyes red-rimmed, face bloated from tears, quivering lips. She walked to a rose-patterned chair, fell into it, stared blindly at the drawn window curtains. Slowly she lifted her hands. Her face sank down. Sobs shook her shoulders.

Was she crying for Cole? Or for herself?

❦

Thankfully, once again I had an emissary's mobility. Dee and I simply thought, *Nick's house,* and we were in the dark living room. I turned on the overhead light and several lamps. The rich chocolate leather sofa and two matching chairs gleamed. Immediately I felt more cheerful. Light is nice.

A stick rose near the drum set. The stick reached the level of Dee's face, likely held briefly to a cheek.

"Dee, he's going to be all right."

The stick slowly descended and lay atop a drum. She cleared her throat. "Let's see to the cat."

I opened the front door. Champ was curled in a ball on the welcome mat. He rose and stretched. When I held the door for him, he strolled inside, tilted his head to look up. Cats can see what people can't. I bent down and petted him. He rose on his back legs, placed his paws on my leg. "Time for dinner."

I started for the kitchen and Champ moved quickly ahead of me.

Cabinet doors were opening, one after another. "Ah." A can of cat food rose in the air. A click and the lid was pulled back. A spoon appeared suspended in air. A couple of quick scoops and a blue plastic bowl floated to the floor.

Champ reached the bowl as it settled on the floor.

I opened the refrigerator. I was ready for a snack. "Old pizza. An egg carton." I picked up the carton. "A week past the sell date."

"That will do for breakfast." Dee clearly had low standards.

"Possibly for you. I intend to have breakfast at Lulu's." I swirled into being. "But the house will suit us admirably as a place to stay."

A thunderous knock sounded at the front door. "Police! Open up! Police!"

I disappeared. "Quick, Dee. I'll toss things around in the living room. You go upstairs, make it appear someone's searched the bedrooms."

"But why—?"

"A diversion." With that, I was in the living room pulling out the couch cushions, flinging them to the floor.

The shouts continued. "Police! Open up! We're armed!"

"Something's going on in there, Sergeant."

An officer must have been at one of the porch windows, peering inside.

I took a stack of magazines, flung them toward the ceiling.

"Johnny, somebody's tossing stuff around." A strained pause. "I don't see anybody."

I swooped by the drum set, picked up the sticks, thumped with vigor, then tossed one to my right and the other to my left. They swooped, then dropped and clattered on the wooden floor.

From upstairs came thumps and bangs.

The front door banged open.

I sped to the desk, pulled out the side drawers, upended them, then yanked at the central drawer.

No one had yet sprung through the door. Likely, the officers were viewing at a slant, being careful not to provide a target.

A distinct rattle sounded as the central drawer slid out at my jerk.

I froze.

A half dozen rifle cartridges rolled toward me.

The cartridges had not been in this almost-empty drawer Tuesday night. Nick had not been at the house since Tuesday night except to feed Champ. In fact, he'd spent most of the day slamming around Adelaide in search of Cole. The police would easily discover the reason for his anger at Cole. If the cartridges fit the murder weapon, it would be another link to Nick.

I grabbed them. I wasn't visible, so I had no pockets. The cartridges hung in the air above the desk as the police officers stormed inside, guns drawn, heads swiveling, looking, checking. One I knew—handsome, dark-haired Johnny Cain. The other was muscular and heavyset with a pugnacious face.

I zoomed up to the ceiling. If either man looked up, they would see the cartridges.

I'd thought myself clever to create a scene of chaos to suggest forces at work while Nick was in jail. Indeed, there had been a force at work. A killer had, at some point, either before or after shooting Cole, brought the cartridges and left them here to incriminate Nick.

A hollow boom sounded upstairs. Dee apparently was getting into the spirit of our project.

The burly cop jerked his head toward the stairs. As he

ran past, I saw his name tag: *Officer E. Loeffler.* He started up the treads, moving with his back to the wall, one step at a time, gun held steady in both hands. Johnny followed, gun ready. Johnny edged from step to step with his back to the railing.

Safe from their observation, I reached the front door and hurried outside. Zooming high above the clearing, I spotted a faint glimmer in the moonlight. I sped over a patch of trees. Not far below gleamed a farm pond. With enormous relief, I reached the center of the pond and dropped the bullets one by one.

Now unconstrained by physical objects, I landed immediately in the upper hall of Nick's house. Officer Loeffler was in a half crouch, facing a slightly ajar bedroom door. Johnny stood at an angle in a similar crouch.

"Police." Loeffler's shout was grim, threatening. "Come out with your hands up."

The only answer was another bang.

"Now." Loeffler launched himself against the partially opened door. The panel crashed back against the wall. Loeffler and Johnny plunged into the bedroom, then, slowly, they rose from their attack stance and looked around. The mattress was half off the bed. Dresser drawers stood open, the contents strewn on the floor. The wide-open closet door revealed not a threatening figure but jumbled piles of clothing.

I popped downstairs, banged the front door.

The officers came pounding downstairs. Again they were cautious as they reached the door, which I had left open. Loeffler stepped near, risked a quick glance outside. He straightened. "I don't see anybody. Let's douse the lights, go out the back way, and circle around."

I returned to Nick's room. A dresser drawer closed. The floor was clear. In the closet, a shirt rose from the floor, was slipped onto a hanger. I leaned against the jamb. "Tidying up?"

"I can't abide a mess." A pair of slacks was slipped on a hanger.

I gave a soft laugh. "Let them work that out when they come back."

After a moment's pause, Dee laughed, too. "I hadn't thought of that."

I wasn't amused long. Nick's desk was no laughing matter. "Someone put cartridges—I'm sure they'll fit the rifle that killed Cole—in Nick's desk drawer. I got rid of them. The bullets were not in the drawer when I arrived Tuesday night. We know Nick didn't shoot Cole and that he never had the rifle in his possession."

A hanger hung motionless next to a shirt dangling from the collar. "The bullets were planted."

"Yes." The conclusion was inescapable.

"The police came to search Nick's house." Dee's tone was thoughtful.

What a near thing it had been. Nick hadn't forgotten Champ waiting at home, so we came here. "If the police had found the bullets, it would be another link to Cole's murder."

The shirt was slowly hung, the hanger returned to the rod.

Downstairs a door banged. "They're back."

"I gathered." Dee's tone was dry.

Outside a siren squalled. And another. I looked out the bedroom window, sensed Dee beside me. Police spilled out of several cars. Two teams started circling the house in opposite directions.

"Rather busy here. We need a place to stay."

"I know a bunkhouse not too far away." Dee's voice was eager. "Dusty Road Stables. If there's no show this weekend, the place will be empty."

⌒

I looked down at three dark barns and several corrals. A light came on in a structure near one of the corrals. I joined Dee inside a double-wide trailer fixed up with a half dozen bunks, a bath, and a galley. "Nice."

The door of the small refrigerator opened. An ice tray arched to a counter. A cupboard door swung out. Two tall green plastic tumblers plunked onto the counter. Ice cubes popped. The water faucet hissed.

I swirled into being.

A disapproving huff. "Why are you appearing?"

I smoothed the expensive material of my slacks. "Unseen clothes don't afford nearly as much pleasure."

"Vanity. All is vanity."

"Shall we balance vanity with pompous adherence to pointless prohibitions? There's no one to see you but me."

A glass approached me.

I wondered if I was going to have a face full of ice water shortly.

The glass went down, remained motionless for an instant, then slowly came toward me. I accepted with pleasure, drank long and thirstily. "I can talk better if I can see you."

The deep voice was cool. "It seems to me you talk quite well enough."

"Don't be small-spirited."

A riffle of laughter. "You're not quite the ass I took you for."

"If that's a compliment, it seems unfortunately phrased."

"Oh well, in for a penny . . . and I spent many happy hours here when I was a girl. . . ." She swirled into being, her Marlene Dietrich blonde hair a perfect foil for ice-blue eyes, a pointed chin with a distinctive cleft, a long, thin nose. She was immaculately attired in a crisp white blouse, cream jodhpurs, high tan leather boots. A riding crop appeared in her slender hand. She waggled it experimentally. "Feels good. If only McCoy were here."

I looked at her in alarm. "Don't even think about it." Bunking with Dee was one thing, but McCoy was quite another.

A slight smile touched her thin lips. "He's in the last stall on the right in the barn." She glanced toward the trailer door. "Perhaps early tomorrow before anyone stirs, I might ride."

"We have plenty to do tomorrow." I gestured toward a sofa, sank onto a wooden chair.

Abruptly, remembrance drew down the corners of her mouth. She flung herself down on the small plaid sofa, crossed her slender legs, tapped the end of the crop against one shiny boot. "That business about the bullets. You see the implications."

I did indeed. I ticked them off, one at a time. "Nick was set up to take the blame from the get-go. The murder occurred at the gazebo because Nick was meeting Cole and had broadcast his anger at him all over town. Someone with reason to kill Cole was aware of Nick's search for him."

"I wonder"—her tone was dry—"if anyone in town *didn't* know."

I understood Dee's frustration. There didn't seem any point in trying to seek out witnesses of Nick's highly vociferous search for Cole yesterday. The murderer hadn't necessarily personally observed Nick's angry stops. Word-of-mouth had carried the tale all across town.

I sipped the wonderfully refreshing water. "We must figure out who wanted Cole dead. We have to find out everything possible about him. His enemies, his presumed friends, even acquaintances. Someone will have the information we need."

Dee looked puzzled. "How?"

I spoke with confidence. "A little conversation here, a little conversation there. It's amazing what can be discovered, especially when questions are backed up by authority."

"Your private-eye gig?" She shook her head. "You can't ride that horse. You're a wanted woman."

My smile was benign. "You're not."

Chapter 10

Dee and I sat at Lulu's counter. In the mirror, she looked aristocratic in a wine-red wool jacket with oversize enamel buttons. As always, her short-cut blonde hair was perfectly coiffed. However, her pointed face was drawn in a worried frown. I checked my reflection. I admired the fit of a pink silk ruffle pullover. The blouse was perfect for the gray and pink plaid skirt I'd chosen. High heels, of course, gray leather with a strap over the instep.

"All right." Her tone was crisp, impatient. "We're here, since you insisted." She, too, glanced in the mirror, but not with pleasure. "Wiggins feels strongly about emissaries appearing."

I'd stayed mum about my plans, hoping a nice breakfast would improve Dee's attitude. Moreover, in order to eat at Lulu's, we had to appear. I hoped Dee would find swirling into being easier the more often she became visible. Her stony expression suggested otherwise. I pulled a sheet of paper from my pocket. I'd worked a bit after Dee rolled over in her bunk and fell asleep. I unfolded the sheet, placed it on the counter between us, and tapped it with my forefinger. Hmm. Red polish didn't complement my lovely blouse. Oh yes, that was much better. I smiled at the new light pink polish.

Dee didn't miss the change in shade. She seemed rarely to miss much. Her cool blue eyes weren't admiring. "Did you spend every waking moment admiring yourself when you were alive?"

I glanced at her colorless nails. "Scarlet would be an excellent choice."

Her cleft chin jutted. "I've indulged you. We are having breakfast at what is apparently your spiritual home. You claim to have a plan. What is it?"

"Dee, it's a Heaven-sent opportunity." I tried to sound as if surely this was meant to be. "You left Adelaide after your teenage years. No one will recognize you as an adult. You can talk to people with motives to shoot Cole, such as Lisa and Brian Sanford and Arlene Richey. There may be others as well."

Dee stirred steaming grits. "Why would anyone talk to me?"

I squeezed a dollop of honey on my toast. "Police officers have every right to ask questions."

"Of course they can. No one disputes—" She stopped, the spoon midway between the bowl and her mouth. "Exactly what are you proposing?"

"The Adelaide police have a very flattering uniform, French blue with black stripes down the trouser legs."

"No."

"Do you want Nick tried for murder?" I regretted the sharp question the minute I'd spoken.

Dee's face twisted. She closed her eyes briefly, opened them. Heartbreak stared at me. "We might do more harm than good. Surely the police will investigate and find out the truth."

"I hope so." My tone was grave. "Chief Cobb is a fine man." Possibly Dee was right. Possibly I enjoyed the hunt too much. As Wiggins always warned, emissaries must fight against being too much *of* the earth.

However, I didn't hear the distant whistle of the Rescue Express, which did not augur well for Nick Magruder.

I felt a sense of urgency. The DA would press Chief Cobb to file charges if the evidence against Nick continued to mount. Even if we managed ultimately to clear Nick, sooner was better than later. Mud sticks. Nick might well want to stay in Adelaide. As a seriously rich young man, he could live wherever he wished, and I thought his wish would be to stay where Jan was.

Was Nick truly in danger of a murder charge?

There was only one way to find out. "It's time to go to Chief Cobb's office."

A gray alligator purse appeared in my lap. I opened the bag and lifted out a matching billfold as I picked up the check. Heaven always provides.

∽

Sam Cobb's brown suit jacket hung limply from his chair. Folders were strewn across his desk. He stood at an old-fashioned blackboard with a thick stub of chalk in his right hand. I was pleased to see the blackboard. The chief had resisted the mayor's effort to replace it with a more modern whiteboard and dry-erase markers. The chief knew who he was and where he came from. He'd used chalk as a high school chemistry teacher; he used chalk as police chief. Today his blunt face, domed forehead, strong nose, and square chin looked formidable.

Although the chief was no artist, I recognized the outline of the gazebo on the blackboard. Steps led up to a horizontal line that represented the floor. Hatch marks indicated the presence of weeping willows at the rear of the structure.

The chief held a sheet of paper in his left hand. He muttered, "Rifle fired from a distance of approximately five feet." He marked an arrow and turned toward Detective

Sergeant Price, who leaned against the stippled plaster wall. "The shot knocked the victim backward, so Clanton was facing the rear of the gazebo when he was struck. Magruder said the shot came from the willows, which is consistent with the position of the body. Magruder claims he was standing near the entrance to the gazebo and was behind Clanton when he was shot."

Price quirked one blond eyebrow. "Why would Clanton turn his back on Magruder? It seems more likely that Magruder was at the back of the gazebo and Clanton faced him. It's pretty shadowy there near the willows. Maybe Magruder hid the rifle there before they met. That works out to about five feet."

Chief Cobb placed an *X* near the hatch marks. "Magruder was found on his knees next to Clanton, and Magruder was facing the willows."

Price waved a dismissive hand. "Magruder's luck ran out. He planned to beat it before anyone saw him. After Magruder shot the guy, he waited for a couple of seconds to be sure Clanton was dead or dying. Unfortunately for him, Smitty heard the shots when he got out of his patrol car and immediately raised the alarm. Magruder started for the steps, and here came men with lights. Magruder knew he was trapped." Price's eyes narrowed. "Okay, he's standing there and lights are flashing and cops are shouting. Maybe he's a quick-thinking dude. He uses the tail of his polo to swipe away the fingerprints on the trigger and some of the stock and barrel. He hurries to the body and drops down by Clanton like he's trying to help the guy. For a little extra, he gives himself a whack on the head and crashes over, wounded hero, the rifle lying next to him."

Cobb looked thoughtful. "That would account for his fingerprints on the rifle in odd places."

Price pushed away from the wall, reached for a tan folder on a circular table near the blackboard. "We have a half dozen witnesses"—he held up a sheaf of papers—"who say

Magruder was hell for leather all over town yesterday looking for Clanton."

Chief Cobb placed the chalk in the tray, walked slowly
to his desk, and settled in the sturdy, worn leather chair.
"Anybody know the reason?"

Price settled on the corner of the desk. "Nobody seems
to know why. Magruder admits he wanted to keep Clanton
off the Arnold property, but last night Magruder showed up
with an agreement to sell the place to Clanton for one dollar.
That doesn't explain why Magruder was running after Clanton and yelling threats."

The chief pulled a folder close, flipped it open. "Something happened yesterday to change the status quo re the
property." He picked up a plastic bag with a single sheet of
paper in it. He picked up a pair of reading glasses, pushed
them high on his nose, and read aloud: "'Upon completing
purchase of the Arnold property, I, Nicholas Duvall
Magruder, agree to sell the land and house to Cole Brewster
Clanton for the sum of $1 (one dollar).' It's signed by
Magruder and dated yesterday. The paper was found in his
pocket when he was taken into custody."

Price's eyes gleamed. "I smell blackmail. Magruder
stormed all over town breathing fire, but he meets Clanton
at the gazebo ready to surrender."

Cobb leaned back in his chair. "If Magruder intended to
shoot him, why make out the agreement?"

Price shrugged. "Maybe he used it as bait, flapped the
sheet but kept it out of Clanton's reach until he could grab
the rifle and shoot. Magruder never intended to be caught
at the gazebo."

"Granted." Chief Cobb pulled out a side drawer, retrieved
a sack of M&M'S. He dribbled candies into his hand, offered
the sack to Price.

Price took a handful and lounged against one end of the
chief's brown leather sofa. He munched, said indistinctly,
"Magruder claims a woman was there. Hilda Whitby."

The chief pulled a legal pad closer, scrawled *Hilda Whitby?* in large script.

Price shook his head. "Whoever she is, she's not Hilda Whitby from Dallas. We've run checks up and down and sideways. No Hilda Whitby in Dallas."

Cobb's heavy face folded in thought. "What'd you find at the B and B?"

"A woman answering her description checked in Tuesday night. She arrived on a motor scooter belonging to Nick Magruder. It's still there. We've dusted for prints and ditto in the room she occupied. We ran the prints. No matches. All the clothing was new and a bunch of tags and a Wal-Mart sales slip were in the wastebasket. She bought the clothes yesterday morning. Apparently, she claimed her stuff had been stolen."

My, how thorough. Of course, I have always had the highest respect for the investigative abilities of the Adelaide police. I hoped Dee was impressed.

"Kind of like she disappeared." Cobb's voice was faintly uneasy.

"We should be able to find her." Price spoke a trifle loudly. "She doesn't have transport. Her purse was in the bedroom." He frowned. "That was odd. The purse had a billfold with money in it but no ID, no credit cards. The purse was part of the Wal-Mart purchases. No ID, but lots of makeup."

The chief frowned. "No ID at all?"

"Nada."

"Kind of like she doesn't exist." The chief moved uneasily in his chair, reached for the M&M sack.

"She exists." Price spoke flatly. "The B and B owner's daughter confirmed that she and her mother talked at length with the woman Tuesday night. Whitby claimed to be a private investigator hired by Magruder. Hilda Whitby of SAM Private Enquiries, Limited. No such firm in Dallas. Or in the entire state of Texas."

"A redhead." There was a curious tone in Chief Cobb's voice.

Price stiffened. Quick interest flared in his eyes, then slowly died. "No way, Sam. Those other times—"

The detective was referring to previous visits to Adelaide when it had been essential that I appear. After my first mission, I'd tried hard not to been seen by Detective Sergeant Price. We found each other much too attractive. I was true to Bobby Mac, and Hal Price needed to find an earthly redhead. In my encounters with Chief Cobb, he and I had achieved an unspoken agreement not to delve deeply into the origin of helpful information.

"—we probably picked up on stuff our subconsciouses knew all along. You know, you tumble to something and you don't quite know how you made the leap, but it all proves out."

Cobb cleared his throat. "Sure. Still, it's odd how she's here and then she isn't here. But," he continued hastily, "what we have to find out is whether there's any truth to the tale she spun for Jan Richey and if she was at the gazebo last night."

Price shrugged. "But who is she? What does she have to do with Magruder?"

Cobb leaned back in his chair, eyed the ceiling. "Let's not worry about who she is or where she is for the moment. The other screwy thing is her telling the Richeys that Magruder hired her to investigate some threats he'd received and that someone had shot at him at his house." Cobb's gaze dropped to the desktop. He moved several files, found the one he sought. "Last night before he clammed up and asked for a lawyer, Magruder said Whitby was at his house Tuesday night when someone shot at him." Cobb lifted the sheet, brought it closer to his face. "Here's the report. Officers Loeffler and Cain answered the call. They found Magruder alone. He told them somebody shot at him. A window screen was poked out. A slug was embedded in the opposite wall.

Loeffler said the whole setup looked phony to him. But he took the slug into evidence." Cobb looked at Price. "I've asked ballistics to take a look. That's rifle shots two nights in a row. Anyway, Loeffler and Cain said Magruder was there by himself. Last night Magruder said the redhead was there but she'd gone to the B and B before the police arrived and she'd insisted he come to the B and B, too, after the police left. She thought he would be in danger if he remained at the house."

Cobb dropped the sheet on the desk. "If Whitby—if that's her name—was there when someone shot at Magruder, why did she beat it before the officers arrived?"

Price popped an M&M into his mouth. "She didn't have ID. She isn't who she said she was. What are the odds she's someone else entirely?" Price pushed away from the couch and walked to a table covered with files. "Magruder's house," he muttered. "Yeah. Here it is." He turned to face the chief. "About the time Magruder was locked in a cell, I sent Loeffler and Cain to his house to look for anything that would link him to Clanton. They had a warrant. The front door was open. According to Loeffler's report, someone was in the house when they arrived. They heard somebody banging on the drums."

Cobb looked bank. "Drums?"

"There's a big drum set in one corner. The report said the drums were hit several times."

Cobb's heavy brows drew down. "Who'd they find?"

"Nobody. They went in, ready for trouble. There was noise upstairs. There is only one stairway to the second floor. They went up. Nobody was there. The house had been searched, drawers pulled out, stuff on the floor. They called in help, made a thorough check inside and out."

Cobb stared at his detective sergeant. "Nothing?"

"Nothing. Except"—Price cleared his throat—"when they first saw the upstairs bedroom, a bunch of clothes were lying on the floor. The second time they looked, some of the clothes had been rehung."

Cobb's expression was sour. "They missed the perp," he said flatly.

Price turned his hands over. "They swear nobody came in or out of the place."

Cobb looked frustrated. "Two smart cops both heard someone upstairs. They went up. They found a mess and nobody there. Was there any exit from the bedroom where they heard the noise?"

Price shook his head.

Cobb growled, "So they hear noise and find a mess but they don't see anyone."

Price was exasperated. "That appears to be the case."

"Appears to be the case," Cobb repeated, his voice heavy. "Just like it appears to be the case that there's a redhead who's sometimes here and sometimes not."

Price looked stubborn. "They saw evidence of a search. They heard noise. The only explanation is that they somehow missed the perp."

Cobb heaved out of his chair and walked with his hands clasped behind his back. "Obviously Nick Magruder wasn't there. He was locked up in a cell. We had him in hand within minutes after the shooting and retrieved his phone, so he didn't call a buddy and suggest a search. Besides, why would he search his own house? If he somehow contacted somebody, maybe by ESP"—the chief's voice was heavy with sarcasm—"he'd give instructions on where to look for whatever he didn't want found. That washes out Magruder, any way you look at it. But"—Cobb's eyes narrowed—"Cain and Loeffler would for sure have checked for guns, ammo. Was there anything in the house to show Magruder was a hunter?" He looked inquiringly at Price.

The detective sergeant was emphatic. "Nothing along that line was found. No ammunition, no gun safe, no guns."

Cobb settled again in his desk chair and reached for a notepad. "Cain's around the same age as Clanton and Magruder. Have him check people he went to school with. It's important to know if Magruder shoots."

"It doesn't take a lot of skill to hit a man in the upper thigh from five feet." Price's tone was mild. He straddled a straight chair by the table.

"The killer had to know one end of a rifle from another. But the search of Magruder's place bothers me. Maybe somebody was in the park, saw what happened, and went to the Magruder house to—" Cobb broke off, then said explosively, "To do what? Search the place? Who was looking for what? What does Magruder's house have to do with Cole Clanton being shot?" Cobb's face furrowed. "And what, if anything, does a shot at Magruder's house Tuesday night and a missing redhead have to do with Cole Clanton's murder?"

Price was decisive. "Let's focus on what we know for sure: Magruder was hot to get his hands on Clanton. Magruder was at the gazebo when Clanton was shot. Magruder's fingerprints are on the rifle."

"Not on the trigger." Cobb made the observation almost absently. "He checked out okay on the GSR test, no barium or antimony on his hands or his clothing. He could have rubbed his hands on the victim's trousers. Like you say, if he heard officers coming and managed to wipe most of the fingerprints off the rifle and get his hands clean, he's one cool-thinking dude." Cobb moved the open folder aside, pulled a legal pad near. He wrote, pausing occasionally. Finally, he ripped off a sheet. "Here's what we need to know."

Price stood and came to the chief's desk. He took the sheet.

I moved to look over Price's shoulder, bumped into something, knew that Dee had gotten there first. Unfortunately, I recoiled from the slight impact and my hand brushed Price's shoulder.

Price jerked his head and craned to see what had touched him. He glanced up at a vent. "I guess you got some funny air currents." He took a step to one side and read the questions aloud:

1. *What was the quarrel between Magruder and Clanton?*
2. *Trace ownership of the rifle.*
3. *Can Magruder shoot?*
4. *Check to see if slug from Magruder's wall came from the murder weapon.*
5. *Check upstairs bedroom at the Magruder house for fingerprints.*

Price looked puzzled. "Whose fingerprints?"

"The redhead's. Check the hangers in the closet."

Price opened his mouth, closed it, and continued to read aloud:

6. *Where is Cole Clanton's iPhone?*

Cobb walked back to his desk, settled in his chair. He picked up the phone, punched an extension. "Cobb here. Where's the ballistics report on the Clanton case?" He leaned over to turn on the speaker phone.

"Just a moment, sir." Papers crackled. "We have a good match between the bullets in the cadaver and the forty-four Winchester rifle."

Neither Cobb nor his detective sergeant changed expression. The information confirmed what they had expected.

Cobb leaned back, and the old leather chair squeaked. "Did you run the check to compare the slug from the Magruder house?"

"Yes, sir." The voice was bright. "Another perfect match."

Cobb jolted upright. "Are you telling me the bullet that went into the wall of Nick Magruder's house and was taken into evidence Tuesday night came from the Winchester that killed Cole Clanton?"

"Yes, sir."

Cobb's heavy face wrinkled in thought. "Send up the report." He replaced the receiver, looked at Price. "Explain that one." The chief shook his head in puzzlement.

Price pursed his lips, finally said, "I like simple. Simple almost always gets you where you want to go. Loeffler thought the shot in the wall was a setup. He knew all about the push and shove going on between Magruder and Clanton about the Arnold place. Loeffler thought Magruder intended to accuse Clanton of shooting at him to make Clanton look bad around town. A lot of people thought Magruder was a horse's ass to muscle the Arnold property away from Clanton. If Loeffler's right, Magruder poked out a screen, shot a hole in his wall, called the cops. The next day he took the rifle to the gazebo to hide it. It isn't likely Clanton would have stood like a shooting gallery pigeon if Magruder waltzed up with a gun that night. The two men met, Magruder retrieved the rifle and shot Clanton."

I felt utterly thwarted. I knew without question that Nick had nothing to do with the shot at his house Tuesday night.

The chief pulled another folder near, riffled through several pages. "Here's the report from the interview with Jan Richey last night. She insisted the redhead was at Magruder's place when the shooting occurred and, in fact, pushed Magruder out of the way."

I felt a welling of relief. Chief Cobb was always thorough. Surely this information proved that Nick had no connection to the murder weapon.

Price's expression was skeptical. "I want to hear it from the redhead. She could have said anything to the Richey woman. After all, Whitby claimed to be a private detective hired by Magruder, and we know that's probably a lie. And neither Magruder nor the redhead sidekick said a word about a shooting when Jan Richey came to his house."

A hand groped near me, touching my wrist. Making contact, long, slim fingers tightened against my wrist, pulling me forward. A faint whisper sounded near my cheek. "Your fabrications have put Nick in grave danger."

I whispered back, "Nick's temper didn't help. Hush for now. I have some ideas."

The chief gazed up toward the ceiling. "Do you hear that?"

The detective sergeant slowly nodded. "Sounded like people whispering." He looked again at the air vent.

I placed a horizontal finger on Dee's face. The cautionary finger missed her lips and landed on her cheek but surely she got the point. Then I moved to the ceiling and rattled the handle of the air vent.

Price looked relieved. "Yeah. Air currents."

Chief Cobb shook his head, like an old dog coming out of water. "Right. Air vent. And I get what you're saying about the rifle. But Nick Magruder's apparently a pretty smart guy. How stupid would he have to be to fake a shooting, call the cops and see the slug taken out of the wall for evidence, and use the same gun the next night to blow Clanton away?"

Price's smile was cool. "Cocky guy from what everybody says. Goes around telling people he's 'seriously rich.' The really rich think they're smarter than everybody else. No other weapons were found at his house after he was arrested, so apparently he had only one rifle. He shot the wall at his place Tuesday night. The next day he hid the rifle at the gazebo after he set up with meeting with Clanton. He had everything planned. The gazebo's remote, right in the heart of the park. He thought he could shoot Clanton and get the hell away before anybody saw him. Maybe he planned to toss the rifle in the lake. Magruder didn't intend to be caught in the gazebo. He intended to shoot Clanton and melt into the night. Maybe he had no idea the police station was across the street. Even if he knew, he probably didn't think the shots would bring anyone as soon as they did. He never counted on our officers immediately taking command of the grassy area in front of the gazebo." Price's expression was satisfied. "Served him right. All he could do then was hope nobody checked the slug taken from his wall with the murder weapon. He hoped wrong."

Chief Cobb slowly nodded. "That could be what happened. Or maybe Magruder's telling the truth. Maybe X shot at him Tuesday night and X showed up in the willows behind the gazebo Wednesday night and shot Clanton."

Price folded his arms. "Do you think somebody had a motive to shoot both Magruder and Clanton?"

Chief Cobb cleared his throat. "It doesn't sound reasonable. Murder, like you say, is usually simple. We know Magruder was furious with Clanton. We'll find out why. We have enough evidence for the DA to bring a murder charge."

Suddenly the stack of folders on the chief's desk slid to the front, toppled over the edge. Papers fluttered toward the floor.

Chief Cobb watched with an expression of bemusement.

I darted down toward the desk, bumped into Dee, who made a whiffing sound.

I grabbed her arm and tugged.

She resisted.

I yanked and though I expected she was much stronger than I from her years of controlling McCoy, suddenly she yielded. We sped up and through the ceiling and the third floor to the roof.

"Let's sit on the parapet." I tried hard not to sound chiding. "Perhaps we can calmly discuss our situation."

"Precept Five." Her deep voice was morose.

I reached out, found her arm, gave it a gentle pat. Obviously she knew that scattering the chief's folders in a fit of pique was a contradiction of Precept Five: "Do not succumb to the temptation to confound those who appear to oppose you."

"These things happen." I was once again the virtuous Siamese princess. At least, in this particular incident.

"With alarming frequency." Wiggins was equally morose.

"I'm terribly sorry, Wiggins." Dee spoke hastily. "But those men are dolts." Dee's voice rose in outrage. "How can they possibly think Nick would shoot anyone? Why, any fool can take one look at Nick and see what a lamb he is."

Wiggins sighed. "Possibly a bit callow."

I forbore to point out that the chief and the detective sergeant might think seriously rich Nick arrogant enough to believe that whatever he wanted he should have, no matter the cost. However, we had to face facts. "How can the police *not* think he shot Cole? Officers arrived on the scene within a minute, and there was Nick with the murder weapon and blood on his hands and clothes. In fact, as the chief said, they have all the evidence they need. Don't you see what that means?"

Dee's voice shook. "They're wrong!"

Wiggins cleared his throat. "A hopeless situation?"

"Of course not. An emissary from the Department of Good Intentions never flags or fails until an assignment is completed with honor." I could almost hear a bugle tattoo in the distance. As Mama always advised, "Tell a man what he wants to hear and he will bow every time." Not, of course, that I would take advantage of Wiggins's good heart, but I had to forestall his instinct to shepherd Dee and me aboard the Rescue Express.

"However, the meaning is absolutely clear." I spoke in a somber tone. "The official investigation will now be focused on rounding up more evidence against Nick."

Dee gripped my arm. "What are you saying?"

"If Nick is to be saved, it is up to us to save him."

There was a strangled sound of dismay a little to my left.

I turned in that direction. "Wiggins, Dee and I will right this wrong, prevent a travesty of justice, bring honor to the department."

"Honor!" There was a definite hint of despair in the pronouncement. "Precepts One, Three, Four, and Five flouted, disregarded, abandoned."

Dee spoke, her voice ragged with tears. "Wiggins, he's such a dear boy."

If anything pleased Wiggins more than devotion to the department, it was evidence of a good heart and now, clearly, a grieving heart.

"Oh well," he said in a rush, "do your best, ladies. Of course, you must make every effort to see justice done. But mind now, follow the Precepts!" The last was scarcely audible.

I waited several seconds to be sure he was gone, then heaved a sigh of relief. "I thought he'd yank us on the Express sure as shooting."

Dee cleared her throat. "Has anyone ever told you that you have a fine command of—" She broke off.

"Bull?" Mama always urged delicacy in language. "I learned it when I was a secretary at the Chamber of Commerce."

She managed a laugh, which ended abruptly. "All right. We're still here. What do we do next?" I imagined an elegant hand gesturing at the gritty rooftop.

"We visit the scene of the crime."

Chapter 11

Yellow police tape fluttered from poles that marked a rectangle enclosing the gazebo. More tape blocked the entrance.

I stood near the dark splotches that marked the site of Cole Clanton's death. "When you yanked the cell phone away, Cole turned to try to grab it. That's when someone shot him. Dee, you must have been right above the willows."

"I was way up high." Her tone was regretful. "When I heard the shots, I thought perhaps Cole had a gun and was shooting in the direction of the cell phone. I'll admit that wasn't sensible, but everything happened quickly, and I was determined to get rid of the cell. I went straight to the center of the lake and dropped the phone, then came back. You and Nick were trying to help Cole, and the police were converging. I realized that you might be placed in an awkward position"—her voice was smooth as butter—"so I promptly sent out an urgent message for Wiggins." A virtuous Siamese princess had nothing on Dee for putting the best face possible on her earlier lack of interest in my being stuck *in* the world.

My mouth opened, then closed. This was no time to let Dee know just how reprehensible I found her callous disregard for my limboed state. Right now, as Wiggins had made clear, we would have to cooperate. I kept on point. "Did you see anything down in the willows?"

"No." Her tone was regretful. "I may have heard a rustle."

"Let's see if we can find any trace of the shooter."

"The police have already looked." She was dismissive.

I was sharp. "How hard did they look? Their focus is on the interior of the gazebo and Nick. I'll start at one end, you start at the other. Look for any evidence someone pushed through the willows."

In the patch directly behind the gazebo, the willow branches parted. "Look"—Dee's voice was excited—"these are broken. The shooter may have stood here."

I agreed. We might be convinced, but there was no way to prove the willow had been disturbed last night. "The strands could have been broken at any time." I eyed the gazebo railing. It was the right height for a rifle to be propped. "We'll ask the chief to test the railing for gunpowder residue."

"Really?" she drawled. "When we next have a tête-à-tête with him? Perhaps over a cup of coffee? We could meet him at Starbucks."

"Don't be offensive. I have my methods." But I spoke absently. "We have to explain the rifle. It definitely was used to shoot at Nick. Did the person who shot at Nick Tuesday night kill Cole Wednesday night? Who would want to shoot both of them? But if Cole's murderer also wanted Nick dead, Nick could easily have been shot at the gazebo."

Dee drew in a breath, realizing that Nick could now have been dead if that had been the murderer's intention. "Nick wasn't hurt last night." Her voice trembled. "Think back,

Bailey Ruth. You were at Nick's Tuesday night. Was the shot simply to scare him, or would it have struck him?"

I remembered the location of the slug in the wall. "The shot would definitely have struck him if I hadn't pushed him out of the way."

Dee gripped my arm, her fingers painfully tight. "Nick may still be in danger."

"Not as long as he's in jail." I thought for a moment. "Here are the possibilities. One: The murderer shot at both Nick and Cole. Two: The shot Tuesday night was fired by another person, but Cole's murderer obtained the rifle on Wednesday. Three: The murderer fired twice last night. One of the shots may have missed Nick. We have to look for someone with a motive to shoot both Cole and Nick or discover how Cole's murderer obtained the rifle from the person who shot at Nick. That argues a close connection between Cole and his murderer." My thoughts raced. Abruptly, I was certain of the identity of Nick's attacker. "Dee, it was Cole."

"What do you mean, 'it was Cole'?" Her exasperation was obvious. "Your inability to engage in a coherent exchange of information doesn't bode well for our progress."

"The rifle belonged to Cole. Don't you see?"

"Not even through a glass darkly." Her tone was acidulous. "That makes no sense."

"Here's what happened." To me, the solution was obvious. "Cole had a rifle and he shot at Nick. Wednesday morning he confided in someone, or someone heard about the attack and knew Cole was likely responsible. That person took the weapon from Cole's apartment. The murderer"—I was triumphant—"saw the opportunity to kill Cole and have Nick be blamed. Everything hinges on the rifle. This was a well-thought-out crime. There was no snatching up of a weapon and murder on impulse. The killer came here prepared to shoot Cole."

"There's a good deal of creative imagining in your reconstruction but"—she admitted—"you may be correct. *If*"—a good deal of emphasis on the conditional—"your guess—"

I wasn't guessing. I was reasoning with the elan of a high school English teacher who entranced even football players by offering hearty dollops of Hemingway and Fitzgerald. However, vainglory does not become an emissary, so I modestly refrained from commenting.

"—is right, we have to find out who knew Cole well enough to obtain the rifle. I can"—her tone was grudging—"almost see how the murderer came into possession of the rifle, but that doesn't explain how the murderer knew Cole was meeting Nick at the gazebo. That's the stumbling block."

"Not at all." I was a trifle acerbic. My good humor stretched only so far. "Once in possession of the rifle, the murderer decided to shoot Cole and have Nick be blamed. There are several possibilities: Cole told the killer of the scheduled meeting with Nick; the killer followed Cole here. Nick told the person with the rifle about the meeting. Or Nick was followed. Almost everyone in town knew he was hunting for Cole." I felt saddened, but a definite possibility had to be faced. "Jan Richey left a message on her mother's cell, telling her Nick was meeting Cole at the gazebo. If Cole had a rifle in his apartment, Arlene would know. Tuesday night, Arlene learned someone had shot at Nick. She also learned Cole was cheating on her."

"She probably had a key to Cole's apartment." Dee was thoughtful. "They clearly were lovers, and almost certainly she would not have met him at the B and B."

I felt a burst of optimism. "We'll follow up each possibility, starting with Arlene."

Instead of quick agreement, there was silence.

"Dee?"

"That approach is much too fragmented." She spoke with great authority.

I bristled. "How many murder investigations have you conducted?"

"It's a matter of taking jumps in proper order. For example, why was Cole Clanton shot last night? What made his murder essential at that particular time? Moreover, you have overlooked the most basic question." A supercilious Siamese princess now. "Who wanted Cole Clanton dead?"

"I've already jumped that fence." I wasn't even a Sunday rider, but if she wanted horse lingo, I would oblige. I ticked off the names. "The possibilities include Arlene Richey, Lisa Sanford, and Brian Sanford. Moreover, all of them knew Cole well and can give us other leads. I can't interrogate them as Officer Loy. They know me as Hilda Whitby, private eye. That's where you come in. If you are wearing an Adelaide police uniform, you can ask every question we need answered."

No response.

I felt that I could almost reach out and grab a great big lump of disapproval. Dee's aura was obviously flashing red. If I had the equivalent of a seismic reading that registered reluctance, the lines would be jagged.

A silence, then a sigh of resignation. "Possibly that may be necessary."

I refrained from a shout of delight. Now we could get busy.

"However"—the word was slapped down like a knight's truncheon on a Viking's helmet—"I have to know more about Cole Clanton. You can't ride a horse if you don't know which way he will jump. Let me see, they would have his address in those papers at the police station. . . ."

"Dee—" I broke off.

She was gone. Delilah Delahunt Duvall was willful, determined, and exasperating, but she had the upper hand. I'd spoken with Arlene, Lisa, and Brian as Hilda Whitby. I could not appear as Officer Loy. I was tempted to let Dee pursue whatever avenue she chose and go my own way, except I needed her.

Where Dee went, I must go.

ᔋ

Chief Cobb poked a French fry into ketchup mounded on the foil paper from his hamburger. Seated at the round table not far from the chalkboard, he read as he ate. I peered over his shoulder. An autopsy report. No surprises there. He flipped to a report from Officer W. Dugan: "Witnesses report that throughout Wednesday Nick Magruder was overheard to demand knowledge about the whereabouts of Cole Clanton and that Magruder was visibly angry. See Appendix II for printout of taped interviews, n.b. Rod Holt, proprietor of Holt's Back Shop."

Chief Cobb flipped through several sheets to Appendix II.

Rod Holt, Interview by Officer Johnny Cain

Background information: Wednesday morning Officer C. Kaufman was on foot patrol downtown when she observed a man (later identified as Nicholas Magruder) storming into Holt's Back Shop. Magruder was clearly in a state of extreme anger. Officer Kaufman followed. When she opened the door, she heard Magruder demanding to know the whereabouts of someone named Cole (later identified as Cole Clanton, homicide victim). Rod Holt, the proprietor, told Magruder that he had no knowledge of Clanton's location. Magruder shouted that Clanton deserved to be horsewhipped and he'd be lucky if he didn't end up hanging from a rafter in a stable. Officer Kaufman believed this was the equivalent of a death threat, as she equated it with local history and the hanging of seven men accused of murder in 1909. Magruder told

Holt that he (Holt) had better let Magruder know if Clanton turned up or he might be in the same boat. Magruder then slammed out of the store. Officer Kaufman asked Holt if he wished to swear out a complaint against Magruder. Holt declined. Officer Kaufman stepped outside. Magruder wasn't visible. Officer Kaufman reported the incident to Sergeant J. Fisher.

Pursuant to instructions from Detective Sergeant Price, Officer E. Loeffler and I interviewed Holt at 9:22 this morning, Thursday, October 14. Holt was reluctant to discuss the situation between Clanton and Magruder, but when pressed with an understanding that he could be cited for impeding a murder investigation, Holt revealed that Clanton possessed on his cell phone compromising photographs of a sexual nature of Mrs. Arlene Richey. Clanton threatened to post the photos on Facebook unless Magruder agreed to buy the Arnold property and deed it over to Clanton for one dollar. Holt said Clanton knew Magruder would do anything for Mrs. Richey's daughter, Jan.

Chief Cobb gave a low whistle, took a final bite of hamburger.

Of course, this information had been almost sure to surface. It reinforced my conviction that Cole's murder occurred last night precisely because visibly angry Nick Magruder chased around town Wednesday hunting Cole. The murderer had taken advantage of a ready-made suspect.

Chief Cobb had opportunity, a weapon, and now a motive. Would the police look further?

I moved to the blackboard, picked up a piece of chalk. The chief was absorbed in the file. I wrote very slowly to avoid a squeak of chalk on the blackboard. I chose my words carefully:

Nick Magruder Innocent. Officer M. Loy

If nothing else, the message would suggest to him that Officer Loy, whom I was quite sure he remembered, was back in town.

At the table, the chief continued to read, head down. He didn't see the chalk return quietly to the tray or the activity on his desk behind him. Folders opened and closed, Dee seeking Cole's address.

One by one, the folders were returned to a tiny stack.

I will admit Dee's next action caught me totally by surprise. The eraser rose from the tray and in two swipes my message was gone.

I launched toward the eraser and grabbed Dee's arm.

She hissed, "Grandstanding."

We struggled and the eraser plopped to the floor.

The chief's head jerked up. Frowning, he stood and walked to the blackboard. He bent, retrieved the eraser, replaced it in the tray, and turned away, shaking his head. He walked back to the table, gathered up the trash from his lunch, and dropped it in a wastebasket. He stood by the table and stared at the blackboard.

I was as sensitive to Dee's presence as a praying mantis to the nearness of a moth. Suddenly, I knew without doubt that once again she'd flown the coop and this time had popped to Cole's apartment. I needed to start after her immediately. Her cooperation was essential, so I had to catch her before she popped somewhere else. I moved from one foot to the other, impatient for the chief to turn away and go to his desk, but he remained standing and staring.

I sped across the room, picked up a pencil from his desk. I tossed the pencil over the massive leather sofa that faced the windows. The pencil clicked on a window pane and fell to the floor with a rattle.

Chief Cobb immediately turned and walked toward the windows, skirting the couch.

I was at the blackboard, chalk in hand. I wish to be clear that I was not shamed by Dee's accusation. However, Nick was best served not by distracting the chief with the possibility of Officer M. Loy's return, but by specific facts that spoke to Nick's innocence. I printed in block letters:

WILLOWS BEHIND GAZEBO HAVE BROKEN FRONDS. CHECK FOR FOOTPRINTS CHECK RAILING AT BACK OF GAZEBO FOR GUNPOWDER RESI

I sensed movement behind me. I whirled.

Chief Cobb's large hand lunged for the chalk, which hung in the air between us. I scarcely had a heartbeat of time, but I managed to elude his grasp. The chalk plummeted to the floor.

Chief Cobb looked down at the chalk, up at the blackboard.

A rapid knock and his office door opened. "Hey, Sam—" A pause. "Hey, Sam, something wrong?" Detective Sergeant Price recognized a man hunkered in a defensive posture when he saw it.

The chief took a deep breath. With obvious effort, he relaxed the stiff muscles of his face and slowly turned. "I just had a thought." He took a step forward and chalk crunched under his shoe.

Price strode across the room, his face furrowed. "Something we missed?" Cobb gestured toward the board.

Price read the message aloud. "You think Magruder's crazy story could be true?"

Cobb spoke carefully. "Strange things happen sometimes. Maybe I'm having a brain snap. But get the crime lab over there. It won't hurt to run the test. Look for footprints."

Happily, they were too absorbed to notice that a folder now lay open on the chief's desk. Cole Clanton had lived in Apartment 3-G, River Oaks Run Apartments, 2018 Magnolia.

∽

All the lights blazed in Cole's apartment. I surveyed the surroundings. I heard a squeak and watched as the center drawer of battered yellow pine chest was pulled out. Dee was here and busy.

The studio apartment was definitely a bachelor pad, with a sofa, a couple of chairs, a small kitchenette, a breakfast table, a desk, and a double bed. Sports and true-crime magazines were stacked on a ledge along one wall. A black walnut four-gun rack was mounted above the ledge. One rack held a shotgun, a second a .22 rifle. Haphazard piles of clothing covered the top of a small bookcase crammed with CDs and DVDs. Bunched cushions at the end of a threadbare sofa appeared tattered. A game console was connected to a flat-screen television, which looked extravagantly expensive in comparison to its surroundings.

I studied the gun rack. "The top rack appears never to have been used. The felt strips on the empty second rack have traces of oil."

"You're here." There was a distinct lack of enthusiasm in Dee's voice.

"I doubt there is any way to prove that Cole owned the murder weapon unless we find registration papers."

"He wasn't orderly." She spoke with disdain. "I didn't find a file or records about any guns. However, there are several boxes of ammunition in the desk. The box with bullets for the Winchester hasn't been opened."

"There had to have been another box." I was certain of my conclusion. "The murderer left a handful in Nick's desk, but I foiled that little trap."

"Even if we prove that Cole owned the rifle, it won't save Nick." The yellow drawer closed. The bottom drawer squeaked out. "The police will say Nick came here and got the rifle Wednesday morning."

I understood her point. Nick spent Wednesday hunting for Cole. Of course he would have tried his apartment.

The chest's bottom drawer closed with a bang—Dee venting her frustration.

I settled on the edge of the desk, noticed it was bare of papers. "Did you find anything interesting when you searched the desk?"

"Not much. No address book. No handy notes with lists of names under a helpful heading: *Enemies I Have Known*."

I'd already offered the beginning of a list—Arlene Richey and Lisa and Brian Sanford—but Dee was too high and mighty to follow my lead. However, to give my unwilling companion her due, the more we knew about Cole, the better idea we would have of those with a reason to want him dead. "If he had an address book or a day planner, it was probably in his cell phone." The cell phone was now at the bottom of the lake behind the gazebo. I surveyed the room again and realized what was missing. "There aren't any books."

"Why would there be books?" She wasn't impressed by my comment.

"He was heading up the Old Timer Days celebration. Where are the books about Oklahoma history?" Now I opened the desk drawers looking for a Kindle or a Nook. "Maybe he had one of the e-book readers."

There was a questioning silence, and I brought Dee up to date on the new means of reading.

She was crisp. "I didn't find anything other than unpaid bills, check stubs, a bankbook. Only about two hundred dollars in his account. He bounced three checks last month."

I wasn't surprised at his precarious financial situation. If he'd had any money, he would have been able to buy the Arnold property. But surely there was something of interest among Cole's possessions. "Have you checked the closet?"

In response, the closet door swung open. "Clothes. Stuff."

I like to see for myself. I put out my hand to prevent the closet door from shutting. Several expensive sweaters and two pairs of worsted wool trousers, all of which looked new and of excellent quality, hung toward the front of the single rack. I wondered if these clothes were gifts from Arlene. Less expensive sports shirts and slacks hung toward the back. Sweat clothes were folded on a shelf next to stacks of magazines. I craned to see. Apparently all were true-crime magazines. A tennis racket leaned against a bag of golf clubs, a pair of skis, and a new shovel. Two pairs of cowboy boots, three pairs of loafers, ratty tennis shoes, and new running shoes were crowded at the rear of the closet.

"Possibly you can deduce the victim's state of mind by the contents of his closet?" Dee was falsely judicious. "Was he cross-eyed? Did his digestive tract trouble him?"

My tone was sweet. "He had good eyesight, because he played tennis and golf, which require excellent eye-hand coordination. He didn't have much money in the bank, but he had expensive tastes. Those sweaters are new and both are cashmere. I'll bet they came from the lady friend. You know why?"

"Tell me, oh swami."

"Pink. No guy buys a pink sweater. And he was big on true crime." I reached out and touched the lurid cover of a true-crime magazine, this one of a scantily clad, curvaceous blonde in extremis. "High fashion, but low tastes."

"Not half-bad." She sounded faintly amused. "A good jump."

Generous praise indeed from my prickly companion.

I stepped out of the closet, closed the door. My eyes roamed the dingy, cluttered single room with its overlying scent of beer and pizza.

"The state of his living quarters"—distaste was evident in Dee's tone—"tells us is that he was broke and slovenly." She wasn't about to admit the visit here was a bust. We would leave with no better sense of Cole Clanton than we'd had before we came.

I glanced at a digital clock. Almost one o'clock. Time was speeding past. "Dee, your instinct was right for us to come here." Was I magnanimous or what? But as Mama always said, "Perfume smells better than a hog lot." Dee was as hard to corral as a skittish horse, and I was willing to do a little sweet talk to secure her cooperation. "I think we agree that the chances are very good that Cole shot at Nick. Our challenge is to find out who hated Cole or feared him or wanted something from him. There had to be a powerful reason for his murder. Was he killed because of sex, money, jealousy, fear, or revenge? Cole was unfaithful to Arlene and threatened her reputation. He made love to Lisa Sanford, then dropped her. Brian Sanford was intensely jealous over his wife. I always think sex is a good place to start."

∽

Dee straightened her name tag. She lifted her hand toward the doorbell.

I was pleased by the choice of names. Dee was now Officer H. Augusta. Saint Helena Augusta was famed for her success at discovery. Hopefully, her temporary namesake would do as well.

"Very nice." My tone was admiring. Dee looked superb in the French-blue uniform of the Adelaide police.

Her aristocratic face, however, was troubled. "Wiggins emphasized that we must observe the Precepts." She glanced down at the uniform.

She needed pumping up, one of my specialties. "As is made absolutely clear in Precept Four, an emissary can become visible only when absolutely necessary." I emphasized *only* and *absolutely* and sounded both stalwart and soulful, a combination I'd always found very effective.

A swift, wry smile lighted her ascetic features. "When next we see Wiggins, I will tell him that you explained the Precepts to me in such an effective way." The smile slipped away. "At this point, it's obvious we're Nick's only hope. I will do what I have to do." She lifted her hand and jabbed the doorbell. Now her face was stern and intent.

Jan Richey answered the door. Her eyes widened in apprehension. She tried to speak normally. "Hello."

Dee was unsmiling and gruff. "Adelaide police. Officer Augusta. Arlene Richey, please."

Jan held tight to the edge of the door. "She's not feeling well. May I help you?"

"It is necessary that I speak with Mrs. Richey in connection with the murder of Mr. Cole Clanton." Dee's gaze was cold and insistent. "She can be interviewed here or at the police station."

Jan looked sick and frightened. "If you'll come inside, I'll call her." Jan led the way to a small room off the main hallway, opened the door. "Please wait here and I'll see if she can come down."

"Her choice. Here or the police station." Dee stepped inside the narrow room with red velvet curtains, an Axminster carpet, a harpsichord, and a spinet. Dee did not sit on the petit-point sofa or in a Queen Anne chair with lace tatting. She remained standing in the center of the small room, an imposing figure with a cold, piercing gaze.

I followed Jan up the stairs. She climbed fast and hurried up the hall to knock on her mother's door. When there was no answer, she rattled the knob. "Mom, the police are here. Please, you have to open the door."

I flowed into the dim bedroom. Neither the rose-shaded lamp on the dressing table or the bronze floor lamp with its fussy fabric shade were turned on. Arlene slumped in an oversized easy chair.

"Mom, a policewoman's here." Jan's voice was muffled and distant through the door. "She insists on talking to you. About Cole."

Panic etched the white face turned toward the door.

"Mom, if you don't talk to them here, they're going to take you to the police station."

Arlene touched her throat with a shaking hand.

The doorknob rattled. "Mom!" There was desperation in Jan's cry.

Arlene pushed up from the chair. She moved woodenly. At the door, she turned the key in the antique lock.

Jan stepped inside. "A policewoman's waiting in the music room." She looked at her mother in despair.

Arlene made a pitiable attempt to appear calm. "I suppose I'd better see her. Not that I know anything about . . ." She bit her lips, and tears welled.

"Oh, Mom. Don't cry."

"I'm not crying." Arlene's voice was harsh. "I haven't felt well today." She turned, stumbled to the dressing table. She found powder and patted several layers, trying to hide the ravages of tears. A shaky hand unevenly applied lip gloss. She combed her hair and squared her shoulders and moved toward the open door. "All right." She walked down the stairs with Jan following. At the music room, she took a deep breath as she stepped inside.

Jan started to follow.

Arlene held up her hand. "I'll talk to the officer by myself."

"But Mom—"

"Please, Jan." Arlene averted her eyes from her daughter.

"Mom, it's okay. I understand."

"I know you do. Not"—Arlene tried to sound bright—"that there's much to understand. He was a friend. That's all. I'll be glad to help the officer. If I can." With that she turned and closed the door, leaving Jan in the hallway.

In the music room, Arlene faced Dee with an attempt at dignity. "You wish to talk to me?"

"Yes, ma'am. I am here in regard to the murder last night of Cole Clanton." Dee was doing her best imitation of officialdom. Fortunately, I doubted Arlene was acquainted with police procedure. The fact that officers worked in pairs was likely unknown to her. Dee pulled a small notebook from a pocket. She nodded toward the Queen Anne chair. Dee had placed the chair directly beneath the chandelier so that Arlene would be in a bright pool of light.

Arlene sank into the chair, but she seemed oblivious to the glare that exposed the puffiness of her face, likely from a sleepless night.

Dee remained standing, a formidable figure. "You are Arlene Richey."

"Yes."

"You were having an affair with Cole Clanton."

"We were friends."

"Intimate friends."

"Friends." Arlene's voice was dull, despairing.

"When did you last see Mr. Clanton?"

For the first time, Arlene hesitated. Finally, painfully, she said, "Yesterday morning." Her lips quivered.

"Describe the circumstances." Dee waited with folded arms.

"He came here. We spoke for a few minutes. He left."

Dee's voice was sharp. "You had discovered that he was betraying you with another woman."

"My conversation with him had nothing to do with his death." Arlene looked pummeled, weary, heartsick.

"Was he angry when he left?"

"I don't know." Her voice was dull. "He may have been."

"In fact, Mrs. Richey, you know he was angry because he threatened to make public photographs of you—"

At the mention of the photos, Arlene stiffened. She stared at Dee in shock. One hand pulled at the lace tatting on the chair arm, wadded it into a tight ball.

"—taken on his cell phone, unless Mr. Nick Magruder sold the Arnold property to him for one dollar. Is that correct, Mrs. Richey?"

Arlene trembled. "I don't know what you're talking about."

"We have a witness. Mr. Clanton told Mr. Rod Holt about the photos. Mr. Magruder came to see Mr. Holt and made threats against Mr. Clanton."

Arlene pressed fingertips to each temple, shook her head back and forth, back and forth.

Dee took two steps, loomed above Arlene, tall and intimidating. "You were desperate to prevent Mr. Clanton from posting those photographs online."

Arlene's face crumpled. She swiped her sleeve to try to staunch the tears.

Dee stared down at her. "You knew Clanton owned a rifle. In fact, you suspected he used that rifle to shoot at Mr. Magruder Tuesday night. You were seen at Cole Clanton's apartment yesterday."

Arlene stared upward, a hand raised to ward off the blinding light. "Who says so?"

"There is a witness."

"I don't care what anyone says. It must have been someone else. God knows he had enough women in his life. I don't know anything about his rifle."

I dropped next to Dee, spoke in a deep voice that sounded uncannily like hers. "You knew Mr. Magruder was meeting Mr. Clanton at the gazebo. You came to the park. Your car was seen."

Arlene breathed rapidly, then abruptly pushed to her feet. "I didn't shoot him. I wouldn't have shot him. Oh God, I loved him. Can't you understand? I loved him."

"You were at the gazebo last night." Dee spoke with utter, damning certainty.

Arlene wavered on her feet. There was horror and the memory of horror in her eyes, the horror of blood and death. "I didn't shoot him."

"You were there. You can swear that Mr. Magruder is innocent."

She wavered. She had only to speak and Nick would be saved. There was that understanding in her desperate face, but the understanding, too, of her peril. If she admitted her presence, how could she prove that it was not her hand that had held the rifle, steadied it, pulled the trigger?

She might be innocent but she may well have shot the man who broke her heart and threatened her with humiliation as well as betrayal.

Was she innocent? Was she guilty?

Her words tumbled fast. "There are lots of cars like mine. No one can prove my car was there." She took a deep breath. "I was driving around. I was a lot of places. I didn't shoot Cole."

She turned and rushed toward the door. She yanked open the door, plunged into the hall. The sound of running feet marked her progress up the hallway and onto the stairs.

"Mom!" Jan's cry was sharp. "Wait."

Dee's face was grim. "Arlene can prove Nick is innocent, but she won't admit she was there." Despair weighted Dee's voice.

I was grave. "She may have shot Cole. But if she is innocent, she may know something that could point to the killer. We have to let Chief Cobb know."

Chapter 12

Only one light shone in the chief's office, a goosenecked lamp on the desk. Folders were strewn across the desk and table.

"He's not here." I spoke with relief. "You check the folders, see if he's had a report on gunpowder residue on the gazebo railing and the search for footprints. I'll leave a message." On the blackboard I printed:

> *Arlene Richey May Have Taken Rifle From*
> *Cole's Apartment. She Was At The Gazebo*
> *When Shots Fired. She Can Exonerate*
> *Magruder.*

Behind me papers rustled. "I found it." A pause. "Oh." A discouraged sigh. "GSR test inconclusive. Heavy dew overnight. Residue would have dissipated." More papers rustled. "Search behind gazebo revealed a partial footprint of the sole of a woman's shoe and a clear impression of the heel print of a man's shoe. The sprinkler system came on at 8:00 p.m. Wednesday, which accounted for wet ground. The woman's shoe print was about eight feet from the willows behind the gazebo. The heel print was nearer the gazebo and in a direct line with the estimated trajectory of the bullets that struck the victim. A reasonable conclusion is that the footprints were made after 8:30, when the sprinklers turned off. However, the ground would have remained soft for at least four hours. That means," Dee's voice was bitter, "they won't pay any attention to the prints because there's no proof they occurred between 8:30 and 9:07, when Cole was shot. How's that for throwing away an important piece of evidence? Obviously, they've made up their minds that Nick is guilty, so why pay any attention to inconvenient facts?"

"Don't be silly, Dee. Chief Cobb is an honorable man—" I was turning as I spoke. I broke off and looked across the table and the desk where a folder hung in the air, the goose-necked lamp turned to beam light upon it, and beyond the desk at Chief Cobb's blunt face peering over the back of the leather sofa, eyes wide, mouth ajar. Oh my. I doubted he had indulged in an early afternoon siesta. I suspected he had taken a moment to stretch out in comfort and ponder the unexplained odds and ends of an investigation. Possibly he might not have been shocked by a chalked message, but a conversation between unseen women clearly disturbed him.

"Put the folder down." My voice was urgent.

"I beg your pardon." Her deep voice was affronted. "I am simply following your instructions, which, I might add, I successfully—"

"Ladies, hush." Wiggins was emphatic. "The roof."

Chief Cobb was on his feet. "Must have fallen asleep . . . odd dream . . . Did I write on the blackboard . . . ?"

As I landed on the roof, I carried with me a memory of his wide eyes and bemused expression.

∽

The wind gusted yellowed maple leaves across the blistered and cracked tar roof. "One would think," I said brightly, "that the city would better maintain—"

"Bailey Ruth, I am not concerned with upkeep of public buildings in Adelaide." Wiggins's voice was stern. "I am concerned with maintaining a respectful distance between Heaven and earth."

"Wiggins, that is simply poetic. As well," I added hastily, "as a poignant reminder of the duty of all well-meaning emissaries. Dee and I have made every effort to avoid any indication of otherworldly intervention as our investigation proceeds. Most especially"—(As Mama always said, "If the bull is thundering straight at you, grab the horns.")—"in Dee's efforts as Officer H. Augusta. I know, Wiggins"—my voice was admiring, suggesting that he was, as always, exercising excellent taste—"you are an especial fan of Saint Helena. Arlene Richey and her daughter have no reason to wonder at the authenticity of Officer H. Augusta, since Dee presented herself most admirably." Maybe a little sweetness would charm Ms. Prickly, though that was a faint hope. "And"—I simply exuded satisfaction—"our sojourn to the chief's office was an unqualified success."

"Success!" Wiggins sounded guttural. Perhaps the dear man's breath had been taken away by the stiff breeze on the rooftop.

"Definitely." I was serene, a complacent Siamese princess. "I'm sure the chief has already persuaded himself that he had slipped into slumber and awakened from a most vivid dream." I reached up and tried to smooth my hair. I would need a brush when we finally exited the roof. I decided I'd create a purse containing an elegant tortoiseshell brush.

Dee cleared her throat. "Certainly no one abhors going outside the rules more than I. But if it weren't for my inquiry, the police would have no way of knowing that Arlene Richey was very likely present when the murder occurred and, in fact"—Dee was judicious—"may well be the murderer."

I smiled. How nice that Officer Augusta was taking pride in her work. "Now it's time for Officer Augusta to speak with Lisa Sanford. We'll find her at the library."

Leaves whirled in a particularly strong gust. I truly needed that comb.

A small wooden structure contained the door that gave access to the roof. The door opened. Chief Cobb stepped out, shaded his eyes, and gazed carefully around the area. Finally, his tense stance relaxed. "Nobody here." A pause. "Of course nobody's here. Just a dream. My subconscious is right. I need to see what the crime scene search turned up. Since there's a print of a woman's shoe near the gazebo, we'll check, see if anybody noticed Arlene Richey downtown Wednesday night." He swung about, moving fast. The roof door slammed behind him.

"Well"—Wiggins's voice was almost cheerful—"perhaps all's well that ends well. However, Bailey Ruth, you too often skirt disaster by a mere whisper. Follow the Precepts . . . when you can."

It was as near carte blanche as we were likely to receive.

⌁

Leaves rose in swirls, cascading across the grassy slope behind the library. Dee—Officer Augusta—and Lisa Sanford stood near a vine-covered arbor in a sculpture garden. Lisa clicked a lighter as she cupped one hand to shield the cigarette between her lips.

Dee waited, her expression imperious.

The cigarette finally lit, Lisa inhaled deeply. "I got a fifteen-minute break." Red-rimmed eyes stared at Dee from a puffy, haggard face.

"Mrs. Sanford"—Dee placed emphasis on the title—"how long were you and Cole Clanton lovers?"

Lisa swallowed jerkily. "What business is it of yours?"

"You can respond to my questions here"—Dee was brusque—"or we can go to the police station. Or possibly you might wish for me to start my inquiry with your husband?"

Lisa's face twisted in despair. "Don't tell Brian. Please. Him and me, I don't know, but maybe we can get things good again. Brian loves me. I don't guess anyone else ever has."

Dee looked away, but I saw a quick flash of compassion in her eyes.

Tears slid down Lisa's cheeks unchecked. "I was always crazy about Cole. In high school, when Brian and I were dating, Cole would come over and we'd go out back of my house. I knew he didn't care. I was just a body to him, but I wanted him. He never had much to do with me in public, but people knew. They always know. Everybody but Brian. When Brian and I got married, I told Cole not to come around and I didn't have anything to do with him, not until Brian lost his job and he was miserable and we didn't have any money. I guess Cole was looking for an easy lay, like always. Anyway, he looked me up and I was so unhappy I started going out with him. And then"—her voice was bitter—"Cole dumped me for that old woman." She drew on the cigarette, made a face, dropped it and ground the stub into the grass.

Arlene was in her late forties, old enough for Cole's choice to diminish Lisa.

"I don't know what he saw in her." Her tone was hot. "But she knows people around town and she was helping him with that dumb Old Timer Days."

I suspected Cole had combined business with pleasure. Older women have much to offer younger men.

"I thought if I went around with Nick, it would make Cole jealous." She gulped back a sob. "Cole didn't care."

"Your husband cared. He's a jealous man. Maybe he figured out what was going on and that you only cared about Cole Clanton. Your husband knows how to handle guns. Did he and Mr. Clanton ever hunt together?"

Lisa shot a wild look at Dee. "Don't you go after Brian. He'd never hurt anybody. He gets mad and makes noise and yells but he's never mean. Never."

"There are only so many people who had access to Mr. Clanton's apartment. You have a key. Your husband could have found it."

"No, he didn't." Lisa spoke in a rush. "He couldn't have had the key. I had the key—" She broke off.

Lisa was certain her husband didn't have her key. Had Lisa used the key that day? Had she entered Cole's apartment? I gave Dee a poke.

Dee pounced. "Why did you go to Cole's apartment yesterday?"

Lisa stiffened. Her eyes rounded in panic.

Dee's voice was deep. "Did you go to get his rifle?"

Lisa's face was suddenly rigid. "Was Cole killed with his own rifle?"

"Yes." Dee's answer was clipped, and her eyes never left Lisa's face. "How did you get the rifle out of his apartment? Did you wrap it in a blanket?"

Lisa's long black lashes fluttered. Abruptly, she shook her head. "I didn't take Cole's gun."

"You had a key." Dee's words came hard and fast. "You knew he had a rifle. You were furious with him, the way he treated you, using you, not caring. We can find your fingerprints in his apartment. Why else would you go?"

Lisa drew in a breath that was half a sob. "I wanted him back. I wouldn't have hurt him. Not ever."

"The investigation has proved"—Dee was emphatic—"that Cole either gave his rifle to the murderer or the murderer came to Cole's apartment Wednesday and took the gun."

"If someone took his rifle . . ." Lisa's words were barely

audible. She looked like a woman remembering, thinking, figuring.

I reached out, clutched Dee's right arm. Had Lisa passed someone she knew in the corridor of Cole's apartment building, or had she seen someone she knew outside?

Dee gazed sternly at Lisa. "If you saw someone, it's your duty to inform the police."

Lisa stood quite still. Finally, her face smoothed out. Dee hadn't offered any proof that Lisa had been seen. She lifted her chin. "I wasn't there. I can't tell you anything. I got to go back to work." She turned and moved swiftly toward the door into the library, her shoulders hunched in obvious fear that Dee would command her to halt.

Dee frowned. "She was there. We need to find a witness who saw her. Until then, she'll lie. My guess is she took the rifle or she saw someone who may have taken it. I have to get this information to the police."

"We'll use a phone in the library. Meet me on the second floor by the fire exit."

Dee stepped behind the arbor and disappeared.

Upstairs in the library, we flitted unseen until we found an untenanted office with a telephone. I shut the door to the hall.

Dee dialed the operator, requested connection to the Crime Stoppers line. "In regard to the murder of Cole Clanton"—Dee's voice was brisk and authoritative—"the murder weapon belonged to Cole Clanton. Test the rifle barrel for traces of the padding on Clanton's gun rack. Clanton shot at Nick Magruder Tuesday night. On Wednesday Lisa Sanford entered Clanton's apartment. She possessed a key. She had been engaged in an on-again-off-again love affair with Clanton. She either removed the rifle and shot Clanton that night at the gazebo, or she knows the identity of the person who did." The receiver moved from its stationary position in the air and returned to the cradle.

"Well done." I was genuinely impressed.

"Perhaps." Dee was thoughtful. "Or I may have added another bar to Nick's cell. If the police trace the rifle and prove that it belonged to Cole, their immediate assumption may be that Nick visited Cole's apartment and took the rifle Wednesday. Nick was all over town looking for Clanton. I'm sure he would have tried his apartment. One way or another, Nick may be linked to the rifle. In fact, I may have made his situation worse."

I reached out, found her shoulder. "You did the right thing."

"I know." Dee's voice was weary. "But if she's innocent, I'm afraid that fool of a woman may think she can take advantage of what she knows. We have to stop her."

⁊

Downstairs we searched the stacks for Lisa. No luck. We started at opposite ends of each floor. When we reached the third floor, it became apparent Lisa was no longer in the library.

Dee appeared in an empty aisle behind the stacks on the first floor. She walked to the main reference desk. "May I speak with Lisa Sanford, please?"

A plump woman with a cheerful smile, murmured, "A moment, please." She lifted a phone, asked for Lisa, listened, then ended the connection. "I'm sorry, Officer. Mrs. Sanford has left for the day. May I help you?"

"It is important that I speak with her. Please give me her home address."

A stranger off the street would have had no luck asking for an employee's address, but the French-blue uniform worked its magic.

⁊

The Jolly Roger Haven Trailer Park was home to about eighteen trailers, most well kept up. On the eastern edge of the park, Lisa and Brian's rusting double wide had one boarded-over window. Towels masked the interior in the remaining windows. The middle plank of the front steps sagged. A lawn chair lay on its side. An old Pinto without wheels rested on concrete blocks. A dead rosebush looked forlorn in a weed-choked flower bed.

Dee started to appear, the first hint of French-blue swirls gathering in the air.

I spoke quickly. "Let's go inside first and see if anyone's home before you knock. Lisa may not answer if she looks out and sees a uniform."

The blue wavered and disappeared.

Once inside the trailer, the darkness was intense. I fumbled near the door and found a switch. No one was home. Dirty clothes were heaped near the kitchenette. Breakfast dishes rested in a small sink. Several roaches skittered away. The trash can was full, the furniture worn, the narrow double bed unmade, the bathroom door missing a hinge.

"Defeated." Dee's tone was more sad than critical.

I understood what she meant. "I'm afraid so." Lisa sought comfort in other men's arms, Brian drank beer until he no longer felt anything. A side table was jammed with papers. I sorted through them. "No bankbook. Lisa took her library checks to a ready cash place." There were bills and a credit card cancellation notice.

"Sticky," Dee murmured with distaste as she flipped through the contents of a drawer in a cabinet on the opposite wall. "Interesting. A thirty-eight. Somebody shoots, likely Brian."

My search didn't take long. "We'll come back after work hours. If Lisa's not here, maybe Brian will know where to find her."

The cabinet drawer slammed shut. "Talk, talk, talk. Our efforts aren't getting us anywhere. What if we find them both here? Lisa won't admit to anything and probably neither will Brian. I'm going to go see Nick. He needs to keep his mouth shut." Her tone was slightly defiant.

"Dee, surely he's spoken with a lawyer—"

The feeling of solitude was now familiar. Dee was gone, and I was alone in the trailer. I could use a quiet moment to consider what to do next, though I would have preferred more edifying surroundings.

In an instant, I was in the cemetery that adjoins St. Mildred's Episcopal Church. Leaves cascaded from maples and oaks, stirred by the brisk breeze that perhaps heralded a change in weather. The well-kept cemetery with its grassy expanses and clusters of trees was as beautiful as always. I took a moment to stop at the Pritchard mausoleum to pet the stone Abyssinian at Hannah's tomb and the greyhound at Maurice's. Hannah and Maurice had been leaders of society in Adelaide, patrons of the arts known for their generosity and kindness. After their deaths, the legend grew that those who stop to admire and stroke their beloved pets are blessed by good fortune. Outside, I drifted above the tombstones. Perhaps a cemetery seemed an odd choice for cheer, but there is solace and encouragement in many epitaphs. Most offered gentle tributes:

> *In Loving Memory*
>
> *Beloved Husband*
>
> *Lifted to Heaven*

There were a few unusual epitaphs:

> *Mercy to him that shows it, is the rule. William Cowper*
>
> *What seems to us but sad, funeral tapers May be heaven's distant lamps. Henry Wadsworth Longfellow*
>
> *Every sound shall end in silence, but the silence never dies. Samuel Miller Hageman*

The acts of this life are the destiny of the next.
Eastern proverb

I stared at the last inscription, which was dappled by the shade of shifting limbs tossed by the breeze. *The acts of this life* . . .

What act led to Cole's painful end at the gazebo? Why had he died on that particular mild October night? Had there been a trigger for his murder on Wednesday, or had someone with a deeply held grudge taken advantage of Nick's public fury?

At the B and B Wednesday, Cole had been desperate to assuage Arlene, but he hadn't acted like a lover seeking to save a liaison. His thoughts appeared centered on the Arnold property. Before his angry departure from the kitchen, he'd apparently realized that he could use the photos in his cell to force Nick to turn over the Arnold property.

Why had he been determined to gain access to that property? What difference had it made whether or not he set up a replica of the original trading post?

Cole had revealed something else on that last morning of his life. Though he had been focused on obtaining access to the Arnold property, Cole had told Nick that first he had some "business" to see to, then he'd be in touch with Phidippus. I was sure Cole had already had in mind the offer of the sexy photos in exchange for the property. The "business" must have been very important to make his pursuit of the Arnold property second on his list.

The natty French-blue uniform of the Adelaide police carries authenticity. If Officer Augusta was unavailable, Officer M. Loy was ready to report for duty.

Yee-hah.

❧

The only sound on the third floor office of City Hall was the slight hum of the air register. October is a challenge for office buildings, being neither hot nor cold, so the room was slightly stuffy. The door to the anteroom to Cole's office was ajar. I peered around the edge. A thin blonde sat at a desk, half-turned to one side as she delicately painted the nails of her left hand a vivid ochre. Unless she was performing in a Halloween play, the color was ill advised. Careful not to muss wet nails, she turned a page of a magazine on her desk.

I glanced up and down the hall, spotted the ladies' room. Once within, I made certain I was alone. I swirled into being. In the mirror, I admired how the black of the visored cap emphasized red hair. The French-blue uniform was crisp and fresh and the black leather shoes well shined. No doubt the police had already interviewed the secretary, so I doubted she would question their return.

I moved toward the door, then paused. Cole's secretary had seen me briefly on Wednesday morning when Nick had stormed out of the office. Perhaps I should try a wig. A black pageboy was boring. I didn't like blonde either. I settled for a rich chestnut. Just in case, I added large aviator sunglasses. I limped as I made my way up the hall. I'd moved swiftly and easily when glimpsed on Wednesday.

At Cole's office, I pushed open the door and stepped inside.

The secretary looked up. Quickly, she screwed the cap on the polish and flipped the magazine shut.

I limped forward. "Officer M. Loy, Adelaide Police Department. I understand you were Cole Clanton's secretary." I pulled out a small notebook, began to flip through pages. "You are . . ."

"Libby Bracken." Her eyes were bright with excitement.

I glanced down at the magazine. "*Woman's Day*! Last week I found the best recipe for chocolate truffle pie. What's your favorite new recipe?"

"Brownies with coconut and brown sugar topping. I have some here." She pulled open her desk drawer, retrieved a plastic container, lifted the lid, and carefully unfolded wax paper. "Would you like one?"

When I was comfortably settled in the chair next to her desk, the brownie on a napkin, we traded several recipes. When we were new best friends and I'd finished the brownie, I pulled a pen from my pocket and placed the notebook on my knee. "Sometimes it helps a witness to recall events again. If you don't mind, please describe Wednesday morning."

"Like I told the officer yesterday, I was scared. Everything turned nasty. Cole—" She paused, and a bit of pink touched her cheeks. "He was my boss, but I called him by his first name. We grew up on the same block. I know Nick Magruder, too, and I don't care what they say, he wouldn't shoot anybody, even if he was awfully mad. And he was. I've never seen Nick like that. But that was later. Everything was ordinary until around nine o'clock. I was in Cole's office. He had a bunch of stuff for me to copy and deliver to the stores downtown, an announcement about the celebration." She looked deflated. "I don't know whether they will go ahead with Old Timer Days or not. It's scheduled for the first weekend in November. That's about the time when Belle Starr and her gang robbed a Katy train. Some people think she brought the gold here to Adelaide that December. My mom says it's all hogwash, and she ought to know. She teaches Oklahoma history. Anyway, I had some announcements that looked like old-time wanted posters with the date, and I was supposed to ask the shopkeepers to put them in their windows. I never even got them all copied that day because of everything that happened. About nine, Cole got a call from Arlene Richey. They'd been hanging out together. I think it's real embarrassing for Jan." Libby sounded prim. "Jan's her daughter, and I went to school with her, too."

"Arlene's call came around nine?" I wrote in the notebook.

Libby nodded vigorously. "I wasn't surprised she called him. She called him all the time. He knew it was her. He looked at his cell and gave me a kind of nod, meaning *You can go out and close the door*, and that didn't surprise me, either. Once I accidentally heard a bit of his conversation with her. It wasn't nice." The pink was more pronounced in her cheeks. "But this time"—her eyes were rounded—"I knew something big had happened. I wasn't even to the door when he said, and his voice was sharp and loud, 'Wait a minute, Arlene. You can't mean—' Then nothing. I suppose she'd hung up on him. I heard the beeps as he dialed her back. Then I closed the door."

The timing fit with what I knew. At the B and B, I'd answered the hall phone and he'd thought I was Arlene. I'd assumed they'd just been speaking. When he didn't reach her, he'd come to the B and B. Arlene had made it clear she was done with him. I'd tried to bluff him about Nick's house and the late-night visitor to the Arnold place. I'd gotten his attention, but not in the way I'd expected. Nick had arrived and told Cole to leave. Cole had made his veiled threat and departed, presumably to take care of some "business" before he dealt with Nick.

I licked a brownie crumb from a finger. "What happened next?"

"Cole rushed out. I didn't ask where he was going. He was moving fast and his face was awful. I wondered if he was going to go see Arlene. He came back a little before ten, and he looked even madder. He stomped past me like I wasn't here and slammed his office door so hard it popped open again. That's the only reason I heard what I did." She rushed the last sentence.

The door to Cole's office was a good eight feet from her desk. I had no doubt she'd eased across that space and leaned near the open door. I hastened to encourage her. "Even a scrap of conversation may make a huge difference in our investigation."

Libby nodded, her eyes huge with memory. "Cole was talking on the phone, and he said, 'Not so fast. You haven't heard the latest. I got a foolproof plan that's going to get me fair and square on the Arnold place. But first I want to be sure you and I are on the same page. I'm coming to see you. I want to know where you were around midnight.' The words don't sound bad, but the way he said them was scary, like he was ready to raise a big stink."

"Do you know or have any idea who he was talking to? Did he mention a name?"

She shook her head. "No. He must not have waited for an answer. All of a sudden it was quiet, and I heard him crossing the floor. He headed out looking mean."

"Did he return later?"

"I never saw him again." Her voice quivered.

I doubted that Libby felt a personal loss, but she had seen a man her own age with only hours to live, and her eyes held the shadow of eternity. She bit her lip. "My mom said I'd probably have to testify at Nick's trial."

"Trial?" The change in subject puzzled me.

She hooked a finger in a long strand of blonde hair, wound it tight. "Nick raced in about an hour later. He was wild." Her eyes were wide. "I've never seen anybody madder. He was yelling he was going to knock Cole flat and he wouldn't listen when I said Cole was gone, and he banged into Cole's office and he kicked over a chair and then he ran out. Everybody says he hunted all over town for Cole and last night he met him in the gazebo and shot him. I wish I wouldn't have to say what happened, but if I'm under oath, I'll have to tell the truth, won't I?"

I snapped shut the notebook. Indeed she would. Nick had left an incriminating trail a blind anteater could have followed. I cleared my throat. "The investigation is not complete. Mr. Magruder is a person of interest, but there are a number of unexplained facts." I eased to my feet, making a show of a stiff leg.

She watched with big eyes. "Did you get shot or something?"

"It's a temporary injury. I pulled a hamstring." I was fuzzy about hamstrings, but the ailment seemed common for baseball players, though the nearest I'd ever been to a baseball field was watching the 89ers up in Oklahoma City.

"In the line of duty?" Her admiration was evident.

How could I disappoint her and let down the side for the Adelaide Police Department? I gave a modest shrug. "Going over a fence after a Peeping Tom. We got him."

It was a nice note for my departure.

I looked up and down the hallway. Certain I was unobserved, I disappeared. I had a plan, but, regretfully, this would not be the right venue for Officer M. Loy.

Chapter 13

Nick sat on his bunk, hands planted on his knees. The orange prisoner's jumpsuit was too big, sagging around his bony shoulders. His eyes shifted back and forth across the cell.

I had come to the right place. "Dee?" I spoke softly.

Nick's eyes jerked toward me. He had excellent auditory skills. "One's all I can take. I mean"—his head jerked a little to his left—"it isn't that I don't appreciate your support, Aunt Dee." His face tried to stretch into a smile. "It's just that I feel like I'm at the end of my rope. Like I keep telling you, I don't know a damn thing about Cole except he was a jerk. Maybe my jerk cousin Bill can fill you in on what Cole's been up to. Bill hung out with Cole. I've only been back in Adelaide a few weeks, but it's beginning to feel like years. Now you say Cole shot at me." Nick looked puzzled. "But that's the gun that killed him. How'd the killer get it?"

Dee was brisk. "We think the murderer came to Cole's apartment Wednesday and took the rifle."

Nick stared. "Were you there? If you know, please tell the cops."

"Nick." Dee's tone was chiding. "Either Cole gave the rifle to the murderer or the murderer took the rifle from Cole's apartment. That's logical."

Nick briefly shut his eyes, opened them. "If that's logic, I think I'll take another aspirin." He looked forlorn. "I'll need more than aspirin. As if the cops don't have enough against me already, I was at Cole's apartment yesterday and pounded on the door loud enough to wake the dead." He looked pensive. "Not that the dead I know seem to take the grave seriously."

Some comments are better ignored. "Did you see anyone while you were there?"

"I blew in and blew out." He cracked the knuckles of his right hand. "I heard a door squeak as I went down the hall to the stairs. Somebody might have poked a head out of an apartment."

I had no doubt he'd been observed. One more dangerous bit of information against him. "Did you see Arlene while you were there?"

Nick clapped his hands to his head. "Oh, wow. If Arlene was there, that's not good. Look, don't let the cops know." His hands dropped and he spread them open in a plea.

Dee's voice was stern. "Arlene created her situation. She must deal with it."

"She's Jan's mom." His voice was imploring. "Please, Aunt Dee."

"You are in jail. That is intolerable."

I hastened to intervene, because this argument could have no good resolution. "Nick, did you see Lisa Sanford?"

He shook his head. "Was she there, too?"

"We believe she was there." Dee was emphatic. "We think she saw someone she knew."

He gave a heavy sigh. "Probably it was me." Then his

face crinkled in puzzlement. "Spoke to her? Voices out of the ether?"

I hastened to explain. "You would be very proud of your aunt, Nick. She appears as Officer H. Augusta. She is very impressive."

"I'll bet she is." A semblance of a grin pulled at his lips. "The Adelaide cops will never be the same."

Dee had no time for diversions. "Who might have a key to Cole's apartment?"

Nick shrugged. "Lisa for sure. Probably Arlene. But I know old apartment houses. I lived in one in Austin 'til I launched *Featherfoots*. It would be easy to get inside Cole's apartment. A credit card can usually jimmy an old latch. Or you can make a lock pick with a butter knife."

Dee cleared her throat. "That seems an arcane piece of knowledge."

"My Featherfoots are big on lock picks. I have a sequence where—" He broke off, shook his head. "Featherfoots can't come to the rescue this time."

I kept on point. "Arlene Richey has a key."

Nick's eyes fell. "Yeah." He sounded miserable. "Please keep that to yourselves. I don't know what's going to happen. I don't see a way out. I just wish it would all go away and I could wake up and think about the good old days when all I had to do was program ambushes that a smart Phidippus could outwit. Maybe you and her"—he lifted a hand, turned a thumb in my direction—"could go someplace and talk to each other."

"You and *she*." I spoke automatically.

"I can't go anywhere." He was aggrieved. "You and her have to beat it."

The door at the end of the hall clanged open. Brisk steps sounded. Heavyset Officer Nelson planted herself like a battleship in front of Nick's cell. Mustachioed Officer Maitland peered over her shoulder, his face a mixture of uneasiness and bravado.

Officer Nelson's voice, deep and rusty, sounded like a barge scraping against the sides of a canal. "Listen, bud, are you nuts?"

Nick looked thoughtful. "I don't know. I may be."

Maitland took a step back, his face folding in wary lines.

Nelson cleared her throat. "How come you want to talk like women?"

Nick made a steeple with his fingers. "I don't think I want to."

"Then why do you do it?" Nelson erupted.

Nick pushed up from the bunk. He waved a hand to encompass the small cell. "When they talk to me, it would be rude not to answer."

"Who talks to you?" Maitland clawed at his mustache.

Nick looked sly. "I can't see them, but I know they're here. And my mother always told me to be polite to ladies."

Maitland plucked at Nelson's sleeve. "He's having us on. We got to stop letting him jerk us around."

"You got that right." Nelson took a step nearer the cell, jutted out her square chin. "Magruder, you better keep it down. Much more out of you, and maybe you'd like to be switched to the county jail. This is kind of like the Waldorf in comparison. You wouldn't have your own cell. You might not like the bad men they could put you with. Do you get what I'm telling you?"

"Threats!" Dee's shout was stentorian.

Nick and I both moved at once. We collided.

I smothered an *ouch*.

Nick winced.

I hissed, "Hush, Dee. Later."

Maitland was backing away. "The guy's a nutcase. You ever see anybody bump into nothing like that? And those damn voices again. Let's see if the chief will let us switch him to county. No point in keeping him here. He's lawyered up and not making a peep. We'll tell the chief he's driving everybody crazy. We got that prisoner in cell eight going to county tomorrow. Be easy to take both of them."

As the footsteps receded, Nick stood in the center of the small cell, rubbing his face like a tired child. If ever a man looked worn down, it was Nick. "They'll probably haul my ass over to the county jail and throw away the key."

"Over my dead body." Dee's whisper quivered with outrage, but it was a whisper.

"Aunt Dee, I can't take a lot of comfort there."

"Nick." She sounded stern, even in a whisper. "Remember that on your mother's side you are a Delahunt."

Did I hear the distant sound of bagpipes?

"There is that." His grin was twisted, but it was a grin.

I admire wry courage. The threat of county jail might have proven the last demoralizing straw. I would have liked to have given him a hug, but I doubted he would be pleased.

As it was, we'd tarried long enough. "Dee." I scarcely made a sound, but I knew she was attentive. "Meet me at Nick's house." I moved close enough to lightly whisper near Nick's ear. "Don't despair. With Dee and me on the case, you have nothing to fear. We're leaving now."

I would like to report that his mood immediately lightened. Honesty compels me to admit that the only expression on his face was relief at our departure.

༄

A sharp meow sounded from the porch.

Champ knew Dee and I were in Nick's living room even though we'd arrived unseen. Cats, dogs, and children look with eyes that fathom more of the universe than most adults ever realize.

I opened the door. The big orange tabby twined around my ankles, and I bent to lift him to my shoulder, taking care to hold him gently. "You've been in a sunny patch." His warm fur smelled of fresh earth. His purr was deep in his throat. At the sound of a snapped-open lid, he twisted free and loped toward the kitchen.

In a moment, two glasses moved through the air.

I took one and drank fizzy cold Coke. "Champion thanks you and so do I."

Her glass was lifted. "Better than cat food."

"Unless you're a cat."

Nick's sunny living room was a cheerful contrast to Cole's apartment. The drumsticks lay on the floor where I'd flung them as the police arrived.

Dee's glass settled on a nearby table. The sticks rose in the air. A blues shuffle beat sounded, the sticks flicking between snare and bass drums. Why, it was perfect for "Stormy Weather." I belted out the lyrics. As I finished, she concluded with a rattling finale.

"Very nice." I always give credit where credit is due.

"Thank you." The sticks were replaced. "All right, we've had a break. Now we need to canvass the apartment house."

I swirled into being. I needed a lift from the gritty atmosphere of the jail. I chose a V-necked tee in a soft violet, fine black corduroy jeans with a paisley scarf instead of a belt, and pebbled black leather ankle boots. I sighed happily, drank half the Coke, put the glass on the desk, and found the phone book.

"Can you breathe in those jeans?" Dee's tone was bland.

Some questions do not deserve a response. "An advantage of your police uniform is that it comes with equipment. If you'll pop here, I'll use your phone." I smiled brightly and held out my hand.

Dee gave an irritated huff, but colors swirled and French blue appeared. "I don't suppose it does any harm to be visible here." She unclipped the cell, handed it to me.

I flipped pages, found the number. The phone was answered on the fifth ring. "La Hacienda."

"I'm supposed to drop something by for Bill Magruder. What hours does he work?"

"Five to ten tonight, eleven to three tomorrow."

"Thanks." I hung up the phone.

"What do you intend to take to Bill?"

"Nothing. Bill works at La Hacienda—"

"Are you hungry for Mexican food?"

"Always, but a visit there will combine pleasure with business. Nick said Bill was friendly with Cole. He may be able to tell us about Cole's sudden passion for the history of Adelaide." I settled in Nick's chair, opened the center desk drawer to search for paper. I settled finally for a plumber's bill that I flipped over.

Officer H. Augusta perched at one end of the desk. Despite the perfect fit and crispness of the uniform, Dee seemed diminished. She was as imperious as always, but her eyes were shadowed and there was a droop to her shoulders. She looked at me soberly. "I'm afraid for Nick, terribly afraid."

"Dee, this morning I went to the cemetery." I quoted the inscription, " 'The acts of this life are the destiny of the next.' I asked myself what actions by Cole or by others led to Cole's death at the gazebo. Here is what we know." I wrote on the back of the plumber's bill:

1. Cole worked on the Gazette until he took leave to head up the Old Timer Days celebration.

2. Cole was not known to have great interest in Oklahoma history, yet he orchestrated a celebration re-creating the early days of Adelaide's settlement. What caused this transformation?

3. Cole worked closely with Rod Holt of the Back Shop.

4. Cole received permission from Claire Arnold to set up a replica of the original trading post on the Arnold property.

5. *Out of spite, Nick arranged to buy the Arnold land
   on the condition Cole not be permitted to erect the
   trading post.*
6. *Tuesday morning Claire informed Cole he could
   no longer gain access to the property.*

I stopped and marked two big *X*s next to number six.
"Claire informed Cole Tuesday morning that he couldn't
come on the property. That night Cole shot at Nick. Nick
and I went to the Buffalo B & B, which is next door to the
Arnold property. Late that night I saw lights next door. Since
I was concerned about Nick's safety, I decided to investigate.
The Arnold property was overgrown with vines and downed
branches on the path. I caught glimpses of a light—I think
it was a flashlight—and I heard an occasional pinging sound.
The light disappeared. I lost my way and went off the path,
and then a coyote howled and I started running. Suddenly
I was wrapped in a plastic trash bag, picked up, carried to
a wooden bridge and thrown into a pond." My nose wrinkled. "A nasty, scummy pond."

Dee folded her arms.

I admired the Adelaide police insignia, a shield with the
Latin inscription *Magna est veritas et praevalebit.* If only
we could make truth prevail for Nick.

Dee looked at me quizzically. "I fail to connect your
introduction to pond scum with shots at Nick and Cole's
murder."

I wrote on the sheet:

7. *Cole was willing to commit murder to place a
   replica of the original trading post on the
   Arnold property.*

Dee tapped number seven. "Isn't *commit murder* too
strong an interpretation of the attack on Nick?"

I remembered the thunder of the shot. "If I hadn't been here, Nick would be dead."

She pursed her lips. "You have a talent for the dramatic."

I pushed up from the chair and walked to the wall. "Come here, please."

Dee joined me.

"Stand there." I pointed at the spot in front of the bookcase where Nick had been. The remnants of the broken vase still remained on the top surface and the floor. "You are about the same height as Nick. Look at the wall."

Dee studied the pocked wall. "I see." She turned away, a sick expression in her eyes. "All to gain access to an overgrown piece of land."

"And replicate the original trading post."

"That is a motive for murder?" Dee was incredulous.

"To build a trading post would require moving materials onto the land. Putting in the foundation would require digging." I wrote swiftly:

> 8. *Rod Holt arranged for treasure digs in City Park.*
> *Digging on the Arnold property while building a*
> *trading post wouldn't attract attention. Rod Holt*
> *has created as many as twenty treasure maps. The*
> *maps carry the legend* Belle's Treasure.

I scored three heavy lines beneath *Belle's Treasure*.

Dee's face curled in utter derision. "G'wan." Her heavy cockney accent would have done justice to Eliza Doolittle. The put-down was inelegant but emphatic. "Buried gold? I can't believe you're serious." Dee pushed up from the desk, paced to the drum set, picked up a stick, and whacked a cymbal. "Belle Starr's gold. That's the silliest thing I've ever heard."

"Why then"—I kept a tone of reason (*Wiggins, don't you see how handicapping it is to deal with this woman?*) and inquired mildly—"did Cole try to kill Nick, if not to prevent Nick from buying the Arnold property? Cole was having fun insulting Phidippus, but Tuesday night he took his rifle and shot at Nick. Nick didn't screw up Cole's affair with Arlene until Wednesday morning. The act that propelled Cole to shoot was Nick's success in barring Cole from the Arnold place. Everything centers on the Arnold place." Ignoring Dee's rolling her eyes, I pulled the list closer, added:

9. *Wednesday morning at the B and B, I described the lights next door and my toss into the pond. I thought Cole might have been on the property, but he seemed shocked, and I don't think he was pretending. He wanted to know exactly what I'd seen and heard.*

10. *Nick arrived and ordered Cole to leave. Cole emphasized Nick's devotion to Jan and said Nick would probably do almost anything to keep Jan happy. I think that's when Cole figured out he could force Nick to sign over the Arnold house in exchange for the photos on Cole's phone.*

"Dealing with Nick, however, wasn't Cole's focus as he left." I squeezed my eyes and tried to be precise. "Cole said, 'I got some business to see to, then I'll be in touch, Phidippus.'" I wrote on the back of the plumber's bill:

11. *Cole returned to his office, clearly upset. His secretary overheard Cole on the telephone make what sounded like a threat. Cole then left. Where did he go? Who did he see? What "business" was more important to Cole than getting the Arnold place?*

Dee was judicious. "You have to do the jumps in order. If your analysis is correct, everything hinges on the Arnold place. We need to be sure that we're in the proper ring. You think Cole"—she gave a head shake—"discovered the location of Belle Starr's stolen gold, and the gold is buried on the Arnold property, possibly near the site of the original trading post. Moreover, you are suggesting a conspiracy based on the conversation overheard by Cole's secretary. Her interpretation may be the result of a heated imagination after a murder. But the big hurdle to my mind is believing that Cole and an unknown coconspirator"—heavy irony—"know the whereabouts of Belle Starr's treasure." She slapped her hands on her hips. "How would Cole come up with information that no one else had ever discovered in the one hundred and twenty years of Adelaide's history?"

"Cole wrote a series of articles for the *Gazette* about the early days."

Her smile was sardonic. "We all know how reliable newspaper stories are. Besides, nothing we've learned about Cole suggests he was capable of careful research. I'd think his approach would be to rehash previous stories." She gazed at me in cool disbelief. "Your conclusions aren't justified by the facts."

"I have facts. Tuesday night at the Arnold place, I not only saw a light, I heard occasional pings. Metal detectors ping. Cole was stunned when he heard about the obvious search. I think Cole knew the identity of the searcher, and that Cole's 'business' was to deal with that person before he met with Nick."

"Hidden treasure." She shook her head. "I don't believe it, but"—her tone was grudging—"there appears to be a connection between the Arnold place and Cole Clanton's murder. Since he never expressed interest in Adelaide history until he wrote those articles, obviously the *Gazette* is the place to start." She swirled away.

I started to speak, then stopped.

Champ sauntered up and effortlessly jumped to the desktop. He flopped onto the sheet with my notes. I stroked his head. "She's gone, isn't she?"

Champ placed a moist nose against my hand.

Independent Dee continued to set her own course. I was exasperated. A visit to the *Gazette* was in order, but the newsroom wasn't where I had intended to start. For now I had to follow Dee's lead.

⁓

In the *Gazette* newsroom, I gazed down at the unoccupied city desk. A page layout filled the screen on the monitor. There was a somnolent air. The minute hand on the big, round-faced clock marked seven minutes before five, the workday almost done. The *Gazette* was an afternoon newspaper, so today's deadline was long past. Several freshly printed newspapers were stacked to one side. One newspaper was spread wide and there were red checkmarks by several stories.

Across the room, a white-haired woman made notes on a laptop. Another reporter watched a rerun of a football game. Albert Harris hunched over an electronic game at his desk. His resentment at Nick's success with *Featherfoots* apparently didn't prevent him from playing video games.

Crisp footsteps sounded. Dee came through the newsroom door from the hall.

Albert slipped the game into his pocket. The city editor would probably consider him on company time. Albert looked over his shoulder.

Dee surveyed the room. "Adelaide police. Who can provide information about Cole Clanton's employment here?"

The sports reporter didn't look away from the screen. "The city editor's in a meeting." He jerked a thumb toward Albert. "They knew each other."

Dee moved to Albert's desk. "Officer H. Augusta. I'm here about Cole Clanton. Is there a quiet area where we can talk?"

Albert looked interested. "You new on the force?"

Of course the *Gazette* reporters likely knew most of the police officers in town.

"I started last week. Used to be a cop in Pensacola. Now, are you the man to see about Clanton?"

"As much as anybody, I guess." Albert's eyes jerked toward a metal desk a few feet away, a desk obviously not in use, the surface empty, no laptop, no papers, no mementos. Albert swallowed. "That was Cole's desk." He looked for a moment longer, his expression strained, then stood. "We can go in the break room."

In a small room with a stained Formica-top table, Albert offered Dee coffee, gestured at a greasy box with two crullers and a couple of glazed doughnuts.

She shook her head briskly, took a seat, pulled a notebook from her pocket.

Albert poured coffee that looked strong enough to walk into the chipped white mug. He dropped into a plastic chair across from her. "Joan said the word on the street is that Nick Magruder's going to be charged."

I tensed. Albert assumed that as a police officer Dee knew the crime-beat reporter, Joan Crandall.

"No formal charge has yet been made." Dee was bland. "At this point, my instructions are to seek personal information about Mr. Clanton. Were you and he longtime friends?"

Albert lifted his shoulders, let them fall. "I wouldn't say so. We went to school together, but we didn't hang out. He played football."

He spoke as if his meaning would be clear.

Dee looked puzzled. "You weren't friends because he played football?"

I realized that she'd been gone from Adelaide for many years and her background was cosmopolitan, so she asked a question that no homegrown police officer would have asked.

Albert's round face flushed. "Football guys hung out with

football guys. My best friend was Nick Magruder, the guy they think shot him. Funny, he and I aren't friends now"— Albert's eyes were cold—"but Cole and I got along fine when he started working here." His expression was wry. "Cole wrote like he had a crayon in each hand. He only got the job because his uncle owns the paper. The only thing Cole was interested in was true crime. He kept trying to talk his uncle into letting him get Joan's job, but that would never happen. Joan knows every cop in town. I guess she's probably given you licorice, too. Every time she quits smoking, she's got a pound of red licorice in her desk and she offers a strip to everyone."

Dee said smoothly, "A woman with red licorice will always have friends. So Cole wanted Joan's job?"

"Oh yeah, kind of like a kid wants a candy store."

"Why her job?"

"He was nuts about true crime." Albert's face crinkled in distaste. "You ought to see the magazines he had. Who wants to see pictures of dead people?" Then he shrugged. "*CSI* racks up the viewers, so what do I know?"

I doubted Dee had a clue about *CSI*. Thankfully she was smart enough not to ask for an explanation. Instead, she used the comment to segue to her objective. "Please describe the articles Mr. Clanton wrote about Adelaide's early history."

He stared at Dee, his gaze speculative. "What does that have to do with Nick Magruder shooting Cole?"

Dee murmured vaguely, "Possibly Mr. Clanton's research into early crimes in some way led to his death."

Albert frowned. "I don't see what Nick has to do with early crimes."

Unfortunately for Dee and me, Albert Harris was not a downy sheep ready to be led.

Dee checked the door to be sure it remained closed, then said quietly, "Mr. Harris, please treat this conversation as confidential. We have received a tip that"—her voice fell even lower—"the motive behind the murder might be connected to Cole's articles about Adelaide."

I understood her decision not to mention Belle Starr's gold. Albert Harris would probably have laughed out loud. Buried treasure has a tendency to evoke that kind of response from smart people and, looking at Albert's measuring gaze, I decided he was bright and quick.

Dee persisted. "When did Mr. Clanton first come up with the idea for the articles?"

"It wasn't Cole's idea. It was around the end of July, and the city editor told him to look back in old files and come up with six or seven stories about unsolved crimes in Adelaide. He spent a lot of time down in the basement, looking at old issues. He talked to the *Gazette* librarian, and she gave him tips on what years to try. He wrote the stuff in a hurry. I think the series started the first week in August."

Dee nodded. "Can you provide me with copies of the articles and the dates when they appeared?"

"Sure." He pushed up from the table. "I'll bring them up on my laptop and have them printed. You can pick up the copies downstairs at the reception desk on your way out. Is there anything else you need?"

Dee rose, too. "When did you last see Mr. Clanton?"

"I hadn't seen him for a week or so, but he called Wednesday." There was an odd note in Albert's voice. A nothing-out-of-the-ordinary call marked the last time he would hear his friend's voice. Albert took a quick breath. "He was supposed to drop by and give me stuff for a feature on Belle Starr's treasure maps, but he said some things had come up and he'd try to come over the next day."

I whirled behind Albert, materialized long enough to mouth, "What time did he call?" and disappeared.

Dee always took everything in stride. Her expression gave no hint of my momentary presence behind Albert. She asked smoothly, "What time did he call?"

Albert frowned. "Maybe around ten o'clock. I was on my way to interview a guy who carves pipes out of corncobs. The city desk is big on local stuff." The words were delivered with the deadpan inflection of a reporter caught up in the downward spiral of local newspapers to irrelevancy.

"What was Cole's demeanor on the telephone?"

Albert's face squeezed in thought. "Kind of distracted. Something was bugging him. He said he had a couple of things he had to see about, but he said he had Nick Magruder over a barrel and the trading post was going to be a go. That's the last time I talked to him."

This confirmed Cole's comment to Nick that he had some business to take care of, but he'd be back in touch with Nick. Cole made the phone call overheard by his secretary, telling his listener that he was coming. Possibly he'd used his cell to call Albert when he realized he didn't have time to drop by the *Gazette*. Cole had been elusive that day, leading Nick all over town.

Dee's lips thinned. Nick's name popped up in every conversation, and that was no doubt being compiled by Chief Cobb's officers as they readied a file for the prosecutors. "Why was it important to Mr. Clanton to be able to gain access to the Arnold property?"

"That's the site of the original trading post. Cole was working with Rod Holt, the guy who runs the curio shop. They wanted to put up a replica, and that's where it belonged."

"Did historical accuracy matter to Mr. Clanton?"

There was a flicker of interest in Albert's eyes. "I wouldn't have thought so. But once he got involved in the Old Timer Days stuff, you would have thought he wrote the history books."

"How did Mr. Clanton become associated with Mr. Holt?"

I was pleased with Dee. That was the important question.

Albert's shoulders rose and fell. "I don't know. Cole left the *Gazette* right after the series ended, and I didn't see much of him. You'll have to ask Rod Holt. I'll get the stuff printed out for you."

True to Albert's promise, a folder awaited Dee at the counter downstairs. She was pushing open the door when running steps sounded behind us.

Joan Crandall, stringy hair flying, careened around Dee. As the crime reporter plunged outside, she yelled at Dee. "Picked it up on the scanner. Better check in. One eighty-seven. Jolly Roger Haven."

Chapter 14

I grabbed Dee's elbow. "That's the trailer park."

"What's one eighty-seven?" Her voice was tense.

I felt sad and weary. "I suspect that is code for homicide."

Dee was shaken. "Lisa?"

"I'm afraid so."

Dee's usually strong voice was scarcely audible. "I told her that Cole was shot with his own rifle."

I was firm. "You also told her to tell the police if she saw someone near his apartment who might have taken the rifle."

Dee glanced down at the folder. "We need to go to the trailer park. Where can I put this?"

I had an idea. "Wait until there's no traffic, then disappear and zoom straight up."

Dee objected. "I foresee mass hysteria if a manila folder is observed streaking, self-propelled, above Adelaide's business district."

A gust of wind lifted a black trash bag above the street. "Hold on." I popped to the trash bag and maneuvered it earthward so that the bag's descent appeared to be the result of the wind. When the bag drooped down near Dee, I explained. "Disappear. You carry the folder. I'll follow below you and keep the bag rippling. Anyone who looks up will think a gust caught the bag. They'll never see the folder."

We arrived at the stable where Dee and I had spent the night. In only a moment, the folder was secreted beneath a thin mattress on a bunk. We were free to travel and travel fast.

လ

In gathering dusk, a half dozen police cars, roof lights flashing, rimmed the dusty yard around Lisa and Brian's trailer. Pine trees partially screened the Sanford trailer from neighbors. Residents drawn by the sirens and lights had ventured close to the end of the grove to watch. Men stood with grim faces, arms folded. Women shooed children away from the police cars. Barking dogs, some snarling, excitedly lunged at the ends of tethers.

Inside the Sanford trailer, there was scarcely room for Chief Cobb, Detective Sergeant Price, and the wiry young man who bent near Lisa's body on a small blood-drenched sofa. I recognized him as the medical examiner.

"Same song, second verse." The young doctor raised a curious eyebrow. "Severed femoral artery. Just like the Clanton kill."

Cobb's heavy face looked dour. "A suspect is being held in that murder."

The ME straightened. "Copycat? Was the severed artery released to the media?"

"No." Cobb was crisp.

The ME shrugged. "Word gets around. Anyway, I'll do an autopsy."

"Time of death?"

The ME turned over his hands. "Takes maybe ten minutes max when the flow isn't stopped. Could have been half an hour ago. Up to two hours." He looked around the small quarters. "Blood could have spurted several feet."

The chief nodded. "Thanks, Doc."

The ME picked up his bag and edged past the bulky chief and the lean detective.

Cobb stared down at Lisa. "We got a tip on Crime Stoppers that she might have seen someone take Clanton's rifle from his apartment. Had anyone talked to her?"

Price pulled out his cell phone, sent a text.

Cobb noted the disorganized clutter. "Hard to say if somebody searched. I don't think so. Anyway, someone either came in with her or she let someone inside. There's no evidence of a break-in. She sat down and the murderer pointed a gun at her leg and fired. Messy, but effective."

Price read a text aloud: "Officer Cain went to library at 4:37 p.m. Lisa Sanford had left shortly after 4:00 p.m., said she wasn't feeling well. Cain proceeded to trailer address. No one appeared to be home and there was no answer to his knock."

Cobb jerked his head. "Let's get out of the way, let the techs get to work."

A few feet from the trailer steps, Cobb stopped. "As far as we know, she was last seen at the library. See if you can find out where she went after she left work." He jerked his head. "Interview the neighbors. See if anyone saw her come home, ditto the husband." Cobb surveyed the terrain. He pointed at a sandy, rutted lane that curved behind a stand of cane. "Anyone wanting to arrive unseen could park behind that cane, cross the dirt patch, and skirt behind the Pinto to the front steps. Find out what time the husband left work. Like the ME said, she could have been shot as recently as a half hour ago, and that's about the time he called nine-one-one, right?"

Again, Price checked his phone. "Call came in at 5:09. Three cars dispatched. First arrived at 5:12. According to Sergeant Pence, husband appeared distraught."

Cobb looked across the dusty ground. "And bloody. I'll see what he says."

His face slack and dazed, Brian leaned against the fender of the jacked-up Pinto. Blood streaked his soiled T-shirt and arms. He stared at the open trailer door.

Chief Cobb strode across the ground, heavy face grim beneath thinning, grizzled black hair, an imposing figure—burly, muscular, and intimidating. He stopped in front of Brian. "Police Chief Sam Cobb."

Brian looked at him dully. Tears welled. "Somebody killed Lisa."

Cobb's eyes narrowed, but his next words were quiet, almost gentle. "Tell me what happened."

"I got home from work. I guess it was about 5:10. Lisa's car"—his gaze slid to a very old Honda parked next to the Pinto—"was here. I was glad."

"Was she usually here when you arrived home from work?"

"Sometimes." He didn't meet the chief's eyes.

I sensed the chief's pity for the grieving figure, a young man who looked old—balding, paunchy, never sure when he came home if his wife would be there. Cobb cleared his throat. "This afternoon you came home and went inside?"

Brian struggled to talk. "I should have known something was wrong. The front door was open and, when I called out, Lisa didn't answer. I went up the steps, and when I was inside . . ." He turned away, crooked an arm to hide his face. His shoulders shook.

"I'm sorry, Mr. Sanford."

In a moment, Brian lowered his arm. His breathing uneven, he turned back toward the chief.

Cobb asked quietly, "Do you own a gun, Mr. Sanford?"

Brian stared at him blankly, then his face worked. "You think I shot Lisa? I never hurt Lisa. Never. She was lying there, all bloody. . . ." His voice quivered.

The chief spoke reassuringly. "It's a matter of procedure.

If you'll tell us where you keep your gun, we can be sure it wasn't the weapon."

Brian rubbed his face. "Oh. I see. Yeah. I have a thirty-eight. Look in the drawer below the cabinet across from the sink."

Cobb nodded at Hal Price, who turned and walked swiftly to the trailer.

Cobb asked quietly, "Is that a drawer with a lock?"

Brian appeared puzzled. "We don't have any drawers that lock."

"So the gun wasn't secured."

"I didn't have any reason to lock it up. We don't have any kids." Again there was a spasm of pain.

"You claim your wife was dead when you came home?"

Brian's face twisted. "On the sofa. Blood was everywhere. All bloody. Somebody shot her. Just like Cole Clanton."

The chief's brown eyes glinted. "It's very similar to the attack on Mr. Clanton. How did you know that?"

"I heard the guys talking. Mickey Barrett's brother is a cop. He told Mickey there was blood everywhere, that somebody shot Cole in the leg."

Cobb's mouth tightened. I suspected a police officer was due for a conference with the chief. "So you knew Clanton died from a severed femoral artery?"

Brian blinked. "Fem—what?"

Cobb let it go. "Your wife and Cole Clanton were lovers at one time."

Brian pushed away from the Pinto. "That's not true. She was just trying to make me jealous. That's all. She didn't care about Cole. She told me she didn't. Where'd you hear that junk?"

"Information received." Cobb obviously had paid close attention to Dee's call to Crime Stoppers.

"It's a lie." But there was misery in Brian's eyes. "Cole was all over that woman who runs the B and B. Not Lisa."

Cobb moved on. "Do you know anyone who had a motive to shoot your wife?"

Abruptly, Brian's face hardened. "Maybe. Lisa called me a little while after four. I was edging the back patio at the Raymond house. My cell vibrated, so I turned off the edger. Lisa was excited and told me she had big news." He pressed his lips together for a moment. "She said maybe our luck had turned. She said she was going to talk turkey to somebody and she didn't owe Cole anything. I didn't know what she meant. She said Cole was a rat and he'd riled a lot of people and she'd seen what she'd seen and there ought to be a nice amount of money in it for us and we could leave town and go to Dallas and hunt for jobs there. I started to ask what was going on, but the boss was walking toward me. I told Lisa I had to go and I clicked off and got back to work."

Cobb's face was thoughtful. "We'll need for you to come to the police station, Mr. Sanford, and give a statement."

Brian sagged back against the Pinto. "Yeah. I don't care. Nothing matters anymore." He lifted his arm and crooked his elbow, again shielding his face.

❧

It was close on midnight when Chief Cobb closed a folder and leaned back at his desk. "We have sufficient evidence to charge Brian Sanford. According to the neighbors, Sanford and his wife didn't get along well this past year. According to some neighbors, his car often came creeping in late and they knew he was drunk again, and hers didn't roll up until midnight. And"—he turned to his computer, opened a file—"the ME says Lisa had a hell of a smack on her jaw and another huge bruise on her abdomen shortly before death." He saved the file, leaned back in his chair. "There was plenty of trouble between husband and wife. I don't doubt we can confirm she was involved—or had been—with Cole Clanton. We found a key in a zipped side pocket in her purse. It wasn't a key to the trailer. We checked, and it opened Clanton's front door. The most damning piece of evidence is the gun that killed her was a thirty-eight, and Sanford's gun is missing. He had plenty of time before we got there to throw a gun in that pond or just toss it into the thicket of blackjacks."

Hal Price smothered a yawn. "Sanford had time to wash his hands. No GSR residue." Price's face wrinkled in thought. "I don't rank Brian Sanford as brainy, but I don't think he would be dumb enough to kill his wife with his own gun, even if there is a pond about a hundred yards behind that trailer."

"Not dumb. Brokenhearted. Furious. Too mad to think." The chief pulled open a desk drawer, lifted out a bag of M&M'S, looked at his watch, and shook his head. "Not even M&M'S sound good at midnight. We'll keep hunting for the gun. Probably it's the murder weapon or it wouldn't be missing. But what gets my attention is the MO."

Price nodded. "Like the ME said: same song, second verse. The intent both times was to make sure the victim didn't survive. There's another important point that could go either way for Brian. We didn't find Lisa's cell phone in her purse. Brian claims she told him she was going to talk turkey to someone and that she mentioned Cole and said she thought she knew something worth some money. If that's true, it seems pretty likely she called the murderer to set up a meeting. The murderer shot her and took her cell to hide the fact of her phone call. But maybe the only call she made was to Brian, and she told him she'd seen him going into Cole's apartment and knew what he'd done."

The chief rubbed eyes reddened by fatigue. "If that's the case, Brian has to be smarter than we think and in control of his emotions. And if he killed her because of Cole's rifle"—a heavy sigh—"we have the wrong man in jail for Cole's murder." The chief reached up, turned off his goose-necked lamp. "We've talked until my brain feels like cheese. Maybe I'm a damn fool just to hold him and not go ahead with an arraignment. Right now it looks bad for him, but we're going to keep looking." He stopped, turned the lamp on. "Let me check one more thing. . . ." He flipped through a red folder. "Yeah. Here it is. Johnny Cain and Ed Loeffler talked to people at Clanton's apartment house. They got descriptions of people knocking on Clanton's apartment Wednesday afternoon that fit Lisa Sanford, Nick Magruder, and Arlene Richey. We didn't find Lisa to interview her. Nick's lawyered up. As for Arlene Richey"—he drew an orange folder close, flipped it open—"she told Cain and Loeffler she didn't go to Clanton's apartment Wednesday and nobody can prove she did." His face tightened in a frown. "Have you turned up anything about this so-called Officer Augusta?"

Uh-oh. Arlene obviously had mentioned the visit by Dee, probably saying she'd already talked to the police and she wanted them to stop bothering her.

"Nada." Price turned his hands palms up. "Richey insisted this tall blonde officer talked to her. And she swears she wasn't at City Park Wednesday night. We'll need a search warrant to check her shoes to see if there's a match with that partial woman's shoe print."

Cobb slapped the folder shut. "Richey's lying about Clanton's apartment. Clanton's next-door neighbor—Mrs. Billiemae Oldham—saw her, along with Magruder and Lisa Sanford. The only other person she says came upstairs was a pizza deliveryman. She didn't see the pizza guy leave. Lisa and Nick went past her door and neither was carrying anything. Richey went by about two o'clock. Ditto—she didn't seem to be carrying anything. Of course, the rifle could have been relayed out of a window to the ground with a rope. It could have been done, but, once again, we'd be talking lots of smarts."

Price quirked an eyebrow. "If these two crimes are connected, the murderer thinks plenty fast."

The chief nodded. "Or maybe there's a way into Clanton's apartment that doesn't pass the nosy neighbor's door. If someone came to Clanton's apartment to take a rifle with the intent of shooting him Wednesday night, that person would have been damn careful not to be seen. Tomorrow, check it out, see if there's access to the apartment other than from the hall. But"—and he pointed in the general direction of the cells—"who are we looking for? We're supposed to have Clanton's killer in jail."

༄

Morning sunlight streamed into the double-wide trailer at the horse farm. Dee found a package of frozen waffles, some canned blueberries, and—horrors—canned orange juice and instant coffee.

Our breakfast was makeshift, but edible. I don't mean to sound critical, but Heavenly food is Heavenly. Bobby Mac was no doubt enjoying eggs Benedict, country smoked ham and red-eye gravy, grits with pepper cheese, and fresh orange juice.

However, Dee had also found frozen brownies and, after a zap in the microwave, the aroma was marvelous. The taste, while not quite divine, was plenty good enough. If a brownie after breakfast seems a trifle decadent, remember that "seize the moment" is a nice creed at any time. I was comfortable in a snazzy Pointelle openwork orange cotton sweater with an adorable cowl neckline and dark brown trousers with boot-cut legs and low brown boots. Even Dee had unbent enough to appear. She was elegant in a white blouse, gray jodhpurs, and, of course, high riding boots.

I glanced at the clock. "Before we set out to make inquiries, let's look over the stories Cole wrote for the *Gazette*."

Dee retrieved the green folder from beneath the bunk mattress and sat far enough away that the folder was out of my reach.

Wiggins, are all horsewomen as controlling as Dee? I squashed the thought, lest I be guilty of uncharitableness, and forced a pleasant smile.

Her quick glance at me suggested my benign expression didn't fool her for a moment. "We'll start at the first. 'Upcoming series announced August second.' Banner headline: 'Missing Gold, Passion, Unsolved Murders from Adelaide's Steamy Past' . . ." Dee raised a sardonic eyebrow. "I'd say the city editor decided to liven up the dog days. The August third article is about Belle Starr . . . born in Carthage, Missouri, in 1848 . . . attended Carthage Female Academy . . . excelled in Greek and Latin . . . played the piano . . . During the war she reported on Union troops to the Confederates. . . . Brother was one of Quantrill's guerrillas . . . killed by Union troops . . . family moved to Texas . . . Belle knew Jesse James and Younger brothers. . . . Belle married a former Quantrill Raider who turned to crime. . . . She was accused of taking part in robberies. . . . She wore buckskins and moccasins and sometimes tight black jackets, velvet skirts, high-top boots, holsters with matching pistols, and a man's oversize cowboy hat with a feathered plume. After her first husband's death, she left their two children with family and plunged into the life of an outlaw . . . spent time in prison . . . returned to robbery when released . . . married Samuel Starr in 1880 . . . Samuel was shot in 1886. . . . In November 1888 she and four men held up a Katy train. . . . Adelaide legend says Belle knew Ezra Porter at the trading post in the Chickasaw Nation from his days as a Quantrill Raider and that she trotted up on her big black horse one snowy December day when dusk was falling, leading a donkey with saddlebags slung across its back. Some people believe she buried the gold near the trading post, but a Chickasaw Indian told a grandson he'd been riding past a cistern in the area now encompassed by City Park and saw lanterns and two figures with shovels digging. The next day Belle rode away. An unknown killer shot her in the back a few months later on her ranch near Eufaula, and the booty from the train robbery was never recovered. The Indian's grandson claimed to have a map, but he was killed in a bar fight and no map ever surfaced.

"The next story is about murder suspects taken from the jail by an armed mob in 1909." Dee raised an eyebrow.

"That gruesome story is known to every Adelaide resident." My parents had been children when the murders occurred. They'd never wanted to talk about that night. "The prisoners were handed from the rafters in the abandoned livery stable behind the jail a couple of blocks from here. Not near the Arnold place."

Dee talked as she scanned. "A bootlegger disappeared in 1932. His cabin out near Allen burned down. It was said to be arson. He was supposed to have kept money at his place. No one knows what happened to his stash. . . . In 1934 a lady of the night was found dead in an upstairs room at a bordello at two forty-eight Buffalo Street." She looked at me. "Isn't that the address of the Arnold place?"

Dim memories returned, Mama shushing a visiting uncle when he'd raised an eyebrow about Buffalo Street. However, the Arnold place had been turned into a genteel boarding-house in the 1940s. "Claire Arnold said that unhappy things had happened there."

Dee raised an eyebrow. "Here's another one. Nineteen eighty-two. Edward J. 'Buster' Killeen was found dead in the backyard of the Arnold place. He'd been shot a half dozen times. The killer was never caught. . . . Killeen was a gambler—"

I remembered Claire's description of the poker table in the basement.

"—and reportedly kept huge sums of money hidden in his house. An interesting twist on his murder is that he was dressed for travel in a topcoat, dark pinstripe suit, and black dress shoes. In the kitchen, the police found two fully packed suitcases. He had about a thousand dollars in his billfold. The house was searched extensively, but no money was found. The murderer wasn't caught. Police thought Killeen knew someone was gunning for him and had planned to leave town. Killeen was divorced. His ex-wife lived in California. The house and land went to his sister, who sold them and used the money for her husband's church."

Dee riffled through the sheets. "Three more stories, all unsolved murders, none with a connection to the Arnold place." Dee replaced the copies of the news stories in the folder, slapped the cover shut. "Cole doesn't quote anybody in any of the stories or refer to sources. He probably got all his information from old *Gazette* files. There's no evidence he did any independent research and no hint he had found a link to buried treasure."

Dee had a good point, but I wasn't convinced. "There had to be a compelling reason for Cole to be so determined to get onto the Arnold property. He wasn't genuinely interested in Adelaide history. He could have set up an 'original trading post' next door at the B and B and it would have been in the right vicinity. I believe he wanted to set up the trading post on the Arnold place so he could dig for gold. Cole may have found something in writing one of the articles about Belle Starr that pointed to the hiding place."

I have looked into the eyes of dead fish that evinced more enthusiasm than Dee's gaze.

Dee's tone was tart. "And, of course, no one else in all these years ever tumbled to that wonderful little nugget of information."

I felt as deflated as a punctured balloon. Dee was right. Anything evident to Cole would certainly have been evident to a person knowledgeable about Belle Starr. Yet, I felt certain Cole had discovered some fact while writing the series that prompted him to leave the *Gazette* and wangle a job that gave him an excuse to gain access to the Arnold property.

"If Cole found out"—I was adamant—"we can find out."

"Buried gold. That's absurd in the twenty-first century." Dee was disdainful. "Everyone assumes Brian Sanford is stupid. Who had a better motive to kill both Cole and Lisa? Obviously, he adored her and she cheated on him. Maybe Brian is stupid like a fox."

"Cole died because of the Arnold property."

We glared at each other.

I took a breath, held out a conciliatory hand. "We can agree to disagree. What matters is that we both know Nick is innocent. The more we find out, the better chance we have to clear him." I lifted my mug of coffee in a toast. "Here's to Officer H. Augusta and Officer M. Loy, who can aid and abet Adelaide's finest."

There was no answering salute from Dee. "My posturing as a police officer resulted in Lisa's murder."

I put down the mug so sharply that coffee sloshed onto the breakfast table. "Lisa's actions led to her death. She had every opportunity to inform the police if she knew the identity of the person who came to Cole's apartment for that rifle. Instead, she apparently chose to ask for money in exchange for her silence. She made that decision, not you. Blaming yourself is an exercise in absurdity and a reprehensible waste of emotional energy."

Slowly a smile softened her thin lips. "Why am I not surprised you taught English?"

I think it was a compliment. I continued full steam. "We need you at your best—alert, quick thinking, and confident."

Dee face was set in a distinctly wary expression. "What"—her tone was gentle, but her eyes cold—"do you have in mind?"

Chapter 15

My nose wrinkled at the scent of room deodorizer. Two brown tabbies twined about Dee's legs. A creamy Siamese stood on back feet and pretended Dee's leg was a scratching post while giving the anguished Siamese howl that resembles the screech of a tortured banshee.

"Sneakums and Bootikins and Shimmysham think you're wonderful." Billiemae Oldham's eyes were wide in approval. Bluish white hair cupped a plump, eager face.

Dee's eyes glinted.

I whispered in her ear as the Siamese howled. "Cats rule." We didn't want Clanton's neighbor to have an unfavorable view of the Adelaide police.

Dee gave a short nod, tried to shake the Siamese loose.

"Oh, oh, oh." Billiemae's wheelchair scooted forward, and she reached to pick up the cat, which hissed, twisted free, and jumped an astonishing distance. Billiemae's glance at Dee was reproachful.

Dee cleared her throat, said grimly, "Sorry. Regulations. No scratches permitted on uniforms."

"Regulations," Billiemae murmured. "Oh, I understand. Well, come sit down, Officer. Yesterday there were two of your nice officers who came to see me. I was so glad I was able to be helpful."

Dee glanced toward the hall. A screen door afforded a clear view of the hallway.

Billiemae's pink and white face was serene. "Wasn't it nice of the owner to let me have a screen door? He thought it was the cutest thing when I asked. But the babies and I don't get out, and this way we can see people come and go."

Dee gazed at the doorway. "Wednesday you observed an attractive, dark-haired young woman, a lanky man in his twenties, a blonde woman in her forties, and a pizza delivery-man. Are those the only persons who passed your door that day?"

"Oh no, indeed. Mrs. Binney in twelve has her groceries delivered, and the girl brought two sacks. The Ozarka man—I know him because he goes to my church—brought water for Mr. Jones in nine."

"As I understand the layout of the apartment house, there is only the one stairway. Therefore, anyone visiting Mr. Clanton's apartment had to pass your door. Is that correct?"

Billiemae nodded vigorously as if Dee were an especially bright pupil. "The stairs are at the front of the building. There isn't any other exit past my door except for the fire escape, and those doors sound an alarm when they are opened."

"That's very clear. Therefore, anyone who came to see Mr. Clanton had to pass your door both arriving and departing. Now, do you recall the approximate time each of the visitors passed your doorway?" There was only one time period that mattered. If Lisa's murder had resulted from her visit to Cole's apartment, the murderer must have arrived while Lisa had been here.

Billiemae ticked them off in order. "The grocery girl—her name's Winona—at nine o'clock. The skinny young man just before lunch. He looked upset, and he made so much noise at Mr. Clanton's door I was afraid the panels would break, and he scared my babies right under the bed. He rattled the knob and yelled. Finally, he gave up and went stomping away. I've seen the pretty girl before." Billiemae shook her head. "I think she and Mr. Clanton . . . Well, young people these days don't act the way they did when I was a girl. I've seen her many a time. She went down the hall a few minutes after noon. Like I told the officers yesterday, she must have gone inside Mr. Clanton's apartment. The pizza man passed by a few minutes later. I don't know which apartment he went to. I heard a knock, and then it was quiet. You know, I hadn't thought about it, but he must have gone to Mr. Clanton's apartment and the young lady let him in, because no one else is home during the daytime. A few minutes later my phone rang and I scooted over to answer it." She pointed at a portable phone in its cradle on a bookcase. "I answered, but no one was there. I came back to my usual place and in about five minutes the pretty girl went by. The blonde arrived about three fifteen and the water man at four, and that's everyone until people who live here came home from work."

Dee opened a notebook, pretended to skim. "I don't believe I have a description of the pizza man."

Billiemae twined a blue-white curl around a plump finger. "I didn't see him that well. Are you thinking he may have seen something interesting and you want to try the pizza places? My, that would be a lot of calls to make. I just had a glimpse. He was walking fast. He was wearing brown slacks. He was carrying the pizza box balanced on his hand with his arm up, like waiters do in restaurants sometimes." She lifted her arm, elbow even with her shoulder, forearm at a right angle.

Oh, clever. Someone knew Cole well enough to be aware of his observant neighbor. The thick pizza box was an effective screen.

I whispered in Dee's ear. "Ask his height."

"How tall was he?"

"Oh"—she was vague—"he wasn't real tall, but he wasn't short. It's hard to judge when you don't see someone clearly."

Dee bent forward. "When did the pizza deliveryman depart?"

Billiemae's rosebud mouth rounded in an O. "I didn't see him leave." Her eyes blinked in surprise. Then she clapped her hands together. "He must have gone by when I went to answer that wrong number."

I imagined a hand lifting the receiver in Cole's apartment, ringing the next-door neighbor, and then a swift, unseen departure. The murderer had planned ahead, the pizza box held up as a screen, the nosy neighbor's name obtained from the downstairs mail slots.

Billiemae brightened. "I'll bet that pretty young woman can give you a good description."

I imagine Lisa Sanford very well might have been able to do so—if she were alive.

*

In Cole's apartment, nothing appeared changed since yesterday, there was simply a little more dust, the same sense of emptiness.

"What's the point in popping into Cole's apartment?" Dee sounded impatient.

I held up a hand, but, of course, I wasn't visible. I do like to be present, because what good are pretty clothes if no one can admire them? I swirled into being. Cole's mirror on the back of the closet door wasn't the finest quality, but I appeared in a pool of sunlight splashing through the east windows. Serendipity or Heaven-sent? I smoothed a red curl and applauded, purely on the basis of taste, my orange pointelle sweater.

"I hope you're satisfied with your appearance." In her usual stubborn fashion, she remained invisible.

"Oh, I am." I beamed a smile in her direction, then surveyed the room. "Lisa arrived shortly before noon. She had a key and came inside. A few minutes later the deliveryman knocked on Cole's door. He either had a key or jimmied the lock. According to Nick, jiggling a credit card will open most doors in old buildings." I glanced around the room. "When she realized someone was coming in, Lisa would have been worried that it was Cole. Where could she hide?"

I strolled around the room, stopped by the closet. "This is almost the only possible hiding place. All right, she stepped inside but she must have left the door cracked. As she watched, the man with the pizza came inside." I pointed to the kitchen table. "First he put the box down, then he got gloves out of his pocket. My guess is that after he bought the pizza, he first took the box home and carefully wiped it to remove all fingerprints. Then I think he covered the box in Saran wrap."

"How do you pretend to know that?" Dee was disdainful.

I walked to the refrigerator, opened the door, looked inside, and felt a surge of triumph. "That's what must have happened, or a pizza box wouldn't be on the center shelf. This murderer would never leave fingerprints."

Dee's tone was judicious. "That makes sense. But if Lisa saw someone take a rifle, why didn't she realize after Cole was shot that she'd seen the murderer?"

"Lisa had no reason to connect Cole's rifle with the crime. Everyone in town knew that Nick was being held. Moreover, I'm sure she recognized the visitor. Maybe she thought the pizza had been brought for a meal later." I walked across the room to the closet, which was ajar, elbowed it wide enough to step inside, pulled my sleeve down over my fingers to prevent leaving any fingerprints, and cracked the door. "I can't see the wall with the gun rack. The murderer wrapped the rifle in a trash bag or possibly a towel. When he crossed the room to use the telephone to decoy Mrs. Oldham away from her door, Lisa saw the general shape but didn't realize it was a hidden rifle until you talked to her. At that point, she would simply be praying that the visitor left without discovering her. The murderer had no idea he'd been seen until she called him yesterday afternoon."

"She'd been in love with Cole for a long time." Dee's tone was pensive. "How could she cover up the identity of his killer?"

"Anger. Jealousy. Bitterness. And"—I felt regretful—"she wanted money, and she wanted to make a new start away from Adelaide where she wouldn't be the woman everybody had tabbed a tramp. Brian loved her. Maybe she wanted to give the two of them a new chance."

"Granting all of that, what kind of fool plans to meet a killer?"

"She felt that she was prepared. When she got home, she took Brian's gun out of the drawer. That gave her confidence. She sat on the sofa with the gun aimed at the murderer, made her demand. Who knows? A thousand dollars? Two? Ten thousand? Whatever, the murderer agreed to pay and maybe pulled out a checkbook, then asked for a pen. When we were in the chief's office last night, he clicked on the ME's report. Lisa had bruises on her jaw and abdomen. When Lisa started to get up, the murderer socked her in the face and the gut, got the gun, moved back far enough to be out of the way of the blood, maybe he even had another trash bag and held it up as a shield, then shot her in the leg."

"And you"—Dee's tone was bemused—"deduce all of that from a box of pizza." The refrigerator door opened. "If you're right—about any of it—there will be no fingerprints on the box. If there are fingerprints, it means Lisa opened the door at the knock and took the box from a genuine deliveryman. So, either there will be no prints, or Lisa's prints and unidentified prints."

I walked to the oak desk and picked up the telephone. I

knew this number well. I dialed and punched on the speaker phone.

"Chief Cobb, please."

"May I ask who's calling?"

I smiled. "Hilda Whitby."

I was on hold for only seconds. "Cobb here." His tone was crisp.

"Hello, Chief."

"You are wanted for questioning in regard—"

"—to the murder of Cole Clanton. I was there. Nick Magruder told the truth. The shot came from the shrubbery behind the gazebo."

He didn't ask where I was. I suspected his caller ID had already identified the number as Cole Clanton's and that he was even now scribbling orders dispatching police units here.

He spoke in a pleasant tone. "We need to take your statement."

"Another time, perhaps." As Mama always said, "There are many nice ways to say no." "I'm calling now to provide you with a definite lead to the murderer of Cole Clanton and Lisa Sanford."

The intensity of his silence was gratifying.

"Cole's next-door neighbor, Billiemae Oldham, saw Lisa Sanford shortly before noon. . . ." I quickly sketched the conclusions I'd shared with Dee, adding, "Now you can eliminate Nick Magruder and Arlene Richey as suspects. And, of course, Brian Sanford as well."

"That's good to know." His voice was heavy with irony.

"Sarcasm doesn't become you, Sa—" I broke off, realizing I'd been about to call him Sam, as if I knew him. I rushed to speak. "Once you arrive at Cole's apartment, you will find the police seal intact. The pizza box is in the refrigerator. If you check, I am positive the box will not reveal a single fingerprint." I hung up.

"Pushing all your chips on top of a pizza box?" Dee's tone was quizzical.

"You sum up the facts nicely, Dee."

She was acerbic. "I can't match your utter disregard for the bounds of possibility."

"Would you care," I asked sweetly, "to place a small wager on the presence or absence of fingerprints on the box? Possibly an abject apology if there are no prints?"

"The pizza box isn't your only flight of fancy. Why didn't you tell him about Belle Starr's gold and Rod Holt?"

"I want to provide proof."

"Oh, the confidence of a woman who *thinks* she's on a roll. You aren't fooling me. You know you'd lose all credibility if you sprang buried treasure on the man."

As Mama often said, "When an uncomfortable truth smacks you in the face, make the best of it."

"Dee, your insight is impeccable. We need more than a theory, we need certainty. Here's my wager to you: If Cole Clanton found a link to buried treasure, we can find it, and our ticket to success is Rod Holt."

"There you go again." But she sounded more amused than irritated.

"Meet me at the Back Shop."

∽

"That's an impressive collection of branding irons." Dee's cool voice was near.

I hovered near the plate-glass window on the left side of the entrance to the Back Shop. "If I had my choice, I'd pick the calico bonnet. You wonder about the woman who wore the bonnet when it was new and the sights she saw and the work she did."

"Would we have been as brave?" Dee's voice was thoughtful. "And now there's only a bonnet in a window. We can be sure of one thing: She never gave up. Nor will we. Now"—I envisioned Dee standing near me in her Adelaide police uniform, arms folded—"is it your thesis that Rod Holt was the brains behind Old Timer Days?"

We had the sidewalk to ourselves, and I spoke freely. "Exactly. Cole was interested in true crime, not Adelaide history. Even if he knew the site of Belle Starr's treasure on the Arnold property, how could he hope to dig there? How about a celebration of old Adelaide and building a replica of the original trading post? Nothing we've learned about Cole suggests he had the imagination or background or intelligence to come up with Old Timer Days. On the other hand, Holt knows everything about Adelaide's early history. Holt could easily feed Cole the necessary information."

"True, but Cole probably spent enough time in a newspaper office to learn how to find information to fake his way." Dee was pleasant but firm.

"Planning the celebration was only the first step. Even if Cole could have managed to dig up the gold, how would he have disposed of it? I think he approached Holt looking for a way to cash in on the treasure. The gold would be worth much more than its original value because of the age of the coins."

"You always have an answer." She sounded amused. "Treasure hunter connects with expert. How much do you suppose he was willing to share?"

"I'd guess he offered Holt half of the proceeds." I looked through the plate glass at the old Winchesters. I wondered if Cole had any sense that he was dealing with a man who not only knew everything about lost treasures but was steeped in an Old West where the man with a gun could take what he wished. "I expect the agreement was for Cole to arrange for construction of the trading post. Holt would have been right there to watch every spadeful. But everything changed Tuesday."

Dee mused aloud, "'Time goes by turns, and chances change by course, From foul to fair, from better hap to worse.'"

I was silent.

"Robert Southwell. An apt quotation, I believe."

Not to be outdone, I murmured, "As the man from Stratford-upon-Avon once wrote, 'Giddy Fortune's furious fickle wheel . . .'" No one ever matched Shakespeare for the bon mot. With honors even, I said briskly, "Right. Tuesday was the sea change. Nick arranged to buy the Arnold place. Claire Arnold warned Cole off the property. Tuesday night Cole shot at Nick and someone hunted on the Arnold property. Knowing that Cole was barred from the Arnold place, I think Holt decided to search with a metal detector to be sure he knew the location of the treasure. Wednesday morning, when the news was all over town about the shooting at Nick's house, Holt figured Cole was the assailant. By then, Cole had heard from me about the searcher on the Arnold property. Cole went to see Holt, demanding to know about the search. I think Holt persuaded Cole that everything was aboveboard. Cole had already decided to blackmail Nick about the cell phone photos of Arlene, so Cole was sure everything was on track to get the property in exchange for deleting Arlene's pictures. However, Holt now knew the location of the treasure, and he decided to take his chances on getting it all for himself. Besides, he may have been afraid that the police might suspect Cole of shooting at Nick, and he didn't want the police nosing close to Cole. Cole's public quarrel with Nick provided a handy scapegoat. Holt retrieved Cole's rifle. At some point, Cole must have told him he was meeting Nick at the gazebo."

Dee made an indeterminate noise, which might have indicated either agreement or disagreement.

I glanced up and down the street. "No one's coming this way and there's no traffic. It's time for Officer H. Augusta's arrival." I spoke as if I took her cooperation for granted, but I held my breath. Dee was quite capable of galloping off on a path of her own.

I was grateful and relieved when colors formed next to

me. After a moment, I looked into the appraising gaze of tall, slender Officer H. Augusta, blonde hair perfectly coiffed, aristocratic face intent and measuring.

She gave a shrug of those elegant shoulders. "I am willing to explore all avenues." She reached for the handle of the old oak door.

The cluttered store seemed even mustier today. The gaslights on the walls flickered, doing little to dispel the gloom. At the rear of the store, Holt's wooden chair in the shadowy corner wasn't occupied. Officer Augusta stood for an instant at the deserted counter, noted an ornate, solid-brass Victorian desk bell, and tapped the ringer with vigor.

"Coming." Rod Holt came through the storeroom doorway and ambled to the counter—thin, slightly stooped, picture perfect as a late-nineteenth-century tradesman with his sleek black hair and mustache, 1890s shirt, trousers, and boots. He looked slightly surprised when he saw Dee.

"Can I help you?" His drawl sounded puzzled.

"Officer H. Augusta, Adelaide police."

His gaze shifted behind Dee and back again. Slowly he inclined his head. "What can I do for you, Officer?"

She pulled a notebook and a pen from her pocket. "I'm here as part of the investigation into the murder of Cole Clanton Wednesday night. You and Cole Clanton worked together closely on the Old Timer Days festivities."

He nodded agreeably. "Guess you could say that. I thought it was a good idea, and I was happy to help out."

"It was your idea, I understand." She spoke as if this were simply a throwaway line, preparatory to her interview.

Holt gestured toward a straw chair. "Sit a spell if you want." He dropped into his seat, stretched his legs out straight. "I can't take the credit." He sounded regretful. "Cole came to me with a gangbusters plan."

"I understood you called him after the features ran in the *Gazette*."

"No'm. Other way around."

Holt could be telling the truth.

I perched on the counter and wondered at the wary expression in Holt's eyes, deep set beneath thick tufting black eyebrows, eyes that looked cold despite the slight smile on his hawklike face.

"Please describe the plan to me."

Holt lifted a hand to tug at his mustache. "What's Cole's plan got to do with Nick Magruder shooting him?"

Dee was brisk. "Information received suggests that Mr. Clanton's murder resulted from his connection to the Old Timer Days celebration."

Holt raised an eyebrow, looked amused. "Do tell. Did some crazed historian take him out because Cole didn't know the difference between a Lazy Q brand and a Lazy U?" He shook with silent laughter. "Ma'am, I don't think your dog's gonna find a coon up that tree. Cole may not have known a lot about history, but he was having a high good time sweet-talking merchants into contributing to giveaways and setting up Old Timer events. His best idea was the treasure dig."

Dee's stare was hard. "Digging for treasure was his idea?"

"Sure was." Rod's tone was easy. "He asked me to make the maps."

"For Belle Starr's stolen gold?"

"Belle Starr has star power around here." He looked pleased with his reply. "Cole's first story told all about her. She showed up here in 1888, sometime in December. That was around the time Adelaide was first settled. There was a trading post and a couple of settlers. Everybody knows about Belle coming here. She knew Ezra Porter at the trading post. Of course, the rest of it may be like whispering a story to one kid and he whispers on to the next and so on to the end of the line, and you end up with nothing like what got started. Some folks think Belle brought that stolen gold in saddlebags and hid them by the trading post, but there's another legend about an Indian on his way home who saw two people digging not far from a cistern on what's now part of City Park. Cole had a nifty plan to make up a bunch of maps and have folks dig in the park. I got permission to dig from the park department. The digging will be where they want to plant some redbuds and sycamores to take the place of the pines killed by wilt last summer."

She glanced down at her notebook as if checking off queries, gave a little nod. "Why was Mr. Clanton determined to gain access to the Arnold property?" She asked as if this were just one more question she'd been instructed to ask.

Holt waved a languid hand. "He wanted to build a replica of the original trading post, and that's where the post was. I liked the idea, too, because"—his thin lips curved in a satisfied smile—"I was going to stock the trading post, and I only had to give ten percent off the sale price to Old Timer Days. I figured I'd make a couple of thousand that weekend."

"Did Clanton believe the original tale that located Belle's treasure near the site of the old trading post?"

"Believe it?" Holt raised both eyebrows. "Maybe he believed in fairy dust. I don't know. It was a good gimmick. But the trading post was his deal; the treasure maps were mine. I sketched out the maps and had them printed up on some stuff that looks and feels like tanned leather with charcoal markings. Cole didn't know much about real treasure maps."

"Yet he came to you with the idea for the celebration?" There was a hint of disbelief in her voice.

"Sure did. I guess he got fired up when he did the stories. He had some of his facts wrong, but the stories all had punch. He got a lot of responses from people." Holt shrugged. "Maybe somebody told him about the Eighty-Niner Day celebrations in Guthrie and he decided he'd try to start something here. Mostly, I think he was looking for a soft deal, and did he ever get it with an office in City Hall and me to do most of the real work. But I played along. I figured I'd sell a bunch of stuff that weekend. I've already talked to the mayor's office. The celebration's still on."

Dee persisted. "Can you explain how Mr. Clanton was able to create a plan for the celebration when he lacked knowledge about Adelaide history?"

"No'm, I sure can't." His smile was bland. "But I got some papers back in my storeroom. Maybe they'd be some help. I'll go see what I can find." He paused, nodded his head. "If you got the time."

"I have time, Mr. Holt."

I followed him through the doorway. He walked to another door, opened it, flicked on a light, and stepped into a closet jammed with old saddles, worn boots, branding irons, and Indian baskets, and closed the door behind him. He pulled out his cell, tapped a number. "Sergeant Bucky Cresswell, Rod Holt calling. . . . Hidey, Bucky. Rod. You got a new cop name of H. Augusta, about six feet tall, blonde, blue eyes, cleft chin, looks whipcord tough . . . ? I thought it was a mite strange, a cop without a partner asking me all about Cole Clanton, and I already talked to Johnny Cain and Ed Loeffler. She's wearing a nice new Adelaide uniform. Hardly looks like it's ever been worn before. . . ." He glanced up at a television monitor. His bronzed face was rock hard. "She's still sittin' there, pretty as you please. I'll talk to her until you get here." He clicked off the cell.

I was at Dee's shoulder. "Disappear. He's called the police."

Holt stepped from the back room. He stopped and stared at the empty chair on the other side of the counter. Eyes narrowed, he moved fast, careening around the corner and into the central aisle. He paused midway and stared at the closed front door. There was no sound in the store except the heavy tick of a grandfather clock. His face puzzled, he strode to the front door, yanked it open. The bell sounded. He looked up at it. He yanked the cell from his pocket, called. "Bucky, Rod. She beat it. . . ."

As he talked, he moved around the store, checking between shelving, peering underneath tables. "She's not here. I saw her in the back room on the monitor, and three seconds later I got to the counter and she was gone. The bell on the front door didn't ring. I don't know where she went. It's like she vanished into thin air. I don't get it. There's no way out but the front and the back, and I'd have heard the bell as soon as I stepped out of the closet. No point in your coming now. But I don't like it. Who was she and what did she want?"

I heard a faint whisper. "I'll make a noise in the storeroom. Might frazzle his nerves. Meet you outside by the front windows."

In a moment a loud crash sounded from the storeroom.

Holt loped down the center aisle, flung himself around the counter. He bent and grabbed a gun from beneath the back of the counter and edged into the storeroom.

As soon as he was out of sight, I opened the front door, heard the distinct ring of the bell. Another unexpected noise might truly demoralize him.

In an instant, Dee was beside me. "Rod Holt's back on his cell. Very likely several police cars will soon arrive."

"Adelaide's good-old-boy network. He and Bucky probably hunt together. Holt thinks fast. Since he doesn't know how or where Cole obtained the link to the gold, he's immediately suspicious of anyone who shows up and asks questions, especially when he knows the police department well enough to realize you were a phony. You can bet he'll be asking his old buddy Bucky all about the search for Officer H. Augusta. But we found out what we wanted. Holt's claim that he's not behind the Old Timer Days planning is hogwash."

Dee was judicious. "He sounded credible."

"He couldn't wait to tell us it was Cole who wanted the Arnold property. The clincher is his insistence that Cole made all the plans. Unless Cole learned an awful lot about

Adelaide history awfully fast, that can't be true. We need to talk to someone who spent time recently with Cole." Lisa was dead. Arlene was unlikely to cooperate. Moreover, I doubted Cole had revealed to Arlene his disdain for history.

I had a quick memory of a face that looked so much like Nick's. "Nick said his cousin hung out with Cole. That's another reason Bill was on Nick's blacklist. It's still early. Let's try Bill's apartment." I frowned, foreseeing an obstacle. "I suppose Bill knows you."

"I rarely visited Adelaide. I saw Nick in the summers when his mother"—her voice softened—"brought him to see me. Bill is the son of Nick's father's brother. Possibly we met in passing at funerals."

Dee possessed a memorable personality, but hopefully a teenage Bill had scarcely noticed. "Even if he vaguely remembered you, appearing as Officer Augusta is an effective disguise."

Chapter 16

I admired Dee's appearance. Tall and trim, immaculate in a crisp uniform, her aristocratic features imperious, she was imposing. She knocked with authority on the door of apartment 6. After several attempts, she spoke too softly for anyone else to hear, "Perhaps he's not here."

I popped inside. The shades were drawn and no lights shone. Unwashed dishes filled the sink. Clothes were draped over chairs and CDs scattered across a table. Through the open door to the bathroom came the sounds of rushing water.

I returned to Dee. "He's there. Keep knocking."

The door opened on Dee's fifth try. Barefoot in a wrinkled T-shirt and red and black plaid boxer shorts, unshaven and obviously irritated, he burst out, "Stop the—" Then he saw the uniform.

Bill reminded me of Nick, the same deep-set eyes, bristly cheeks, and pointed chin. I had a sharp memory of Nick hunched in the Adelaide jail cell. Somehow we had to find facts that would convince Chief Cobb to seek the man I believed had conspired with Cole to find Belle Starr's gold.

Dee said crisply, "Mr. Magruder?"

"Yeah?" He had the expression of a driver who scooted through a light turning from yellow to red, wondering if a traffic cam had caught him.

"Officer H. Augusta. I am investigating the murder of Cole Clanton. I have some questions for you." Her face was stern. "May I come in?"

Bill scratched at his unshaven cheek. "Yeah. Well, I just got up." He glanced down at his tee and shorts. "I'm not dressed, but come on in." He led the way, grabbing a ragged pair of jeans and stepping into them. He zipped and buttoned, stumbling slightly, before turning to face Dee. He looked around, hurried to dump a pile of shirts from a chair. "Yeah. Why don't you sit down."

"Thank you."

Bill blinked, looking hung over and miserable. "I haven't had any coffee. Would you like a cup?"

Dee was pleasant. "No, thank you, but please prepare a cup for yourself."

"Yeah. Gee, thanks." In a rush, he sloshed water into a mug, put it in the microwave, punched twenty-five. He found one of the small tubes of instant coffee from Starbucks, emptied it into the steaming water, stirred, then dropped onto the sofa. "Gee, it's too bad about Cole. But"—and he hunched forward—"listen, you got my cousin in jail, and Nick never shot anybody. Not even Cole. I mean, he didn't like Cole, but Nick can't stand to see anything get hurt. That's how Nick got crossways years ago with Cole. Cole was gonna kill this spider, and Nick's nuts about spiders. And cats. And dogs. And rabbits. Nick never even hunted. So, my cousin didn't do it."

"I will share that information with my superior."

Bill sagged back against the cushion, lifted the mug, drank

deeply of the coffee. He swallowed and his expression became more benign. "What can I do for you?"

"Were you a longtime friend of Mr. Clanton's?"

"We hung out together, me and Cole and sometimes Albert Harris."

"Are you aware that Mr. Clanton wrote a series of articles about old crimes in Adelaide for the *Gazette*?"

Bill took another gulp of coffee. "Yeah. But only 'cause he had to."

Dee frowned. "Please clarify that response."

Bill looked blank.

Dee said gently, "What do you mean?"

His shoulders lifted and fell. "Yeah, well, Cole actually didn't want to work at the *Gazette*, but his uncle pretty much said he had to do something, and that seemed easier than a lot of things. The city editor told him to write about all these old crimes. Cole liked a good murder, but he was interested in current stuff, like *CSI*. He was totally freaked about having to flip through those musty old papers. I mean, who cares what happened in Adelaide a long time ago? Cole sure didn't. He bitched the whole time he was writing that stuff."

If we'd needed confirmation that Cole Clanton was not a student of Adelaide history, we had it from a guy who knew Cole when he wasn't putting on a good face at his job.

Dee looked perplexed. "If Cole didn't care about old Adelaide, why did he quit the *Gazette* to head up the Old Timer Days celebration?"

Bill smothered a yawn. "Sorry. Didn't get in until real late last night. Karaoke night at the Blue Note. Well, it was like some kind of karma." He looked doubtfully at Dee. "You know, something happens that leads to something else and you draw an ace and it blows your mind. I mean . . ." He trailed off, apparently despairing of communicating serendipity to the police officer watching him with an unblinking gaze. "Anyway, it was kind of funny. I guess maybe after the crime stories had been printed, we were hanging out one night and his cell rang. It was a lady at the *Gazette*, the one who'd helped him look up all that stuff. He almost didn't answer, then he muttered something about Uncle Curt being such a jerk, and if she complained to his uncle he might get fired. Cole said he'd probably made some mistake and she wanted him to fix it, like it mattered when it all happened a long time ago. Anyway, he answered and talked for a minute. When he hung up, he was really pissed." Bill cleared his throat. "Excuse me. He was kind of irritated. He said some old lady had called up the gal who'd helped him and told her to send the reporter to see her—the old lady that called—because she had kept some papers—"

I felt a moment of sheer euphoria. I had been certain that somewhere along the way Cole Clanton had discovered the site of Belle Starr's gold. What papers? Who had held them?

"—that he should see, and she gave Cole the old lady's phone number. After Cole hung up, he shrugged and said, what the hell, he'd go see her, but for sure he would do it on *Gazette* time, and maybe it would take him all morning. We had a big laugh about it."

"Did he mention whether that interview came to fruition?"

"Fruition?" Bill repeated.

Dee was patient. "Did Cole talk to the old lady with the papers?"

"I asked him about it a couple of days later. He said he talked to this old dame and it just went to show that kissing his uncle's ass was going to pay off big time, very big time. I asked him what he meant. He said he had some big plans in the works. It was the next week that he quit the *Gazette*."

Dee leaned forward. "Did he describe the big plans?"

Bill took another swallow of coffee and appeared slightly energized. "Not exactly. He said he was going to make a bundle and blow town, and maybe he'd buy a Maserati and

I could come along and we'd drive out to LA. But I thought he was just talking big."

⁓

I carefully lifted Champ and buried my face in his fur. He nuzzled me in return, then wriggled free when the can opener sounded in the kitchen.

Dee lifted her voice. "Come on, big guy."

I joined her in the kitchen. Nick's cabinets didn't run to coffee, either real or instant. However, all was not lost. I retrieved two Dr Peppers from the refrigerator. I popped the tabs, held out one.

Dee took the can.

I held up mine in a toast. "Here's to crime."

"That doesn't seem in the best of taste, given the current circumstances." Her distant tone clearly indicated reproof.

Honestly, I wondered if the woman ever found anything funny. However, she was still my very own Officer H. Augusta, and this was no time to find fault.

"Albert Harris can tell us who helped Cole with the background. We'll pop over to City Hall and use the phone in Cole's office." Then I realized that Officer Augusta could appear and use her cell phone—

"Ladies." Wiggins's deep voice brimmed with good humor.

I was so startled, I spilled Dr Pepper on my sweater. I was glad I'd not asked Dee to appear. Wiggins found us in compliance with Precept Four. I can't abide being sticky. A new outfit—even if I couldn't see it—was a necessity. An open-throat, white cotton blouse with a lace trim collar, slim-leg aqua twill trousers, and matching aqua slingback pumps immediately made me feel spiffy without a trace of sugary residue. After an instant—half an instant?—of calculation, I threw Precept Four overboard and swirled present. As Mama always said, "Men are much more susceptible to feminine charm if you smile and look deep into their eyes. In a very nice way, of course."

"Wiggins!" Bobby Mac once told me I have a smile with more megawatts than stadium lights on a Friday night. What a guy, both then and now, my handsome, exuberant, ebullient, sexy husband. "How grand for you to take time for Dee and me. We have so much to report—"

In the distance, I heard the faint rumble of wheels clacking on the steel. Oh, surely not! With an ingenuous expression indicating utter certainty of wholehearted approval, I segued into my pitch.

"—and a great deal more to do. We're here to feed Champ, then we'll be off to use a phone."

Champ, gentleman that he was and probably missing the man of the house, twined around Wiggins's ankles. I couldn't see Wiggins, but I knew he stood a few feet from me, dark cap riding high on curly brown hair, high-collared white shirt stiffly starched, arm garters between shoulder and elbow pulling the cuffs up a trifle to reveal strong wrists, plain vanilla suspenders, and a thick black belt holding up gray flannel trousers.

Champ rose into the air and appeared draped in space. "Good boy." Wiggins's voice was deep. "Good boy."

"Now that we've taken care of Champ, even though we are in a rush to wind things up"—it didn't hurt to emphasize both our thoughtfulness and the necessity for further action—"Dee needs to call Albert Harris at the *Gazette*. As soon as we know the name of the woman who helped Cole with his research, we'll track down the information that will lead us to the gold."

"Ladies, that's why I'm here. Although I *deeply*"—great emphasis—"regret the wholesale contraventions of Precepts One, Three, and Four, I am hopeful that once these wicked crimes are solved, the activities of an unauthorized policewoman will fade from the memory of those involved."

His tone lacked conviction. Poor, dear Wiggins. Perhaps

I might suggest he try those positive affirmations made so popular by Oprah, something on the order of, "If I try, I can believe six impossible things before breakfast." One can't go wrong with *Alice in Wonderland.*

"Exactly, and that's why Dee must call as soon as possible."

The woo-woo of the Rescue Express was nearer now.

"I fail to see why further activity by Officer Augusta is necessary." Champ was lowered to the ground. Oh, dear. Wiggins was all business now. "At the very most"—Wiggins's voice was stern—"a final call to Crime Stoppers can provide police with the necessary information to complete the investigation. Chief Cobb is an able and thorough investigator."

Coal smoke tickled my nose. A whistle blasted as the Express pounded down silver rails to pick us up. It was all or nothing. "Wiggins, how credible will the police find an anonymous tip claiming that Cole Clanton and Lisa Sanford died because of Belle Starr's gold?"

The shriek of the Express rattled Nick's house.

After a pause, Wiggins cleared his throat. "I had not considered the likelihood that the authorities would scoff at the suggestion of buried treasure."

Dee's deep voice was brisk. "Regrettably, Bailey Ruth's analysis is correct. So far, no one is aware of our suspicion about the gold. We need proof that Cole Clanton indeed had information about a treasure for that motive to appear credible to the police. Therefore"—she could make a pronouncement with the force of the "Hanging Judge," Isaac Parker, who had once convicted Belle Starr and had been the scourge of outlaws in Indian Territory—"if two innocent men are to be saved, Wiggins, only Bailey Ruth and I have the skill to finish this jumper course."

Wiggins was a stalwart man, but Delilah Delahunt Duvall was not a rider to be bested.

The thunder of the Rescue Express receded.

"I see that the obstacles you face are almost insurmountable, but I have confidence in you." A pause. "And Bailey Ruth."

I would have been more impressed if the addition hadn't seemed a bit perfunctory.

"Ride hard." He spoke as a man rallying his troops.

The scent of coal smoke vanished. Iron wheels no longer clacked.

Wiggins was gone.

"Well done, Dee." No one can say I'm not a magnanimous spirit. Mostly. "And now, to City Hall."

∽

Cole's office door was closed. The telephone receiver floated in the air. Dee punched speaker phone and dialed. "Albert Harris, please."

"City room. Harris." The tone was abstracted. Likely he was pressed on a deadline.

"Mr. Harris, Officer Augusta here. I'm seeking information about the archives of the *Gazette*." She spoke briskly. "Who is the woman who assisted Mr. Clanton in his research of old crimes in Adelaide?"

There was a noticeable pause. Then, he repeated, "His research?"

Since Dee had just spoken with him the afternoon before about Cole's series, the reporter's hesitation seemed curious. I whispered, "I'm off to the *Gazette*, Dee." With that, I disappeared and arrived unseen at Albert's desk.

Albert sat with his back to the city room, the receiver gripped in his hand. Eyes narrowed, his rounded face looked puzzled, wary, and very alert. "The old news stories? Kathryn O'Connell dug stuff up for him. She runs the *Gazette* library. A lot of the old stuff is on microfilm. I'm not sure about the hours. You can call the *Gazette*'s main number, ask to be connected. . . . Sure. Glad to help." He put the receiver down, swung his chair around, came to his feet. As he crossed the room, he called out, "Hey Joan, that fake cop just called, the one you got a story on. She's on her way here to talk to Kathryn."

"Albert, honey, you just bought yourself a steak at Lulu's." The crime reporter grabbed her cell, punched a number. "I got a big break for you, folks. That fake cop's on her way to the *Gazette*."

In an instant, I was in the basement. The corridor was empty. I didn't worry about Dee. Whatever happened, no one would trap either Dee or me. My concern was not with Officer Augusta. Hilda Whitby swirled into view, business-like in a subdued cream silk blouse, belted black wool pencil skirt, and circumspect black pumps with only a tiny gold bar as decoration.

I opened a frosted door, stepped into a room with several oak tables reminiscent of an old-fashioned library, a row of microfiche readers along one wall, and a no-nonsense metal desk in one corner. A woman with a mass of snowy curls held a telephone receiver. "Really? That will be interesting. Certainly. I'll keep her talking." She replaced the receiver, turned to me. Thick-lens glasses magnified appraising but kind blue eyes. "How may I help you?"

"I'm Hilda Whitby from City Hall"—my expression was earnest—"and I've been asked to continue the promotional efforts for Old Timer Days. I know you've heard the sad news about our director, Cole Clanton."

She nodded.

"I'm sorting through files and notes and memos and dealing with matters on his schedule. Unfortunately, I sometimes have difficulty deciphering his handwriting." I opened my purse and drew out a small notebook, turned several pages. "Ah, here it is. Can you give me the name of the older woman who contacted you wishing to speak with him about one of his *Gazette* articles describing early-day crimes in Adelaide?"

"Oh, I'm afraid that won't be of any help to you." Her

tone was commiserating. "Mrs. Barnett passed away yesterday in Oklahoma City. She was ninety-two and bright as button, though she couldn't see well at all. They took her up for hip surgery and she didn't make it through. We'll miss her."

The door opened. Dee walked in, tall, crisp, and commanding as Officer Augusta.

Kathryn O'Connell's expression was bland as her gaze scanned Dee. "I'll be right with you."

I turned until my face was out of view by the librarian, and mouthed, "The police are coming."

Dee blinked in quick acknowledgment. She glanced at her wrist. "I'll be right back." She turned and was through the door before the librarian could respond.

Kathryn grabbed her phone, punched. "Joan, in regard to the personage of whom we spoke, she was here but left. She should either be in the basement hall or the elevator."

"Do you know why Mrs. Barnett wished to talk to Mr. Clanton?"

"Mrs. Barnett?" The librarian was clearly distracted. "Oh, something to do with one of the stories. She said she had some information he might find interesting."

"Did Mrs. Barnett indicate which story?"

The librarian looked amused. "Sadie Barnett played her cards close to her chest. She instructed me to tell Cole she had old family papers that put a very different twist on one of his stories, and she gave a huge cackle."

"Does she have family here in Adelaide?" My only hope was that someone else in her family was privy to her secret. I wasn't terribly hopeful. If she'd found a map to Belle Starr's treasure, surely someone would have made an effort before now to dig up the gold.

Yet the facts seemed clear: Cole went to see Sadie Barnett; he quit his job; he became an instant expert on Adelaide's past and the director of Old Timer Days; he worked closely with Rod Holt; he proposed re-creating the original trading post on the Arnold property; he shot at Nick after Nick had arranged to buy the property; he agreed to delete compromising photographs of Arlene Richey in return for the property.

"The Barnetts are an old Adelaide family." The librarian's eyes moved past me toward the frosted door, her head was cocked for any sounds. Voices rose in the hallway. "I'll see if there are any survivors." She faced her computer, clicked the mouse several times, reached for sheets of paper curling out of her printer. "Here's the obituary that will run in this afternoon's paper. Now, if you'll excuse me, I must check on a matter."

She crossed the room and opened the door.

Voices called:

"Nobody on the elevator."

"Check the rooms down there."

"Has to be trapped."

She left the door open as she stepped into the hall.

The crime reporter's breathy voice demanded, "Where is she, Kathryn? You were supposed to keep her talking. . . ."

I disappeared and rose to the ceiling with the obituary copy. As I moved toward the doorway, I folded the sheets into the form of a paper airplane, using that simple design we all learned in first grade. In the hallway, I held the plane by the fold below and skimmed high above the police milling about, opening doors, seeking, searching.

The librarian stood with her hands on her hips. "I had no chance. I was getting information for a woman from City Hall. I told the policewoman I'd be right with her, and she turned and walked out. What could I do?"

"What did she look like?" Hal Price's face was intent.

"Tall, blonde, piercing blue eyes."

I felt a faint tap on the hand holding the paper airplane. A whisper. "Got your back."

Dee would have been a superb police officer, looking ahead, foreseeing that a partner (and how nice to think she considered me as such) might be at risk.

So intent were the police on opening every door, moving warily into the huge area with the presses, and beyond that to the concrete-floored, starkly lit room that housed the massive heating and cooling system and air transfer unit, not a single officer ever looked up.

The paper airplane slipped just beneath the ceiling tiles to the stairwell. Possibly I was a bit too exuberant. The paper plane shot straight up and out onto the ground floor. For an instant, truly no longer than heartbeat, the little plane nosed straight up, heading for the ceiling.

"Hey, Betty!" The raucous voice behind the counter belonged to a buxom woman in a too-tight blouse, who obviously was not attending to her job. "The cops arrive like a B-movie SWAT team and somebody's got time to play with paper airplanes. Hey, I'm going to catch it."

She pushed through a swinging gate, stood in the middle of the area by the front counter, staring upward. "It has to come down. Just another example of your taxpayer dollars at work." This witticism reduced her to cackling laughter, but she never took her eyes off the plane, leaping to try to snatch it.

"Vick, you'd better watch where you're going. What if someone comes in?" The cautionary call came from a thin-faced woman looking over her shoulder from her computer terminal.

The plane glided beneath the ceiling toward the front door. Vick careened after it, making occasional jumps, red-tipped fingers outstretched. "Look at that sucker go. There must be a current of air coming from somewhere."

The front door opened.

Dee was indeed at my back.

The challenge lay in the height of the doorway. To clear the transom, the paper airplane would be within reach of those predatory fingers, which were beginning to take on the shape and size of mobile tree stumps in my mind.

Now for a swoop and elude.

Vick was more agile that I expected. We collided as she leapt and I sped.

Her fingers grabbed at the airplane, tearing off a corner as she tumbled to the floor.

"Not to worry. Make the jump." Dee's voice was cool and confident.

I rolled to one side, grasping most of the airplane, and fled through the door.

Outside I looked through the plate-glass window.

Vick rolled heavily to her knees, then went rigid as her fingers bent apart, the scrap retrieved, the door opened, and the remnant of the airplane zoomed outside.

"Roof," Dee said crisply.

As I reached the parapet, I had a last glimpse of Vick as she plunged out onto the sidewalk and stared upward with an expression of disbelief.

The wind was brisk on the rooftop. I must confess that I paused for a moment to catch my breath.

The scrap of paper approached. "I should be repentant. Precept Six prohibits alarming earthly creatures, but I haven't had that much fun since the time I told an arrogant ass that not only was he an inept horseman, his pickup line would embarrass a slobbering clown." Her laughter was a satisfied gurgle.

I don't know which offense most irritated Dee, but her good humor was infectious.

The scrap was thrust at me. "What's this?"

I was ready for a moment's respite. I settled on a raised wooden top to a trapdoor, opened the torn sheet, and held it and the scrap in my right hand. "Sadie Barnett's obituary. The librarian didn't think there was any family, but maybe there will be the name of someone we can contact." Cole Clanton had learned something from her that prompted him to create an elaborate excuse for digging on the Arnold property. However, no one else may have been privy to Sadie's information.

I read the obituary aloud.

Sadie Watkins Barnett

Sadie Watkins Barnett, 92, departed this earth following surgery in Oklahoma City. She was the daughter of the late Robert Armand and Nettie Louise Killeen Watkins. The Reverend Robert Watkins was well known in Pontotoc County as an evangelical preacher who warred against the evils of alcohol and gambling. He founded the Come to the Glen Missionary Church. His wife, Nettie, played the organ. Sadie was a native of Adelaide. She graduated from Adelaide High School and from the University of Oklahoma with a degree in education.

Sadie returned to Adelaide and taught first grade at Alcott Elementary for 47 years. She married Daniel Barnett in 1947. Daniel Jr. was born in 1950. She was predeceased by her parents, her husband, Daniel, her son, Daniel Jr., who was killed in combat in Vietnam, her uncle and aunt, Emmett and Louise Watkins, and her cousin, Edward J. Killeen. Sadie loved children. . . .

As I read, it was like watching a roulette wheel and seeing the ball stop on my number. Now I knew what Cole must have discovered when he spoke to Sadie Barnett and she revealed information that had been left out of one of his stories. Sadie had had "family" papers, and in those papers Cole had learned enough to believe that the Arnold property was the site of hidden wealth. It would likely have been a simple matter, except Gabe Arnold had permitted no one on the property, and his dogs had made a nighttime intrusion impossible. Now Gabe was dead and the dogs were gone. I wondered how and when Gabe had died. If his death had been "accidental" and occurred after Cole spoke with Sadie Barnett, it would be further proof of my theory.

I turned to Dee and started talking. Fast.

When I finished, she gave a low whistle. "Officer Augusta?"

"Hilda Whitby, I think."

"Oh, all right. I suppose it's your turn. But I would have liked to have been in at the kill."

"If all goes as I expect, we'll both have that opportunity."

Chapter 17

I opened the front door of the Majestic Buffalo B & B and stepped inside. The only sound was the tick of the grandfather clock and the distant rush of water in the kitchen. I swirled into being. In the long, ormolu-framed mirror, I nodded approval of my white drop-shouldered cardigan, pale blue blouse, and matching spandex slacks. Blue boots, too. I smoothed curls tangled by the ever-present Oklahoma wind and my hurried departure from the *Gazette*. I glanced at the clock. A few minutes after ten. I called out, "Hello? Jan?"

The kitchen door began to open. Jan, wiping her hands on a dish towel, stared at me in surprise. "I didn't think you would come back. The police are still looking for you."

"Don't be worried. I will be speaking with the police quite soon." That was definitely my hope.

"I'm glad." She spoke simply, but with obvious relief. "I felt dreadful not telling them I'd talked with you."

Jan clearly believed in following the rules—normally, of course, a laudable attitude. I hoped I wasn't going to hear a celestial snicker, but surely Wiggins wasn't privy to my thoughts and in any event would be too much of a gentleman to indicate amusement at my expense. I always have the best of intentions. "I have great news for you. Nick will soon be released, and your mother is cleared."

Invisible but whipcord-strong fingers gripped my arm. Dee apparently lacked faith and very likely felt it was unkind to make promises I couldn't keep.

I would keep them.

I spoke with emphasis. "The police have received information that will prove Nick's innocence." I had no doubt that Sam Cobb would realize the importance of the pizza box without fingerprints. No fingerprints was definite proof that the pizza deliveryman was a fake. The presence of the box in the refrigerator proved the "deliveryman" had entered the apartment. There could have been no reason other than to obtain Cole's rifle.

The pressure on my arm increased.

"I'm hoping you can provide a time frame for me."

She looked puzzled.

"Cole's stories about early-day crimes appeared the first week in August. When did Cole become involved with your mother?" It was another way of finding out when Cole and his partner had put their scheme into motion.

Jan looked pained. "It was right after the mayor appointed him to head up the Old Timer Days event. I didn't see how there would be time to organize a program by November, but I have to admit Cole worked like a demon. He rushed around town and whipped up enthusiasm and got a lot of people on board, like Rod Holt, and that gave him some clout. Rod knows everybody. Cole came to see mom because he thought the B and B"—she spread her hands—"was a great venue for an early-day book club."

I maintained an expression of pleasant interest. Indeed, the old Victorian house was an excellent background for pioneer-day activities, but more important, the B and B was next door to the Arnold property.

Jan looked half-sad, half-mad. "He gave Mom a huge rush. I tried to tell her he was a creep, but she wouldn't listen. She tried to persuade the Arnolds to let him put up a replica of the trading post."

I heard the plural. "I thought Mrs. Arnold was a widow."

Jan nodded. "He hasn't been gone long. He died on Labor Day. He drowned."

"An accident?"

Jan shrugged. "No one knows what happened. He loved to fish. But he was such a loner, he never went where there were other people. He had a favorite fishing hole on a private lake about twenty miles from town. He didn't come home for dinner, and Claire called for help. A deputy sheriff found his body not far from the end of the pier. All his fishing stuff was on the dock. Apparently he fell and struck his head on the dock and drowned. He was a strange man, a real recluse, but nice as pie if you ever talked to him. That was hard on Claire, because she's as friendly as can be. She's a social director at the Sunshine Serenade retirement home. I understand everybody loves her. She plays the piano and arranges bingo and takes people around town in a minivan. I guess having fun during the day made it possible for her to put up with being all cooped up at home."

"Cooped up?"

The pressure on my arm had eased. I imagined Dee was listening just as hard as I was.

"Cooped up puts it nicely. Gabe surrounded the place with ten-foot-tall fences, and all the gates were padlocked. It's only been since he died that Claire opened the gate between our place and hers. Now she drops by sometimes for breakfast on her way to work. The funny thing is, she was really crazy about him, but she can't wait to get away from that place, and I don't blame her." Jan shivered. "All that wild growth of shrubs and vines and Gabe not letting anybody step foot on it."

"So he wasn't receptive to Cole putting up the trading post?"

"Absolutely not. I told Mom it wouldn't do any good to ask Gabe, but she tried because she wanted to help Cole. Everything changed when Gabe died. Claire thought the trading post was a fun idea, and I think she hoped it would help sell the property. Then Nick said he'd buy the place but nixed the trading post. For the amount of money Nick offered, she was quite willing to tell Cole the deal was off."

I reviewed the time frame. "Cole wrote the articles in early August. About a week after they ran, he quit his job and persuaded the mayor to support an Old Timer Days celebration. He wanted to build the trading post near the original site, but Gabe Arnold wouldn't agree. Arnold drowned on Labor Day. Claire said Cole could put up the trading post until Nick blocked him by promising to buy the property. I suppose Rod Holt came up with the idea of digging for treasure. Or did Cole get interested in the history of Belle Starr and the gold?" I watched her carefully.

She raised an eyebrow. "Cole's idea of Adelaide history was the football team's record twenty years ago. Rod Holt was over here one afternoon after Cole's article on Belle Starr ran, and he was really disgusted. Apparently, the article put way too much emphasis on that legend about the Indian who saw people digging near the cistern. Rod said if the gold was anywhere, it was somewhere on the Arnold property, but he thought the whole thing was a myth. Why would Belle Starr hide gold around here? She lived on a ranch up by Eufaula. Rod said the idea of her bringing gold to Adelaide didn't make any sense."

"But he's selling treasure maps for City Park?"

She grinned. "As any good merchant knows, you sell what you got. Rod will make the treasures fun, maybe with glass beads and fake gold coins. The city will get the ground spaded up after, of course, and they're requiring diggers to sign waivers for any injuries incurred, and Rod will pocket all the money from the maps as well as sell a bunch of stuff at his store."

The bell tinkled behind us, signaling the opening of the front door.

Jan's expression formed into the pleasant receptiveness of a hostess, then joy lighted her face. "Nick, oh Nick." She plunged past me.

Nick looked even scruffier than usual, his T-shirt wrinkled, his jeans hanging low on his bony hips. He never looked my way. There was only one person in his universe at that moment. He grabbed her in his arms and held her close and pressed his bristly face into her hair. "They let me go. Janny, I was scared."

"Nick, I was scared, too." She held him tight for a long moment, then looked into his eyes. "I knew you were innocent. You'd never hurt anyone, ever. You even love Featherfoots."

He touched a gentle finger to her cheek, traced a line to her lips. "You're as beautiful as any Featherfoot."

Oh my. What higher praise could this lover offer?

I decided to slip quietly away, but a board creaked beneath my shoe, a hazard in an old Victorian foyer.

Startled, Nick's head moved toward me. Abruptly, he stiffened. His eyes widened. His gaze jerked around the entryway.

He was looking for Dee.

"What are you doing here?" His voice was combative.

"Nick!" Jan looked at me, then back at him. "Isn't she helping you?"

Nick swallowed. "Yeah. But . . ." His gaze again circled the foyer. "Where's Aunt Dee?"

His head jerked up. He touched his cheek, managed what could only be described as a pitiful imitation of a smile. "There you are. Great. One big party."

Jan's face folded in concern. "Nick, I'm right here. Don't look past me."

"Of course you are." His laughter was hollow. "You and me and the two visitors from—" He broke off, and I was sure Dee had placed a firm hand across his mouth.

Jan took his arm, tugged. "Come into the kitchen. You must be tired. There's only me and Hilda. You must be imagining things."

"Imagining?" His voice skidded up an octave. "I wish. Listen." He turned toward me. "Everything's okay now. You and—" He took a breath, jerked a thumb at me. "You can go back where you came from. Both of you. As soon as possible. Like immediately. I'm out of jail. No charges. It turns out"—and now he looked utterly bewildered—"that I didn't have on the right pair of pants."

"Nick, let me fix you some breakfast." Jan's eyes were filled with concern and uneasiness. "Then you can go to bed and rest."

"Jan, I swear." Nick's voice wobbled. "That's what happened. The big guy, the police chief, had me brought to his office. He had a folder and he looked at it and he told me where I'd been seen all day on Wednesday. I guess I went kind of nuts trying to find Cole, and people saw me everywhere. Cobb said the descriptions all tallied, that I had on grubby jeans with one knee out. And then he said, and it was as if he quoted, 'from information received, you were not at any time on Wednesday dressed in brown slacks.' He said they'd obtained a search warrant and didn't find any brown slacks in my house. I told him I only had one pair of slacks and they were gray, and who needed slacks anyway? I think he almost laughed, then he said I might not have much of a wardrobe but this time it may have saved me from a murder charge, and he said I could go."

I could scarcely contain my delight. Brown slacks mattered because Chief Cobb had followed up on our tip. He had checked the pizza box in Cole's refrigerator for finger-prints and none had been found. From there, the pieces had fallen into place: Nick, wearing jeans, had arrived and departed before pizza was delivered by a man in brown slacks. Cole had not been home. The pizza box could only have ended up in the refrigerator if the deliveryman had been a fake and either had a key or jimmied the lock. The pizza had been left and Cole's rifle taken.

"No fingerprints. Yee-hah." Validation satisfies the soul.

Nick and Jan stared at me.

Mama always said to leave while on a high note. "It's time for me to go. If we don't meet again, raise a glass of champagne in a toast to those who love you"—I looked meaningfully at Nick, and I knew he understood I meant his aunt Dee—"at your wedding."

As I opened the door and stepped onto the porch, I felt certain my departing words would add luster to Nick's morning and possibly to the years to come.

∽

When the door closed behind me, I felt a yank on my arm. "Do you think she's the right girl for him?" Dee's voice was gruff.

"Absolutely. You can add Jan to those who love him, even if he is seriously rich."

"She seems nice. And he cares terribly." She knew her Nick. "Bless him. It hurts to care that much, but"—and now Dee's voice took on a lilting tone—"love makes life worth living." A pause. "Along with horses, of course."

Everyone has his or her own qualification. For me? Bobby Mac, along with our kids, Dil and Rob, sunshine, laughter, good friends, and kind hearts.

"Do you suppose he'll tell Jan about us?"

"Not in this lifetime. All's well with Nick and Jan, but

there is still a murderer to find. It's time to talk with Claire Arnold."

I disappeared.

ℒ

Maples and cottonwoods dotted the grounds, with soft hills rising in the background. Sunshine Serenade retirement home was built with wings extending from a central core. Recently painted white shutters were cheerful. Rich purple pansies filled several flower beds. Still-green weeping willow fronds wavered cheerfully in a brisk breeze. Rockers, most of them occupied, were scattered about a shady, screened-in front porch.

Stepping inside the main foyer, I smelled the good Oklahoma aroma of crispy fried chicken. The tables in the dining room were set for lunch. I saw Claire Arnold, her brown hair shining in a patch of sunlight as she bent to arrange chrysanthemums in a pebbly blue vase. A basket of mums lay on the table beside her, and other vases across the room were filled or waiting to be done.

"Claire." I walked swiftly across a parquet floor, easy for wheelchairs to navigate.

She looked up with interest. I imagined Claire was always interested, whether in memories of an old lady's reminiscences or the newest app for an iPad. As I neared, her face took on a forlorn expression. "I'm sorry about Nick Magruder. I can't believe that nice boy had anything to do Cole Clanton getting shot."

My voice was robust. "He's been released from jail and is no longer a suspect. I'm gathering up evidence about what really happened, and I know you will be excited to learn how you can help."

She looked eager. "I'll do anything I can. I knew Nick's arrest had to be an awful mistake."

I glanced toward a terrace. "Could we step outside and talk for a moment?"

She picked up the basket. "Of course. Come right this way."

We stepped out onto the flagstones and into the joy of a crisp, clear Oklahoma day with the blue sky arching cloudless above us and the breeze stirring green vines in the pumpkin patch across a white board fence.

Claire plopped the basket on an outdoor planked table. "You just tell me what you want to know, though I only met Cole Clanton when he started coming over about the Old Timer Days. He tried to talk Gabe into letting him put up that trading post, and then after Gabe died, he was nice to me, and he said he and Rod Holt would give me part of the proceeds of sales they made during the Old Timer Days if I'd let him put it up. I figured Gabe was too busy finding out all about the streets of gold to pay too much mind to what I was doing, and if he was watching over me, he knew I didn't have much money and every little bit helped. When Nick offered to buy the place, why it was an answer to a prayer, because I sure want to move out to my sister's house. Bea's real sick right now and she needs my help. I thought Gabe would be mighty pleased since Nick didn't want the trading post to go up. I know that's all off now." She sighed. "I don't like to feel sorry for myself when there's so much trouble for Nick and poor Cole is dead, but the real estate agent told me he didn't think I'd find anybody else who would buy the place. It needs a whole lot of work."

"Nick will buy the property." I had no qualms about committing him.

Claire clapped her hands. Her face shone. "I can't tell you how happy that would make me."

A sharp pinch shocked me.

Dee would have to hold her peace. I spoke ostensibly to Claire, but for Dee's benefit. "Nick will be delighted to buy the place, restore it to its old glory, and create a companion inn to the Majestic Buffalo B & B." Nick was seriously rich, the price of the Arnold place was a drop in his monetary

bucket to him, and, if all went well, Nick would owe me—
and Claire—big time, and this would be a nice thank-you.
"However—"

Claire's face drooped, foreseeing the end of a very brief
dream of escape.

"—I need information about Buster Killeen."

⌢

Shoulders hunched, feet wide apart and solidly planted,
Chief Cobb stood behind his desk. He had the look of a bull
hunkered down against horseflies.

His particular horsefly loomed as large as a vulture in
the middle of his office—lacquered blond hair in odd spikes,
puffy face with overdone makeup, bejeweled hands on
plump hips. Jagged black stripes against the white background of her silk dress numbed the eye. The Honorable
Neva Lumpkin, mayor of Adelaide, was on the attack. ". . .
absolutely a dereliction of duty. The DA made the situation
clear to me. There is more than adequate evidence to bring
charges in not one, but two cases, yet you are not holding
either suspect! The town of Adelaide is unprotected from
murderous assaults. The city council shall be informed. An
inquiry shall be instituted. I insist that Nick Magruder be
arrested. If he is not in jail by this time tomorrow, you will
answer to me. I will call a special meeting of the council.
The DA will present his evidence. You will no doubt be
relieved of your duties. It is my sacred pledge to protect dear
Adelaide. I will not rest, I will not pause, I will not—"

Once launched into campaign mode, her rhetorical range
was nearly inexhaustible.

I tapped her on the shoulder.

She broke off and swung around to berate the dolt who
had dared interrupt her.

No one stood between her and the closed doorway to the
hall. Her features froze.

I slipped to the other side, again tapped her shoulder.

Despite her bulk, she pivoted, her face purpling. "Sam—"

Sam Cobb remained behind his desk, brows drawn down in a puzzled frown. "Something wrong, Neva?"

She looked up. She looked down. She looked to her right. She looked to her left. She yanked around again to look behind her.

This time I gave her a sharp poke in the middle of the back.

With a yelp, she swung around, mouth working. "What are you doing, Sam?"

"I'm not doing anything." Innocence has its own authenticity. He, too, had a haunted expression.

Carefully, taking one step at a time, she backed to the doorway, hand behind her to reach for the knob.

I delicately tapped her upturned left palm three times.

With a muffled cry, Neva turned and yanked open the door, slamming it behind her.

Dee's laughter was muffled. "I don't blame you. But there goes Precept Five."

"Surely Wiggins will understand." I spoke without confidence, already ruing the fact that I'd once again succumbed to the temptation to confound those who appeared to oppose me. "Chief Cobb deserves support. That woman—"

"Ladies." Wiggins sounded grim. "The roof."

∽

The sunny roof was unoccupied. I settled on the parapet, my back to the street.

"Regrettable behavior." A heavy sigh. "Reversionary." His voice came from a few feet away. I knew he faced me, his genial face now set in stern lines. Wiggins always worried that emissaries might revert to earthly attitudes. That accounted for his insistence that we remember always that we were *on* the earth, not *of* the earth.

"Repugnant?" I offered. As Mama always said, "Be the first to say you're sorry and you'll be the last to cry."

"Oh, well." Wiggins had a big heart. "I wouldn't go so far as to deem your actions repugnant. You are much too well meaning, dear Bailey Ruth, to be characterized in such a fashion." A sigh. "If only you weren't so impulsive, so impetuous, so uninhibited."

"But then"—and Dee's voice quivered with amusement—"that odious mayor would have made life miserable for Chief Cobb. Besides, did you see her face?" Dee erupted in merriment.

Her gurgle of laughter and perhaps even a shamefaced chuckle or two from Wiggins masked the gritty scrape as the roof door opened. Chief Cobb slipped out, moving quietly for such a big man.

"However—"

That Wiggins continued to speak indicated he was looking toward me and was unaware of the chief's arrival on the roof.

"—Nick Magruder has been released, and therefore your mission is accomplished."

Chief Cobb's face indicated careful attention. I had no doubt he heard every word. Wiggins always spoke in a robust tone. Chief Cobb inched backward and eased behind the small structure until he was out of sight but our conversation would still be audible.

"Wiggins, I have a plan." I was tense at the prospect of our mission ending when I had the necessary information to trap our quarry. However, I didn't hear a train whistle in the distance. "Dee and I will leave first thing in the morning if the police apprehend the murderer tonight."

"How can that be accomplished?" Wiggins was skeptical.

"Claire Arnold will announce that she intends to dig for buried treasure tomorrow afternoon near the site of the original trading post, and the public is invited to attend— five dollars a ticket. Late tonight—well after midnight—the murderer will slip onto the Arnold property with a metal detector and a shovel. The police will be waiting, hidden in the shrubbery."

"Buried treasure!" Wiggins's exclamation was incredulous. "Oh, my dear Bailey Ruth, surely you don't believe that after all these years Belle Starr's booty will be found. I never thought you, of all people, would succumb to the lure of buried treasure." His voice expressed disappointment and embarrassment at my intellectual gaffe.

"Not Belle Starr's gold." I was romantic enough to believe that on a long-ago cold November day Belle Starr might have left a fortune in Adelaide, but rotting saddlebags filled with coins would remain undisturbed now and perhaps forever. "Belle's gold was a stalking horse, just as the Old Timer Days celebration was a diversion. Rod Holt designed the Belle Starr treasure maps to draw attention away from the Arnold property. Holt claimed that Cole Clanton contacted him with plans for the celebration. Cole didn't care about history. Cole cared about money."

Dee's deep voice was crisp. "Bailey Ruth deserves credit here. When Cole wrote about early-day Adelaide crimes, Sadie Barnett contacted him. She has since passed away, but Bailey Ruth discovered in her obituary that her cousin was Buster Killeen. One of Cole's stories told about the murder of Buster Killeen at the Arnold place. Then Bailey Ruth talked to Claire Arnold, and that's where she hit pay dirt. Buster Killeen once owned the Arnold property. He was found murdered, presumably just as he was preparing to leave town. In the kitchen was a briefcase containing ten thousand in cash. But according to Claire Arnold, there was an even larger amount of money that was never found."

I spoke in a resonant voice. I definitely wanted Chief Cobb to hear. "Claire's husband, Gabe, grew up hearing stories from his father about Buster. One of those tales involved more than half a million in cash in a strongbox. Gabe believed Buster had planned to escape the night he was shot. Knowing he was in danger, Buster had hidden the money, hoping a threat from a disgruntled customer would blow over and he would return. Sadie Barnett gave Cole some old papers, papers she wasn't able to read because of her failing eyesight. I think Cole found confirmation of her story and directions to the location of a steel box full of cash. Mrs. Arnold said her husband was convinced the money was hidden in the house, but Cole's actions make it clear the money must be buried outside. Cole soon discovered he couldn't gain access to the Arnold property. That's when he and Rod Holt hatched their scheme. Pretty soon Cole was director of the celebration with an office in City Hall. Cole wanted to build a replica of the original trading post on the Arnold property, which would make it easy to dig without arousing suspicion, but he was blocked until Gabe Arnold drowned. I think Gabe's death was murder."

"Wiggins, one jump follows another." Dee was emphatic. "After Gabe drowned, Cole charmed Claire Arnold, and everything was set for the replica to be built until Nick came to town ready to settle some old scores. That's when Cole found his horse was hobbled. Nick promised to buy the Arnold property on the condition that Claire prevent construction of the trading post."

It all seemed clear to me, one domino falling and then the others. "When Rod learned the trading post was blocked, he searched Tuesday night and found the site. Wednesday Cole came to see him, demanding to know if he had been on the property and had thrown me into the pond. Rod must have satisfied Cole that he was just checking out the site and that they were still working together. Cole told Rod about his plan to trade the photos of Arlene for the property, but Rod had heard about the shooting at Nick's house, and he decided Cole was a liability. Rod made up his mind to kill Cole and retrieve the money for himself. Nick's quarrel with Cole made Nick an excellent scapegoat. Rod took a pizza to Cole's apartment and left with the rifle. That night he shot Cole at the gazebo.

"Lisa Sanford had been hidden in Cole's apartment when Rod retrieved the rifle. When she realized Cole's rifle was the murder weapon, she attempted blackmail. On Thursday Rod came to the trailer presumably to give her money, but he overpowered Lisa and shot her with her husband's gun. At this moment, he is basking in success, but tonight Rod Holt can be trapped."

"Why would Chief Cobb agree to follow your directions?" Wiggins did not sound persuaded.

Dee's laughter was again robust. "When Bailey Ruth gives him a chance to solve two murders, he'll jump at the chance. He'll relish the expression on the mayor's face when he holds a news conference to announce the solution to two crimes, which only he and his department realized were connected."

"Possibly you have a good point." Wiggins was silent.

Would Wiggins agree? I hoped he would make a decision quickly. It wasn't quite noon, but there would be much to do to create a successful trap for a highly intelligent and ruthless adversary. I had no illusions that Rod Holt would be easy to fool. We would have to be exceedingly clever.

"Very well." Wiggins was brisk. "The Rescue Express will be here at nine in the morning." A pause. "Do make every effort to communicate with Chief Cobb without creating a sense of otherworldly intervention."

"Oh, Wiggins, of course." My voice was as smooth as butter, since what Wiggins didn't know would never cause him distress. "Dee and I will be utterly circumspect." After a fashion.

Fashion . . . I was a bit chilly. The sun had slipped behind a cloud. Perhaps a crisp, new double-breasted blue blazer with shiny gold buttons in lieu of my current white drop-shouldered cardigan. *Mmm. Very comfortable.* "You can count on Dee and me and the chief." It was my sincere hope that Wiggins would be reassured and depart to some far corner of the world.

A hand came from behind the wooden structure, a big, strong hand closed in a fist with the thumb pointing up.

Chief Sam Cobb was on board.

Then the thumb curled below three fingers and a forefinger pointed down.

Chief Cobb was in agreement and directing Dee and me to report for duty.

The chief eased quietly from behind the structure, opened the door, closed it gently behind him. He was en route to his office to await inspiration—certainly not otherworldly—for the best way to bait a succulent trap for a greedy, dangerous, and resourceful adversary.

Chapter 18

In his office, Chief Cobb walked to his desk, punched the intercom. "Sheila, no calls. No visitors"—he glanced at the wall clock—"for twenty minutes." He settled into his desk chair, opened the drawer to his left, plucked out a big bag of M&M'S. "Ladies?"

"That would be lovely." I took the sack and poured out a generous handful.

Dee took the bag from me, filled her palm. "Thanks very much."

His brown eyes watched the sack move through the air, the mounds of M&M'S apparently suspended in space, the deposit of the sack on his desktop. His big, square face was studiously inexpressive. "Who knew M&M'S floated? Not that I intend to share that fact." He popped a half dozen in his mouth, munched.

For an instant, there was a crackle of candy being devoured.

When the floating M&M'S were gone, Cobb pulled a legal pad close, picked up his pen. "Sometimes I like to think aloud, jot down ideas. The first step is to contact Claire Arnold, ask for her cooperation. . . ."

As he wrote, Dee and I offered suggestions. In fifteen minutes, the campaign was mapped.

As Dee put it so well: "Now it's time to ride."

∽

Another time, I would have been fascinated by the interior of the Arnold house, a big central reception area with rooms opening off either side and a wide staircase leading up to the second floor. I could easily envision its past use as a bordello and as a boardinghouse. In a sitting room off to one side, a wide-eyed Claire Arnold listened to Chief Cobb.

". . . so that is all you need to do. If you agree, Officer Shirley Abbott will remain in your house tonight as a pre-caution, though the activity will be confined to the yard."

"Of course I'll help. That nice young man threatened with jail, why it's dreadful." Claire's voice was stern. "Now"—there was a sudden, teasing smile—"I'll make the call if you'll come over tomorrow and tell me all about it."

Chief Cobb's smile was easy. "That's a promise."

I saw admiration and possibly something more in her faded blue eyes. I heartily approved. Chief Cobb was not only a fine, upstanding man, he was very attractive—grizzled hair above a strong-featured face, a husky build with strong shoulders and tree-trunk legs.

"All right." She took a deep breath, picked up the receiver. She punched numbers. "Hi, Rod. Claire Arnold. I just wanted to give you a heads-up. I'm sooo excited. You know how Gabe always kept looking for Buster Killeen's strong-box. Well"—her voice was slightly breathy—"I only wish he could be here now. I found a map that shows the strong-box isn't in the house after all, like Gabe thought. It's buried about twenty feet from the old oak tree, you know, right near where the trading post was. Anyway, it may not amount to a hill of beans, but I've arranged for a bulldozer to be here at four tomorrow afternoon. I'm going to make an announcement in the *Gazette* and sell tickets for five dollars each, and anybody with a ticket can come and watch. Whether we find anything or not, holding a dig here will be a great way to promote Old Timer Days, and if you want to come and sell the Belle Starr maps, that would be fine. . . . Oh yes, I think it will be a lot of fun. I thought you'd be interested. . . . Right. Four o'clock. . . . I hadn't thought about refreshments, but that's a good idea. I'll whip up a bunch of brownies and make some lemonade, and I can sell that, too. . . . I'll see you tomorrow." She hung up and expelled a great whoosh of air. She looked at Chief Cobb, her eyes huge. "He thanked me for letting him know and said he'd be here with bells on."

☙

The city editor put down the phone, swiveled in his chair. "Hey, Albert . . ."

At his screen, Albert frowned and looked up at the clock, but he obediently popped up and crossed to the city editor's desk.

The editor ripped off a sheet from a notepad, thrust it at him. "Need it today. Big dig planned tomorrow in a hunt for hidden money. People love those kinds of stories. No time to get out for an interview, but give her a ring. For now, give me ten inches and rustle up a file photo. Cover the excavation tomorrow."

I looked over Albert's shoulder. The city editor's notes were neat:

> *Claire Arnold—319-0809*
>
> *4 p.m. Saturday—bulldozer excavate/ claims to have map/ buried steel lockbox/ half mil in cash/ ck files Buster Killeen/ murdered '82/ tickets $5*

Albert hurried back to his desk, studied the notes, his rounded face drawn in a tight frown beneath his mop of curly brown hair. Finally, he grabbed a pencil and picked up the telephone. "Mrs. Arnold, Albert Harris at the *Gazette* . . ."

Mission accomplished. This afternoon's *Gazette* would carry the story reporting the planned excavation. Likely the feature would run on page 1, because the editor was right that buried treasure fascinates. This would confirm Claire's call to Rod, give the announcement authenticity. Moreover, in accordance with Chief Cobb's request, a bulldozer had duly been hired.

Wherever Rod looked—if he did—there would be another proof that in less than twenty-four hours Buster Killeen's hidden cash would belong to Claire Arnold.

∽

The wind stirred the leaves in the oak tree, rustled the shrubbery. An owl hooted, the wavering cry mournful. I strained to hear and tried not to shiver. The temperature was likely in the low fifties. Dee was perched nearby, both of us on a sturdy limb that poked above the area where the intruder had searched Tuesday night. I tried not to lose hope. It was now past two o'clock in the morning. No one had approached the Arnold property. If no one came, Chief Cobb might face suspension if Nick Magruder didn't go back to jail.

Had Rod Holt sensed a trap, decided he had no cards to play?

A twig snapped not far away.

Police dressed all in black ringed the area, some behind shrubs or trees, others posted in the shadows of the house and outlying sheds. They would be chilled now and stiff from the long, quiet hours when no one had come.

I scarcely dared to breathe.

Rustling in the grass. More crackles of leaves and twigs. Suddenly a flashlight illuminated a square patch of ground.

The breeze rippled a tiny orange warning flag atop a wire poked into the ground. Whenever construction is planned, buried lines are located and little flags placed every so often to prevent accidental rupturing of phone or gas or utility lines. How easy to retrieve one of those flags and place it atop the spot where a metal detector would give its loudest ping. No one would notice or remark upon such a flag.

The shadowy figure, dressed in a dark Windbreaker, jeans, and running shoes, appeared slightly bulky. There were no features, the face hidden beneath a black cotton face mask. A backpack was dropped to the ground, a flap opened. Gloved hands pulled out a collapsible field spade, opened and locked the handle to the blade. He waited for an instant, head cocked to listen, then moved quickly to the little flag, plucked it from the ground, and began to dig.

"Police." The shout was loud and clear. "Hands up. Police."

The intruder whirled, flung the shovel in the direction of the voice, and kicked the flashlight into the dense shrubbery. In a scramble, he jerked a metal canister from the backpack, yanked. Smoke billowed, dense and choking. He grabbed the backpack and swung toward a path that plunged into darkness. As he ran, his hand came out and moonlight glinted on metal. His arm rose.

Shots.

Shouts.

"Hold your fire by order of the chief," Chief Cobb shouted, his deep voice clear and recognizable.

Officers crouched with weapons drawn behind trees and shrubs were hampered by darkness and smoke, unable to fire because of risk to their fellow officers.

"Dee!" My call was urgent. "He started off to his left." I took a deep breath and whirled through the smoke. Just over the bridge at the pond, a dark figure ran, heading for the grounds of the Majestic Buffalo B & B. Pausing long enough to tuck the gun beneath his arm, he pulled out another canister, yanked the pin, and lobbed it over his shoulder. The gun once again in one hand, he darted toward the gate.

Behind us Maglites shone muzzily, obscured in swirling smoke. Men shouted.

At the gate to Arlene's garden, shadows wavered, changed, shifted into a huge black horse. His rider stood in the stirrups, right arm uplifted. Snaking through the sky, clear now in the moonlight, a lasso whirled through the night and fell neatly over the running figure. In an instant the horse thundered close. Dee swung to the ground and with several jerks bound the figure tightly. When he was immobile, she pushed him over with her boot. The backpack lay on the ground next to a pistol.

I swirled into being and bent down to pull the face mask up and off.

Albert Harris glared at us, his stare malignant, his round face twisted in fury.

Running steps sounded.

Dee swung back aboard McCoy, reached out for my hand.

I swung up behind her. I smiled as I settled on McCoy's rump. That was how we began our adventure near the entrance to the Department of Good Intentions.

∽

Saturday is a morning for pleasure, especially this Saturday. I smoothed the sleeve of my cotton blouse, admiring the soft autumn-foliage design against a butterscotch background. My suede riding pants—a tribute to Dee—weren't visible, since I was sitting at Lulu's counter. Breakfast was superb: country bacon, two eggs over medium, cheese grits, orange juice, and black coffee. I ate with the Saturday morning *Gazette* propped against the menu holder. The *Gazette* is an afternoon paper on weekdays, morning on weekends.

I looked with interest at Albert Harris's story about the

planned Saturday-afternoon excavation on the Arnold property. This was an expanded version of the shorter announcement that had appeared in the Friday afternoon edition. Of course, the Saturday *Gazette* had also gone to press long before he crept through the night, armed and dangerous, seeking the payoff for his crimes. Albert—smart, quick, and clever—had been the guiding force behind Cole. Albert had taken the interest generated by Cole's stories and come up with Old Timer Days as a means of gaining access to the property, and Albert had prompted Cole to enlist Rod Holt. Albert quite possibly had followed Gabe Arnold to his lonely fishing place, knocked him out, and pushed him off the dock to drown. Probably Cole would never have lived to share in the loot, but once Cole had shot at Nick, Cole's hours were running out.

I looked at the clock as I took a last sip of coffee. I paid the bill, strolled outside, stepped into a doorway, and disappeared.

Dee had decided, not to my surprise, to spend her remaining hours in Adelaide near Nick. I popped from place to place to observe just for a moment those I'd assisted on earlier visits and, of course, I paused briefly in my daughter Dil's kitchen—

"Hugh, the funniest thing yesterday. I was out visiting Margie Patton's mom at the retirement home and I caught a glimpse of a woman walking out who looked so much like Mom. Much younger; I could tell by the way she moved. I wanted to talk to her. By the time I'd reached the porch, she was gone. Do you remember how Mom and Dad used to lead the senior class in a rumba line and it just scandalized . . ."

—and hovered about my son, Rob, his red hair thinning and touched with white as he jogged through the park. I hoped he wasn't overdoing it.

I soared up high and belted out "Oh What a Beautiful Morning." I heard the church bells chime the hour. I was sure Chief Cobb was always at his desk by eight.

✍

Sam Cobb swiped a handkerchief against watering eyes, still weepy red from the acrid fumes of the smoke bombs. His face looked doughy, muscles slack with fatigue, but he walked toward the blackboard with a spring in his step. He picked up a piece of chalk, wrote:

EVIDENCE LINKING ALBERT HARRIS TO CLANTON/SANFORD HOMICIDES

1. *Possession of the .38 pistol belonging to Brian Sanford. Slugs that killed Lisa Sanford a match.*
2. *Heel print of Harris's right brown oxford matched print found in patch of damp grass behind gazebo the morning after Clanton's murder.*
3. *Search of Harris apartment yielded the brown slacks he wore Thursday, which match description of those worn by pizza deliveryman. A notebook contained detailed descriptions of all Old Timer Days events, several with notations to advise Cole to add to the program.*
4. *A partial thumbprint on Cole Clanton's refrigerator matched Harris's fingerprints. Otherwise refrigerator surface had been polished and was clean of all prints.*
5. *A Jolly Roger Haven resident out walking a dog noted a red Mustang parked behind a stand of bamboo Thursday afternoon at the approximate time of death of Lisa Sanford and recalled the license plate. The car is registered to Albert Harris.*
6. *Harris's cell phone records indicate two or three daily calls to Cole Clanton or receipt of calls from Clanton.*

Cobb swung around and moved heavily to a chair by the table, sat across from Hal Price. "There'll be more. Once you know, it's pretty easy to untangle all the knots." The chief sounded hugely satisfied.

Hal Price lifted a hand to his face, yanked it down again. "I've got to stop rubbing my eyes. I've got a hot date tonight, and if we turn off the lights and my eyes glow red, she'd start to shriek and leave." Instead, he massaged the back of his neck and gave the chief a quizzical look. "So how come you played it so close to the vest? Don't you trust your staff? Were you afraid there'd be a leak to Harris?"

Cobb looked startled. "Not trust—hey, knock it off, Hal. Nope, here's the skinny. I thought the perp was Rod Holt. I got a tip from the horse's mouth."

I reached up, touched my lips, not sure I cared for the simile.

"Nobody was more surprised than I was." Cobb shook his head. "I took a chance on an anonymous source." His expression was benign. "Sometimes you have to accept what is given and not worry about the whys and wherefores. Anyway, everything worked out. We got our man."

"Yeah." Hal Price forgot and rubbed his eyes again. "But how do you explain the rope trick?"

"Ah, the rope trick . . ." Chief Cobb turned his big hands palm up. "Maybe somebody else was there." He spoke carefully, as if the words had the fragility of crystal glass stems. "Maybe somebody didn't want him to get away."

"Somebody?"

Cobb's shoulders lifted and fell. "Don't look a gift horse . . ."

The man was almost as obsessed with the equine kingdom as the woman who was likely even now astride a huge black horse, out for a last gallop before the arrival of the Rescue Express.

❧

Bright sun bathed Adelaide in gold. I hovered near the steeple of St. Mildred's, gazed at the wooded park on one side, the cemetery on the other. The bell chimed the hour, and I saw the twisting curl of coal smoke and heard the clack of the great iron wheels on steel rails.

I heard a snuffle nearby. "Dee, let's see if he'll agree."

"I'm with you." She was genial and relaxed now that Nick was safe.

Wiggins's shout was exuberant. "Come aboard, ladies."

I swung aboard the rear platform. I wasn't at all sure Wiggins would grant my plea. I spoke quickly, my voice full of entreaty. "Wiggins, since there is no time in Heaven, would you be kind enough to swing back and pick up me and Dee at five o'clock this afternoon?"

After an instant's puzzlement, he laughed. "Don't tell me you truly think there's a steel box full of money in Claire Arnold's yard?" His tone was teasing.

"You don't run a horse into a lather and not sponge him down." Dee's deep voice was firm. "That's leaving a job half-done."

"Life is full of surprises, especially if you look for them." That's what Mama always told us kids.

"The two of you make quite a pair. Partners in crime." He found that hugely amusing. "Very well. Five o'clock it is."

❧

Smoke belched from the yellow Caterpillar bulldozer as the bucket dumped a couple of feet of rich black dirt to one side. Kids perched on tree limbs. Casually dressed adults holding paper plates and cups stood behind security tape that kept the crowd back from the bulldozer and the deepening hole. Nick's arm was draped around Jan's shoulder. He looked proud and happy. Jan's face glowed. Arlene Richey was pale but composed. Claire Arnold pushed back a strand of brown hair and looked shyly at Chief Cobb, burly in a blue polo, jeans, and worn cowboy boots.

In the broad seat, the muscular driver looked bored. He manipulated the bucket down to jam into the dark, dark dirt.

Clank.

The driver leaned forward, peered. "Got something down there."

Cobb turned to Claire. "Do you want me to see?"

Her eyes wide and excited, she nodded. She lifted her fingers to press against her cheeks.

The chief eased into the two-foot ditch, knelt. He pulled a handkerchief from his pocket, brushed away tendrils of roots and clods of dirt to reveal a rusted oblong steel lock-box. With an expression of amazement, Cobb worked the box free from the soft earth and stood. He climbed out of the hole.

"Oh my, oh my, oh my. Oh, Sam, please open it."

Cobb placed the lockbox on a picnic table. He fumbled in his pants pocket with a dirt-stained hand, drew out a pocketknife, flicked out a small tool, inserted it in the rusted lock, and wiggled the blade.

A screech.

Claire drew in a deep breath.

Cobb used a stronger blade to pry along the rusted seams until he could prize open the lid.

The only sound was the rustle of leaves in the breeze.

Yellowed newspaper lay atop the contents. Cobb removed the paper and fragments broke and drifted in the air. He picked up a packet wrapped in thick plastic and carefully unfolded the covering. "By God, look at these!" The chief's big hand held up a thick stacks of bills bound with rubber bands.

Tears streamed down Claire's face. "Now I can take care of Sis."

ᔕ

Dee and I stood on the platform of the caboose as the Rescue Express streaked toward Heaven.

She clapped me on the shoulder. "I'll ride with you anytime, Bailey Ruth."

Wiggins thumped my arm. "As they used to say when I was a young man and we settled around the poker table, if you can't be good, you'd better be lucky. This time, Bailey Ruth, you were good and lucky."

The wind stirred my hair. The wheels thrummed as the Express picked up speed. Heaven-bound and glad to be. I reached out and grasped a callused hand and a firm, rein-strong hand. "I'd never claim to be good, but I've always been lucky."

From *New York Times* bestselling author
Carolyn Hart

Ghost Wanted

A Bailey Ruth Ghost Novel

With mixed feelings, Heavenly supervisor Wiggins assigns irrepressible ghost Bailey Ruth to check out acts of vandalism and theft at a haunted library in Adelaide, Oklahoma. When an innocent girl is arrested, it's up to the spirited detective to book the real culprit.

PRAISE FOR THE SERIES

"Bailey Ruth . . . will delight readers."
—*Boston Globe*

"Blends an enjoyable fantasy with . . . an engrossing plot."
—*Publishers Weekly* (starred review)

carolynhart.com
facebook.com/AuthorCarolynHart
facebook.com/TheCrimeSceneBooks
penguin.com

FROM *NEW YORK TIMES* BESTSELLING AUTHOR

CAROLYN HART

Death at the Door

A DEATH ON DEMAND BOOKSTORE MYSTERY

Annie Darling—owner of mystery bookstore Death on Demand—has a dual murder to solve: a local doctor and the wife of an artist. Someone may be trying to frame the artist, and Annie must discover who wanted both victims out of the picture.

PRAISE FOR CAROLYN HART

"Hart's work is both utterly reliable and utterly unpredictable."

—Charlaine Harris, #1 *New York Times* bestselling author

"One of the most popular practitioners of the traditional mystery."

—*Cleveland Plain Dealer*

carolynhart.com
facebook.com/TheCrimeSceneBooks
penguin.com